The
Solution

FRANCISCO MADEJA

The Solution

39 West Books
Campton Hills, IL

Madeja, Francisco
The Solution : a novel / by FRANCISCO MADEJA—1st Ed.
Fiction: 1.   . Title: THE SOLUTION:

ISBN: 0-9764306-4-9

39 West Books
Campton Hills, IL 60175
630-513-8064

ONE

What is The Solution?

Many years before the American military invaded the countries of Iraq and Afghanistan, a small group of people met in Lordsburg, New Mexico with a single agenda; the complete loss of democracy in the United States of America, and they would take as much time as they needed.

The overwhelming majority of automobiles arriving at the New Mexico hotel extolled the virtues of youth, with convertibles, hot rods, and old beaters; jalopies, with milled engine heads and twin tailpipes; cars of youth and adventure, where no driver had yet achieved a status of wealth. These were students from colleges and universities all across America and a few foreign countries.

Seventy-five vehicles took over the establishment's parking lot, all filled with excited and motivated young people, each with the same driven purpose; to develop a top-secret organization to end democracy in the United States of America, but in a decidedly different way than most envision could ever be accomplished. It would happen through the ballot box, not with force. Voters would freely choose their new rulers without seeing what awaited them when their selection was completed. They were already unknowingly familiar with that process.

Each of the participants received a request to attend the meeting from a man named Russell Harrington, along with his personal check to cover all of their expenses of travel and lodging. The youngsters had met and thoroughly engaged Harrington on political possibilities during his author tour to promote a new book he had written. They knew only that he had become a multi-millionaire in the oil business, and would almost surely run for political office in a few years. He was only twenty-five years old.

Jim Miller was a man in his late thirties and unknown, as was Sara Principle who was twenty, and from the same small Indiana town as Miller. As the principals of the conference, they had created eager excitement and intrigue in the minds of the young men and women, some of whom had received their degrees and would return to graduate school, and beyond. Harrington selected all of them with his own intricate yardstick of how solidly each individual was against some government policies, beginning with the Theodore Roosevelt administration, up to the current one of their own time. The more the youngsters listened to the three organizers, the more certain they were that the impossible could actually take place and they all could be instrumental in creating a new American Revolution.

They also understood it would take many years to complete—so many years that they might not be alive to see the finish line, but the way to end democracy had to be with people voting, not with open revolt. When the seminar was over, Sara Principle gave a wrap-up talk to recommit the seventy-five as a newly created force.

"By now I think you understand what we want to accomplish," she said. "It will certainly take a lot of years, if it happens at all. The chances are *incredibly* slim, and let's not *kid* ourselves! We're all young and inexperienced, but even so, we've decided to try to do the *impossible*! The fact that we actually believe we *might* be successful is fantastic by itself. It'll be a lot more than that if we *do* pull it off, but it *might* wind up being our kids or *their* kids, 'cause it's gonna take a really long time. If it *does* happen, it will be just as amazing as the original American Revolution. Maybe even more so, for even though that was a creative upheaval from the *entitlement* mentality of Europe, they ultimately *failed* from our perspective. *We* must not fail. The survival of America may very well be in the balance. I know that's heavy, but we really *do* think it's true. If it is, we *have* to set things right no matter *how* long it takes before it *is* too late. Let's hope it isn't too late *now*!

"The two parties have had things locked up for a very long time. We've all made a vow to each *other* to move forward with this project and pass it along to others *regardless* of what takes place in our own lives. When we get married, our husbands and wives must be with the mission and understand that it's in *their* personal *self-interest*. I know it sounds weird, but we *have* to get commitments from them up front just like people do with religion. If we can't, we'll have to find a different person to marry, because this comes ahead of *everything*. This is *our* religion, *our* sacred *honor*, and we've all agreed to that principle!

"We'll work in our own communities to create a false perception among the general public that the candidates we unfold are nothing more than basic clones of the two major parties and have nothing at all to do with a secret organization. We'll be locked-down tight—as tight as Skull and Bones, and a few of you know what I mean about that. But we can't forget that as the years go by, it'll probably be easier to get information on people, and that means us too! Another thing you also have to remember is to trust no one, except those we bring into our organization. We *must* keep our little group hidden, 'cause if we *do* succeed, it won't *stay* little for long and it'll be even more crucial to keep it secret *then*. You have to keep everything, and I mean absolutely *everything* hidden. Things will happen as the years go by. Technology may end up being our friend, or our *enemy*. We don't know right now, but we *do* know that change will come whether we like it or not, so we'd better be ready to use it for *our* benefit. There's just no way to tell what it'll be like. Keep the lines of communication open. If you're not sure of something or *someone*, call your team leader. Call Jim, Russell, or me. Secrecy is the single-most important point. It *has* to be preserved at all costs. It'll also have to be super-secure with your husbands and wives. I'm sorry, but it really is that important. Nothing like this has even been considered, let alone *tried*! We're talking about taking down the United States *government*!

"The fact that most Americans can't conceive of such a thing is to our advantage. At least that's what I think now. I might change my mind later. I *do* know that most people think war or an a-bomb might conquer us, but not Americans actually *voting* for their masters. That's just something they don't even think about, and *that's* what makes it *possible*! They have to take for granted they're just selecting Republicans and Democrats when they vote. They'll be comfortable with it 'cause it's what they're *familiar* with. By the time they're able to see their mistake, it'll be too late for anyone to do anything about it. If we *are* exposed, as we very likely *will* be to some degree, we should just say that no one could believe such a preposterous yarn. At least not in America, for we're nothing more than the two major parties! We're just Republicans and Democrats!"

With each passing year, the participants became even more dogmatic and bold, as they methodically worked to reach their ultimate goal, and with a more than forty-year journey, their time had finally arrived to complete their once impossible venture. They had seen many presidents come and go throughout the several years, and now they watched the first female President, Hadley R. Crawford stand before her convention absorbing the chant for four more years. She was the most popular Democrat president in nearly eighty years…and that even included Barack Obama. In the minds of the vast majority of delegates and voters, Crawford would easily prevail in November. She was, they said, a sure winner—a landslide titleholder. This time it would be even worse for Republicans than when Obama was re-elected for a second and even more dramatic term than his first four years.

Even with her concern over the sudden rise in popularity of Sara Principle, Crawford knew that she alone held the ultimate response to any pretender to the throne. Obama had demolished Republicans. Now, as far as reaching the White House was concerned, they were finished. Soon Crawford would make an announcement that would guarantee her victory and secure her enduring place in history. What American in his right mind would not gleefully vote for a woman who would end weapons of mass destruction worldwide forever? Crawford had promised to rid the world of the most dangerous weapons ever invented in her first campaign for the Oval Office, and even to expand on the progressive policies of those who came before her.

At the end of the celebration Crawford said, "My friends, we must do as our revered President Kennedy urged so many years ago. You know the words he spoke then. We have all used them for a long time but now, once again, we must recommit ourselves and seriously ask what we can do *for* our *country*, because as all of you know we can *always* do more! We can always *give* more. Let us see that *all* of our fellow men and women have the opportunity to realize their dreams together; dreams not just for millionaires and billionaires, but also for *every* American! The time is now, and we all must answer the call to band together for the *common* good, *not* the individual! This is *your* country! What are you prepared to *do* for it, see that progress stops with another Republican in the Oval Office? Is that what you want for America? Do you want to let Senator Principle steal this election and put working families in danger of not receiving their full benefits from our government? Do you think that another obtuse Republican should be in charge again?"

"*No! No!*"

"Do you want another *conservative* government?"

"*No! No!*"

"Have you had your fill of Republicans?"

"Yes! Yes!"

"That's right; we've been down that road too many times. It was made moral again with the impressive work of President Clinton in the 1990s, but then we lost our footing for eight years until President Obama turned the tide around in 2009 with the stimulus that stopped another great depression. Then he established *single-payer* healthcare. In the days ahead, we will continue to provide the innovative and *progressive* leadership our people want and need, to have a nation where all Americans are truly *equal*. This is the only way our country can have full freedom. Our democracy is alive and well, and we will continue to lead the world's *progressive* governments.

"Because of our bold initiatives, global unrest is now ending. There will even be peace in the *Middle East*, *Korea*, and *China*, whose human rights problems have ended. I have warrants from General Tso of China and President Jafari of Iran. Things are very different in the world today, thanks to *our* efforts and the hard work of President Obama. Let those who continue to vie for their own *selfish* interests, and we all know who *they* are, come to the know that we will not allow some to reap the benefits of the world's resources at the expense of those less fortunate members of our society. If asking is not enough, let us enact legislation to *mandate* these most *human* requests! Our people are compassionate toward their fellow citizens, and we can harness that *American* empathy by recapturing the House, maintain our majority in the Senate, and continue to be the world's most caring and *progressive* citizens!

"We are on the threshold of achieving an atmosphere of permanent peace; a time in our lives when all governments will lay down not just *some* of their weapons of mass destruction, but *all* of them to the benefit of mankind as a family unit. I will deliver it *fully* next year! Together we can do it! We *must* do it, and I ask all of you for your help! Let's do this for America, and let's do this for the *world*!"

When the Republican National Convention began two weeks ahead of the Democrats, it opened with a stylistic flourish reminiscent of the Reagan years, and rallied around Sara Principle, the New Mexico junior senator. She was so popular she had won nearly every primary race with speeches of inclusion and full commitment to conservative values and the Constitution. She spoke fluent Spanish that was inviting for Hispanic participation, and was in many ways reminiscent of Barack Obama's opposite brand of speeches. Principle frequently issued quotes from the Party Platform even though she made it clear to everyone that she did not fully endorse the final draft. In the stillness of Chicago's McCormick Place, she concluded her acceptance speech.

"Ladies and gentlemen, many years ago a Democrat President, Lyndon Johnson, conducted one of the most vicious smear campaigns on record. He even used the image of an atomic bomb explosion in calling Senator Barry Goldwater a warmonger. After that gross vulgarity, there was no saving the Arizona Senator. He was thoroughly defeated and the war the president spoke of escalated broadly, but it did so under President *Johnson*. Sadly, false charges have always been a part of the political landscape by members of *both* parties. They are not new. We are here in very liberal Chicago with our conservative message, but there can be no doubt that America has developed a more liberal mindset with bigger and bigger government that plans our lives from Washington, to an increasing desire of many of our citizens to acquire something for nothing, and *that* is what scares me more than anything. Yes, my fellow Republicans, this potent *Atlas*, America, is indeed shrugging its once mighty shoulders—bending *downward* from an excessive government that has taken the one *moral* nation of the world and turned it into a bastion of socialistic *free goodies* for all. It is closer to breaking than it was even under Barack Obama, and our own party must share a large percentage of the blame.

"You've heard these words before Republicans, but this time it has to really *mean* something. We must end the practice of debilitating *investments* by our government. That is the code word both parties have used for *spending* without saying the word *spend*. Governments *spend* they don't invest, regardless of what the liberals say. The 1990s had a surplus because of *Republicans*! The benefits in that era actually came as the result of the free market succeeding with one hand tied behind its back, and lower taxes. Democrats are spending us into a Debtor's Prison. America will *self-destruct*! It will be difficult to change, but we are *Republicans*! If we fail, America will stay like the France and Greece it has become, but America can make a *comeback* if we simply *let* it.

"In 2008 governments worldwide once again interfered in the marketplace by injecting fiat money to continue a false economy built on easy credit, consumer spending, and the Federal Reserve. Then they blamed the problems on capitalism, and it *worked*, but for the politicians of both parties who were in power, *not* for America. Barack Obama tried to *collapse* our system and create a new socialist wonderland—a communist democracy like the kind he wrote about in one of his books, in spirit telling how he would kill capitalism by using the *transforming* language he *did* use to get elected...*twice*! Voters didn't understand his words, and gave him the benefit of the doubt...*twice*!

"Inflation is running at breakneck speed. We must have *new* leadership, and we must return to the *conservative* principles of Ronald Reagan and Barry Goldwater, not those of progressive *Republicans* who advocate big, not limited government to make us more like Western Europe, and be in lockstep with *Democrats*!

"Our country is no longer the one it used to be. Inflation is *blazing* down the street. We must have new direction and support candidates who advocate *freedom*, not those of Republicans who promote government interference in the marketplace just like *Democrats*! I tell you honestly, these liberals have nails in place in the coffin lid and are ready to pound it down *tight*. We must chart new frontiers! We must declare that socialism is un-American and we must *call* it socialism! Don't be *afraid* of the word. Don't be afraid to say that government no longer answers our needs not because it spends too little, but because it spends too *much*! This is the United States of America, but it became the United *Socialist* States of America. We are *better* than that, Republicans! We are better than Hadley R. Crawford and all of the Democrats who control the Senate, and we are better than the likes of *FDR, Clinton*, and yes, even *Barack Obama*!

"We must be *true* Republicans and pound the pavement in every congressional district. We must rally the people to action to bring the *real* change we need to register voters in every district, and get their commitment to elect *real* Republicans *everywhere*! And in the doing we must get a lot better at communicating information to our constituents, or our nation will be forever lost." Her voice became hushed as she added, "In fact, as much as it grieves me to say it, we may already be lost, but soon," she bellowed, "we will be *found*, and then we will take our country *back* and return it to limited government and maximum freedom!"

The delegation cheered wildly, while inside Sara Principle a growing confidence stirred. A smile imperceptibly touched the corners of her lips. The plan of many years was working. *This is how it is! They really do believe I am just another in a long line of political sameness.* The meeting in Lordsburg would indeed rise from the ashes of the past, still secret, and she was ready to carry on to the final destination.

Now the race was on for the changing of the guard, the end of democracy, and a major alteration to the Constitution.

The presidential election settled in place between the liberal Democrat and the conservative Republican. Elections had been that way for as long as most people could remember, and this year the standard policies of the two major parties were to carry onward as they had in the past. This historic election would be no different, or so it seemed on the surface with no investigation.

At midnight of the same day in a residential section of New York City, Clifford Cantrell met with an elite employee of the CIA; a top-secret assassin. "Crawford's popularity is sinking like a rock!" snarled Cantrell. "You're the one to stop Principle now, for whatever else takes place in this fucking election she must not be elected president! Be ready to move fast! And one more thing…your future depends on carrying out the mission *I* set for you when the *time* comes!"

Cantrell understood that he must take care of things himself. Now holding the dual role of National Intelligence Director and the Director of the Central Intelligence Agency, Cantrell was the most powerful head of covert operations in the history of the nation. He was also an intimate with the president, and clearly understood that Crawford would never sanction any killing, even with the knowledge that the future of democracy might rest on her own re-election. From the long hours of negotiations, the DNI/D/CIA knew that the price of Crawford's defeat would be the start of a second holocaust in Europe and the Middle East. Not just of Jews this time, but the entire European Continent, the Arabian countries and even North America. If it got that far, nothing could stop it, and that included the wisdom of Hadley R. Crawford and Clifford Cantrell's continuing manipulation of her.

TWO

President Hadley R. Crawford gazed through the windows of the Oval Office not seeing the brilliant sky of Indian summer, or the variety of small creatures that flitted about, all permanent inhabitants of the White House grounds. She was not able to understand her growing loss of support in all the published polls that even included the Internet and her own Internals. The data of the two campaigns were always more precise than nearly all of the celebrated polling groups, and they too showed her sinking popularity.

Press Secretary, Chet Forbes, and Cecil Price, Crawford's chief of staff, waited to hear what was on the president's mind.

"Were either of you able to listen to the Stanley Schwartz commentary this morning?" asked Crawford. Price quickly said that he had not heard the report but Forbes had. He said, "Yes, ma'am. I listened while I worked on my notes for the briefing."

"There's something strange going on," said Crawford, "and I just don't get it! Schwartz also reported our slippage. I thought we had his support locked *up*, but it seems we've lost him *too*. All of this seems *impossible* for the first *female* president. I'd like to know how it happened if it's true. What do *you* think, Cecil? Are they right?"

"Chief," said Price. "I've looked at the data and I sure don't get it either. It really *does* seem impossible! But I have to tell you, it *is* in line with our own internal polling and focus groups."

Crawford sat at her desk; her inner mind heavy, and filled with a clear sense of dread, pulling her lips into a tight, tense expression, with clenched teeth and a furrowed brow. "It doesn't make any *sense*!" she said sharply. "How in the hell has a secure lead evaporated *overnight*? Can either of you tell me that? I know we all agreed that this started sometime in January. We knew then the party was in some disarray, but all of you assured me it would be put *aside* by now. What do you know about *that*, Cecil? Is there anything *more* that I'm *not* aware of?"

"Nothing I can put a handle on, Madam President. It *is* very mysterious. When you think about it, though, it isn't any more bizarre than how

Principle has become a national leader. Think about *that* for a little while. It just seems that everything *about* her is strange. The only thing I've ever seen like it was that explosion of support for Obama when *he* burst on the scene a few years ago, but I sure don't think Principle's in *his* league. I really do think that was a once in a lifetime occurrence, and this Principle thing doesn't mean very much when all is said and done, even though she's female. She's not another Obama, Chief."

"It's more than that, Cecil. I appreciate your position in possibly feeling like you need to tell me what you think I *want* to hear all the time, but that's not your job. Especially now, when I need expert advice, not something invented to make me *feel* good.

"We've all been together for a long time, Cecil, and you *know* there's more to it than that. We've never run into *anything* like this! I don't think *anyone* has, and don't start comparing him to Obama. That's *nuts*! I want to know how Principle has come so far so fast with only three years in the *Senate*! That's the only valid comparison you can make with *Obama*, but the similarity *is* really strange when you think about it."

"Madam President," said Price. "I'm *not* comparing the two, and I really do think it's just happenstance and not serious. Remember back when John Kerry's surge was similar to this against Bush, and Obama's against McCain. It's just a given that a nominee gets a bump right after the convention, but I *can't* tell you why it hasn't happened with you. Maybe you should start talking about the conversations with the Russians! You said it was going really well."

"No, Cecil, not just yet. Before we tell the people we need to have it wrapped up *completely*, and that hasn't happened. We *will* have it finished soon, though.

"I think we need to concentrate just on *Principle*. We need a lot more information on her than we have right now. Whom do I go to for *that*? I *used* to hear lots of rumors flying around about a so-called Secret Society and that she might be a part of one, but I haven't heard anything on it for a long time. Have you, Chet?"

"Those rumors have been around since she ran for the Senate, Madam President," said Forbes, startled by the sudden question he had not anticipated. "She's said over and over it's absurd, and I *agree*. I mean she's been a Republican for a long time. I'm *positive* such a charge has no foundation. Nothing has *ever* come up to show that she's anything *else*, at least as far as *I've* heard!"

"But why is she such a *mystery* in this very strong information age? Where did she get her money? Oh, everyone in the world knows about her husband, and he's worth a lot, but how did she make a living *before* she became the Mayor of Las Cruces? She certainly has great skills as a *politician*, but sometimes she's a *contradiction* of the term conservative. She's even supported some of *our* legislation when most of her own party didn't, yet somehow I think she was really *against* them. There's just something about her that *feels* dangerous."

Price fidgeted in his chair and said, softly, "Why not have Director Cantrell look into her background more *thoroughly?*"

The president rose, indicating the meeting was over, even for her chief of staff. She said, "I intend to do just that, Cecil. Take care of your other work and come back in one hour."

Crawford contemplated the possible results of the coming election as the two men left the Oval Office. She was certain the United States could ill-afford another conservative in the White House, particularly one that seemed to be even dumber than George W. Bush was. People should understand that by now from recent liberal triumphs by administrations that actually cared about people.

Voters clearly affirmed their desires when they elected Crawford. Her new social programs helped the continuation of liberal policies with a passionate rejection of all that was Republican except for the House. Now, perhaps, the Democrats could regain their majority there, and increase their wide margin in the Senate to an unstoppable power as President Obama had in his first two years in office. That would certainly flout the Second-Term Blues just as Obama had managed to do, and Crawford still had her announcement of the Quadripartite Federation to reveal. Americans were clearly smitten with collectives and science fiction TV shows and movies of a single interplanetary federation of leaders. Now the time was finally right for a real one, and with the permanent peace it would offer, voters would not protest in any serious way. They would welcome and embrace the new age...she hoped.

Still there was the matter of the latest polls and growing support for Principle. If they were right, then the Schwartz comments and acknowledged support of Principle could allow her to overtake the president with her newly gained popularity of an empowering conservatism. If it happened, it could set Crawford's progressive plan back by years, perhaps not even achieved in her lifetime. Possibly, it would never take place at all because of the natural, fierce loyalty of Americans to their own constitutional government and the inability and fear to accept a new one. In particular, it would be true if Principle became as popular a president as she had a United States Senator, and there was no reason to believe she would not. She had mysteriously already obtained vast support in the Senate from both sides of the aisle equally.

In the new progressive era, fully aided by the perceived incompetence of George W. Bush in contrast to Bill Clinton and Barack Obama, Principle was now a GOP folk hero. It was made even more surprising by her boldness that she would not seek a second term if she won. She purposely insulted Obama by calling it the Audacity of One, instead of Hope, and then directly labeling Obama as Comrade. Most people thought that kind of attitude was certainly not consistent for someone who wanted to be a leader committed to ideals impossible to accomplish in a single term. It would automatically make her a lame duck. The process was, however, the consistent record of the New Mexico Senator. Everything about her was baffling, starting with her impressive ascent from political obscurity just seven years before. She even seemed to be a growing and constant mix of contradictions, yet had a mercurial rise to national prominence with private funding that appeared to be unending. It was a continuing source of frustration for her opponents and reporters.

Near the end of her four years as the Mayor of Las Cruces and with no known national constituency, Principle announced that her time was over. She would not seek re-election as she had so stated at the beginning of her administration, but would instead become a candidate for the United States Senate. In a brash display of political arrogance as described in many newspapers, most notably the Albuquerque Sun, she threw her support to a novice politician.

Principle introduced Hector Madeja to Las Cruces, who then went on to win the mayoral election with room to spare in the percentage of the vote, thus defying numbers from every polling organization.

With help from the New Mexico governor, Principle quickly established herself as one who would become a national figure, relentlessly urging for a return to the ways of Washington, Jefferson, and Adams. At the same time she inexplicably maintained a consummate state-of-the-art image, even as the bulk of commentators brusquely dismissed her as nothing more than a passing fad—a political throwback who was not in tune with modern times. What Principle wanted in government could not be like the era of America's first president more than two hundred years past. The nation had already been down that road with the Ron Paul candidacy of 2012 and soundly rejected it in favor of continued progressive leadership, and a compassionate government.

Principle entered the New Mexico primary with the same one-term message against an opponent who was a popular incumbent. Sara said their friendship would remain strong whatever the outcome. When all the votes were counted, Principle was victorious. At the start of the general election, she began a series of televised debates with her Democrat opponent Armando Munoz, a member of the Las Cruces City Council. Munoz was also a highly regarded man, and a native of the city.

Publicity surrounding the campaign suddenly swelled to a baffling frenzy. Some said the two men would have very little to debate because they had identical outlooks. Newspapers surprisingly jumped on the idea in reverse with the implication the debates would be exciting instead of dull. Principle caused some confusion with reporters baffled by contradictions, after she told them that contradictions were not even possible. Journalists could not explain how one New Mexico paper, the Albuquerque Sun claimed the debates would be bold, while another paper printed the exact opposite. Political insiders speculated that an unknown, but powerful force was at play—one they should be familiar with but that remained a mystery. It was as though a secret new form of political engineering was creating a massive amount of notoriety beyond that which had ever occurred.

On the evening of the first debate, the two candidates waited for the opening. Bill London, the erudite publisher of the Albuquerque Sun was the first panelist to begin the question period, which followed strikingly similar opening statements by the two candidates that appeared to have them in complete agreement with one another.

"Councilman Munoz" said London. "You have been at the forefront to repeal New Mexico's new open carry restriction for some time. Since the polls clearly show that the public has changed its mind and no longer support open carry with guns in plain view but that you *do* support it, my question is this: *Why* are you for it? Do you also support a constitutional amendment to that end?"

Armando glanced at Principle and smiled. "I've given my answer to that question many times Mr. London," he said, "and it is still the same. I am for open carry, but not as a written law because that is *unconstitutional*! The Constitution *automatically* allows a person to carry a gun open *or* closed. A constitutional amendment is not necessary. The Constitution limits *government*, not individuals."

London bristled. "That is an extremely simplistic answer!" he snapped. "We live in a *complex* era, Councilman. This country has gone through a great many changes since the passage of the Constitution, sir. The Constitution is very *old*. Mayor Principle, what would your answer be to the same question?"

At age fifty-eight, Laura Principle more resembled a retired athlete. She was a trim five feet tall with light brown, shoulder-length hair, swept back softly from her forehead revealing a hint of gray at the temples. Her ice-blue eyes were pale, intense, and formidable, and one of her most substantial assets. Turning to London, the Principle eyes quickly pierced through all obstacles and went directly to the mechanism of the brain that controls reasoned thought, bypassing emotions not required for the moment. The look was a quality that always seemed to bring out the most rational responses to her words, even when the listener disagreed with what she said. When she spoke to an audience, each member felt as if she was speaking to them directly, and personally.

"Actually I *agree* with the councilman's answer," she said. "As far as it goes that is, but that is certainly not far enough for me. The Constitution issues a *blanket* permit to keep and bear arms with the Second Amendment, and the Supreme Court recently *confirmed* that. I forget the year. It makes no mention of so-called controls, and if that constitutional Right is not upheld, then the Constitution is really nothing more than an old piece of paper that no one chooses to honor, *or* obey, which has been the case with all four branches of our government for some time now! Sorry! I include the Federal Reserve in that description.

"Just imagine what would have happened in some of the mass shootings that have occurred. Killers *might* have been stopped! We've certainly seen *more* murders in places where people *cannot* carry, not less, and that is true everywhere that prohibition of *any* kind exists. There is also an abundance of data to support that statement, just like all government injunctions on *anything*. If what you want is *more* of something, just *ban* it. When you ban guns, you'll have *more* violence!

"The so-called gun-control law isn't about gun control in the *first* place. It's nothing more than a vehicle to control *people*, not guns. It is lawful to own a gun for the same reason one own anything, because of the *Constitution*. Of course, modern liberals have been working with collectivists in the United Nations for many years in an attempt to use that world organization not just to subvert, but also to bring our Constitution *down*! Their bottom line is to *destroy* our Constitution!

"The issue has become nothing more than just an emotional, knee-jerk reaction by misguided people who claim, on the outside, to hate seeing others shot down. I do also, but that is not the *true* concern in this instance. It's either that or they simply have contempt for the Constitution, which is *certainly* spot-on for many people, including some past and present *politicians*! I also think there are many Americans who would *agree* with that statement. If held to the same perspective as some of those people see the gun, it would be even more urgent to outlaw *cars*, since they are directly involved with more deaths than guns by a large margin. Yet no one is proposing such a law. Why do you think that is? The answer's simple as far as I'm concerned. It doesn't make any sense. It's not the fault of the car. It's the *driver's* fault! Yet they refuse to apply that same logic to guns. This is just fraudulent, feel-good/feel-bad language that some use to appeal to *emotions* in a disingenuous way to gain support.

"There *is* something over and above the so-called gun control issue, and that is the Constitution itself. What I mean is the Constitution really *does* mean what it says, not what someone *says* it means.

"Those who advocate gun control, for instance, have a far different agenda than they are telling you, in my opinion, and it's what they're *not* saying that you should fear. Unfortunately, we must always look for hidden plans. Gun control advocates *do* know that when a government gets its hands on the guns all controls are absolute, and that is what they want. *Power* is what they *really* covet...*total* power. Look at *Cuba* for a comparison."

"*Mayor Principle*," said London, angrily interrupting her. "I'm not sure I *heard* you right. Just what in the world are you *saying*? Are you trying to compare New Mexico to *Cuba*? If you are, I think that is *very* offensive! Is that what you're saying?"

"No, I'm not Mr. London. I'm just trying to explain that the first step officials have used to gain unchallenged power everywhere is to take control of *weapons*! It's happened repeatedly throughout history with plenty of models outside of Castro. Take for example what Chairman Mao said. 'Political power grows out of the barrel of a gun.' I once heard a cabinet member of President Barack Obama *agree* with that quote. It really isn't hard to see and understand when you remove all of the emotions and see things logically. They *always* appeal to feelings, never to reason."

The debate continued with such complete agreement between the two it bewildered the panel. In newspapers the following day, editors wrote of the great difficulty facing voters. If you liked one you had to like the other, was the consensus of the majority of reports. Bill London wrote a scathing reproof, calling the debate a joke. He formally accused the duo of a conspiratorial effort, writing that if the audience had to pay for the privilege of sitting in the room they would have rightfully demanded a refund. Still the mysterious hype swelled, almost as if an unseen public relations office was orchestrating everything for both candidates. At nearly the same time political commentators began to make the Secret Society charge. In a late night hookup with the television program, Night Side, the conspiracy issue was again raised, but differently, as it was from a friend—the single journalist with access to the Principle inner circle who was also an associate member of The Solution and knew what he was doing.

"Mayor Principle," said the substitute host and hidden member of The Solution David Breyer. "Persistent rumors continue to fly that you are involved with a secret organization of people; a covert cabal of individuals who want to establish something different in government. I've had many inquiries on this, and I've received them from liberal *and* conservative areas of the country. Care to comment?"

Principle's face tightened to a gritty look of disgust and dismissal as she said slowly, carefully; "Yes, I certainly would like to create something different like a smaller and more efficient government, but no, I do not have some kind of secret plot to achieve that end."

"Then why do you think this question refuses to die? What could be keeping it in *play*? Do you think it's a planned and concerted effort by some individual or group of individual's? Why does it keep coming up if there's nothing to it? I know I've been asked these questions and more, not by those who have a political agenda, but just regular folks, and lots of them wanted me to ask *you*."

"I really don't know," said Principle, her lips clamped together in frustration. Then she said, "Maybe it's because people like you just keep on asking about it over and over without having any *evidence* except that you heard a *rumor*! I really do think that needs to change in journalism."

Now she would go on offense, as they had agreed she would do before the program began. She said harshly, "So let me ask *you*! Are you caught up in a plot yourself to keep bringing up this preposterous charge? I'm a *Republican*! Everyone knows this because it is extremely well known, and frankly, I'm getting really tired of this idiotic question. It simply has no basis in truth and constantly making the charge time after time just serves to take *away* time from the *real* questions. We need to talk about *them*! This is not *authentic*! Let's talk about *real* issues, like taxes and government *spending* and *spying*!"

"You should forgive me, Mayor, but I've frequently seen that when something like this persists with *anything*, regardless of what it is there is more often than not a *story* there! Where there's smoke there's fire, so to speak. That's all I'm saying. And I'm not the *only* one. It's being talked about on television, in newspapers, on the Internet, YouTube, Twitter, Facebook, all the social sites, and by a lot of other people, many of whom keep saying they'd like answers *they* claim you're not giving."

"All right David. What do you want me to say that I haven't said time after time? How about, yes, I *am* a part of a vast right-wing conspiracy to overthrow the government. Would *that* make all of you happy? It sounds more like something Hadley Roman Crawford might have come up with in one of her less lucid moments, like those that got her into trouble in the Democratic Primary race.

"Don't you see? The idea is completely way out in left field! I *am* involved with an organization, but not a *secret* one. It's the Republican Party in case you've forgotten! I've been a Republican for a very long time. It is well *known*. I also have many friends who are Democrats *and* Republicans. I really don't know how any of this got started, and I actually thought it was finally over until this very *moment*! Mr. *Munoz* sure hasn't mentioned it. The whole thing amazes me. How anyone could believe such a bone-headed charge like that is beyond me, and how a respected journalist like you could ask about it is even *more* confusing. So let me say it one more time and then maybe it will be the last time I'll have to deal with it.

"I have been and continue to be a Republican, and as far as I'm concerned you and the rest of the press corps ought to be *embarrassed* about bringing up such a seriously goofy idea. I mean, it's just *loony*! I can't figure out how so many of you have been so caught up with it. It's silly! Or that is it *would* be if it wasn't so serious."

Nine days before the general election, Councilman Armando Munoz suddenly called a press conference. He was a quiet, soft-spoken man with a slight Hispanic accent. As he waited for the reporters to gather he stood quietly, his arms held loosely by his side with an occasional nervous gesture to his head, twirling the black curls around his fingers and stepping foot-to-foot before he was comfortable speaking to the press.

After several minutes, he thanked the press and the public. However, due to pressing family matters he could no longer ignore and would not be comfortable discussing, he was withdrawing from the race. While it had been an extremely difficult decision, he could find nothing meaningful to take issue with Principle, who he urged his own followers to support. Principle would serve the interests of the people of New Mexico well, and Armando just had too many personal considerations to stay in the race. He could no longer set aside his concerns and disregard his family's well-being. With no time for the Democrats to field a replacement for Armando Munoz, the election was a landslide victory for Principle.

On the morning after the election, Armando resigned his seat on the Las Cruces City Council. He then moved his family to a home adjacent to the property of Sara Principle, where he remained sequestered for three months, refusing all requests for interviews. During the period, he accepted a teaching post of political science at New Mexico State University, along with a part-time position as an aide to the newly elected senator. Then he set up an office in a nearby warehouse.

To the chagrin of her staff, Principle proceeded to honor requests for appearances on television and radio programs, invitations that even included eastern newspapers known for their liberal biases against the conservative movement that was sweeping the nation much in the same way as the wave of change developed for Barack Obama in 2008. Principle's picture appeared on the covers of several online magazines, with in-depth analysis of her known conservative philosophy that continued to remain largely undiscovered to most voters—nearly a parallel to Barack Obama when he ran for the nomination against Hillary Clinton.

While President Crawford gazed through the window of the Oval Office, she was only aware of the potential threat to her presidency, but not of the summer meeting in Lordsburg more than forty-years before this day. At that meeting, Principle dubbed the new organization The Solution. Twenty-seven years later, and armed with the knowledge of past administrations and the current policies of that White House, Principle once again summoned the foremost Solution members to Las Cruces to consider a new idea. The organization had grown to such a large degree it was now necessary to hold the gathering inside the warehouse to assure privacy, and the press received no invitation.

She told the members of a change in their original strategy as it related to that election. Americans had seen several years of conservative administrations. They knew what would happen when a perceived right-winger was president—quickly becoming the opposite of their free market image, and working with progressive Democrats and Republicans to drive the federal budget to astronomical proportions while promoting events in private, which they publicly disdained. The Solution must now turn their efforts toward the election of a hidden liberal, who, when linked together with conservatives, were the complete antithesis of what the group believed in and stood for. They needed time. Perhaps they would need more than one liberal administration to make their point with the electorate to help them show voters that both conservative and liberal concepts were equally destructive to freedom. The goals of the organization had not changed. Their mission to create a top-secret party-within-a-party of Democrats and Republicans was steadily moving forward and growing. They would carry on with full secrecy. Skull and Bones would be their privacy model, with effective instruction along the way from Jim Miller. For now, however, twenty-seven years after their inception, a new and even more courageous path needed to occur. The original concepts would remain intact except for this one necessary detour. The diverse contrast between the elected conservatives and liberals ending with nearly identical results of government policies would help the full membership of The Solution in their final assault. Afterward, they would begin anew, and return to the old ways and methods as their guide in the mission.

More than forty-years had now passed in the long road. They continued to grow to meet the older and more deeply entrenched collusion of the two major parties to break up everything they had ever created, and they would meet them on their own terms to control America even greater than the American Revolution.

When individual members of The Solution had reached the top of their own hidden itinerary, the Republican and Democratic Parties would no longer be a factor in national politics, because the takeover was to happen in this year. Their demise was now only a few weeks away, and about to crumble like a house of cards. The Solution would institute extreme control over the legislative and executive branches of the federal government. Then, a changed Constitution would follow, with new Articles to suit the ultimate plan. After the occupation of the Congress, they would go after the Supreme Court. When the agenda was completed, very few Americans would recognize their own government. This was the year democracy would collapse.

THREE

Throughout her political tenure, Hadley R. Crawford believed she had seen just about everything there was to see. She had worked all of her life to help the less fortunate, and in her political realm to end war. Now she was seeking re-election to the most powerful position in the world. It was a world that needed serious instruction on what was necessary for a permanent peace from Crawford's perspective, made even more essential by the impact of 9/11 and the subsequent invasion of Iraq that left America seriously wounded and divided, even as George W. Bush was re-elected in 2004. Because of this glaring fact, a quality president like Crawford would have no trouble at all, aided in part by the incredible success of the ultimate progressive elected to two White House terms, Barack Obama.

When Crawford contemplated the outcome of the election and her top-secret meetings with the Russian Foreign Minister, she began to feel old and tired. In three months she would be sixty-six, and the closer her birthday and the election came, the more she wondered if it was worth all the aggravation and personal sacrifice she believed was vital to people in a moral society. She was also growing tired of being on call at any hour of the day or night, but power always beckoned her.

In her heart-of-hearts, she believed she was a good president, even a great one—a chief executive who cared more about people than politics. Though some of her actions were under the tightest security, it was essential for a positive outcome not just for America, but the entire world. This was because the idea behind the treaty with the Russians and the other two powers would serve humanity as nothing had ever done before. Everyone wanted a lasting peace. Americans longed for it, and Hadley R. Crawford would bring that peace and security to them where all presidents before her had failed. For now, however, an attractive, self-assured newcomer to the national scene was daring to challenge the President of the United States and believe that her positions were superior to those of the president. In Crawford's mind, it was extremely presumptuous. This was especially true for a rookie senator no one had ever heard of. Crawford would have to call Principle out in the debates and cleverly belittle her with the live audience to help show Principle up as a rank amateur, with those citizens who were following the debate on television and radio.

Crawford's grey-blonde hair, thick and salted throughout, gave her a regal appearance, even with a waistline that was beginning to show from an overabundance of rich food and little exercise. Her physician had declared her to be in fine physical condition. In fact, her health had improved since moving into the White House. Being the president was good for her. Principle, on the other hand, just four years younger was a woman with a strong, flat stomach looking more like a retired athlete.

The office intercom sounded sharply from the desk of Ronald Davenport, Crawford's personal secretary. The president looked at her schedule and as she did so, Clifford Cantrell bolted through the door with the swift, purposeful steps he always took when he was irritated, as he so obviously was at this moment.

"Hadley," he said quickly, eager to get his message across and equally intent on knowing the president was in fact not just hearing, but listening as well.

"My report to you today is that your chances in this election have dropped to *fifty-fifty*, and you are the first *female* here. If we don't get off our butts and *do* something, Principle just might have the momentum to pull off the upset of the century by unseating the first woman elected president! You *have* to get out of here and hit the road as hard as you did four years ago, maybe even *harder*! You can't keep up with this shit-ass Rose Garden strategy.

"All of our Internals show us that the public thinks Principle is a lot more independent than you…" "Go on," said a resigned Crawford. "Tell me everything."

"Your association with James Johnson and Matt Weeks is hurting you badly. It's not producing the results you want except in the black community, and everyone knows the fucking niggers don't get their asses out there to vote most of the time unless the candidate's a nigger too, like Obama."

"Just stop it right *there*, Cliff! I won't *stand* for it. Stop it right *now*! Keep it to *yourself*! I don't want to hear it again!"

"All right, all right, I'm sorry! I forget sometimes. Please accept my apology, Madam President, and I *mean* it."

"Well, *don't* forget. I don't like it! You've known that for a long time, maybe for *too* long! *No*! I'm *sorry*. I don't mean that, Cliff."

Cantrell could see that he had clearly overstepped and said, "But I still have to tell you. I think it's put you in trouble with the white vote generally, and the Jewish vote in particular, and you really need them 'cause you're losing the goddamn *Hispanic* vote to Senator Pinciple!

"One more thing Hadley! More and more people are starting to think you're grooming Johnson to run for this office just because he *is* black, so *capitalize* on that! The photo-ops in the Rose Garden may work for the press, but not for you in the *election*. You *need* the black vote 'cause Hispanics will vote *Republican* this time. *Listen* to me!"

"I know, Cliff, and I *am*," said Crawford, her face reflecting her concern. "But we desperately need to move the nation into an even *newer* age than what happened under Obama. Even *he* wasn't able to get it done fully, although he *did* stop the demonization of gays. It's the right thing to do Cliff. That's what the photo-ops are all about for me. I *have* to do them. Obama *did* make it easier, but *we* haven't succeeded either, even though I'm certain we'll get the black vote, but not as much as Obama got.

"Think back, Cliff. Bush hurt Democrats with the minorities he put in major spots. That helped *him* get re-elected. We also need the Quadripartite Treaty. That will help people in all areas of the country see that government has finally reached the point in history where it's *fairer*—where it's more charitable, and yes, more *human*! It *will* help us with blacks *and* browns *too*. It is *right*, Cliff, I *know* it is! I've studied this extensively and I know it may be the *only* way, especially since Obama didn't get it done either."

"Excuse me, Madam President," said Cantrell. "*We* know that but the voters don't. They just aren't sophisticated enough to understand all that. The average American just doesn't get it. They don't appreciate the absolute fact that we have to align ourselves with the rest of the world in this way, and that's why we've kept the treaty a *secret*. It *has* been easier, though, with fewer newspapers left operating in the country."

He paused, wondering how a woman he had known for so many years could believe such drivel, and then realizing in the same moment that he had always known it. He also needed the moment of silence to look at Crawford's face to see if she was buying what Cantrell was selling, and then he continued.

"Hadley," he said. "You have to remember that Bush and Clinton were just plain *lucky* in the grand scheme of things. How *else* can you explain it? They *did* have some *very* qualified people, but Johnson and Weeks aren't like that. In any case, you really do need to keep the treaty secret, because the people of this country are ignorant about such things and they always *will* be. But that's to our *advantage*!"

Crawford smiled. That advantage was not the true purpose. Still she would allow Cantrell to believe it was. When the announcement of the treaty did come, it would show the people that world peace had finally arrived in their lifetime. Only governmental concepts would change. It was essential in such a dangerous world, and people must finally understand that individual nations could no longer exist as they had in the past. The treaty, in line with the new North American Union, would bring the various governments under one umbrella with one currency…a true axis. They could easily handle any outbreaks of hostility wherever it occurred. For the first time, even Middle Eastern countries, North Korea, and China would participate. There would be no more war, with force used only where it was necessary. The elusive dream of universal peace and cooperation would prevail in this starting point to bring the world together as a true family of nations for the first time in history…a new *League* of Nations, aka Woodrow Wilson.

"I understand what you're saying, Cliff," said Crawford, as she paced back and forth thinking of the treaty to come, her back turned to Cantrell. "But as far as Johnson and Weeks are concerned," she continued, "I am *certain* they're too important to the *Group*!

"Forget about them!" she said sharply, turning to confront her D/CIA face-to-face. "Let's get back to Principle. *She's* the threat, not them. I can't accept it that she has as much support as you and the others are saying. She's just a clone of George W. These conservatives today are all alike, preaching to the altar of *Reagan*. And one more thing—we seem to know so little about Principle on a personal level. Why *is* that? What about Opposition Research? I mean she doesn't live on some damn *island*! What about the Secret Society thing we used to hear people talk of? Where did *that* come from, and when did it go away? Can you tell me if there's anything to it? I keep asking, but no one has any answers so far. What are we paying those people who do the investigations?"

"Principle's always maintained the idea's absurd, and I agree. It's just too far out to imagine, even for *me*. You've seen what *she* says about it, and it makes a lot of sense. You know we didn't find anything before. If there's a smoking gun somewhere, she has it *very* well hidden, because I assure you my man would have found it, and so would PRISM.

"I also have to remind you that she's no *fluke*, and she's also not as dumb as you think. She's also shown a good capacity to know where she is and where she's going. She has some very top-flight people with her and she won't be easy to defeat, even for *you*. I hope you aren't *underestimating* her. She's done everything right up 'til now, and I guess my biggest fear is the Hispanic thing! She speaks Spanish fluently.

"As far as this Secret Society idea is concerned, I'll look into it again if that's what you *want*, but it'll probably draw a blank just like before. We really can't come up with *anything*. I hired an Internet geek several weeks ago. He told me that nothing's there, and he's certain we won't *find* anything, especially since PRISM didn't come up with something. I think you ought to just forget about that and concentrate on dealing with her positions, *and* in getting out of *here*! The people are clamoring for it *too*. They want to *see* you! You just can't keep staying here in the White House."

"I know, Cliff, and I will. They're putting more appearances in the schedule. But I just keep thinking about this Secret Society thing! If something wasn't *there*, we would never have heard of it!"

"Okay. One more time, I'll see what I can find. In *any* case, there *is* a bright side to all of this. We're certain Principle can't win the popular vote. In fact, we *know* that's true, but we also know she's not even trying for it. They've concentrated enough efforts in key states that she *could* win the electoral count better than Bush did against Gore in 2000. *We* have to keep working for Florida, Ohio, Pennsylvania, Wisconsin, and even New York.

You can forget Texas. Harrington's a key force against us down there, but if we win three of those five battleground states, you'll win the election without any doubt. That's the main reason you have to get out on the trail. At the very least, you have to make a few more appearances in Florida, Ohio, *and* New York, and New York won't be easy to win. There's not much time *left* now! It's really *necessary* to get out of here, Hadley."

As she listened to her D/CIA, Crawford continued to wonder about the mystery of Sara Principle. Even though she was now a national figure, very little of substance was known of her. It often seemed as though she had been a part of the federal witness protection program with no previous identity. Much of the time she was a paradox; a peculiar sort who confused even her most ardent supporters with what seemed to be contradictory positions. She was even odd to some Republicans because she kept saying that a contradiction can't exist, and if you think you see one, you should check your original idea.

From the time when she first appeared on the national scene as a freshman senator, Principle inexplicably managed to influence large numbers of Democrats to follow her lead, even against their own leadership. The impact was made even more baffling because she presumably had no national following, only her power base in Las Cruces. In the Senate, she quickly established her leadership qualities by obtaining generous support from the opposite side of the aisle in what appeared to be an astute awareness and political acumen for any freshman senator. This was especially true for one that came from New Mexico, a vast desert state filled with unsophisticated Hispanics and white know-nothings. It was nearly impossible to comprehend her rise other than being female. New Mexico senators simply did not ascend so far, or so fast, and they certainly did not ever become president. At least Obama was from an open-minded state like Illinois, where the third largest city, Chicago, had a degree of sophistication.

In her rebuttal before the full Senate, Principle spoke effectively on the president's new pet project. The Ethical Awareness Act was a natural outgrowth from the legislation for prescription drugs for senior's many years earlier by a Republican. Believing the bill would easily pass the full Senate, the Majority Leader called it up on the floor, where Principle began a surprise attack. No one, it seemed, ever saw it coming.

"Mr. President," said Principle from the floor of the Senate. "This bill sponsored by the president is designed to funnel millions of dollars for an adult-type school to teach morality and decency to our fellow citizens. Americans are the most decent people in the *world*. Whose ethics is she talking about, her own? This bill has even been the subject of comedy routines for some time now and rightly so.

"If my fellow members of this august body do not see the absurdity of this bill, then all of you need to see a physician, and while you're at it, take her *with* you. Where does the president get off trying to impose her own brand of morality on *anyone*? How can she be so bold in trying to force the people to fund this bill when they do not agree with it and certainly have no *need* for this type of education? Is it because she's female?

"This package is nothing more than an attempt to brainwash the American people even more than they already are. The president wants them to become a nation of human robots dancing to a government tune! It will be just another pork-barrel laden project to transfer more of America's wealth. This nation is still reeling from the *stupid* invasion of Iraq by a *Republican* president who was ill informed, along with the equally moronic spending by the Obama administration. The Bill of Rights exists to limit *government*, not *citizens*! *This* bill is just another reassignment of wealth to benefit *politicians*, not our constituents. It must be strongly rejected, and then it must be discarded into the scrap heap of outrageous demagoguery with a decisive defeat *now*!"

It was a bitter loss for the president. In an emotionally charged press conference, Crawford accused Republican members of the Senate of being irresponsible and insensitive to the needs of working people. She promised to use the defeat in her re-election campaign, and to call on voters to fight with her against the Republicans who voted against the bill. To do less would be an open invitation for them to keep working *against* everyday citizens and unions. She made no mention of Democrats who also voted against the bill.

Following the legislative loss, Crawford met with Chet Forbes, Cecil Price and Mo Dobrosky, the National Security Advisor. "Principle's old ideas are *obsolete*!" screamed Price. "*Everyone* knows that! It shouldn't be a secret to *anyone*! We have to *get* her. We have to get her *soon*! We can't let this go *unchallenged*! It's just too *much*, and you need to make a strong statement *right away*! Don't let her get away with this."

Crawford reflected quietly to herself about her own evaluation of the outburst. Cecil Price was an astute official and a very qualified chief of staff whose opinion was highly regarded in all Washington circles. Having been present at the beginning of the administration, he induced many members of the press to write glowing reports on the president's expertise in both foreign and domestic policies, and Crawford must let him vent his emotions for the moment.

"Like it or not," said Crawford, trying to calm the room, "we still have to deal with her, and we can't let our emotions get in the way of what we're trying to get done, Cecil. In spite of what you might think, Principle's become extremely popular. Yes, her approach is very different from ours, at least on the surface, but she's also *joined* us many times. So calm down Cecil, because I promise you we'll get her, and we'll do it a lot sooner than you think right now. *Trust* me."

Mo Dobrosky had become Crawford's most intimate advisor on security issues. Crawford valued all of Dobrosky's advice, privately in awe of the distinguished Russian immigrant who was the one open hawk that

Crawford had nominated to any office. Dobrosky's influence on the more pragmatic president surprised everyone. He was a very thin, drawn man, nearly emaciated, with a severe, close-cropped haircut trimmed flat on the top, who nearly always called for an increase in NSA surveillance. His voice was crisp and distinct, as he said, "Even though she's a Republican, I believe we could use national defense *against* her! She's even more draconian than President Obama was. She wants to cut the NSA budget in half, and that is unacceptable. She's *dangerous*, Madam President. I am certain you should be able to expose her in the debates on that single issue."

The president rose quickly and said, "I know it's difficult to get a handle on this woman. As far as *we're* concerned, I think it's important to keep stressing the issues and our record, which is damn good on many levels. All of you keep me up to speed on anything you *do* find out, but I will not play the game of dirty politics even to save my job. I never have. It's not who I *am*! I'm also certain I will not have to do that, not because I suffer from a Pollyanna outlook, but quite the opposite. Let me just tell you that I have inside information you do not have."

Crawford was increasingly concerned with the substance of all that Cantrell had to say about getting on the trail. "Cliff," said Crawford. "I've heard all that you've said. I really *have*! I also realize that it might not be comfortable for you because of my position, even though we've been so close for such a long time. Don't be concerned. Just know that I *am* listening to you."

"Madam President…Hadley, we both know that the survival of the nation is at stake and maybe the rest of the planet as well. You *must* win this election. It's *imperative* that you win, and yes, I *do* consider your position, and I do so all the *time*. I know, I've heard what people say, and I'm not without feelings for that, in *spite* of all the rumors. I do respect you, and I do respect the office." Cantrell silently hoped he would not throw up to reveal his true feelings.

"I know, Cliff," said Crawford. "But I also know that what I said before is true, even if you *don't* agree with me, and I *know* you don't. That's okay. The quadripartite must happen. It's the only way for the world to continue to exist. I know none of my *conservative* friends have any understanding on this. Principle *must* lose. President Zgonina hasn't been able to convince the Russian Commonwealth that they have other options. I know he doesn't want war. The same is true of General Tso and *his* people, but we sure as hell can never really know what Jafari and Iran are going to do next. Because of that, I'm certain the Russians will invade Europe if I lose. China will move in on the Middle East at the same time. Tso will remove Mullahs and the Muslim Brotherhood. He'll quickly turn the Middle East into a Chinese satellite with *nukes*, and you know we can't let that happen. At the same time, Russia will get rid of English royalty. I'm convinced they won't be able to deal with Principle, and they believe it too. Also, I'm female, and that makes things even more difficult in dealing with some of the men around the world."

Crawford suddenly felt a chill engulf her body over the prospect of World War. She shuddered, wishing she could tell the nation, but understood that it must remain hidden for a while longer. She couldn't even use the information to help in her re-election bid.

The president also worried over Cantrell. She knew her D/CIA was a man who relished covert violence. Crawford understood that even though progress continued in Russia, she did not want to force Zgonina to a point to risk public safety to the stubborn old men of the newly created Russian Central Committee because they had to deal with a woman in the White House. The Muslim Brotherhood increased the religious problem in the Middle East after the military removed them from power, and with Cantrell's gleeful propensity for violence against anyone who crossed him.

In person, Cantrell was a difficult man to ignore from his outward persona, and the way he seemed to be always on edge. He was a portly man in his late sixties, always appearing to others to be perpetually angry and ready to erupt from the slightest provocation. His closest friends, of whom there were very few but did include the president, knew the opposite was true. On the outside, Cantrell could seem to be ready to swoop down on an unwary victim, while inside, a calculating, computer-like mind plotted precisely how he would have his way on any particular issue. As he was the supreme powerbroker of the moment, he made it clear to every person that it was his way or the highway. There were never any exceptions for the D/CIA, even with the president. Crawford was aware of that attitude, resigning herself that since Cantrell held his position and was the president's close confidant for so many years, it was a problem without a fix.

Cantrell's oiled, salt and pepper hair was slicked back from his face with a precise, off-center parting. The hair defined his black eyes and accentuated the deep creases that slashed the entire width of his forehead, helping to create the always-angry qualities in his appearance that he very much enjoyed. His voice was strong and coarse, a deep smokers voice, with an odd synchronization to his speech that was nearly reminiscent of a talking computer. He possessed great cunning; intense and boiling on the surface, and, who delighted in the knowledge that he was never as he appeared to others in any way, but always in control of all of his own thoughts, and actions.

One of his greatest coups was an operation he created in Colombia, South America. In consort with a wealthy plantation owner, Cantrell brought in gangs to destroy the crops of two major coffee growers. They were men who had gambled away their fortunes and were in very tenuous financial positions. His principals, the largest private consortium in South America, called in markers of both growers and acquired their acreage. In appreciation for his assistance, the consortium gave a sum of $10 million to the President of Colombia, who then made a deposit of $1 million directly into Cantrell's Swiss account. Thereafter whenever the D/CIA drank coffee, he reveled in his good fortune in life, seeing the event as nothing more than a simple, yet superior business transaction to add with several others he had also created in the United States.

When they were in their early twenties and with the help of David Rockhold, the New York City banker, Cantrell helped to introduce his young friend, Hadley Crawford, to the little-known international society The World Council Group. They became members of their American affiliate, The Committee on Foreign Affairs, but Crawford received only enough information to keep her interested in their activities. She did not know the full purpose of the *Group*. Upper echelon leaders pursued Crawford early, deciding that she would be their key to ultimate power simply because she was female.

As she grew older, Crawford learned more details, but only what they wanted her to know; that peace could never happen in the world as long as governments engaged in their own selfish brand of nationalism. One ideology had to surface, with the *Group* as its overseer, to become, over time the Supreme Government of the entire planet. This was the only way to end war, they taught her, and their power would stop even the threat of confrontations worldwide.

Through their offices in Paris, London, and New York, the *Group* would work to manipulate the international monetary fund. All nations were to become tightly controlled, to enable the organization to provide for their general welfare. In the United States, the door would open to allow the *Group* to begin to change public perception of private property and ownership by slowly developing a policy of government issued permits over the course of many years. The licenses would be on the usage of property and assessment of values to establish necessary control of the masses of people throughout America, and then to collect revenue on a continuing basis worldwide.

Long before she became president, the *Group* settled on Crawford to become the principal pawn in their ascendance as the controlling factor in their *New World Order*. It had taken them more than one-hundred years to be ready when the right moment came, and it was now. With Crawford in place and with her re-election, the *Group* was nearing the climax of that very long and very secretive effort.

Most of their success was subtle. They induced politicians to do the *Group's* bidding, even without the official's knowledge. Terms such as government funds, democracy, progressivism, and The New Federalism became commonplace phrases, slowly taking effect as normal language in the intentional program of massive misinformation.

A portion of their credo stated: *If the New World Order maintains the illusion of consent, people will be easier to control. If they come to an understanding that complex issues are for those who are more qualified to comprehend them, they will be easier to control, and in time will learn to love their servitude and permanent dependence. This they will accept for a world forever at peace and devoid of personal risk.*

It was a long process, but Americans clearly showed they were ripe for the plucking. Through their intimate relationships with inner circles in Washington, they influenced numerous decisions in World War I and II, and America's worldwide military presence. They discovered the American government was for sale to the biggest and most continuing spenders. They were also a quiet factor in the establishment of the Social Security Act and the United Nations.

Still there were modern problems coming from the American people in recent years. Voters were starting to end their love affair for massive programs in a wave of conservative demands for fiscal restraint that began in 2014. It helped explain the unexpected popularity of Sara Principle in a strange way, though it seemed there was a huge diversity of opinion as to why she had risen so quickly. Some believed she had rescued the Republican Party from the label of being the *Party of Theocracy*, a nametag that arose from the George W. Bush era. Others chose to believe the principal reason came from the acclaim of Principle's famous husband. If that was not the answer, just what was? The true answer was completely unknown to most Americans.

FOUR

The light drizzle of rain forecast the coming of fall in the nation's capital, as the city awakened to prepare for the imminent election for president that was now just four weeks away. Washingtonians were fraught with gloom in light of the sudden and surprising explosion of support for Sara Principle. Editors wrote of the possible downfall of a benevolent government if the president were defeated, as it now seemed possible. Principle's popularity had soared to new and remarkable heights, and the people of the District of Columbia were worried. They listened to the accolades of the local television coverage and made their collective decision. The president must be re-elected.

Crawford had become the matriarch of D.C. Massive programs created thousands of new jobs in balanced harmony with private business, and the administration even took credit for drastically reduced inner-city crime. They would change the subject, however, when asked about the effect on crime that came from the 2008 Supreme Court decision on the Second Amendment, when the Court declared that it was an *individual* Right to own guns. Now, however, with the Court fully stacked in the liberal administration's favor behind the effort in the United Nations to ban weapons worldwide, they were not concerned.

In a flood of new, government-financed construction throughout the entire district, the president made it clear that the vibrant economy existed because of a caring, committed government, while local union leaders bestowed their accolades on the administration for their efforts in creating thousands of new jobs. D.C. was America's wealthiest community.

In Lafayette Square, directly in front of the White House, WSC, (Workers Supporting Crawford) a national organization, were busy setting up a counter-demonstration to the radical CFL (Citizens for Liberty). WSC was a nexus of union members united to re-elect the president, urging the Congress to set up a repeal of the Twenty-second Amendment. It was their view the Amendment had prevented truly great presidents from having more than two terms in office, and would do so again this time, should the president be re-elected and then not be eligible to run for a third term. It would be just one more tragedy in a continuous lineup of major proportions to go against the working people of America, a blight that ordinary folks would be forced to deal with once again in their fight for their just rights for working families.

On 16th Street, in a building near the National Geographic Society, Sara Principle, Armando Munoz, and Thomas Farley, worked in Principle's alternate office away from her Senate workplace in the Russell Senate Office Building. They were writing Farley's CFL rally speech. Farley was the brilliant and well-known professor of economics from the University of California.

He announced his support of Senator Principle one year before the Republican National Convention. As an independent, he said his commitment to persuade Principle to run was so strong that he would take a leave of absence from the university to tour the nation and speak on Principle's behalf. His journey would be strictly limited to black communities and black organizations as an advocate of breaking the Big Brother stranglehold on his own people. It would approximate methods used some years earlier by the fundamental Campaigner-in-Chief, Barack Obama.

Farley announced that he would appear in person and on black media with the goal of changing attitudes with a simple message for all races and economic situations. His principal focus would be on the black experience for his own people to stop depending on government. He wanted individual black citizens to step up and remove themselves from the control of politicians, and take charge of their own lives.

"Join with me!" he would bellow in churches and public events. "Come forth and *take* your life and your *freedom*, or at least what is *left* of your freedom! You must *take* it because you have given it away to people who use your need for them to hold you in bondage, and yes, that *includes* Barack Obama and Jeremiah Wright and *his* crowd.

"Do not ask that it be *given* to you! It is not yours for the asking or for others to do the giving, and get *rid* of the word, *give*! It *is* yours for the willingness to *work* for it and to have the intestinal fortitude to go out and make it on your own and declare that you are a person who will announce to the world that you really do care about your *own* life and the lives of your neighbors. Success can only happen if you care enough to take *rational, selfish, individual* action to help yourself and your brothers and sisters. Do not embrace *victim-hood*!

"Let the word go out far and wide to remember, that, just with Dr. King's dream for people to be judged by the content of their character, I say to you that *we* have not yet arrived at that grand standard ourselves as *individuals*! Many of us still cling to the groupthink mentality that we *deserve* different treatment because we have a certain skin color, promoted by famous black people. That was an idea foisted on us for a very long time. *We* must *stop* it—*you* must stop it, and you need to begin to *think*, not as a member of a group, but as *individuals*.

"One example is this: It is a fact that many blacks have been freely accepted in *white* communities *voluntarily*, and that is how it *must* be in a great and *moral* society. If the effort is not voluntary, then the society in which it takes its residence is not free *or* moral. Yes, there *are* many white racists, but here is another truth…an unspoken *fact*! Institutional racism is not exclusive to white people. It also includes black, brown, red, and yellow people. We all do it *too*!" He paused then spoke more softly and said, "We also, as men, must care less about pleasure and live with our babies *and* their mothers…just *one* mother!

"Perhaps we did learn racism from whites. I can accept that, but I *will not* accept the altruistic and stupid idiom, African-American. According to scripture, *everyone* came from Africa. It was the first *neighborhood*! Does that make *all* people African-Americans? My own heritage *is* from Africa, but many of my friends do not have that background. As the former Democrat governor of Virginia, Doug Wilder once said, 'I'm not an African-American I'm an *American*!' However, the politically correct crowd wants to lump all of us together. Well, here's what *I* think. We are all different—and as *individuals*, we must rejoice in our natural differences and work to *preserve* them for our own *integrity*. As *black* people, we must also recognize that so-called corrections of wrongs of the past must *never* be legislated on the backs of the people of the present and thus become *new* wrongs! We also have to see and *understand* that groups do not *have* rights. Rights belong *exclusively* to *individuals*!

"As to our history in the building of our new nation and the way we were once treated in the South, *and* that there were *many* wrongs and abuses, whites did not conduct *all* of them. Black people also participated in *very* wicked dealings against each *other*. *Both* races hid their *individualism* within those factions. Don't *hide* your uniqueness. That *is* America…or at least it *used* to be America.

"But racism in the Constitution, as is widely believed by many people was not there. As the great orator, Frederick Douglas proclaimed even better than I can, on March 26, 1860 in Glasgow, Scotland, the Constitution as *written*, was *anti*-slavery. He said many words to authenticate that statement, and here is one quote. 'A wise man has said that few people have been found better than their laws, but many have been found worse. To this last rule, America is no exception. Her laws are one thing, her practice is another thing.' He tried to teach us many things that even now we have not yet learned!

"We must accept what some did against us *then*, but not now, and also, that the Constitution has *never* been against us. When we *do* begin to recognize that the people of today have no responsibility for *past* actions, it is *mandatory* to realize that some of *us* do *not* have a right to a piece of a pie that another person has made. It is acceptable only if the exchange is *voluntary*. In other words, we must be who and what we are as individuals, not as members of a *group*!"

He was an elegant man who enunciated his words carefully, with a robust, bass baritone voice that easily reached the rear of a classroom or auditorium. He commanded so much attention to the spoken word that he was often solicited for voice-over commercials by talent agencies, to which he always declined, saying he had no interest in being in the entertainment business.

The books and lectures of Milton Friedman influenced Farley as a student at the University of Chicago. Friedman, according to the California professor, was the only economist who taught common sense in addition to economics. He should never be lumped into the economist bin who, when lined up in a straight line all pointed in different directions.

At nearly the same time, Farley enrolled in speech classes to help eradicate the unintelligible black lingo he shared with his peers on Jeffery Boulevard in the heart of the black community, and to help him overcome a stuttering problem that naturally disappeared, as he grew older and more self-confident.

The three friends crowded around the computer, their voices mixed in an animated triad of mutual trust, respect and camaraderie. Principle appreciated Farley's academic input in the ongoing work, and gave explicit instructions that there was to be no interruption until they were finished. She was, however, unaware of an event in the outer office, an arrival of the only person who could instantly make the work come to a sudden and screeching halt. No thought was adequate to deny his admission for any reason, including the preservation of his right of entry to other offices in other cities or countries.

When the door opened, he was immediately recognized. Amid the flurry of a busy office, all activity quickly stopped, for Allen Davis, husband of Sara Principle for forty-years, was the most unlikely visitor they had ever seen in this office. He had never before participated in any political campaign, preferring to spend his time only with his own vast career. For more than twenty-five years, he was a leading actor in New York and Hollywood. He was not handsome in the manufactured sense of the movies. Instead, he lived his career as he did his personal life, under his own terms that commanded great respect for him with a powerful, independent presence. He never made any kind of appearance outside of his profession for any reason or for any person...not even for his wife. He was fiercely committed to his craft, not puffery, or open politics.

Allen was an actor extraordinaire with a natural, but refined grace, tall and elegant, and now with white hair. He frequently wore a plain shirt over his two-button sport coat for any appearance, and was lauded for his incredible talent, self-assured authority, and outlandishly direct persona. He always spoke his mind with no pretension. Because he was rarely seen in public, a substantial mystique developed around him, in part because of his steadfast refusal of awards, believing they were not in line with his art form or personal character. Allen was an enigma in the entertainment business normally devoted to self-aggrandizement.

Politicians, bureaucrats, and lobbyists of all stripes were old hat to Laura Hammond. She enjoyed her role as Senator Principle's manager, gleefully dispatching senators and members of the House alike in a precise, jovial manner in the Russell building, but this office was covert; off the record except for David Breyer, a trusted friend and valued member of The Solution. Outsiders were not welcome or even admitted here, but Allen was another matter entirely. Though they knew each other, it was always from a distance, and Laura was unsure how to greet Allen in this setting.

"Mr. Davis," she said, in her most collected and business-like voice after making the decision to be more formal. "May I help you?"

"Yes, you may, Miss Hammond," said Allen, speaking in a smooth, relaxed, baritone voice, and in the manner of an aristocrat accustomed to having his way but without the appearance of presumptuousness. "I've just come in from New York and I'd like to see Senator Principle as soon as it can be arranged. She is *here*, isn't she?"

It seemed to Laura that she had barely enough time to replace the receiver when the door to the private office opened. She looked stunned. Long ago, they agreed to keep their professional lives separate and apart. It was a very important feature in their marriage and in their public lives. Her mind raced. *Why is he here*? He was not the kind of person who ever acted on impulsive whims of the moment, even with her. He was indeed a different kind of celebrity, frankly direct and straightforward, yet friendly. It was a unique skill that many of his colleagues envied and admired all at the same time.

"Allen!" she said matter-of-factly, making a rapid recovery from her initial surprise. "I thought you were going to be in New York today. What has happened?"

He was the only person to detect the faint hint of annoyance in her voice as he embraced her with a light kiss on the cheek. "Why you do, Sara!" he said cheerily. "I've decided to get involved in the campaign and I wanted you to hear it from me first. I've been thinking about it for a while but just never said anything, so I thought I'd come down now and see what *you* thought about the idea."

"Well, I'm just *delighted!*" she lied, and she knew that Allen knew it was a lie. "Come on in. I'm working with Mondo and Tom on his speech for the rally. Maybe you could help us with that. We all know how good you are with words, but I'm *surprised*, Allen. I really *am*! You've never worked on *any* campaign before, and I thought you were going to be in New York for a couple of *weeks*! I was going to try to make it up there *tomorrow*. Has something changed with the play?"

She gestured to the door and as Allen went through, she saw all of the volunteers standing at their workstations with mouths agape in bewildered admiration at the sight of her movie star husband. This would certainly be something to tell their friends. The mysterious and very private man was now out in the open, and in the office of a United States Senator, no less, even though it was not her most important office. They knew Allen had been to the Russell building office, but never to this one because of its inherent nature. Outsiders were not even aware of this workplace. It was in fact a covert office, listed in all Internet phone book editions and on the building directory for one of the oldest members of The Solution, Howard Samuels, Attorney at Law. The undercover office opened and closed with the highest secrecy.

Principle closed the door and then quickly reopened it to issue instructions. "Laura," she said, making an instant decision. "Put someone at your desk and come in here as soon as you can. Also everyone, I do not want anything said to *anyone* about Allen being here today 'til we figure some things out—not even to your parents. Don't forget that you are all here with security clearances. I'll let you know when you're free to speak about it outside these walls, but for now, I don't want *anything* said, and I need to see all of your heads nodding in agreement."

Armando and Thomas were still at the computer with their backs to the door. When Armando saw who was with his boss he could not contain his enthusiasm, as he leaped from his chair and physically lifted Allen from the floor in a bear hug.

"*Allen!*" he yelped. "Is everything okay with you? I *never* thought I'd see you *here*! What's happening? We haven't seen each other for a really long time...Sara too, huh?"

They wrapped their arms around each other with a familiarity acquired over many years. Thomas Farley extended his hand because it was different for Thomas. He had only been an active member of The Solution's inner circle for five years.

Allen greatly admired Farley for the enormous contributions he had made to the campaign, and to his race, even though the bulk of those efforts remained largely unknown, and it would more than likely stay that way for the near future. Reason was difficult to publicize because it had no personal agenda...but along with truth, it could change your mind.

He stepped back to look at Armando, still sleek and trim even after so many years. Built like a long distance runner, his skin was the color of dark coffee with cream. They had not seen each other since they gathered at the convention in Chicago.

Principle watched the three of them, transfixed with Allen's usual brand of open delight and directness. He immediately became just one of the regulars. It continued to amaze her even after so many years together. Then she said, "Allen, what's going on? We agreed that you would stay out of my campaigns a long time ago. Why now...what's changed? I mean we could have talked about it first. Couldn't we?"

In the blink-of-an-eye, the actor's acknowledgement of a new, diverse set of circumstances took over. His gleeful expression quickly became serious and intense, business-like and single-minded, the amusement of the moment over even with his wife.

He stared straight at her for several seconds and then said, pointedly, "Sara, we *did* agree to keep our professional lives separate. We also never knew I would be the success I am, but even *as* those green kids that we *were*, we were still centered enough to know where we wanted to go and how we wanted to *get* there. And one of those ideas was the new and radical belief that we don't need each other's permission for any action we *individually* want to take on our own. We've lived our lives that way for more than forty-years, my darling, with no apologies to *anyone*. Have you *forgotten* that?

"While I think it isn't necessary to *justify* myself, for the record my public stature might be helpful right now. And I *want* to do it. I think I *can* be a positive influence on rally and *voter* turnout."

His face softened. "Perhaps you're way too close to what's going on," he said. "But *realistically*, the campaign needs all the help it can get right now, even though you're ahead in the polls. That might not last. You're trying to unseat a *sitting* president who is *popular*, *female*, *liberal*, a *Democrat*, and that's what people have been voting for in this country for a very *long* time. As for me, it's just one of *my* ways, like the mini-series was. You haven't forgotten how popular *that* was have you? Also, I didn't want to phone it in, Sara.

"And one more thing—I've made all the arrangements with Sid, my publicist, to do the Barbara Langdon program in five days. He's getting it out to all the media right away! You *do* remember *Sid*, don't you, Sara? He's the one who speaks really fast."

He had silently worked through the plan for several weeks by himself, wracking his brain to think of any possible way he could hurt her with the decision, since he had not discussed it with her ahead of time. She would have automatically said no. Her need not to use his celebrity was a vital part of the way she was naturally, and the way her mind continuously worked on everything with which she was involved.

She smiled as he gave his explanation and said softly, "My love, we really do have a unique relationship as far as the rest of the world is concerned, don't we? I bet that if you held a press conference to say what you just said, everyone would have a great laugh and think it was at *our* expense. We could try and explain it for hours and they still wouldn't get it."

When they all laughed, Principle began to listen to them as they bantered back and forth to each other about new tales and hills to climb, Allen to Armando, Farley to Allen, around and back to each other, their voices soft, quiet and soothing, as if from a distance. She listened until the sounds became a light drone, ever so slowly dimming into the recesses of her mind until they were lost in the present, moving to times long since past when everything was possible to the young and inexperienced, and where the only thing that mattered was virtue.

The vision she now saw was how her final year at the university had ended. It was a moment similar to how she had finished her high school years, but greater—a year like no other, except for the historic possibilities of this one.

Sara Principle grew up in New Castle Indiana as the only daughter of traditional, union-member, work-ethic parents. When she was sixteen, she took a job at the soda fountain in one of only three drugstores in the town. It was a very different kind of job from her morning paper route, with a greater opportunity for the precocious girl to meet and talk with a wide variety of people. She was a serious young girl, different from most of the boys she worked with who mainly thought about the New Castle Trojans and girls, and it was at the soda fountain where she met Jim Miller.

On an evening about one hour before closing, Sara struck up a conversation with Miller who owned the local Plymouth dealership just five blocks away. Even though Miller was thirty, a ripe old age to a sixteen-year old, he somehow seemed much younger than his generation, more vibrant, smarter, and more open to teenagers. He had lived in New Castle all of his life in an era of undemanding people. They were Indiana citizens who unconsciously exercised their small town right to be uninformed about the politics of their nation, and what they should and could be doing to make it better. They believed that everything was well with their government for the most part, and polite people just did not go around discussing religion and politics. That was what most of them said to a young girl who craved information. No politics, no religion was the rule of the day, but not for the owner of the Plymouth dealership or his long-time friend, Junkyard Dan Samuels.

Miller had gotten into the habit of stopping in the drugstore for a milkshake with Dan when they knew Sara would be working. They both liked the skinny girl and her ability to think logically, and decided she would be someone to watch. Over time, they began to develop an ongoing friendship, with long conversations at the soda fountain and then at the dealership on slow days, but without Dan, and that was most of the time.

Sara soon learned that Jim Miller and Dan Samuels were not members of a union or a political party. They had, in fact, never even voted, yet seemed to know so much about politics, the one subject that Sara was the most interested in due to her mother and father. Unlike most of their fellow citizens, the Principle parents wanted to talk politics constantly. Sara's mother worked part-time for the governor of the state, and her father was a highly opinionated political junkie. Both parents were strong Republicans. Jim Miller did not attend any church in town, and that was especially true for Dan. He was one of a very limited number of Jews in New Castle.

When Sara Principle went away to Northwestern University on a full academic scholarship, she was certain that her major role in life would be in politics, but in what way she did not know. From that time forward, she stayed in constant touch with Miller. It would be a liaison of intense development and changing patterns for many years, and it would be the starting point to create a new government in the United States of America and finally destroy democracy. It would also be the opening of a central theme to obliterate, over time, the power of the two major political parties in Washington. Junkyard Dan's son Howard also sat in on a number of meetings and participated eagerly. He was set to graduate from high school and then go on to Yale University and Yale Law.

At Northwestern, Sara Principle presented an unusual point-of-view in a political science debate. As the program developed, she made eye contact with a young man in the audience. When it was over and she was preparing to leave, he walked toward her, lifting his hand in the air to show that he wanted to speak to her.

He was tall and slender. His long, over-grown curly hair matched his eyes—dark brown eyes that seemed to touch her own in a way she had never before experienced with anyone, especially men. Her familiarity with the boys in New Castle was extremely limited, due in part to her own lack of interest that was primarily centered on politics and history, both of which she studied constantly, making a major obstacle in having time to develop any relationships with the boys in her class, and she seldom dated.

"Miss Principle," he said, smiling as he reached her. "I really enjoyed listening to what you had to say and wonder if I could talk with you about some of your ideas sometime.

"Everything I've ever heard or read about politics has always seemed wrong to me. I can't really explain it well. It just seems wrong and kind of out of focus, if that makes any sense. I'm sorry, but I just have a hard time describing what I mean when it comes to politics even though I'm attracted to what *you* said. Your ideas are unique, but they confused me even more than I was *before* tonight. I didn't understand all of it! It's hard see how it could fit in with what goes on all the time. You know all the stuff you read in the paper and see on TV.

"This was all very new to me. I've never heard anything even close to what you had to say, and I was wondering if you would be interested in talking one-on-one sometime? I really *am* interested in what you *said*, and I'm not coming on to you. What do you think?"

She hesitated, the astonishment on her face real. It always surprised her when she met someone who did not respond to what she said with illogical platitudes—commonplace phrases caused by emotions, not reason. Of the few people, she met who agreed with her none had ever captured her as quickly as this young man had.

"Why yes, certainly," she said. "But that's not a topic many people seem to be interested in though…Mr.?"

"I'm Allen Davis," he said, seeing her apprehension. "Although my major interest is drama, I also take poly/sci. I've heard so many people talking about you that I had to come and see for myself. I'm glad I did! I wonder if you know there are lots of students who think you're really weird, but from what *I've* heard you don't fit that description at all. Why you don't even have two heads!" He threw back his head and laughed, exuberantly, breaking the momentary tension of new introduction. She liked the way he laughed.

Laura Hammond walked into the inner office, breaking the spell of the past. Allen and Armando were engaged in a lively exchange about his possible role in the campaign, comparing the past with the present, laughing and smiling in the manner of old friends. In spite of the agreement they had made long ago, Principle now realized that it was right for him to be there. His instincts were always sound. Now she could see that she had really wanted to have him there all along and didn't understand why she did not realize it long ago.

It was obvious to Laura that the presence of Allen brought a subject to bear that had thus far gone unsaid with her boss. She had been taken aback many times over the more than ten years she worked for Principle, beginning in the Mayor's office in Las Cruces and then in Washington; but this was the most sensational surprise of all.

Laura sat next to Allen as Principle said, "Laura, I want you to connect with Sid, Allen's publicist, and make arrangements for a press conference tomorrow unless Allen doesn't agree." She leaned forward, her elbows resting on her knees, eager to begin moving with the new approach she'd just decided on. She folded her hands under her chin as she contemplated what to say further.

"Allen," she said, her face with the appearance of a woman suddenly full of new possibilities that did not exist even a second before. "I realize now that I've made some serious mistakes all these years, or at least as it relates to *this* election. I'm glad you made me see the light. I really *am*! If this sounds right to *you*, I'd like you to become my chief spokesperson for the duration, and I want you to hold a press conference tomorrow and make the announcement. I think this will grab some really good headlines, but I want to reiterate the need for The Solution to stay hidden. For now, that must stay at the top of our list.

"There's a lot of information you don't have, Laura. Things I now want you to know. Forget the front for a while because this is more important. Tell the kids to keep working, and let them know you will fill them in before they leave. Allen, I want Armando to bring you and Laura up to speed on everything, and Mondo, tell them *all* of it. It's time they knew the whole enchilada.

"Laura, I want you to learn precisely what we're going to do if we win the election, along with other information you don't have right now, and it's all true. Thomas and I will leave here separately, and right away."

Two hours later Allen left the office followed by Laura, her face pale and drawn. Her body trembled from the new information—news the nation would only hear when she gave her inaugural address, if there was to be one. That would be when she revealed the shocking facts of The Solution and what the organization would do to confront ongoing treachery in the United States government.

The volunteers were blind to Laura's outward appearance. They were only concerned with Allen, as they immediately surrounded Laura, begging for inside gossip. Without elaboration, Laura gave instructions to shut down the work for the day. She cautioned them to say nothing about Allen until after the press conference the next day.

Allen approached the microphones in the lobby of the elegant Hay-Adams hotel the next morning. Cameras clicked furiously as reporters jockeyed for position. While he waited, he began to think about the continuing effort of so many years to reach this point in time. He wondered if the people were ready for the kind of government that awaited them if his wife actually won, because it would be without telling the truth. Shockwaves would erupt around the world, from nation to nation, making its biggest impact on Russia, China, the Korean peninsula and the Middle East. It would astonish the Asians, and Muslims to a point they could never have imagined—an advantage that would benefit them in an enormous way and it would come from the Satan America. With that inside knowledge, Allen could not shake the constant, foreboding images of America that began to flash through his brain; pictures of open revolt, of death and panic, of riots and open demonstrations against the new American administration, when voters finally learned the stunning secrets of The Solution.

FIVE

At 5 a.m. on September 30, one day after Allen's press conference, Sara Principle walked out from the gleaming marble structure of the elegant Ritz Carlton hotel on Chicago's near north side with her running mate Robert Wilcox.

The air was crisp; clean smelling from the light rain that had fallen overnight, and she was pleased. All of the signs indicated that her run for the White House was on the right track, the winning track, and as they walked, she mentally recalled the interview of last night. She and Wilcox were guests on the CBS evening news for a full ten minutes, a prerequisite they had negotiated with network chiefs. They were close friends, and hidden members of The Solution for many years, in sharp contrast to their perceived liberalism of themselves, the network, and some on-air regulars.

"Senator Principle," said Terry O'Neil. "I regularly receive a lot of mail about you, and one thing people keep asking about is the steady rumor of some sort of Secret Society you and other members of your campaign might be a part of. Nearly all the Social Media sites have been talking about it. Could you expand on that concern?"

Principle stared, her brown eyes irritated and cold. "Terry," she said, "the problem comes from all the way back during my time as the Mayor of Las Cruces. I'm not sure *how* it first got started, but I *am* a Republican, and I've been a Republican for a *very* long time. It is very well documented, only now I'm starting to wonder if these concerns you say some members of the public have are instead some of your *own* fears."

"Is there a Secret Society, Senator?"

Principle maintained her icy glare and then said calmly, "Not one that I'm aware of. But let me ask *you* a question. Do you stay up late at night thinking of dumb questions just to avoid *real* issues? It's absurd! Let's move on to something that's relevant, like taxes and spending."

O'Neil was not yet ready to concede as he said, "Senator, we've heard from other journalists that you've only acted to squelch the rumors through denial, not proof. They tell us that you are not leveling with the American people. I often hear that charge."

"Do you now? Guilty 'til proven innocent—is *that* what you're saying? I thought you were *better* than that Terry. I've responded in the only way possible. I can't prove a negative, and I'm starting to think that this might in fact be some sort of media *conspiracy. I've* heard *that*! Maybe some of *you* people actually *want* me to lose!"

"Well, if that's true Senator, I'm not *one* of them," said O'Neil with a puzzled expression. Then he added, "But you *do* know there has been a lot of digging going on into your background, don't you?"

Principle smiled and said quietly, "I suppose that's true, and I think they *should*, considering the job I'm running for is president. You all wouldn't be doing your jobs well if you *weren't* looking at me thoroughly, just like you *failed* to do with President Obama. I say that my background has been an open book for many years, unlike his, which clearly wasn't."

She paused, smiled, and then continued. "Let me ask you another question, Terry. Don't you think that if that Secret Society charge were true *something* would've turned up by now? The election is nearly *here*! Just think about that for a second—think about all of the hours the President's Opposition Research team has spent on me. You *know* it's a lot. That *can't* be a surprise. So let me say it again. I am not aware of any Secret Society as it relates to *my* campaign, *period*!

"However, there *is* a famous Secret Society called Skull and Bones. Do you ever talk about *them*? No. So I issue this challenge to you or any other news organization. If you can come up with one that *I'm* involved with, let's hear about it. Tell the people the truth; but if you can't, then quit talking about it and stick to the *real* issues!

"And just to refresh your personal recollection, I went to Northwestern, not Yale. Here's some *more* news for you. I *do* know a lot about Skull and Bones. I'm not willing to talk about it with you. At least not right now, but they *are* secret, and I will have *something* to say about them if I win this election. And just to add a little interest, what I say might even be called a *bombshell*!"

"All right, Senator. Then tell us this. How would you sum up a Sara Principle administration, and just how different would it be from other administrations? Our viewers have been led to believe you would completely destroy all efforts for equal work laws."

"My basic theme is to return our government to a manageable size that's responsible to *constitutional* dictates, not the *invented* ideas of some modern progressives *and* conservatives. If I'm fortunate enough to win this election, it is my intent to expound on just what is and what is *not* constitutional. Many, many areas of our government are clearly outside of what the Constitution calls for, and I *am* for equality in the workplace.

"Beyond that I'm also for lower taxes, less spending and fewer regulations—a return to times long since passed where government exists for and by the people, tells them the truth and isn't secret. It isn't complex. Our leaders need to operate under the provisions set down by our Founding Fathers, especially the Bill of Rights. Much of that has been missing for a long time, especially since the *Obama* years."

They walked south on Michigan Avenue past the historic Pumping Station on the east side of the boulevard, and the landmark Water Tower of the same classic architecture on the west side of the street. Both buildings had withstood the ravages of the 1871 Great Chicago fire. They were a pleasing contrast to the stark, forward-looking lines of Water Tower Place, the shopping complex adjacent to the hotel with million-dollar condominiums rising above the Ritz Carlton.

No Secret Service personnel accompanied them. Principle declined their protection, believing it un-necessary. This time the taxpayers would not pay the cost for what should always be a private bill, as she chose to take on that responsibility herself. It would become a freedom of choice issue later on with other campaigns.

Their destination was the studios of the ABC television station in the heart of the Loop. They would be the only guests on the nationally televised program, David Breyer Now. Breyer had become a valued source of knowledge and friend over the many years, mainly from the time when he became a participating associate member of The Solution, to give them a wealth of inside-the-beltway information to help maintain the secrecy of the organization over the many years.

They walked slowly and in silence. Principle and Wilcox both smiled as they passed the large windows of the Neiman Marcus store just south of the hotel. The windows were trimmed in a style to trumpet the fast approaching Election Day with fashions in red, white, and blue, in a bold statement of patriotism. Voters developed strong interest in the Republicans in a way never seen in Democratic Party Chicago. The enthusiasm was now rampant, but also bizarre. Many Chicagoans were responding to pollsters that they had little to no interest in the election, creating a conundrum—an intriguing challenge to the city's political reporters. The answers were not consistent with known facts.

Principle stopped short as they reached the last window and saw an indication that Allen's impact on the campaign was beginning to materialize. One mannequin fashioned to look like Allen stood to the right side of the window, flanked by an enormous banner that stretched the entire glass and read; *Our New First Gentleman*? Principle smiled at the insertion of the question mark. The display clearly showed that Allen would have a strong effect even in major, liberal cities. The adoration of celebrities would also include many of Hollywood's elites, not usually known to be supportive of any conservative since the end of World War II, as it concerned a Republican candidate. It was also a strangely developing story in New York City, the full state of New York, and California as well.

Principle noticed a man on the opposite side of the nearly deserted street, a man who seemed to be keeping pace with them as they walked—a man with dark hair who carried an oddly shaped case over his shoulder that was neither large nor small. He was also difficult to see clearly in the darkness, even with streetlights on.

The presidential candidate wondered if he might be the same man, she had seen in Manhattan only a few days earlier. She was on her way to the Plaza hotel that morning when she first became aware of a person. She thought then that each time she stopped just to look in a store window for a moment that dark-haired man had also stopped. *Was he waiting for some kind of opportunity then? Was he carrying a shoulder case? Was it this guy?* Principle could not recall and dismissed the appearance of the man as merely something out of the ordinary.

"Have you ever seen that guy over there?" asked Wilcox, motioning with his head.

"I don't think so, Bob. Why?"

"*You* do not sound *convinced*!"

"I'm not, completely. I remember someone in New York, but it's probably not the same guy, and I wouldn't worry about it."

"All the same," said Wilcox, "I've written down a description as best I can and I'll send it to Fred when we get back to the hotel. I don't think it'll amount to much though, since you really *do* seem not to recognize him. I guess it is okay, Sara, but it's also a long walk that we're taking to the Loop studio, and I think we need to be alert."

Principle shrugged. This time Wilcox sounded unconvinced, but then, three blocks later the man suddenly vanished.

"There, you see," said Wilcox. "He's gone."

Near the intersection of State Street and Wacker Drive, no people or moving vehicles were visible. It was just another quiet, very early Sunday morning before people began to stir, and for a few minutes, they were alone in the middle of Chicago's Loop just before sunrise.

The streets perpendicular to the westbound thoroughfares intersect to cross over the Chicago River with walkways and high railings. When combined with the concrete retaining walls, ongoing construction and darkness, direct vision is somewhat obscured from street to street, and even more difficult to see anything in the darkness.

Wilcox sensed movement to his right the instant they reached the curb. He remembered his feeling of unease about the dark-haired man. His first thought was of him. He was right. The man held a gun. Wilcox shouted. He violently pushed Principle into the middle of the street. He turned back. He looked directly into the cold stare of the man with the dark hair—the same man who had walked nearly side-by-side with them on Michigan Avenue only moments before.

His knees were bent, the .38 caliber Smith & Wesson snub nose gripped professionally, with both hands. His eyes were cold, resolute, and his face void of expression, of any outward emotion as he stared for a split second with business-like precision.

It was the last thing Robert Wilcox saw as he began his downward plunge toward the pavement. He heard none of the sounds and rapid-fire explosions that followed. Robert Wilcox was lying face down in the middle of the intersection. He did not move. He was dead—killed instantly from the power of the single bullet that pierced his chest. His skull cracked open from the sudden contact with the asphalt. Blood splayed all around his head from his broken nose and the head fracture to flood the area around his upper body with an ever-enlarging pool of deep red.

Police heard the crack of the gun from their position on Dearborn Avenue. One squad car screeched to a stop, followed by a paramedic unit. Two more police cars raced up State Street past the Langham hotel, sirens blaring loudly in the once quiet Sunday morning air—but the dark-haired man had vanished as abruptly as he had appeared.

In the middle of the intersection, Sara Principle knelt over the dead man, cradling the lifeless form in his arms. They had been classmates at Northwestern and shared a part of their youth that brought them together nearly as siblings. In her mind, they *were* siblings.

The candidate was enraged and grieving at the same time, unaware of the shock to her psyche as she painfully tried to gather her mind into focus from the sight of Wilcox and the pain in her left arm and leg. *How? Why?* She was spinning into another world. Her brain was a mass of raw nerve endings, each one exposed, raw, tender and pressing against the other. Covered with the blood of Robert Wilcox, she refused to believe her friend was dead. She rocked back and forth, moaning and crying out, anything to bring Wilcox back to life. Suddenly she began to shake and scream at the same time, her fingers locked in a vice-like grip, as the reaching hands of paramedics pulled at her arms. "No! Bob, get *up*! No! Get *away* from me!"

The paramedics managed to move Sara to an ambulance that had just pulled up to the State/Wacker curb. She looked backward, calling out to Robert Wilcox to move and stand up. "*Please* get up, Bob!"

When police discovered the identity of their victim, they placed a call to the Station House to find Armando. Principle's wounds were not serious, and as the ambulance moved toward the Wesley Pavilion of Northwestern Hospital, Sara Principle wept. Terror was new in her life. It had never been present, and yet, events still to come would be even more savage than anything she could ever have imagined or thought possible, if she had managed to even have such a coherent thought calling out to her from her brain.

In Marina City, the iconic round towers apartment complex on the bank of the Chicago River and the west side of State Street directly opposite from the hotel, the dark-haired man appeared on a twenty-second floor balcony. He peered through the morning haze, as did other residents who had heard the sirens that shattered the once peaceful morning. He held a cell phone to his ear and looked through binoculars south, toward the LOOP, speaking calmly, as if it had been just the start of another quiet Sunday morning, except for the shrill sounds of sirens.

"Yeah," he said. "There's been a shooting here on State Street. *No,* goddamn it! I'm standing here on the balcony. No, well, I'm not sure. Wait a minute! Don't rush me! They're helping someone up. It's a woman! Shit! She's standing. What? Shit! Yeah, I got it. I'll be on the flight this afternoon, but by god, Cantrell, you better be gettin' me what I want! You haven't sent anyone for a hell of a long time and that shit's gotta stop! I'm not *takin'* this shit anymore, and you had better get your fuckin' ass in gear or you just might lose one very good hit man if you *don't*...in spite of the problem today! I'll get her later."

News of the shooting quickly reached the ABC studios. In minutes, a film crew and two reporters rushed to the location. Principle was en route to the hospital desperately trying to fight off the fury and pain raging in her head with lightning speed. Her face was contorted, grief-stricken and pained. She had not listened to her friends. No one wanted to harm her...she thought.

"Mondo...where's Mondo?" She forced the words from her mouth in a violent explosion of emotions welling inside her head, taking over from her usual steady persona.

"I'm right here, Sara," said Armando, quietly. Police had found him at the ABC studio four blocks south, and he arrived at the scene just seconds before the ambulance pulled away. "Take it easy," he said.

"What? *Easy*—Mondo, what in the hell to you mean? Bob is dead. *Dead*, goddamn it and I didn't listen."

"I know, Sara, but try to calm down."

"How the hell can I do *that*, Mondo? *Look* at me! This is *Bob's* blood and it's *my* fault! How can you *say* that? He's *dead*! My dearest friend and running mate is *dead*!"

"I know, but there's nothing we can do right now. The doctor will fix your wounds at the hospital and give you something for the pain. Then we'll go back to the hotel if they don't have to keep you overnight, but it's *not* your fault, Sara. Nobody knew there was a lunatic on the loose in Chicago...*nobody*!"

"I can't *believe* it! You and Russ were right! I was *wrong*! My own stubbornness got in the way. I should have listened! Goddamn it Mondo, what's the use? Someone meant to kill *me*, not Bob. It's not *worth* it, Mondo! It's not *worth* it. Let them get someone else. What if Allen had been there? Let them have the goddamn country! The people don't really give a shit anyway, and I can't *change* that."

"You don't mean it, Sara. You're in a state of panic right now, and I know you don't mean it."

"You're *wrong*! I *do* mean it, Mondo! Just look at the state of this damn country! It didn't get that way because the voters cared enough to elect people who want to follow the *Constitution*...like Bob Wilcox! None of it matters anymore, and it all started more than one-hundred years ago *Mondo*, with Teddy Roosevelt, and he's on *Rushmore*! That's when the downfall of the country really took off. Then it was that fucking Woodrow, FDR, Carter, LBJ, Bush, Clinton, Bush and Obama. Who's next, Daffy

Duck? *No*! That's an insult to *Daffy*! Voters don't want value. They want *goodies*! If the people really gave a damn Mondo, they wouldn't have gone along with all that crap in 2010 when Obama got that immoral healthcare package through *Congress*, but they did, Mondo, they *did*!"

Two hours later Armando Munoz brought a heavily sedated Sara Principle back to the Ritz Carlton. She was unable to think of anything but the death of her friend and running mate. Her emotions had completely taken over, and she was desperately lost.

David Breyer was a highly respected journalist and moderator of his own television program for many years. When informed of the shooting, he recorded an announcement that said the program would be aired at a later date or time or not at all, but that would depend on the condition of the candidate. At the hotel, he met with Armando.

"You must be out of your fucking *mind*!" screamed Armando. "Just how in the hell can you even consider making the *suggestion* that Sara still do the interview? Tell me *that*! Wilcox was *murdered*! They were like *brother* and *sister*! I can't believe you would try this. I thought you were a *friend* David. What's the matter with you? You've been a member for a long time. You must be *crazy*!"

Breyer persisted. "I *am* a friend Mondo, and that's something you *know* is true. I've helped our movement more than a whole lot of other people. I think she'll be able to go on if we just give her enough time, and I'll wait as long as I need to wait. That's all."

"*No*! You know she's been fighting the ongoing ignorance of the American people all this time from behind closed doors. It's been forty-years, David, and we're this close!" He held two fingers together and said, "She *knows* you've helped make the difference many times, but the answer is no. She's in *shock*! Shit, she *can't* go on television, and I think you're crazy if you honestly think she *can*!"

"I *do* think she can, and I'm gonna wait. You at least have to let her know I'm *here*, Mondo. The crew's in the other room and we'll wait, and think about this. Don't tell *her*, but *think* about it. As crazy as it sounds right now, she can show good colors by *doing* the interview—by acting *fast* in the middle of a crisis. I guarantee you that if the only difference was the name of the candidate and that name was Barack Obama, *he* would take advantage, and he got *two* terms."

Armando hovered for two hours, pausing only once to phone Allen. Then, little by little, slowly, carefully, Principle began to regain some of her equilibrium. In spite of Armando's continued spirited opposition, Sara called for Breyer and his crew. The presidential candidate would do the interview.

Sara Principle looked older when she emerged from the bedroom. The naturally hooded corners of her eyes were more pronounced and covered, weary, dark, and with a guarded sense of loss and vitality. Her voice shook as she reluctantly agreed to proceed with the discussion.

She instinctively understood she would have to fight the pain she felt. Tiny bulges throbbed noticeably at her jaw-line—her face tightly stretched, her lips turned inward and fixed. Still she would say as much as possible. She could not remember a time in her life when she did not want to keep going, to fight one more battle down to the last breath to reach the particular point she was looking for. Sara Principle knew she might want another fight down the road for today, but that time was not now.

David Breyer was a political commentator. He was also an analyst of international acclaim and widely popular, not only for what the public thought of his integrity, but also from his speaking style. He was quiet and uncharacteristically subdued as he readied himself. Gone were the words clipped so sharply at the end of a sentence or phrase that made it appear he had more to say but had forgotten what it was. His voice was hushed, gentle and quiet, as if he sat in the serenity of a cathedral instead of a hotel room with bright television lights and a full camera crew.

"Senator," he said, "tell us this if you can. The national tracking polls showed you with a slight lead over the president yesterday, and they have been that way for one week. Do you think they had anything to do with this heinous crime?"

Principle's speech was normally full and rich. Now it was thin, without color, the intense pain from the shooting evident in her total bearing. She said very softly, nearly inaudible, "Anything's possible David. Public figures have become targets for a multitude of despicable people since the time of President Kennedy, and long *before* him. Now I see that we have to take extraordinary steps for protection. I didn't know or understand that before today. I was blind to the possibility of danger and didn't listen to my advisors. They warned me, but my own idiocy got in the way. I honestly did not think anyone wanted to hurt me. We will correct my stupidity."

Her eyes blinked rapidly as she fought to control emotions racing through her brain, mentally searching for a scintilla of what was left of her control and sanity, and now starting to regret doing the interview.

"It's my fault Bob Wilcox is dead, even though he agreed with our mutual decision to not allow Secret Service protection. We both thought it was necessary if we were to conform to our own ethics. I *do* have a security advisor, and I will instruct him to put a larger team in place for the rest of the campaign. As you know, we are very well funded from our Internet programs, so we'll be able to afford the added expense and keep this a private matter."

Suddenly Principle realized she was not responding to the question, something she had always tried to do quickly with all reporters. Her mind raced with the image of Robert Wilcox lying dead in the middle of the street, with the dark-haired man, and with the admission that it was her own fault. *Come on! If you're going to speak do it right! Snap out of it! Remember where you are and what you're doing! You're a presidential candidate. Act like it, not like some sniveling female!*

She stammered, "I'm sorry David. I'm usually better than this. Let me try to answer your question. I think that if violence were going to happen then the polls, regardless of what they say would have no effect on this election. I have to believe it if for no other reason than my love for Bob Wilcox and what we put together to help change the course of this nation, because if it isn't changed *this* time, it will *never* be changed. Bob and I wanted our politics to be in line with the Constitution. That's not the case now, and the Constitution is routinely violated and *meaningless* to most people. There have been various groups trying to whittle away on the Constitution because they actually want to completely get rid of it, *especially* since President Barack Obama."

As the interview progressed, slowly, question-by-question, some part of her composure began to return, bit-by-bit, inching forward to a recovery, painful but still moving ahead. Seeing the change Breyer made the difficult decision to press the candidate further with a hard question, for he was still a working reporter.

"Senator," he said quietly, "why did you agree to the interview this quickly after Robert Wilcox's murder? I have a hunch you'll be criticized, so what do you *say* to those critics if you are? Americans would like to know the answer to that question, and they'd like it *now*, not later."

"I was really shaken. I still *am*. Bob was the brother I never had. He was one of my most valued friends. We know the gunman was after me, not Bob. He shoved me out of the way. That's why I'm alive! I think the shooter didn't realize it at the time but he could have finished me off too. Maybe he thought he *had* killed me. I think he thought he did, but he just wanted to get away at that point. The police responded very quickly. I don't know how, but that too may have saved me.

"During the past couple of hours, my assistant, Armando Munoz, has been with me. *He* got me here, even though he opposed doing the interview. I know I'm still in shock, but, I came to the conclusion to go ahead in part to show the American people I can be counted on to act quickly in a time of crisis, and this is definitely one of those times. I'm also sure Bob would have wanted me to do it. We had zero disagreements over the things we believe in and want to accomplish.

"I don't want to give the impression that I'm taking his death lightly, because I'm not. As I said, Bob was one of my closest friends and I will *never* get over his death. I didn't see Bob when the shooter killed him, but I did feel the bullets that hit me. Maybe the killer saw me grimace and think he had killed me too!

"Did you *see* him?"

"No, I didn't see him. By the time I even knew what had happened, I was trying to pick myself up from the pavement where Bob had pushed me. It was all so fast, so very, very fast, and there was a fourth shot, at least I think there was that landed just *inches* from me. It probably missed me because I was tumbling end-over-end, head over heels from the force of

Bob pushing me really, really hard, and then the shooter was gone when I was able to look around."

"Can you say what you will do now as far as a running mate is concerned? Did you have others in mind *before* the convention?"

"No. When I chose Bob, he was my only consideration. I had no list of aspirants for the job, only him. We have been on the same wavelength since college."

"When we sat down I had a list of questions about your running mate, beginning with this one. What criteria will you use?"

"The same as before when I always knew it would be Bob. The only reason someone should be the vice president is that he or she is qualified to be president, and constitutionally, there is only *one* job for a vice president. If I win the election, the vice president will fulfill his role *everyday* as President of the Senate *fulltime*. He also won't be making trips outside the country or to various states when Congress is in session. It will be his fulltime job unless a President pro tempore is needed to fill in for him."

David Breyer leaned forward, placing his familiar clipboard on the table in front of him. When he leaned backward his expression changed, as he silently asked himself if he should go on with the interview because he was not just a member of The Solution, he was a working reporter. For several seconds the airwaves were silent, as he mentally struggled to make his decision.

"Senator," he said finally after making the evaluation. "Before we sat down I wanted to try and clear this up. Will you shed some light on your husband, Allen Davis? He is extremely reluctant to make public appearances, but now it seems that he's all *over* the place! What will his role *really* be? Have you lined him up just for publicity because he is so famous, and isn't there a question of ethics here? It seems that you might also be concerned about possible comparisons to Mrs. Clinton and her substantial role with President Clinton and then his with *her* when *she* ran?"

Sara Principle's mind was swirling in a vortex of emotions from the darkness of the hour and of her own thoughts of Allen. She needed his special presence now more than ever because she was in very bad shape, and unaware that his flight was in its final approach to O'Hare.

She shook her head. "David," she said. "I was just thinking of him and wishing he were here right now, but he's in Washington. I'm very tired. As to your question, I have to point out that mates have always been involved in campaigns, and Allen is no different from any other mate of a presidential candidate except that he's famous. As to the other part of that question, I actually *admire* Hillary's part in Bill's campaigns, *and* in his presidency. It takes a lot of guts to do what she did, but when she ran for the nomination in 2008, she really wasn't a very good candidate *or* a manager, and managing is *very* important. Obama had her beaten hands-down even though she *was* catching up at the end. She closed really well, though, a lot better than *he* did. There's a lot of necessary work behind the scenes, more than most people can *ever* imagine. I think she should have *won* the nomination. He just ran a very superior campaign!

"Though Allen has never done anything like this, he decided on his own to be involved as a voice for the campaign. He made the decision without any consultation with me, and due to his status both as my husband and his public image, we agreed that he would become my primary spokesperson. It seemed natural then, and it still does. He's put *all* of his previous commitments on hold 'til after the election to give it all he's got, and that is considerable. It also includes the play that he's scheduled to do on Broadway. He *is* very popular, and I don't see anything wrong with his participation, but I'm here to tell you he won't be a traditional first mate if I *win* the election. He still has a career and he won't give that role up for any *reason* or any *person*, including *me*!"

Slowly, a metamorphosis began to take place and spread across Principle's face as she spoke of Allen…her weariness seemed to vanish.

"Is there any chance you would change your mind about a second term if you win this election?"

"No. I'm positive we can do everything in one term. In fact, I'm very sure we will get much of it handled in *two* years. I also think politicians need to get away from making a long career in Washington, and a single term for a president *voluntarily* would be a good start. The job is to be the president, not the king, and we need to add *term limits* for Congress!

"This nation's problems will not just go away and meekly hide in some distant backroom while our leaders go on conning the people, if America is to really be America, that is. I think our institutions cannot survive in the ever-increasing climate of collectivism that government *forces* on the people. They try to make them believe it can be all things to all people, but it can't, and that's not its job. Bush and Barack Obama created *massive*, *immoral*, and *unconstitutional* debt and *regulation*.

"Here's a small part of what I mean. From the Revolutionary War to the end of 1980, our government ran up a *total* debt of $1 *trillion* in a two hundred or so year period. Then, in only *twelve* years—think of that for just a minute, in twelve years, it *quadrupled* to $4 trillion. That's outrageous, but it was just chump change when compared to the actions of the Obama administration. I believe *they* actually set out to collapse the system on purpose, and I really do *mean* that! They intended to annihilate capitalism in one stroke, not gradually, as progressives *usually* do their work, and they nearly succeeded. But capitalism is *very* strong."

"You've made harsh accusations against several administrations of both parties. You said that the invasion of Iraq was unconstitutional, along with what you just said very strongly about President Obama. Many people agree with you, but tell us what *you* mean."

"David, our government's power has gone virtually unchecked for more than one hundred years. Part of that is by conducting unconstitutional wars. Another is using the fear factor, as Bush did with WMDs and Obama did with the words, depression, recession, and *drones*. Then there is the Congress working *with* the White House to create war *resolutions*. You must know the Constitution compels the *House* to declare war—it does not okay the invention of *resolutions*, executive orders, or signing statements!

"Americans have been coerced to hand over their liberties one-by-one and give them to *politicians* in return for a false sense of wellbeing and the *presumption* of security. It happened, I believe, in much greater measures after 9/11 with some very bad and very *unconstitutional* legislation like the Patriot Act, along with government spying programs that would have outraged the founders of this nation, especially PRISM. People have said that the first job of a president is to keep Americans safe. That is not *true*. The first job is to keep Americans *free*, and most of them have failed at that standard. When you give your freedom away slowly, day-by-day, unnoticed as the years go by, you risk turning around another day to find it *completely* gone while you were asleep and comfortable with the status quo. When *that* happens, people do not understand what went wrong. The result is that the succeeding generations just got used to it, little by little and thought it *was* normal. Well it wasn't normal when the country *began*! We desperately need a change in leadership to restore our liberties and reduce our debt. Americans are *hungry* for it. What they are *not* hungry for are lies from the president and Congress to take us to war, and lies about so many things like the obscene spending and spying programs.

"A very wise man, Robert Houghwout Jackson, Associate Justice of the U.S. Supreme Court and the chief judge at the War Crimes Tribunal in Nuremberg, made a very interesting statement on citizen and government errors, and this is what he said, in part. 'It is not the function of our government to keep the citizen from falling into error; it is the function of the citizen to keep the government from falling into error.' But that's what it is when our military is used without a declaration of war like past leaders have done, and in other areas as well. It just has to stop, and I promise you I will stop it if the people give me the opportunity. I am not a Johnny-come-lately to all of this, and I've spoken about it for a very long time.

"I also want to say something else. It is obscene; at least it is to me, that when the leaders of our country exhort citizens to make *sacrifices*, they themselves do not understand the true *meaning* of the word. You frequently hear this said in relation to our military forces when officials and political candidates *thank* soldiers for their *sacrifice* in foreign wars. This is because they want to confuse the definition of the word, in your mind. The guiltiest in recent years were John McCain and President Obama! They know what the word sacrifice *really* means. They just do not want *you* to know.

"When you choose to fight to protect your nation *defensively*, you are also protecting your own family…self-interest. That is *not* a sacrifice, but when you fight and die—when you are *maimed* for life in a war that was trumped up by politicians to buy *votes*, and that is precisely what they do, that *is* a sacrifice because your life is your highest *value*. The very idea of sacrifice is something deceitful leaders put forth as a feel-good slogan to gullible people. It is not something a Principle administration will *ever* be involved with in *any* way."

The interview ran slightly more than one hour without interruption. Breyer was ready to explode with anticipation as Principle talked smoothly about her concept of having a conservative administration. It was an extraordinary statement. The more she spoke and engaged with the host on issues, the more her face began to take on her normal appearance.

At the close of the program, Breyer made an instant decision to use the opportunity to give an enthusiastic, yet stern commentary he planned for just one week before the election. He said at the time of the Republican convention that he thought Principle could not win. Now, however, he had changed his mind, and Principle was a serious threat. With the death of Robert Wilcox, the Justice Department must conduct a thorough investigation on the possibility of a conspiracy against the senator reaching into the highest levels of government.

Seated in the Oval Office were Clifford Cantrell, Cecil Price, and Senator Edward Kendall of Pennsylvania. They watched the news of the Chicago shooting and the subsequent interview without speaking to each other, including President Crawford.

Eyes darted from Crawford to each other. Kendall silently feared the natural style of Principle would boost her standing in the media, especially with her movie star husband. She displayed the easy charm of Reagan, and was now as popular in the Senate as she was in her home state.

Crawford's demeanor was completely unruffled and calm. She decided it would not be wise to tell her friends of the impending statement and said, "Gentlemen, I strongly urge you not to worry. The voters will not want a return to the days of a female *Great Communicator*...not in our lifetime. I *guarantee* it! In the end, Principle will be just another asterisk in presidential sweepstakes."

Kendall stood up. He was aristocratic in his appearance and spoke in a rapid flourish, a style very much in keeping with his flamboyant, white-haired personality.

"Madam President," he said. "I do not think you understand! I do not think you understand at *all*. I *know* Allen Davis personally. He alone is capable of stimulating $20 million worth of pure publicity between now and November—maybe even *more* than that! They will certainly use him to their fullest advantage. The public may even become *enamored* of them and vote for Principle simply out of reverence for *him*! There *is* one other thing you need to see, and that is this country is a lot more conservative than you think it is. Don't you remember how Obama ran into it in 2010 and 2014? It's still *there*!"

Crawford listened unaffected. The senator did not know it but the president had all the answers. Her coming statement on the first debate day would effectively end the Principle threat for good. The President of the United States held the high card, and she would use it to her fullest advantage. The election would not be close.

SIX

Russell Harrington was a man for his time…and beyond. A native of El Paso, Texas, he was the youngest of seven children and understood at an exceptionally early age the disadvantage of being poor. He was also certain he would not become one of them. Instead, he would imitate the men he read about in his schoolbooks by working as hard as he possibly could to achieve not just common wealth, but extraordinary riches, and then he would be powerful. It was something he had learned from both his parents and his own daydreams.

When he was nine years old, he went to work at a variety of odd jobs. Unknown to his father and mother, he did not contribute all of his earnings to the family coffers. As an alternative, he withheld twenty percent for himself. He stored the cash in a metal container that he kept buried beneath the corner of the fence that separated the Harrington house from their neighbor in the rear. This would be his seed money for a higher education far away, and an escape from El Paso.

Russell did not want to hide his funds away from all eyes, and often carried the money wad of the moment in his pocket for several days until the most secure opportunity came to stash his loot in the back yard. He was a secretive boy with a shock of curly, blonde hair, who would steadily work at four different part-time jobs. By the time he graduated from high school he had secretly accumulated the astonishing sum of $10 thousand.

He earmarked the money for his higher education at the prestigious university, Northwestern, in Evanston, Illinois, where he went on to receive extremely high grades, along with his degree. Afterward, using some of his newly acquired knowledge of geology and other sciences, he began to explore developing opportunities in oil near El Paso. His first success as a wildcatter came shortly after his twenty-second birthday, with a string of hits lasting uninterrupted for two years. At age twenty-four, he had amassed a personal fortune of $15 million and owned a large, independent oil company based in Las Cruces, New Mexico. Being a proud entrepreneur, he bragged about his success to any listener. One year later, he received a request from his alma mater. Harrington was impressed with Northwestern, because they invited him to address a business forum on university grounds.

He sent aides to learn the mood of the campus. Their job was to bring reports back to El Paso to inform Harrington if there were many divergent opinions in business and politics among the student body. The discovery report both intrigued and delighted the wily Texan. One student, in the vast number of what he believed to be pampered rich kids, emerged above all others as having original ideas. Though she had the ability to lead, the university regarded her as a rebel. It was generally true of such people, the radicals of the world. Harrington believed himself to be a rebel, but not like these students. They were different. For the most part, in his mind, they were just spoiled brats, longing to be nothing more than a reflection of each other in a collective mentality, void of original ideas and perseverance, of guts and fortitude. They were only able to see how they should think and act from other people for the groupthink of inclusion, to give them permission for decisions they would make in their lives, especially after graduation from college. That was certainly not for the world of Russell Harrington.

When the Texan arrived in Evanston, he was one week early. He wanted to meet the student rebel and knock her down to size—to prove that the rich and powerful movers and shakers of commerce and industry were the individuals who exercised their superior qualities of leadership. They were the ones to make progress a reality, not the collectivists of the world, the Progressives or Communists.

They met in Harrington's hotel in the elegant, upscale north shore suburb of Lake Forest, one of many real estate ventures he owned, all of which provided him with a substantial income. None of the properties owned by Russell Harrington ever lost money. He became a very astute investor as the years passed, developing an extensive real estate portfolio of shopping centers, large apartment buildings, residential housing, and a string of warehouse buildings that would eventually provide needed space for a still uncreated secret organization that was even beyond his own personal ideas about the future.

Harrington sent a request to the dean to send three of his brightest students to the penthouse suite to review the forum outline and possible results, along with one additional request. Over the dean's protest, Harrington wanted the student rebel, and he would not take no for an answer. The radical student must be included. Then, using his powerful position as a generous benefactor to the university, Harrington sealed the deal by saying he would have his personal driver pick them up at the campus and deliver them to Lake Forest.

He expected Sara Principle to arrive as a sullen, oddly dressed freak. That seemed to be the norm these days with wealthy elitists. They were the privileged class with the financial recourses to attend an institution like Northwestern simply because of their parent's wealth.

In the suite, the anticipated confrontation did occur, but not from Sara Principle. The students with her verbally attacked Harrington as nothing more than a self-involved, trashy capitalist; a man concerned only with profit and money, not the welfare of those who actually worked for a living. Harrington was totally frustrated and unable to communicate any of his ideas, much less try to educate them to a new way of thinking.

When the students first arrived, Sara Principle stood for a few minutes as she watched and listened to Harrington. She was in the process of making up her mind about a feeling that slowly enveloped her brain. After a short amount of time, she finally sat down directly across the low-slung table from the wealthy oilman in quiet observation, and in silent acknowledgement of the cantankerous Texan's power.

As the conversation with the students moved forward, Principle spoke very little, while Harrington saw an abiding self-assurance the others lacked...and more. The longer they talked the more Harrington realized that Principle, just five years his junior was not his enemy, but rather a parallel partner to Harrington's deepest convictions, nearly an identical brain in another body...a *female* body. Russell Harrington had the feeling of having been to the mountaintop of a unique, nearly mystical discovery, and he was extremely confused. He did not believe in mysticism of any kind including religion or the notion of a Creator of the universe. Two days later an animated Sara Principle reappeared at Harrington's suite unannounced to ask for a private, one-on-one meeting.

"I wanted to speak with you," said Principle, "because you remind me a lot of a friend of mine from my hometown in Indiana. He's not rich like you. He's well off, but he's not in *your* league, at least as it has to do with money. I think he *is* in your league with a certain kind of knowledge very few people have. He *does* know a lot about some of the things you talked to us about, and some of the things I think you *wanted* to talk about but didn't."

"You understand that, Miss?" said a very surprised Harrington. Then, based on what he had previously seen and heard, he said, "All right. What's on your mind?"

"You talked a lot about free enterprise. How do you think that applies to the Constitution?"

"Well, Miss, just about everything," Harrington said in his gruff Texas drawl. He frequently called all of the *men* he met, son, even those who were older, but now he had to use the word, Miss. "I don't have a lot of time, Miss," he said. "Now, don't take this the wrong way, but I know things *too*. Is that what you wanna talk to me about, the *Constitution?*"

"Yes, in part. Are you aware that the men who wrote the Constitution were men of property who never meant for people to be *equal*? They also made some very bad mistakes in the writing, but they clearly understood that people could *never* be equal, and that's what I want to talk with you about, the concept of freedom, the Constitution, *and* my friend, Jim Miller. I know he has some very serious things to say that might surprise you if he were here.

"I really think the country is in serious trouble, Mr. Harrington. May-be *dangerous* might be the better word, and that maybe you might become interested in working with me to do something about it. I know that sounds presumptuous on my part considering where we are in life, but when you talked about the politicians, I got the distinct impression you really don't like them very much. I don't either, and I have an idea. It's about freedom and the Constitution. I think most politicians are actually *against* those two things!"

"Hell, Miss, that's *obvious*! Those people are gonna *destroy* this coun-try, but I don't see what it has to do with *us*! What do you mean?"

"Just this; why not try and *stop* them? I'd like to put a plan of action together that *could* stop them in their tracks to make the country better at the same time, and put you on *board* with us. I'm pretty sure you'd like to make the country better! Wouldn't you?"

"I see," said Harrington in his own condescending way that seemed to indicate he might have been wrong about this student. "I'm pleased you wanted to talk to me, Miss Principle," he said with a strongly dismissive tone. "But there's nothin' anyone can do, especially a *college* girl! Those politicians are all the same and it ain't gonna change 'til it's too late. Only *then* we won't *like* the change."

"Well, maybe something *could* be done. I'm reluctant to tell you all of what I have in mind because it's so unbelievable and maybe even danger-ous for me, but I'd like to try if you'll hear me out for just a while. I won't take up a lot of your time, but I think it's very important. Will you listen? It really *is* important!"

"I'll listen. I'll listen for a while, Miss, but I sure as hell can assure you that nothin' can ever be done with people like that, the damn politi-cians and the damn lobbyists! I've been dealin' with those hucksters for a few years now and hell, I know what I'm *talkin'* about! But go ahead and say your piece anyway."

"Okay. Here it is. What if people who see things the way we do ran for office and got elected as Republicans and Democrats but were actually something else? In other words, these people would only *seem* to be mem-bers of the two parties—they would carry their political banner, but not be one of them, and all the while, the politicians *or* the parties wouldn't know what was going on. Do you understand?"

"I'm not sure. Let me get this straight. You wanna have some citizens *pretend* to be members of the two parties? That's the *dumbest* idea I *ever* heard. Just what *is* your status with this university? I've been impressed with you at the outset, but now I'm startin' to think I was wrong. Is that what you're sayin' *make-believe candidates*?"

"Yes. I mean we know the people will only vote for *them* in large numbers. So what if candidates grew *inside* the two parties as a secret, *par-ty-within-a-party*? It seems to me they could run for office all over the country under their banner, using them so to speak, and when there were enough people like that, they could change things in a *very* big way! Does that make any sense?"

"I see, but it's *laughable* young lady! I've heard wacky ideas in my day but that beats all of 'em hands down! I thought you had somethin' *serious* to say. Think about it for a second. How could they do it? In the first place, it would be *impossible* to keep such a thing a secret from party bosses. In the second, it would take one hell of a long time even if it *were* possible. It's wacko! It's even *silly*. It could never happen—no way, not in a million *years*! Not in *ten* million years!"

"Perhaps, you might in fact be right. But maybe you're *not*, and even if you are, wouldn't you at least agree that it *might* be possible, that a sort of parallel progression *could* take place side-by-side and *inside* the parties all at the same time? And if it *is* possible, even to a small degree, wouldn't you at least think it might be worthy of finding *out*, especially if it could straighten out America?"

"Miss, I suppose anything's possible. I guess pigs might even be able to fly someday too, but not this...never this. I do have to say, though, it's an interesting idea I never heard before! Not a *doable* idea, but damned *creative*, and I'll give you *that* much."

When the meeting was over, neither Harrington nor Principle realized it was 6 a.m., as Harrington's mind began to change. They had talked uninterrupted for more than twelve hours.

Three days later Russell Harrington left Lake Forest a changed man. Dazed and bewildered, he had the feeling of having seen a type of history in the making—history that was thus far unrecorded, but long needed for the welfare of the American people and their government.

When Harrington announced the formation of a special grant for students who wanted to pursue a course of study on natural law, it came as no surprise to any person who knew Harrington. He had always been a generous benefactor to Northwestern. With the sale of his company for $350 million, along with his retirement, newspapers emblazoned their mastheads: What is next for young Russell Harrington?

With his disappearance, complete and absolute, shock waves rang out on Wall Street and in financial communities worldwide. Russell Harrington, multi-millionaire wonder boy industrialist, had dropped completely out of sight. Even his family did not know his whereabouts.

He was beyond discovery. Several newspapers began a series of informative articles about his contributions to the oil industry in developing new techniques of exploration. Some speculated about abduction. Such conjecture continued, even after his chief executive officer assured investigators that young Harrington was taking a much-needed rest and would remain unavailable for an indefinite time. But Russell Harrington was indeed alive and well and ready to begin a new chapter in the dynamic life that had begun in El Paso. During the spring break, he quietly returned to Illinois to start the project of his life.

"All right Sara," he said gleefully, as Principle burst through the door of the suite. "The car's gassed up and I'm *ready*! I feel more alive than I *ever* have, but if I told the folks, they'd have me put in a loony bin, and maybe they *should*!"

Principle rubbed her hands together briskly in anticipation of the venture and said, "I've made all the arrangements with Jim. He's willing to teach you everything he knows, which is considerable. When you think you've learned enough we'll get started. Just don't forget Russ. I know how impatient you are, but this is going to take a long, long time. If we finish we might even be very *old*!"

Using the guise of being a distant cousin of Miller, Harrington lived in obscurity in Miller's home over the course of two years, devoting his time to the study of history, geography, other natural sciences and philosophy, as they all related to politics. He also learned a variety of ways to develop secret actions and ideas from Miller, who was thoroughly educated about them through his membership in Skull and Bones, eagerly discarding the oath of secrecy he had taken.

Under Miller's tutelage, Harrington became a man obsessed with acquiring new information. He eagerly devoured the weekly shipments of books and articles from Sara Principle, spending hours on end with her during her now frequent hometown visits and then in three way conferences with his host.

Miller tutored Harrington, taking him from the inception of the first types of government, its cause and effect within a civilized structure, up through the first Nixon administration. Harrington unearthed the existence of an international network of people who worked inside the political systems of numerous countries. They carried on in partnership with politicians and major corporations with the proposition that only a select group should supervise the entire world. It was the hardest of the new ideas to accept. Active, hard-core capitalists, scheming to develop one federation worldwide with a small group of their numbers in control just did not wash, and it would be impossible to achieve. Finally, he could no longer ignore the mounting evidence, as it started to become clearer. He also began to recognize that what the world federation crowds were doing was a parallel progression with his project with Principle, but on a much larger scale, as they had been active longer, and with the backing of progressives *and* conservatives long established inside many governments.

He studied into the early morning hours of each day, valiantly trying to know the unknowable. Little known books with documentation on one of the wealthiest families in the world and their quest to move America into the fold of the world collectivists did not make sense at first. One family could not openly practice capitalism on one hand, while believing in an oligarchic form of government on the other, so he studied, absorbing the information like a sponge. Miller quietly taught and listened to all of Harrington's ideas, and reported his progress to Sara Principle.

After many months of intense investigation, the material began to stick in Harrington's mind and make some kind of logical sense. For the people described in the various reports, the desire for wealth was the same as the quest for power. They worked in unison, each feeding the other, but power was always first. If the family could rise to the top of the federation, they would be able to eliminate all serious competition to their own enterprises. On the day he made the connection, Russell Harrington developed extreme nausea and was bedridden for two days, as Miller nursed him back into focus and action.

Jim Miller's insight of history and government both amazed and depressed Harrington. He became aware that with the passage of many years, people the world over became lazy and smug with a particular way of life. It was especially true in America, as they were unwilling to look for a better solution even when introduced to one. The less they knew about their own politics the more they liked it. He had seen it in his own world. He knew it was true. Even though people saw many facets of wrongdoing by their chosen leaders, ordinary citizens were impotent to correct them. Life had always been that way, they rationalized, which made it comfortable and easy to live with. People liked familiarity, and then they embraced contempt, until finally, full capitulation. Anything else would be frightening to their ordered and obtuse lives, and it was certainly not as compelling or exciting as movie stars, TV game shows, or mindlessly walking through a shopping mall simply because it was something to do. It was what America had become in the evolutionary process. He had no way of knowing it would devolve in an even greater way in the very near future with electronic devices. As far as politics was concerned, the rule in American families was that along with religion, the two subjects were not open for discussion.

When the oilman emerged from his New Castle cocoon on South 18th Street two years later, he had received the equivalent of a full four-year education devoted to history, the natural sciences, philosophy, and a vastly expanded knowledge of politics well beyond anything he thought could ever have happened in the life of his country.

While cloistered in the small town, he managed to write a book entitled, Wealth: How to get it, How to keep it. The book advocated the value of natural conservation and saving; of learning as much as possible about their chosen profession before attempting to land at the top, and above all else to not be afraid of risk and to not give up—to do the best work possible regardless of how low a person was on the ladder upward. These traits ultimately made the difference and separated the successful from the so-called failure.

Stepping forth from self-imposed exile and using the wide connections he determined were necessary to obtain a publishing contract he got the manuscript published, and began a promotion tour. Reviews of the book gave the impression that he should have stayed in the oil business. Much to the surprise and delight of the publisher, however, the book made staggering headlines, was a runaway best seller, and stayed there ahead of several well-known authors for many months.

By late spring of the following year, Harrington had met and listed thousands of people on the tour. He formed strong bonds with some, placing them in various and complex niches of political persuasions until a scant seventy-five remained, intricately selected from the rest. He journeyed to the city of Lordsburg in New Mexico, where he made reservations for three days to accommodate the seventy-five. Four meeting rooms were set up to conduct small symposiums the participants could attend, each according to their own preferences. In the end, a gala dinner was prepared. Harrington and Miller each addressed the group briefly, leaving the main speech for Principle. It was, after all, her idea.

A wide assortment of literature was dispensed to advise the group where more information could be obtained about the individually chosen subject matter. In the end, they spoke with one voice. They were poised to attack the system of government in America. The ideals and aspirations of the new organization would remain top secret. For now, only they would know, and their name would be The Solution.

One of the jobs for each member was to establish a personal goal of finding new recruits, gradually increasing to larger and larger numbers. They knew it would require many years of concentrated effort. Only when a potential new member arrived at a point where no doubt remained as to an unwavering commitment, would that individual move to a starting point as a participating associate. The membership of The Solution was mainly comprised of people who naturally shunned any form of connection to groups, which would make the endeavor even more difficult and time consuming to achieve. The road would be long...interminable to some. Many would not live to see its finale, if they even got that far.

Because of the painstaking, rigorous selection process started by Harrington, along with the participation of Miller and Principle, those individuals chosen would stay with the program regardless of what happened in their personal lives. They went through demanding tests to satisfy the principals that no problems would arise indiscriminately. They would then fight behind the scenes to circumvent an older, and more entrenched covert group created by a number of well-financed executives. These were some, of many, who ostensibly controlled and ran America. They achieved their goals by electing politicians of all stripes who only wanted to have the perpetual illusion of power in carrying out their puppet masters bidding, while the controller's remained invisible to everyone else.

Millions more Americans would have to be secretly indoctrinated to the theme of The Solution, without frightening them along the way with charges of paranoia. People not brought in as members but still influenced to accept the primary goals could not be told of the alliance started by the David Rockhold family in the early 1900s. To do so would cause widespread disbelief in the movement. People simply did not want to hear of conspiracies. If they did, they would not support the stated principles of an organization whose name they did not even know, and certainly not the ultimate goal of destroying democracy.

The higher echelons of The Solution members would begin the process of using a small number of people to manage and direct larger and larger numbers of individuals. They would assist their family members in a wide variety of ways, both financial and personal, and as the years would pass, the numbers would grow exponentially in both camps, as one person told another person, and so on.

It was obvious to The Solution leaders that Americans did not believe people existed who wanted to rule the earth with a single government and currency. To that charge, they would not respond. They had listened and rejected all of the conspiracy theories about the death of President Kennedy and the Trilateral Commission. They had made a collective decision as a nation. Secret cabals were simply from the imagination of novel writers and other paranoid people.

SEVEN

Russell Harrington worked for fifteen years to define his presence in the state of Texas and increase his wealth, and then he entered a hotly contested primary race for the United States Senate as a Republican. He was victorious. At age forty, he had made his face and name one of the most recognized throughout the state. When he was triumphant in the general election, a smug, gravel-voiced Harrington publicly issued a challenge to all other senators as a notification that he would be sending each senator an urgent message. He would be there, and the entire Senate would feel his presence—not as a typical freshman senator, but one from a powerful state with knowhow. The Majority Leader would need to arrange for Harrington to be on powerful committees, as the full Senate would now have to deal with a strength they had never before encountered. It would be a continuous force, not airy-fairy or soft and sedate, for Russell Harrington, United States Senator and now a billionaire, would crash into the legislative body with a dynamism they had never seen.

He was a ferocious supporter of free, unregulated, laissez faire trade. Any piece of legislation designed to tie the hands of business in any way would encounter his full opposition and considerable talent and wealth to generate publicity. He was also prepared to spend a great deal of that wealth to carry the message of liberty to the nation.

As an outspoken critic of what he defined as a continuous, senatorial scheme to promote socialist programs, he declared both parties guilty. If he decided it was necessary, he would inform the people of the full ramifications of socialist policies by purchasing time on television and radio. He would use plain language, charts and graphs, and he had the money to do the promotions frequently. He hired a personal publicist to book him on both early and late night television programs.

Harrington was a fearless fighter for what he believed was right. Whenever possible he boasted of his wealth, boldly pontificating on the wonders of the entrepreneurial spirit and the willingness to reach ever higher to achieve a thoroughly planned and charted goal. He was tired of listening to other rich people apologize for their wealth with self-imposed guilt, and how it was up to the government to make sure poor people got their fair share. "Fair share of what?" he asked. That was certainly not the way for Americans to become prosperous, according to the gospel of Russell Harrington. Nor would it ever be a legitimate purpose or function of government regardless of how many people thought it was. Government really had only one job, and that was to protect Americans from physical aggression, not to spread wealth or create jobs. Many people had just lost sight of the true purpose of government, which was to protect their individual rights.

Harrington started making impromptu statements that received avid press coverage. He was becoming very good copy for reporters. "Hell," he would chuckle in his gruff Texas drawl, "just 'cause the president and I are both Republicans, that don't mean I cain't criticize him! That ain't *ever* gonna happen. I ain't ever played that kind of game with *anyone*, even when I was in the oil business!"

In his first re-election campaign, the gravelly voice would rumble from the microphone. "Listen here all you people!" he would say. "My name is Russell Harrington and if you ain't heard of me, why then you must have been *hybernatin'* all these years! I'm *rich*! R*eally* rich! I'm one of those bad apples that those bleeding-heart limousine liberals whine about—worth more than $1 *billion bucks* by now, I guess. Hell, I don't really know for sure. I ain't goin' back to the U.S. Senate to get *richer*! Hell, I cain't spend all the money I got *now*! I like to tell folks I'm rich. Then they know I won't be tryin' to steal their money just 'cause they send me to D.C. *Hell yes*, and just so you don't forget, I earned every damn penny. Not one red cent came from *taxpayers*!

"I ain't goin' back there to make all you people spend more of your hard earned money on a bunch of bums who are too damn lazy to get off their butts and work, either. Let 'em go out and make it on their own just like *we* do...just like our *folks* did!

"I ain't goin' back to help those people who've been there since the time of Christ, either! All they want is to increase the budget and write a whole bunch of new regulations to bring a whole lot of hurt on business. I'll work to stop that crap, and you should too!"

He was bigger than life—the most dynamic force to arrive on the Hill in twenty years. He made the evening news more regularly than any other member of Congress except for John McCain, and was inundated with requests to appear on a variety of radio and television programs. More than one dozen publishers tried for the rights to his personal biography, never understanding that Harrington's motive was not self-aggrandizement, but changing minds for a secret plan for a new American government.

In the middle of his second term, he received a personal invitation to meet with the president, who wanted to elude Harrington's one-man tribunals on government. In front of the Capitol Building, however, he held with reporters what he called, a street-side *Harrington Court*. One ABC reporter, popular for his criticism of the conservative movement of the time, stood up and asked him to make a comment on the poor and what he thought the president should do to help them. It was a mistake of the highest degree. The reporter also wanted to know if the president would receive a better report card from the oilman than other presidents did because they were in the same party, or if the Texan would be honest in his evaluation and not spin the information.

Lifting one of his meaty hands, Harrington roared with gusto, "Son, I'm not *about* spin. Just get the hell out of the way is what I say! That's all! It's plain and simple. If he does that, you bet he'll get a higher grade, but he should do nothin' to help the poor, whoever *they* are. Just get out of the way. That'll help 'em more than anything will, and besides, it ain't up to the president. Did you all learn *nothin'* from my *court* appearances? I think you weren't payin' very good *attention*!"

He laughed, raised both arms for quiet and said, "Now, now, before all you boys and girls start to go off half-cocked with all of that nonsense about Russell Harrington not carin' about the poor 'cause he's rich, let me clarify my position one more time. Maybe this time you'll all write it down so you don't *forget* it again.

"Now, as far as poor folks are concerned, I think I care more for 'em than all the damn do-gooders in the world *combined*, and that sure as hell includes anyone in the government. I don't want 'em to be dependent on anyone but themselves or someone else who *volunteers* to help 'em! Not 'cause someone in the government *forced* it on 'em, like you folks seem to want.

"There's lots of reasons for poor folks. Some of 'em actually decided that they'll take all the handouts they can get instead of gettin' a job. But if they wanted, in America, still, they could also decide to work and make it on their own, but that comes from applyin' yourself. If you took all those programs away that supposedly aid poor folks, then those who're *able* would go to work. Those who cain't for one reason or the other would get help from charities and other *people*. There's *lots* of charities, and there'd be even more of 'em if there were *no* welfare programs, and hell, they'd do a better job. Families can help too! That's one thing that used to go on before those programs even existed and all the politicians suddenly saw that if they put 'em in place and made you *feel* good, well then, they could buy your vote with your own money! What a deal. Perot was *right*!

"Also, I just don't cotton to people talkin' to me about poor folks in the usual way. *Sure*, there are poor people! Lots of 'em *too*! Trouble is most of you folks just see 'em as members of *groups* that no one can really define, and as far as I'm concerned, that's a form of *racism*! You should see 'em as *individuals*, instead of always lumpin' 'em into some human *pool* like you all seem to manufacture all the time. And hell, everyone's idea about who's poor and who's rich is just a damn opinion! It's *relative*! It's just a mixed up way of thinkin' about things. I'm also *positive* there are poor folks in this country that some of you would flutter over 'cause of what you see as their *poorness*, but they think they're *rich* even though they don't have a lot of money. It's *always* just an opinion. Trouble is you wanna force your point-of-view on the rest of us, and I'm against that *too*!

"Now, my investment of extremely large amounts of money and a hell of a lot of time enabled people other than me to profit just by havin' a damn *job*! And hell, it's not like I underpaid those boys! Had 'em workin' year 'round and the damn union made sure they got paid forty bucks an hour. Hell, that's about eighty thousand bucks a year! What's so poor about that, especially back then? You people really need to start thinkin' in a different kind of way and then just get a life, 'cause the likes of you ain't gonna do anything for America."

On October 14, Sara Principle met with her team of advisors in New Mexico for the final preparation for the first debate in two days. With the president now trailing in the polls, the debates were crucial for maintaining the lead. This would be her last time to prepare, and Principle wanted to be certain she was ready. After the meeting, she would fly to New York ahead of the debate, then to Washington, and back once again to New York before returning to Las Cruces, where she would spend time with Allen at the reunion of the members of The Solution. Then she would go to Baltimore for the second debate.

Seated in a circle in the middle of Principle's living room was Armando, Fred Spans, their head of security, and Russell Harrington, who decided one week earlier to make a final attempt to reason with Principle to convince her to change her mind. He and Armando both agreed. It was essential for Principle to use notes in the debate to help combat the aggressive attack on her credibility that would come from the president. Now, however, in spite of himself, Harrington was having second thoughts. Thomas Farley was en route. Russell Harrington began to pace back and forth in front of the un-curtained windows.

Sara watched the oilman-turned-senator as he walked the floor and said, "I think we should just wait for Tom before we get in on all of this. His flight should arrive soon, Russ. Let's wait for him, 'cause I think he would want us to."

Harrington stopped at one of the windows. Looking out onto the dry desert landscape, he seemed anxious, distressed—at odds not just with himself, but also with what he now thought. For weeks, he and Armando had tried with no success to convince the senator to use notes in the debate. Harrington turned abruptly and said, "Mondo, I've changed my mind. I think we're wrong. I've thought about this a lot, Mondo, and I've decided that we've been wrong all this time that we've tried to hit our gal here with logic as *we* see it." He turned to face Principle.

Harrington's Texas drawl was always less obvious out of the public spotlight. He had effectively learned to use it to his advantage with the Washington press corps and the Texas media throughout his long tenure in the Senate, and before he even ran for office.

"Let me put it this way," he said, speaking to Armando but looking at Principle. "Thus far Sara has handled herself pretty damn well and we all *know* that's true. Hell, you just have a look at how far all of us have come. If we make the final goal, we all know it'll be on her back. Because of that, we damn well may see her elected *president*! Just *think* about that! I've seen her in action for more than forty-years. We *all* have, and not once in all that time has she *ever* used notes. She doesn't even need them for a reference when she quotes people who've either been dead for a lifetime or who said what they said just two weeks ago. She doesn't *need* them. She has that phenomenal recall ability where she can pull up quotes from her brain on the *spot*! Beyond that, she says what she knows is *right*. It all has so much logic it can't be *refuted*, and the president *will* have notes. Next to Sara, she'll look damn clumsy using them. I think we should go along with our gal. Her instincts have been damn good so far."

Principle smiled at her old friend. She held a deep admiration for the man. Not many people could have accomplished what Harrington had thus far in his life. At their first meeting, she believed Russell Harrington was destined for phenomenal greatness, and yet, just like Farley, voters would not grasp the impact of his efforts. It had been that way for many unsung heroes. Harrington had done so much for the nation. If only they could be told the truth. One day they would.

Russell Harrington's instincts were rock solid. He understood that the human spirit has a relentless desire to blossom and bloom on its own if left alone. He knew it should never be a part of the account of an altruist—the ever-present phony do-gooder with the built-in need to force-feed their own beliefs on all people at the same time. Harrington understood that individuals of normal intelligence could succeed as long as the natural drive to accomplish something always stayed secure, but if their livelihood came wrapped in government aid many people would choose not to make an effort. Why should they? It would not be necessary. Government would provide, and in taking responsibility, the individual would have no risk.

Harrington also knew that the taxpayers who provided the funds would not protest the usage of their money because they would never see a direct bill from well-schooled politicians, who understood the welfare laws presented voters with a feel-good rationalization that was obtainable nowhere else. This was a continuous, never-ending cycle to benefit not the citizen, but the ruling class of any nation-state.

"Thanks, Russ," said Principle. "Whether you know it or not, I was hoping to hear you say that, and *believe* it. The day after tomorrow we really begin. We're almost there, and I'm bursting at the seams to tell the country, even though we obviously can't do that now. We still have to play the game, and it's getting rough. We were right forty-years ago Russ. All our efforts will pay off big on Election Day. Soon we'll tell the world. I'm certain the jig is up for the president. I'm equally confident about the debates, and, I really don't need notes. I never have!"

President Crawford cleared her schedule. She spent a portion of the late afternoon boning up on the possible questions, focusing on Principle's likely responses that added to the skill she had gained in rehearsals. She wanted to be prepared to crush Principle with facts only a president could possess. She also wanted the people to see that she was a good president, a woman for all the people of America—a caring person who was under siege by a dark and dangerous enemy, a rival who could very well destroy the good works of progressives.

Throughout the briefings, Crawford's mind recorded all of the information, cognizant of the Senator's natural ability in a live hearing. She was acutely aware of Principle's personal allure, but deep within the inner recesses of her intellectual contrivance, she wondered if any of it really mattered because of what would come on the day of the first debate. She alone knew of the explosive statement to come…an earth shattering decree. Even Chet Forbes, her press secretary who would make the announcement did not know what he would be required to say in the statement. Crawford had left nothing to chance. She would give Forbes a mere thirty minutes to prepare the announcement. It would more than likely turn the poll numbers around instantly.

The stirring words of John F. Kennedy left a distinct and lasting mark on Crawford when she was just a girl. After she graduated from high school, she served a short stint in the Peace Corps before college, and came to understand that leaders the caliber of the slain president, true leaders of the people, were uncommon in any era. Because of that singular quality the nation must work to select strong persons of substance—individuals who held the people's interests above their own, and in their hearts. Now, more than ever, they needed a caring woman like Hadley Crawford.

Kennedy had shown her a special vision—a unique image of youthful vigor, of hope for the future, of caring and concern for others. Then he fell to an assassin's bullet.

The president thought about the legacy of Kennedy and believed that she was the one to carry that fallen banner, even though it happened so long ago. In her mind, history would show her to be the best one ever, including TR, Wilson, FDR, and even the great Barack Obama. It would be especially true after the coming announcement. She smiled, pleased with all she had and would accomplish in her life, a life that had started in the suburbs of Chicago, walking down a privileged path to do great deeds.

Crawford was from Park Forest Illinois, with a heritage dating back to the Continental Congress. Her birth came late in her parent's life, and from her earliest memories, she believed she was a descendent of high-line aristocrats from what her mother had told her. She spent her summers with influential families in the east, where she attended the best prep schools and learned the ways of the upper crust. With her introduction to David

Rockhold, Crawford was enchanted with the trappings of super-wealth and power, never knowing that her parents had struggled many years for acceptance in Chicago's elite culture.

She graduated from Harvard with honors, and then Harvard Law, living out the highly structured life her parents had planned for her when she was born. After her graduation, she spent the summer as the guest of the David Rockhold estate. Rockhold was the principal owner of the Rockhold Manhattan Bank, and fully connected to national power at the highest levels possible for a non-politician.

By the end of the summer after her introduction to Rockhold, Hadley Crawford's indoctrination to super-wealth was fixed, and growing. She was encouraged by Rockhold to stand up and be an official member of the Democratic Party. Crawford was stunned. She had grown up with the belief that the only true politics for everyone was in the Republican Party. Her parents were tried and true Republican's along with Rockhold, whose brother, Wentworth, had even tried for the Republican nomination for president many years earlier, but then found himself ousted from any position of influence in the party.

In the library of his mansion, David Rockhold said, "The summer is nearly over now, Hadley, and I do not want you to fight me on this. The conservatives now rule in the Republican Party, which is one of the reasons my brother never got very far, and it is getting worse with each passing year. Democrats are now the ones who care about people. Republicans no longer feel any concern. I cannot think of one person who is concerned with poor people"

Still having problems following Rockhold's speech patterns that precluded the use of contractions, Crawford was very confused. She said, "I don't understand. You say I should be a Democrat, but all of you are *Republicans*! Even my *parents* are Republicans. How can you possibly think I can understand something like that?"

"You will, in time, Hadley, but for us it is just too late to change. It would be ruinous for business and for many other reasons, but you can begin your political life fresh! Just know that what has taken place in the Republican Party is a disgrace. They no longer care about the everyday people as they once did. Today it is all about big business and tax cutting for rich people. That is *very* sad. It *is* the reality of what we now have to contend with, and there is another part of that, Hadley. I know it is not going to change. I know because I have been a part of it for many years, and now you can too in Chicago, or even on a national level.

"This country needs new committed leaders—men and women who are concerned about people, particularly women. You have so much talent. You can succeed where we have failed. One person *can* make a difference, Hadley, and you are definitely that kind of woman."

"You really think so? I hope you do and you're not just saying that to make me feel better."

"I *know* so, and I will make our financial resources available to guarantee that you *do* succeed. Do you understand? *Guarantee*! You will not have to worry. When you are ready, I will also give you some information known only to a few people in the entire world, but is *vital* to achieving peace *everywhere*. It will be necessary for you to learn it when you are older and start moving up the political ladder."

"Can't you tell me now?" pleaded the young Crawford, her face contorted with unknown disappointment.

"No!" said Rockhold sharply. "You are not *ready*! You are not *old* enough. You are not *ready*! Let me just say that it is clearly a national shame for so many people to be living in poverty in such a rich country. You will learn, as you get older. I *do* want to introduce you to a young man I know. His name is Clifford Cantrell. I think he will be able to help you in your political life, but you will go much further than he will. At the same time, I am certain that both of you will be rare leaders because you *do* care about others.

"When the time is right, Hadley, I will give you the information. I know you do not understand now, but you will, and you will know it much sooner than you think right now. The time will pass quickly, and then you will thank me, but now is not the time for you to have this information. You are not mature enough. You will have to acquire a few more years, but it *will* come, Hadley."

Rockhold introduced Cantrell and Crawford to The World Council Group. Important leaders of the *Group* agreed with the Manhattan banker that Crawford was a young person to watch—that she would one day hold a powerful and important position in the world. What they did not say was that they would be grooming Cantrell as a shadow to the young Crawford, and continued to flatter her with words of praise, as long as she was willing to take their advice. They did not tell her that the organization would see to it that she did take their advice working through Cantrell and Rockhold.

One year later, Crawford decided to get involved in the presidential campaign. That was when she met a young man named Alfred Bradford. He was the son of the Bradford's of Boston, upper echelon merchants to the elite of Massachusetts' society and other wealthy people around the world. They had developed a reputation for the highest quality merchandise and customer service long before some of the newer, more flamboyant establishments that came after them.

Crawford was immediately attracted to Alfred and him to her. Alfred was also impressed with her credentials and experience working in the Peace Corps, as he was on the prowl for a woman who would go far along with him. He instantly knew Hadley Crawford was that woman. Much to the delight of their families the young activists' courtship became a whirlwind romance. At a kickoff political party at the home of one of the New York banker's associates, they discovered they were very well suited to each other. It was late in the evening as many of the guests were leaving when Alfred Bradford seduced Hadley Crawford on the far reaches of the back lawn.

A very tall man, Alfred was blonde and very masculine in his appearance. He was also a delightful surprise to the young women in his life, filled with a sexual lust and hunger that enraptured the inexperienced Crawford. From her first exposure to his excesses, she became so obsessed with him that she was ready to break all of the rules regarding people of their station in life. She would risk everything to have him, which even included the opportunity for a successful run for president in the future, what David Rockhold told her to plan for her ultimate goal. Ten days later, they eloped to the Catskills.

Mostly they stayed in their room. Alfred was what she often tried to fantasize how a virile man must be like, but with a decidedly different approach to satisfy his ravenous appetite for sex. He was her dream come true. His main interest was in oral copulation both ways, and of that, he could not get enough.

Each morning he awoke his new wife, teasing her with his tongue, biting and nibbling her clitoris until she was to a point near pain. And Crawford could not contain her own propensity for oral gratification, returning his ministrations eagerly. They made love with the relentless stamina of youth, in their own personal way.

Crawford was surprised that her husband's desires did not diminish with age, but instead increased in direct proportion to her political fortunes. She found that she could not keep up with him and politics at the same time. Not surprisingly, politics won out. Then things changed.

Their thirty-eight-year marriage produced no children. Of late their relationship had grown so cold and strained it was as if no life to it had existed before her time in the Oval Office. Though she could not be certain, she believed that Alfred had taken a lover many times over since she assumed the office of president, yet she refused to have it investigated.

In happier times, Crawford pursued her winning ways to victory as the Governor of Vermont, and then on to the White House. In the middle of her second year as president, however, she began to experience a myriad of difficulties that paralleled a similar path with Sara Principle in terms of Principle's mounting successes and widespread notoriety that nearly matched certain unknown qualities similar to Barack Obama in 2008, when he easily defeated Hillary Clinton in the Democratic Primary.

When Crawford's Social Enrichment Act came to the Senate floor, she was certain it would become her greatest triumph. Her other sponsored measures had sailed through both Houses of Congress with strong approval that even included good opinions from Senator Sara Principle. The president made the personal decision to announce the bill was coming out of committee the next day to the full Senate, and she made a hurried, last-minute decision to quote Martin Luther King Jr. for her own protection, a choice she would come to regret.

"Thank you all for coming," she said in the Rose Garden. "The expected passage of this bill will help carry on part of the great work of Dr. King. He was an exceptionally heroic American who stood for all of the downtrodden and said this many, many years ago."

'I have the audacity to believe that peoples everywhere can have three meals a day for their bodies, education for their minds and dignity, equality and freedom for their spirits. I believe that what self-centered men have torn down, other-centered men can build up.'

As Crawford spoke of the bills introduction, she had no concern about its passage. It was clear, however, that with the final vote, the victory belonged not to the president, but to Sara Principle. Her forces defied the Senate headcounters and made it appear that everything was in place for the President's wishes. It would enable them to flex their political muscle openly, and to announce to the president and other senators the surging power and popularity of Sara Principle.

The bill was mysteriously defeated in a bipartisan vote. Principle delivered the final nail in the legislative coffin, in a forceful demand for fiscal sanity and moral philosophy. She also seemed to have no regard for any possible backlash that might swarm against her from a potential appearance of being anti-Martin Luther King Jr.

In a steady, fervent voice, Principle said, "This bill is the product of a president who has no regard for the American people and the dollars they work so diligently to earn. She believes she can ramrod anything through this Congress regardless of the consequences of cost, or the immoral ramifications to millions of taxpayers who want no part of this bill but would have the responsibility of paying for it all the same, in another liberal/progressive power-grab.

"So let us analyze that revered message from Dr. King that the president quoted from. On the surface, it sounds grand, and let me add that he *was* a great man in many ways, but not in this message.

"The president knows this basic fact. Equality and freedom cannot live side-by-side as peers. They are bitter and natural enemies, and we want them to stay that way. The closer you get to one the further you get from the other…and make no mistake. I am certain that Dr. King knew it then, and I am also certain that President Crawford knows it now! However, she wants you to overlook the clear and inescapable fact that it is impossible for our freedom to remain intact while being forced to foot this bill against our wants and needs.

"President Crawford asks us to believe that we can be free and equal at the same time, knowing full-well it is not possible *or* desirable. Freedom means, in part, to be exempt from political restraint or autocratic control. How can we be free if we are *compelled* to pay for programs that should never be a part of government in the first place? Well, we cannot, and the president is very much aware of this simple, basic fact. There are already too many such programs in this country.

"She also knows that *only* self-centered people can enrich the world and its people by providing employment and creative innovation. She and Dr. King want us to believe that self-centered people are evil and care only about money, that they are simply greed-filled despots. But the president knows, and so too did Dr. King, that only where there are people willing to risk it all can the rest of us obtain the better things of life for ourselves and our children. But if it is going to be provided by some far-off entity, especially a remote government, the people will regard that which they receive for nothing as being worth nothing. It is well-known human nature. They will believe the goods and services become their just reward simply because they exist. It is a basic and indisputable *fact*!

"And when she speaks of culture for their minds and dignity, does she mean culture that is imposed by some group of *bureaucrats* in Washington? Well, she does, because the purpose of politicians and bureaucrats is self-perpetuation and nothing else!

"I say to you that this bill must never see the light of day. It is time to end the practice of forcing people to do what *some* in government declare is good for them at the expense of our liberty, and limited government. It is time to recognize that individuals can decide what they do or do not need. We have to get back to the government our Founding Fathers created, and we can start here and now by dismissing this legislation for the fraud it really is and put it in the scrapheap *convincingly*!"

On the same day, an angry President Crawford went before television cameras to denounce Principle and accuse her of being an elitist who was concerned only with the desires of the rich and powerful figures of corporate America.

EIGHT

On 222nd Street in New York City, a two-story house stands that is like no other house anywhere…on the inside. Externally, its looks are the same as thousands of other such houses all across America, but only in its facade. Unassuming and indistinguishable from other such homes, the house is very different in its construction, for it has a covert purpose known only to a very select group of people.

The front of the house has a small box built into the wall by the door. Four-feet inside is a second door that leads into the interior, and past a stairway that ends abruptly on the floor above at a blank wall.

Entrance to the second floor is through a rear door that leads to the upstairs floor rooms, staffed by CIA specialists. Their current, but periodic changing role, is to monitor satellite transmissions of mobile nuclear missile systems in place around the world on a twenty-four hour basis. The structure of the house is like a fortress, able to withstand all attacks short of a direct hit by a powerful bomb. The first floor is also the permanent residence of a man with dark hair…a man named Dominick Caputo. Only the D/CIA, Clifford Cantrell, David Rockhold, and past CIA Directors know of its existence and location. The house has escaped all presidential daily briefs to keep the presidents clean.

Rockhold, the New York City banker, is the ranking member of the powerful international alliance, The World Council Group. While still in his youth after graduating from college, he single-handedly put the house into operation with his inside contacts.

Headquartered from Paris, London, and New York, the *Group* is an organization devoted to establishing accord among nations by promoting benign interaction and information between countries…but that is not their true purpose. Instead, they are a covert, Anglophile Society comprised of wealthy industrialists and government insiders, motivated by the desire for unrelenting power. Over a period of more than one-hundred years, they have succeeded in implanting themselves in Washington nearly as a government in their own right, but invisible. They have caused sweeping changes in the policies of nearly every phase of government procedures, and their influence is in the same concentrated degree with other nations as well. However, only a few individuals know of their ultimate goals or plans to covertly attain and hold power. They are also racist and misogynist, with a completely white male membership.

Under an agreement with the *Group*, David Rockhold arranged for the house using his influence in government circles to keep all of its expenses off budget, or, *Black Budget*. It was the ultimate benefit for the *Group*, whose single-minded goal is to control and direct the four major power centers of the world, to divide the planet into a Quadripartite Federation patterned in large part after the American tripartite system of government, and the World War II Axis. The heads of state in the four regions would develop a single government to oversee the entire world, now simplified by the creation of the new North American Union, answering only to the World Council Group, with the results of elections around the world easily known in advance.

The organization first began to infiltrate the upper echelons of the United States government in the early 1900s, with the understanding that world domination would not come in the founder's lifetimes, as it would require a vast number of years to complete. Ultimately, the Progressive takeover would occur at the start of the next century, and now they were ready. The administration of Hadley R. Crawford had unwittingly laid down the groundwork to carry out the plan. The president was unaware that she would be nothing more than a figurehead in the *New World Order*. She was convinced the coalition was the only true way to end war. It was especially true now with the new, sophisticated nuclear weaponry mutually developed by Russia and China that was now online and ready for action against any nation, including America, and with their own government's permission.

The quadripartite would become the new world authority, taking control of all military weapons worldwide. Records in a mainframe computer in Paris would oversee the recruitment and affairs of all countries. Insurrections would go to a review committee for recommendations to the four leaders. Designated as the initial heirs to the federation throne were Casimir Zgonina, the Russian President; Salvatore Ripoli, the President of Western Europe; General Tso, Chairman and Prime Minister of China; and Hadley R. Crawford, President of the United States of America.

For Dominick Caputo, the streets of New York City became his home by age twelve. Deserted by his mother as an infant and then later by his father, he managed to scratch out his existence living in condemned buildings and stealing food from open markets. By the time he was fifteen years old he had committed armed robbery countless times on his own, graduating to become the leader of a small, but ruthless independent ring of thugs.

They began an organization for hire that caught the attention of a Little Italy Mafia family who enlisted Caputo's gang to conduct raids against a competing family. Then, when he was twenty, the FBI apprehended him. The Bureau coerced him to give testimony against the family who had hired him, which led to a price on his head. At that point, CIA entered the scene. They would use Caputo's services as a paid assassin. His knowledge of the criminal element and the psychiatric profile that indicated he was a genuine, cold-blooded killer made him a perfect candidate for a new project. The Company would use him for special assassinations separate and apart from all others. His role would be Black Ops—geared to overthrow a few tinpot dictators around the world and high-level targets domestically, even though it violated the CIA charter. That would not be a problem. It was in fact an ongoing program blessed by many administrations.

Violence walked hand in glove with Caputo. He was a completely odious man, holding contempt for the world at large. He also hated women and wanted to inflict humiliation and degradation on as many of them as possible. One of the criteria he insisted on as part of his negotiation was to have women, many women for a variety of sex acts. He made no pretext for passion. He simply wanted to hurt as he had been hurt, and he regarded his own preferences as completely normal. Nothing he did was ever unusual…to him.

Caputo was on call for more than thirty years to fulfill high-level as-sassinations. He became a master of cover-up, completing his tasks fully, with an uncanny precision for detail. Never captured, his very being was unknown to all local enforcement agencies. As the years passed, his methods were greatly simplified. He would carry out his assignments to include a handpicked scapegoat, made easier within the passing years from newly developed manufacturing methods. His greatest success came with the murder of a prominent official in Texas, where he took great pride in giving local authorities someone to try, and then convict for the crime for which they knew he was not guilty. As his most major contract, the man used as a patsy proclaimed his innocence and tried to tie in a shadowy man with dark hair who had recruited him. He continued to argue his lack of guilt until his own mysterious death. Years later when a vast amount of evidence surfaced from a Southern lawyer, authorities accused him of being nothing more than a Publicity Hound. No legal authority ever took his evidence and eyewitness statements seriously.

Caputo was now fifty-eight years old and a virtual captive of the house except for limited excursions the D/CIA allowed him to have on his own. Late one night he decided that he had had enough. It had been many weeks since Cantrell had sent a woman to him, and he wanted one now. If the D/CIA thought it was in his interest to play hardball, and not live up to their agreement, that was fine with Caputo. Only now, he wanted a street hooker. He had grown tired of the fancy women with their elegant clothes and constant complaints. Now he wanted a common whore, a woman he could easily subdue and intimidate, and he would have the kind of whore who would not report to the agency because the agency would never know about her.

He telephoned for a taxi, taking the extra precaution for pickup not at the house, but at the corner of the block. Then he went to Harlem. Over the entire period of time he had spent in the house, each new D/CIA kept him supplied with high-priced call girls in a Manhattan apartment. He would take the woman there.

In Harlem, he made contact with a black woman and one very young white girl. He decided he would have them both. With large amounts of cash on hand to purchase needed equipment to use at a moment's notice, he agreed to pay each woman $500. He made it clear they would also have sex with each other, if that were what he wanted at any given time, or anything else he decided. In turn, he would give them liquor and all the hard drugs they wanted.

En route to the apartment, however, Caputo abruptly changed his mind, giving the driver instructions to change his course. He wanted to go to the house. When the women objected, he agreed to give them an additional $100. On the way, he told them to stay only in the bedroom area, and not attempt to go elsewhere. At the entrance, he made them stand to the right side of the door as he inserted a plastic card to bypass the second floor monitor. Inside, the white girl, Margie, started up the stairs. When she had reached the third step, Caputo yanked her backward, his face angry and red.

"*Common* baby!" she protested. "What's with the *strong-arm* shit? I was just goin' up to the *bedroom*!"

"Listen bitch!" snarled Caputo. "You're not allowed to go up there! No one is! Get it! The bedroom is down here. *Nobody* goes upstairs! Understand...nobody! So don't try it again!"

The black woman, Sheila, was the first to respond. She said softly, "Sure, sure, Sugar. Anything you say."

As he led them through the hallway they felt a slight vibration from somewhere in the house. Only the smaller night shift worked in the main computer room on the second floor. The slight pulsing sensation, along with Caputo's explicit warning made the atmosphere seem bizarre and frightening. All at once, an involuntary chill engulfed Sheila. Turning to Margie she whispered, "I don't know 'bout you, Sugar, but this place give me the fuckin' creeps. I got a good mind to get the fuck *outta* here."

Sheila watched as Caputo walked to a tall mahogany cabinet in the bedroom. He opened a fold-down door to a professionally stocked bar, on which he spread a small amount of cocaine on its mirrored surface. He divided the powder into four very small thin lines with a razor blade. Sheila was the first to move toward him.

"Whew-ee, *Sugar*!" she squealed. "You really had me *goin' Sugar*! You said you had it, but I really didn't *believe* you 'til now!"

Caputo was incensed. "*Listen*, you fucking bitch, and listen good, both of you!" he snarled. He repeatedly pointed his finger at the two women and said, "I'm paying you a lot of money! More than you'd make all night." He paused, still aiming his finger and looking even more menacing, as he quickly settled the point he was making. "So just keep your fucking mouth closed and believe *everything* I say!" Then he added with a menacing firmness and finality, but in a voice barely above a whisper, "you'll regret it if you don't."

Instantly the women were more than just docile. They were completely submissive, except for Sheila's continuous ogling of the tiny coke lines on the mirrored door.

He ordered them to remove their clothes while he watched, making lewd comments and thinking about what he eventually wanted to do to them, and how and when he would do it.

Margie was a small, natural blonde, and attractive in a rough sense. He liked blondes. He also liked black women with thick lips and dark skin. Though he was not certain what he would do to Sheila, for Margie, he was. He would save the electric device for her. Even though she was a prostitute, Caputo could tell that Margie was far too young to have had much experience. She wouldn't understand the true purpose of the electric dildo when she first saw it, but she would explode with pain when he inserted the unit, strapped it in place and turned on the current. He would force her to keep it inside until his warped mind was satisfied with the extent of pain he wanted to inflict.

Then he thought of Sheila. She was very experienced. He would have to think of something very good for her.

His voice was crude and gruff and filled with a lurking rage. The women understood that he was not the type of man they could easily manipulate. They were just simple street girls working the darkened alleys to provide quick oral release to a variety of men who used them for a million different reasons and a million different needs, that more than likely had nothing to do with pleasure, or with the woman who provided their sexual release…any woman would do.

Sheila had a pimp she despised and loved at the same time, and continued to turn over her earnings like the rest of her sisters on the street. It was the only way to survive. He gave her the drugs she needed and told her she was beautiful. No other man had ever told her that. All they wanted was to use her for their own gratification, but he was different. At least that was what she had always told herself, but her personal reality knew it was not true for him, or any other run-of-the-mill-pimp.

Caputo told them to go ahead and help themselves to the coke while he went in to the bathroom. He knew they would be much easier to control under the influence of the drug, and enable him to excite his senses by conflicting serious pain against them. In his absence, Sheila told Margie to try to relax. As Sheila greedily eyed the white powder, she said that she had been wrong. They had a good thing going and Margie should not be so uptight. They were making great money, and they needed to just relax and enjoy their good fortune.

Margie was nervous. She liked sex, even though she was a hooker, but she'd never been with another woman before. Her most real experience was with her boyfriend a few times each week, except for her new profession. She never used drugs and she had managed to avoid them completely, but not on purpose.

Sheila immediately went to the white powder and Margie said, "What do you do with this stuff? You sniff it up your nose, right?"

"Like this, Sugar!" squealed Sheila, as she expertly rolled one of the hundred dollar bills into a tight cylinder. Quickly she snorted the line. "That's how, Sugar, jus' like *that*!" She did the second line and said, "Take my word, Sugar. You gonna *love* it!"

She helped Margie do the coke and then poured whiskey into two glasses. She said, "Now look, Sugar, don't you worry 'bout a thing. This is *good* stuff. I'm already gettin' some action, even though he didn't give us very much, and besides, Sugar, you know how these guys *are*! It won't take long for him. Think of it like that, and think 'bout the *money*! And if this guy wants to get off watchin' you an' me fo' 'while, well then, that's it—that's what we'll have to do. *Relax*, Sugar. Just make this a learning experience." She laughed.

Sheila saw the glaze in Margie's eyes just as Caputo walked into the room completely nude. He made it clear he would not countenance any faked responses they might have cooked up while he was gone. Any ideas the two women may have had started to evaporate with the effect of the liquor and cocaine. On their own, they began to fondle each other, laughing and falling down to the floor, while Caputo just watched. He would continue watching and not participate this early. He would take his time, especially with Margie.

Coming down from the influence of the coke, they descended on the bar. Caputo laid out more lines. He always seemed to know exactly how much to give them, making it last only a short time. He thought to himself that this was going to be better than he had planned, and that he would have to do it more frequently.

By 1 a.m. they were putting on a remarkable show, performing on each other, and on Caputo, without the slightest objection to whatever he told them. At 3 a.m., Sheila told him she wanted something stronger. Caputo went to the bathroom. He returned, armed with needles and syringes. If they wanted something stronger, he would give it to them and enjoy the results.

He was exhilarated watching the performance of the two women, but he was also tiring, Thirty minutes later, he fell asleep, but Margie was just getting started. She was flying in a world she had never experienced, and had not had enough of either the sex or drugs. But Sheila was also tiring, and Margie decided to have more of the heroin after Sheila fell to sleep.

When he awakened, Caputo saw that Sheila was still asleep, while Margie sat on the floor leaning against a wall not speaking. Her head was against the wall, her eyes closed and her mouth gaped open. Now he would have some real fun. He did not know that Margie had sampled more of the heroin, nor did he know of her inexperience. He walked to her, viciously slapping her face, hoping she would wake up screaming. Instead, she crumpled to her side. Then he knew…Margie was dead.

NINE

Luther Johnson was in his final year at New Mexico State University when he first started to intern for Mayor Sara Principle. Luther believed Principle to be a rare person—a creative and wise politician who would go very far and have an uncommon destiny to generate change, but not the type of change touted by Senator Barack Obama when the future president campaigned for that office. Principle's change would be even more revolutionary and daring than Obama could ever imagine—different from any other politician in either political party, in America's entire history. It would be groundbreaking not just for obtuse voters, but also for deceitful and even honest politicians, individuals who were in many respects not as well educated as those they represented, and they were completely obtuse.

Having a strong interest in politics when he was very young that mirrored Principle's at the same age, Luther also discovered he was developing deep personal conflicts with the policies of the Democratic Party. As a boy, he was greatly inspired by Obama, and pliable enough to buy in to his soaring oratory...but only for a short time. That was when he decided the new president was simply wrong-headed all around.

For most of his life, Luther had listened to his parent's rail against the Republicans in an incoherent way, trying to convince their son that the only place for a black person in politics was with the *Party of the People*, the ones who actually cared about the working-man, but the proclamations did not make sense. As a young black man, Luther felt his race had not made gains from what the Democrats espoused, and never would, with political assumptions that made it appear the people could not take care of themselves without the Democratic Party. He also believed their policies were institutionally racist, notwithstanding the great success of Obama. Luther confused his parents even more when he tried to explain to them that the great orator was not really a Democrat, but a Progressive. In many ways, normal Democrats historically mirrored Republicans, but not Barack Obama and his friends. They were intent on establishing a new paradigm based on the works and progressive beliefs of people like Teddy Roosevelt, Woodrow Wilson, and Saul Alinsky. That was not what true Democrats stood for. At least from everything he had heard his parents say, even as the bulk of them were unable to comprehend the real difference.

Luther moved on to a full-time job in Principle's administration after he graduated from NMU. His role then changed when he followed Principle to Washington, and discovered the newly elected senator had something special in mind for her young aide. Principle's intimate circle was a nearly even split of Republicans and Democrats. She wanted Luther to begin working on a new project—a pilot program to gain information but away from D.C. It was also a venture paid for with private funds.

Luther went to a section of Harlem that had not yet seen the full effects of rehabilitation. It was a still a blighted area, filled with neglected property and people out of work. Devastated by poverty, it even included individuals who were unemployed, but still did not have to work to survive. They received government aid, while at the same time they moved to petty crime and looted their own kind. It did make any sort of sense when Luther thought about it, though it was a convoluted, yet prevailing attitude. If the government sanctioned the taking of property by force from some people to give to other people, then surely it was permissible to steal from one's own kind.

Luther's job was to explain new ideas and teach about the benefits of individual achievement. It would be a type of domestic, one-man mini-Peace Corps in a private sense. In the short time he was there, he managed to make some inroads because of his race and youth, working diligently to maintain a casual, optimistic approach to everyone, he met, and he seemed to be gaining more and more respect.

Early on a Monday morning in a diner, a black prostitute came to his table. She was an attractive woman with strong features and deeply colored skin. As he sat drinking his coffee, the woman boldly sat down after his nodded invitation from their eye contact. Had the meeting taken place when he first arrived in Harlem, he would not have made the connection about her profession. He was just a middleclass suburban kid who was new to the ways of the big city. Now, however, he effortlessly understood.

"Hi, Sugar!" she said, fearlessly, but hesitatingly at the same time. "You don't mind if I sit down, do you?"

He said, "Help yourself. What can I do for you?"

His approachable, civil attitude surprised her. "Well," she said, cautiously. "I heard 'bout you from some people I know and thought I'd look you up. I know you know what I do, Sugar, but I jus' wanna talk. I'm not tryin' to turn a trick, so don't get nervous. Okay?" She seemed genuinely sincere, and she was very easy to look at.

She told him her name was Sheila Larkin, and that she had had a slow night. She just wanted to have someone pleasant to talk to, and everyone said he was nice. She didn't tell him that she also liked his lean body, his handsome face and his killer smile.

They talked for nearly one hour. Luther made the discovery that Sheila had a personality to match her looks, once she was able to get beyond her natural suspicion. She was open and friendly, with a positive outlook on her life. It surprised him. Hookers were supposed to be the kind of women who hated themselves, being on the lowest rung of society and put down by nearly everyone.

"What do you think 'bout what I do?" she asked.

"Well," he said, puzzled. "I never really *thought* much about it, but I guess it just hasn't been on my radar at all. Why?"

She smiled and said, "I jus' wanted to see what you said—see if you *judged* me. But I'm *satisfied*! Anyhow, at least I'm not on *welfare*, but I'll get out of the racket one of these days. Maybe not this year, but I *will*! Know what I mean?"

"Yes, I sure do, but let me ask *you* something. Has anyone told you what I'm doing and why I'm here in Harlem? You know I'm not *from* here, don't you?"

"Yeah, that's another thing. They say that you work for this woman named Principle. Who's she?"

"She's the Republican candidate for president."

She pulled her lips backward baring her teeth, but without smiling. "Well," she said, looking straight into his eyes, "how the fuck could you expect me or anyone else here in Harlem to vote for some fuckin' *Republican*? I'm *black*!"

"Well, in case you missed it, so am *I*! So *what*?"

"*Because*! Those fuckers don't like black people. What does your honky boss think 'bout what *I* do? I don't like any of those motherfuckers! What are *you* doin' *workin'* with 'em?"

He knew he must be careful and said, "Whoa! Hold on! I'm just trying to *help* people…*our* people! Young *black* people! I'm working to get them to understand that they can't just keep on living the way they do and not give a damn. People *have* to work in this world, and the best way to do that is to get an education, and I don't necessarily mean colloege. You have to *know* things! They really need to get it that it's *their* life, and it's up to *them* to care enough about it to start developing goals and good work habits. They need to stop expecting someone to *give* it to them. It seems to me that that's what *you're* doing, Sheila. I've only known you for about an hour, but I can tell you aren't looking for any handouts. *And* it's not just here in Harlem, Sheila! *Lots* of young people are like that all over the place. Before I came here, I saw it in other areas too. How come *you're* not like that? And don't make excuses, 'cause I *know* you're not like that."

In the brief time they spent together, they were connecting in a way neither thought possible when they first met. Luther asked if she would have any interest in going around Harlem with him on occasion. Sheila was thrilled that someone would want her help instead of her body, and for the next five days, they were constant companions, caught up in their own unique discovery of people…and each other.

They went everywhere together, talking to people about their inability to make ends meet with dead-end jobs that paid little, or who had no job at all. Sheila was becoming more than just a new friend. Now she was an advocate, with the natural ability to understand that the only way to arrive at a higher economic plateau was to work as diligently as possible to attain a specific goal. It was what she had always tried to do, even though she was a prostitute, but now it was somehow easier for her to see it. Still, it was a dream not yet achieved.

One morning they met for breakfast, and Sheila told him of the night she and Margie had spent with Caputo at the house on 222nd Street. She had not seen Margie before or after that night, but they had made a lot of money all the same. At least she remembered that much of the nightlong affair, if little else. It was mostly like a far-off dream she could not completely recall, but she was certain of one thing. The dark-haired man was dangerous. She could not give Luther the specifics he asked for, only that she thought the man might be unstable.

She told him what she could about the house and the man. When she awoke the next day, she was lying in a cell; arrested, they said, for being drunk in a public park. She did not remember the park, and she did not even remember leaving the house. Everything about the long night was a blur. Afterward, her pimp was teaching her a lesson by locking her out of her apartment that he paid for with money she had earned. She stayed with a friend, and finally the ugly bruise under her left eye was gone. She received the shiner because she did not report the money, and her pimp would not be taking care of her for a while. She would have to learn just how important he was to her life.

Luther was an exceptionally handsome young man, and Sheila was inching toward infatuation. He was nice to her. She decided not to see him for a few days. When she finally went out searching for him, strung out from several days with hard drugs, she felt the need to be with him. He made her feel safe, and he was easy to be around without other company. This was something that was very rare for her.

When Luther saw her condition, he immediately took her to his apartment. She was asleep on the bed instantly, while Luther took the sofa. The next morning he awoke to the smell of sizzling bacon and coffee. Sheila was cooking.

He sat down at the table to the steaming cup of coffee she placed in front of him and watched as she went through the motions of preparing food. It was a fascinating metamorphosis. She was at once like a young housewife, swishing back and forth from stove to toaster. In another time, he thought, and under very different circumstances, Sheila would probably enjoy the everyday routine of making breakfast for a husband. Knowledge from her profession had added to her instinctive wisdom to provide certain necessities of life without puncturing a more traditional desire that was lying dormant beneath the surface.

Suddenly something clicked in his mind. It was about a back page article in the paper from a few days earlier. He remembered the story Sheila told of Margie and the house. She was young and blonde like the girl in the story. *Can Margie be the girl in the article? No. It's not even possible! It's just not possible!*

"Tell me about that crazy house again," he said casually. "Think you could remember where it is or how to get there? I'm curious to see what a place like that looks like. Is it just a *regular* house? Maybe if you saw it again it would jog your memory. It'd also give us a chance to get away for a couple of hours, and might be a nice break for *both* of us. I think it'd be a good time off. How about it?"

One hour later, they were driving in the general location where she thought the house was. On the way, she told him about the plastic card. It came to her suddenly, as she then remembered how the man used the card to open the front door. Slowly some of the events of the night came back to her as she saw more of the area. There was a small box by the door, she told him, and when the man inserted the card, the door opened freely. It was the same for the second door just four feet inside. Now she wondered why there was another door.

She told him about the camera she had noticed, and of her feeling that there were machines on the floor above. At least the vibrations made her think of machines.

When they turned the corner on 222nd Street, she shrieked out. "That's *it*, right there! *That's* the one! Only I don't wanna stick around here! There's somethin' *wrong* there!" She pleaded. "I don't know what it is! *Please! Luther!* Let's get the fuck outta here!" Luther was stunned. Sheila was screaming, shaking, and genuinely frightened.

He made a note of the address without understanding why, and then they made their way back to Harlem. At this point, he operated primarily on instinct, as he quietly vowed to himself to do a thorough investigation. He wondered if there was any possible connection to the newspaper article. Probably not, but still he would check it out.

Luther spent a sizeable amount of time in New Mexico training with Fred Spans, the former Secret Service agent who oversaw Sara Principle's presidential security. Fred instructed Luther on a variety of ways to watch, listen, and recognize a wide range of consistencies and inconsistencies in a given situation. He cautioned the youth to be constantly aware of unusual activities with people and locations. Certainly, the house fell into both categories, but not with any link to the campaign. Still, he would look into it if only to satisfy his own need to know, but people in normal homes did not use plastic cards to open doors, nor did they have cameras at their entrances. It was a natural state of affairs for luxurious apartment buildings and hotels, but not for a typical two-story home in an ordinary neighborhood.

When he returned to his apartment, Luther settled down to read the back issues of newspapers he had stacked in the corner of his kitchen just a few days earlier. He had dropped Sheila off at the diner with the promise of a movie in a day or two, telling her that he wanted to read up on some things without mentioning the story, or possibilities that could turn into realities.

As he skimmed the pages, thoughts of the house and the fantastic tale Sheila had told continued to trouble him. The strange behavior of women ordered into submission by money and drugs, along with their fear of a man who demanded that they not stray from the bedroom area, caused him to feel unsettled. First, he thought, the women were picked up in a taxi, not in a car. *Inconsistencies—why was he adamant about not leaving the bedroom area?*

Second, she said the man told the driver to change directions to go to the house. He even agreed to pay more money. Why? Then there was the matter of how the man gained entrance to the house. All events leading up to the nightlong affair were consistent with the man's conduct, yet inconsistent with the nature of the neighborhood and picking up prostitutes in a taxi. Luther was also starting to question his own motives. Was he looking for something that was not there because things had gotten personal with Sheila? No! *I can't get involved with a prostitute*! Maybe there were conflicts with *his* thinking.

He continued flipping through the pages. His mind was now obsessed with Sheila's story and the nagging feeling there might be an element of truth to it. Her story was far too detailed to be a complete fantasy, and she did not seem to be the kind of woman to have phony dreams in spite of her profession. She was more a realist living in a world not of her own making, but one that most people would see as unreal and appalling. Then there were the things Fred had taught him. Finally, he came to a follow-up on the shooting of Robert Wilcox. The only clue was centered on a man with dark hair, a man seen on two separate occasions by Senator Principle, and then by Wilcox.

Bang! *There is* a *connection*! Why had he forgotten the man seen by Principle? Sheila said the man had dark hair and a gruff voice. No! It just couldn't be, but it was, and what was the other thing she had said...*the case*! *That's it, the damn case*! She said she noticed a black shoulder case that was leaning against a wall—a strangely shaped case, not large or small, or for anything familiar. Principle had given Luther a complete description of the man on Michigan Avenue, along with the case with the irregular shape. The two distinct descriptions were essentially the same. *That's it*! *It can't be, but it is*! The pounding in his brain about a possible tie-in to the campaign was on track after all. Now he was certain. It was the same man...or was it? It was clear that some of the information made sense and some did not. What was the answer? He just could not shake the nagging doubts that filled his brain. If true, he had to find out right away.

Suddenly a small headline to an even smaller story on a back page of the paper caught his eye, the one he was looking for. The story was about a young woman found on the outskirts of Harlem who had died of a drug overdose. Her body showed possible signs of rape. The police had no clues in the case, although they had discovered Margie's one-count rap sheet that clearly showed she was a pro. Still they could not be certain a rape had not occurred. That doubt, and the drugs, kept it an open case.

The article seemed to leap from the pages. It had to be! He knew he was right, but the reservations stayed with him. If he was right, he must get in touch with Sheila and go back over her story for one more look, but he had to get rid of the questions. She could wait for her pickup. He needed to get more information first.

He called Fred for permission to continue with what amounted to a probable false lead in the Wilcox shooting. He told Fred the full story, telling him he could offer no positive connection to the campaign. At this point, it was simply a hunch.

From his limousine, Cantrell dialed the private number. "What is the current disposition of Shawn and Phillips?"

"They are working on the Oriental Project."

"Tell them to shelve that for now and meet me in New York. I need them for an operation in Harlem immediately!"

After getting the okay from Fred, Luther was able to find a sleeping room very near the house on 222nd Street. It was on the opposite side of the street facing the front where he set up his high-powered telescope fitted with infrared sensors and waited, for how long he did not know, or for what. He knew only that he could not contact Principle with anything less than verified information.

The reward for his vigil came after one full day of monitoring the house. One hour before the arrival of the black limousine, Luther had repositioned his camera in line with the telescope. He was ready for something, but for what he did not know. Everything at this point was a visceral reaction to events with which he was not involved, working only with second hand information.

To the untrained eye the vehicle was merely one more symbol of conspicuous consumption, in a city where it reigned supreme and was even commonplace. To Luther Johnson, the car had all the earmarks of the CIA even before its occupant emerged from the rear of the vehicle. Fred had taught him that much. The limousine had an oddly shaped antenna with plain license plates.

Even though he was overflowing with trepidation, when the car door opened, he was ready. In the same moment when he began to snap the shutter, he was certain the lone figure was Clifford Cantrell, the Director of the Central Intelligence Agency.

Luther photographed the D/CIA as he walked up to the house and the brief time he spent at the door. The entire process after the door opened took less than eight seconds. He watched for more than thirty minutes until the director reappeared to leave. The entrance and exit was uneventful. No curious onlookers stopped to peer into the car's darkened windows. It was a simple, anonymous event.

He wanted to notify Senator Principle but fought off the inclination to watch the house for another five hours. Nothing further happened. It was just another normal day in the life of an ordinary section of the city, and the director had been nothing more than a typical part of that day. Then he called the Plaza hotel.

"Senator, I got the okay to work on this directly from Fred, and I've been at it all day and night," said Luther. "I'm sorry for the hour, but he said to call regardless of the time if I thought I had something, and I sure think I *do* have something! I photographed the D/CIA at a house in New York, and I think you should see the pictures. Even though I was busy with the camera, there was a dark-haired man there. I can't be certain, but I *think* he matches your description of the guy in *Chicago*. In fact, I'm *positive*. Well, *almost* positive. That's it."

Luther didn't try to hide his excitement, and was surprised when Principle agreed. She told Luther to deliver the film to an address on the Upper East Side and to wait. When ready, he must immediately bring the prints to the hotel and wait for Principle to look them over.

Two hours later a haggard Luther Johnson presented himself at the Plaza, placing an assortment of photographs and notes in front of his boss. He had not slept in more than eighteen hours, and was grateful for a short break to lie down and close his eyes, but the time-out was short lived. No sooner had he drifted off than Principle urgently awakened him. He would have to get his sleep on the plane to New Mexico. The pictures must go to Fred Spans now, and in person. Principle did not have the capability here of sending them over a secure line.

Principle questioned him as to anything he could remember about the front door of the house, or if he was able to see inside. One picture clearly revealed a man inside the house—a man with dark hair—the same man Principle had seen in Chicago.

After Luther left the suite, Principle telephoned Fred. "I'm sure the worst is yet to come," she said, "especially now, with all that's happened. Either the CIA must have been in on Bob's death or they know who was. You be there when my flight gets in at three. Allen gets there at eight. This is too much of a coincidence."

Luther found himself to be a courier when Fred met him at the airport with a new ticket. He was washed-out when he finally reached his apartment and slept most of the day. Sheila never showed up which was good, because he was too tired to be with her anyway. The next morning there was no activity at the house, so he made the decision to return home for more sleep. He would resume the reconnaissance the next day when he would be fresher and more alert.

In the early morning hours before daylight, he awakened with a jolt. Light sounds from his door—scratching sounds, as if someone was trying to get in the apartment. He sat upright in his bed, startled, anxious, and somewhat afraid.

He tiptoed to the door, pressing his ear to the crack of the opening side, waiting, listening. There! Again! Now he was more fearful.

His mind raced to the newspaper story on the dead girl. Luther was no spy. Whoever was responsible for Wilcox's death had found him. Now he was fully frightened. He thought of Sheila. He had befriended her! He had seen and photographed the Director of the Central Intelligence Agency in a covert way!

My God, I am a spy! Somehow, they knew he had watched the house. How could it be? On this, he had not bargained.

Please! *I'm not a spy*! *I'm just working for something I believe in*! *Oh, God, there it is again*! His fear was now absolute.

Beads of cold sweat welled on his forehead. He had no gun. He didn't even know how to use one. He raced to the window. No escape there...the windows were fitted with protective grills.

Quickly his imagination began to work overtime. Could they really have found out about him? Never before had he felt so terrified or helpless. That had to be it. Somehow, they had found out and tracked him down. It would be easy for the CIA. It was true! It had to be! They were going to kill him. Then again, softly, the scratching continued.

My God, they're trying to pick the lock! *Oh, God, I am a spy and they're going to kill me*! *Maybe they found Sheila. Maybe they forced her to tell them where I live*! *Why, Sheila*? *I was good to you*! *You said so*! *Why*? *They're the same people who killed Margie*! *It has to be*! *Please, God, somebody somewhere please help me*!

He wiped his forehead, shaking his head from side-to-side to help clear his mind. Instinct began to take over his movements in spite of the crushing fear. He listened for more of the sound.

Oh, God, they're trying to pick the lock! *They killed Margie and Robert Wilcox too*! *What chance do I have*?

He dashed to the telephone, terror gripping every part of his mind and body. He reached for the receiver. Why him? He was just a young activist committed to a cause. People didn't die for political beliefs in America anymore, did they? Certainly, they did back in the civil rights years, but things were not like that anymore, and this was *Harlem*. Mississippi burning happened more than sixty years ago. America had risen above racist organizations like the KKK, as random ideas swept through his mind...but wait! What could he do? He listened, unable to make his fingers dial a number...any number. His body was made of ice, frozen in place. Then it came. Now the sound was a voice, a faint moaning-like sound that was nearly undetectable, but there all the same.

He replaced the receiver. He moved cautiously back to the door once again, stepping as softly as possible to avoid squeaking the old wooden floor. *Easy*! *Take it easy*! *Don't rush*!

He listened. Now the voice sounded agonized and more like intense pain. Then he made his decision. He moved the chain lock very softly and then with his left hand on the doorknob and his right on the lock button, in one rapid movement, he pushed the button while simultaneously turning the knob to yank the door open. He crouched, his body tense, his arms cocked, ready to confront an unseen enemy. In the same instant, Sheila Larkin slumped forward, her bleeding face and head a mass of raw, exposed pulp. She hit the floor with a nauseating thump not moving.

Luther stood there horrified, not believing the sight before him. On one of her arms the blood still flowed, slashed on the outer side in a line extending the entire length of the arm. A portion of the bone protruded outward where the arm was fully broken. Her dress was soaked with her own blood from the deep wounds over her body, her eyes swollen closed, as a dark blue color began to spread over her face.

Thundering bolts of terrorized shock ripped through him, making him sick to his stomach. His head pounded from the sight of the crumpled, unconscious form that had once been beautiful and seductive. Sheila Larkin was dead.

TEN

Majestic! Imposing! Monumental! Just three of the words she knew to describe what she saw, and they were not enough. Very possibly no words existed to illustrate the event taking place before her eyes. Even if she knew all the words, she was certain they would not be adequate. The ever-changing look of the mountains and desert surrounding Las Cruces always made her feel energized—full of possibilities, not small or insignificant to nature, but the opposite of such a powerful emotion. She experienced the sensation of the possible force of humans to control even their own environment here in the desert. She had felt it the first time she arrived from Indiana. She did not understand the why or the where of it that a Hoosier could have been so moved by such an arid climate. Yet it was here in this grand and astonishing place of vast open land that stretched for miles, bordering rugged mountainsides, the desert climate where she gathered her strength to think, and where she was now in the unique position to become President of the United States of America. Life sometimes moved in very extraordinary ways.

She thought of all of the events that had taken place over the many years, all-encompassing moments of what could and should be yet remained unreached. This year's election cycle, however, would see them fully accomplished. She especially felt it here with all that had taken place and all that would occur in the debate to come.

Armando and Fred were gone, leaving her to the quiet stillness and solitude she required before Allen arrived. In just one day, she would stand on the same platform with President Crawford. The debate of untold, unrewarded, secret opposing schemes was actually going to happen, and she needed this private time to reflect after the more than forty-year effort. The end was now in sight, and America would never be the same. No election that came after this one would ever rely on polling organizations, the two parties, or the current tripartite system of government, finally destroyed by two terms of Barack Obama. He had managed to do much more harm than Woodrow Wilson's reign that began in 1913, also a very bad year for liberty when the fourth branch of government, the Federal Reserve, came into being in direct violation of the Constitution, along with the Sixteenth and Seventeenth Amendments. The Solution would correct those mistakes.

She believed information on the assassination of a prominent leader in Texas many years earlier was still unexplained, and that the circumstantial evidence in the files of The Solution was true. That information showed someone other than the individual named by the commission was the real assassin; data painstakingly collected over many years and saved in precise detail by the one reporter who knew every element of the case.

The files had taken many years of research to put together. If they were accurate, as she now believed they were, the people responsible had resurfaced and were now attacking her. How many more victims would fall to the evil of that tracking, dangerous enemy?

She thought about the mindset of the dark-haired man. If he was the one mentioned in the files, how could he have achieved such feats? Did political ideology motivate him, or was he just a hired gun—and if he in fact was the triggerman, who had hired him? Who protected him? He must have operated then, as he did now, with explicit orders and complete protection from the highest levels inside the government.

Soon Principle would update many associate members of The Solution on a wide range of subjects. They would reconvene here in Las Cruces in five days, and that would include Jim Miller, even though he was extremely ill. Special arrangements made it possible, for nothing would stop Miller at this point. It would be a glorious event for many families and new converts to regale each other with tales untold. They had not held a meeting like this for many years, and this one was much larger. Jim had already cast his absentee ballot, making it the first time in his life he even voted. At least he had been able to do that much, though he must recover to see their work to a positive conclusion, and even with that he continued to wonder if they were only self-delusional and would lose in the end.

She turned the television on to watch the early news. Allen's flight arrived at eight, which meant he would be home by nine. As the program began to break for a commercial, she had the uneasy feeling that something major was about to happen. It came out of left field. She tried to shake the foreboding from her mind as scenes from the past strangely flashed through her thoughts, along with images of Robert Wilcox, the dark-haired man, and of some type of impending doom that was lurking in the background unseen and unknown.

The screen changed to fadeout, with words scrolled at the bottom to promote the next segment—the coverage of the Thomas Farley speech in Chicago to the Progressive organization, EAD, (Education and Diversity) a group known to be fiercely opposed to Farley and all that he stood for. Farley frequently cited Memories of Milton Friedman, highlighted by EAD as their whipping boy.

When the news anchor reappeared, he covered the story. As the report was ending and he was preparing to start a new one, his expression suddenly changed. He appeared shaken, moving his papers around the anchor desk in a semi-circle to re-check the lineup that was now different from his written copy. Quickly he became re-oriented with the new story that took precedence over what was to have been the next report.

"This is just in," he began. "It is believed, though not confirmed, that flight 719 from Los Angeles, California to Las Cruces, New Mexico *may* have been hi-jacked. At present, the location of the aircraft is unknown. On board that flight is Allen Davis, the actor and husband of New Mexico Senator, Sara Principle. She is the Republican candidate for president. We hope to have more details later in this newscast."

Sara stared at the screen in disbelief, her senses jolted, taking powerful command of her brain until she could not even grasp the meaning of the statement or anything that followed. It was as if her hearing had suddenly vanished. The telephone rang at that moment. She leaped to the table. On the line, was the muffled, coarse, yet quiet voice she immediately had the impression she had heard before, and as she listened, she became even more certain she was right.

"Listen tight, Senator," the voice said. "I will not repeat! He is all right. We have merely diverted the plane as a demonstration. It will land in Las Cruces in one hour and he will be in his seat. We can seize him at any time and if you do not follow these instructions, we will. Only then, he will not return.

"We believe that you have a good chance to win the election, and that we will not allow. Tomorrow, Senator, you will hold a press conference to announce that you are withdrawing from the race and Governor Kayne will replace you. Use any reason you like. If you do not, we will act. We have the power. If it is possible for you to keep him secluded, our other option will be to kill you, and we will exercise that option if you force our hand. I strongly urge you not to do it."

As quickly, as the call arrived the line went dead. She replaced the receiver, realizing in that same moment she had at least enough presence of mind to have turned on the recorder. She stared at the phone unable to believe what she had just heard, as the sight of Robert Wilcox lying dead once again passed through her brain.

She listened to the recording. The message lasted just under twenty seconds, and whatever method the man used to disguise his voice worked. It had a peculiar synchronization and coarse sound, and she was certain she had heard it before. But where? The horror of Allen's condition on the plane and the sinister mind behind the voice snapped her attention to Fred Spans and the photographs taken by Luther Johnson. Could this possibly be the dark-haired man, or was it someone even more threatening and evil? Was it possible?

The telephone rang again. Had they changed their minds? People like this were always unpredictable. She answered, thinking that the worst might just be happening.

"Sara?" The familiar voice immediately eased her mind for a split second. "It's Mondo. Do you have your TV on?"

Principle sighed with relief. She said, "Yes, I do Mondo. Are you at your place with Fred?"

"Yes."

"All right Mondo. I want both of you to come over to the house right now."

"Okay. We'll probably want to make some notes, so let me grab a clipboard and we'll be right over."

"Wait a second, Mondo. Come in about twenty minutes. If I'm right about what I just thought, I'll let you know then, but something just occurred to me, so come in twenty minutes. And Mondo, wait *outside*! Do not come *in* the house. I'll tell you why then. I have to make a call and it shouldn't take long. So wait for me outside near the gate, not the house. Tell the guards to be on alert."

She stared at the phone still in disbelief, but as she talked to Armando, she felt a blow that quickly awakened her inner sense of action. She was no longer numbed and weakened over fear for Allen. All of her systems were now charged and full of purpose. She picked up the receiver and dialed the long distance number. Now she was in firm resolve. Of course, there would be no dropping out. That was too absurd to consider. The Solution had come too far and spent too much to back down now. She would not allow a lunatic to prevent them from reaching their goal through intimidation. The answer to it all came in the few seconds she spoke to Armando. It had to be! She knew who it was! She knew the voice because she had heard it once before, just as she thought she knew as soon as the first words of the threat were spoken. It was also a smoker's voice, deep and resonant.

"Good evening," said the pleasant female voice with no apparent accent, "The White House."

"This is Senator Sara Principle," she said calmly. Her mind was working perfectly now. She knew what to do, and she would do it with incredible speed and resolve. She was a United States Senator running for the office of president. She could not be intimidated. "My clearance code is J-3-PO4. I want to speak to the president now!"

Seconds later the male voice answered in a soft, distinctive style, moderately pitched with a Southern accent...and stimulating.

"Senator, this is Ronald Davenport. I am President Crawford's secretary. We've been working late and the president has just retired for the evening. Is there something *I* might be able to help you with?"

"Mr. Davenport," said Principle, offended by his dismissive demeanor. "My clearance code entitles me to speak to the president even if she's asleep. Would you like me to repeat it?"

"That won't be necessary, Senator," came the curt reply. "If you will hold a moment longer, I will get the president for you. It may take a few minutes, so please hold."

They're all alike these macho egotist's. Just give them a little power and they're all the same!

Principle understood the procedures for calls like this. The secretary had his instructions. He must follow an exact procedure set down for him by a harried president. When Crawford was ready she would answer, and the process would take the required amount of time decided on by the Chief, not by Principle. It took ten minutes. While she waited, she thought that one of the President's so-called poor would not be able to afford paying for minutes of unused long distance charges. Especially all over the Southwest, where the cost for land-based lines was so prohibitive most people were forced to use cell phones for their principal service even though they had to pay for calls both ways. The culprit that few understood was the many sets of rules and government regulations, too numerous to even try to count, and even the poor had free cell phones.

When she answered, the inimitable, style and sound of Hadley R. Crawford was clear to anyone who had ever listened to a radio or watched television. It was as distinguished as dozens of other male politicians who came before her, and who also stood out from the crowd exactly as Hadley R. Crawford did now.

"Sara," said the president, with a blithe elegance to her voice. "How are things out west? If you're calling to concede, I accept!"

"You should excuse my directness, Madam President, but I didn't use my special clearance for a chat. Have you heard about flight 719 out of Los Angeles?"

Crawford was startled and genuinely surprised. She reacted with brief silence. She had not heard of the incident, and with good reason.

"Flight what?" she asked, fully confused by the nature of the call. "Why no, Sara, I haven't. Should I? Nothing has been mentioned here at the White House by anyone!"

"Madam President, my husband is a passenger on that flight," said Principle, struggling to remove any trace of panic from her voice, mentally fighting for control.

"Yes, Sara, but I still don't understand what that has to do with *me*. Please clarify. I know you're aware of the time difference where you are, but it's awfully late here in Washington and I had a very long day! I was just getting ready to *retire* for the evening."

"Ma'am, that plane may have been hi-jacked! I just got off the phone with someone who sounded very much like your Director Cantrell. The person made certain threats concerning Allen's safety! If the voice *did* belong to Mr. Cantrell, and if *you* know *anything* about it—if you are a *part* of it, I'm calling to tell you in no uncertain terms that it will not work and you may relay that message to the director at your earliest convenience! Am I quite *clear*, Madam President?"

"Now hold on, Senator!" snapped Crawford, irritated by the personal assault. "Just calm down, Sara—I understand your concern but I honestly do not know *what* you're talking about, and frankly, I resent your insinuation that I *do*! However, it just so happens that the director is here on a matter of national importance, and he arrived just a few minutes ago. With your permission, I'll put you on speaker and you may ask him yourself."

Then it fell apart. The voice that said hello was not the same as the one that had just terrorized her only moments before. It was grainy but not as harsh, deep, but without the same uniqueness. The synchronization was also similar, but it was not the same voice. It was impossible but true. How could she have been so wrong?

"I heard the president's part of the conversation," said Cantrell. "What can I do for you Senator?"

Principle was seriously confused. She was supremely confident when she made the call. Now it was obvious that she was wrong. She wondered if Allen was frightened, or if something had happened to him. Maybe they had changed their minds after all. *Where in the hell is Mondo*? Damn! She forgot. Armando was outside. She felt as though she was about to lose her mind, her brain fighting at the same time to retain what was left of the power to control her emotions.

"Director Cantrell," she said, her voice breaking with uncertainty. "There isn't *anything* you can do. In fact, I owe you an *apology*. I mistakenly thought you had just called with a threat against my husband and me. I'm very sorry. Since we've only spoken once before, I hope you will forgive my presumption. I was wrong. Please excuse me."

"Sara," said Crawford. "Tell the director what you told me about the plane."

"It isn't necessary, Madam President. The caller said the plane was not hi-jacked, only diverted, and it's almost nine o'clock now. That is when his flight will land according to the caller."

"What do you mean, Senator?"

"Mr. Cantrell, I defer to the president to tell you. Please excuse the interruption and please excuse my clumsiness, Madam President."

She couldn't wait to hang up. It was a preposterous idea in the first place. A President of the United States did not do things like this. She had been so certain, but she also had counted chickens too soon. Now she was beginning to think that she might be losing all that was left of her sanity, along with any control to protect Allen.

Police escorted Allen from the plane to the tarmac and a teeming mob of reporters, along with the captain of the aircraft who was one of his friends. They were laughing as they walked, unruffled and collected, until the barrage of questions began.

"No, ladies and gentlemen," said the captain, laughing as he spoke. "There was no problem! *Believe* me! Where in the world did you get such ridiculous information? Didn't any of you check the Automatic alert? You all have access!" He laughed again.

When the reporters said that it was an anonymous phone tip, everyone roared with laughter. The captain said it was not true, and that due to extra heavy air traffic it had been necessary to go to a holding pattern to wait for clearance to land. The reality of the event known only to Cantrell, enabled him to conduct his demonstration with the lasting effect he wanted to shake the confidence of Sara Principle—to make her think of possibilities of what could be…and it worked. There had been no actual diversion, only a successfully planted seed.

Sara leaped to her feet and raced to the front lawn. She approached the two men with her index finger between her lips, pointing skyward to ward off any remarks until they were well out of range of the house. She somehow instinctively understood that she could not speak in close proximity to her home, or even on the inside of it.

"Sorry, guys," she said. "I just had a tough telephone call to make with the president, and…"

She quickly related the substance of the threat and the conversation with Crawford and Cantrell, adding that she now believed her home was wired for sound. Fred said he would have the house and grounds swept for electronic bugs but Principle vetoed the plan. Fred must do it alone. The big boys were playing for keeps now and quite possibly with the blessing of the President of the United States. It was now essential that Allen have protection around the clock and three men with him at all times. Principle still could not accept any Secret Service personnel in her campaign for any reason. She made a silent vow not to overreact to anything else that happened, and hoped that she had not already been guilty of that mistake.

Allen leaped to her arms when the limousine reached their home. Principle quickly embraced him and consciously worked to control her emotions. She held him close and whispered about the possible surveillance bugs. Her voice was steady and reassuring, yet cautious. She did not want him to blurt out any information. In the house, she motioned with her hands for him to watch. He clenched his teeth with a firm resolve and began to respond as if they were alone, assuming the actor's role for a possible unseen audience.

As he watched the deliberate movements of Sara and her security chief, the memory of the first time they made love strangely began to enter his thoughts. He loved her for so many reasons, but mostly, for the kind of person he knew her to be. She was not at all like her ongoing public persona of a woman with no emotions. She was in fact a caring, deeply patriotic woman with strong emotions she kept well hidden from all but four people; Allen, Armando, Russell, and Jim Miller, the man who had schooled her on politics in ways she could not have imagined, well ahead of any other person, and long before the idea of The Solution even began.

He was calmer than he had been on the drive from the airport, able to begin the ritual of two people filling each other in on recent events. She told him that she had heard about the plane incident on the news. At the same time, she motioned for him to pay attention to Fred, because any number of people could have planted audio or video devices. A small group of workers outside their circle had been to the house over the years with routine maintenance projects. Were there any bugs, and if so, how many, and what had they seen or heard?

Soon Fred pointed with his clipboard to the bottom side of the mini-blind anchor in the bedroom and began to write. The note said that so far there were two audio and one video device. One audio was at the window, with one on the inside rail of the bed. The video was a button in the tufting of a chair. All three devices were in excellent locations in the most intimate area of a home.

Principle thought about the membership of The Solution. Had they been penetrated as a unit, and if so, how extensively, and were there units in other homes and offices across the country? What did the opposition know, and when did they learn anything? Then it hit her. The bugs were new! They had to be! The Solution was safe, at least for now. If that were not true, evidence of the organization would have surfaced, but thus far, the only information was in the form of a string of allegations of a Secret Society. They had managed to keep everything secure through the years, in part because of extra special and exotic software protection from J.J., with bouncing and disappearing email that confused and eluded the spying program, PRISM, they had discovered. Neither Sara nor Allen had been in the home for a long time, and even when they were, they did not discuss the business of The Solution. Eavesdropping was always a concern, but now it was more urgent than ever to tighten up on any possible slipups.

It was essential to conceal secrets from the public. They would not understand the mission. If they did, it was very unlikely the mess the nation was in would have occurred.

She remembered the early days when she and Harrington first put the impossible idea together. It developed as a plan to change the political course of America, and ultimately, the Constitution. They would also have to be constantly diligent to shift public opinion covertly, and as she mentally recalled the beginning, she remembered the countless times someone said it could never happen. Not in a million years, some had said, because the idea was far too complex for the secret to stay completely hidden. Even Harrington had said it, yet The Solution had grown in numbers unimaginable, with millions now participating all across the nation. It was how they had shattered the huge number of contributors Barack Obama had amassed in 2008 to produce his incredible war chest, and even if they failed in their final objective, so many inroads had been made within the two parties they could still claim a successful conclusion. It was also ironic that in a classic struggle of the individual against the collective, it had to take place as their own closed communal effort to restore individual rights. In years to come, the movement would not go away as others had before them. They had made their mark. They would be a factor—The Solution factor, and all elections that followed would feel what they had created and left for others to continue, a truly free nation. All governments that came after them would govern not by opinions of representatives and judges, but by the specific text of the Supreme law...the Constitution. They would establish the very first truly free nation never before seen in the world.

They had begun an impossible mission more than forty-years before this day with a mere seventy-eight people. Millions more could now be counted on to continue the endeavor, even though the majority of those individuals did not thoroughly understand everything they were doing. In this election, as in the past, voters would only support the two major parties in large numbers. The result this year, however, along with the method millions of citizens would use to make their ballots count would be the biggest shock in the history of America. Another part of the plan was to confound polling organizations by first declaring for one candidate, and then for the other. The establishment would never be the same. The members now held national offices as Republicans and Democrats in every state, but now they must obtain a controlling two-thirds majority in both the House and Senate, in addition to winning the White House. They were close enough now to taste the win. All of their Internals confirmed they would be victorious in this election, for to do less would enable the opposition to continue as they had for one hundred-twenty years in ignoring not just the original intent of the Constitution, but the written text as well.

Cantrell tried to reassure the president. So great was Crawford's repugnance to violence that the majority of operations requiring its use were kept from her in fact, and in all of the Daily Briefs she received from the agency. She would never knowingly approve an act of violence. Not even for her own benefit, or belief that the future depended on her victory not just for America, but the world as well.

"No, Hadley," said Cantrell. "I assure you we had nothing to do with it. I *will* check it out if you like."

"All right, Cliff. Principle made a serious charge. That is, she *almost* made one. I'll put *Patterson* on it. It's really more a job for the Bureau because of your charter."

Cantrell smiled as he picked up the phone in his car. The obvious location was frequently the best place to hide something...in plain sight. It was amazing. Neither the president nor Principle thought about the president's speakerphone, as Cantrell knew would happen. It altered each person's voice naturally, but Crawford's had been modified even more. When Cantrell spoke on the presidential phone, he knew it would change the way Principle heard it in New Mexico. She was bamboozled by technology and unaware of its existence in the presidential phone.

The answer was simple and direct. "Yes?" the voice said. "Get a plane ready for New York."

When the black limousine pulled up to the house on 222nd Street Cantrell was unaware of a secluded observation post operated by a very angry, Luther Johnson.

In the house, Cantrell barked out orders. "Get going, Dominick, and do it fast. Come out to the car when you're ready, and make it snappy!"

ELEVEN

Across the street from the Russian Embassy in New York City is a four-story mansion from a bygone era. It is the home of the Committee on Foreign Affairs. Opulence of old walnut panels, marble floors, stained glass and crystal abound within its walls of privilege. The house belonged to the well-connected industrialist, Harvey Pitney. His widow donated the property to the *Committee* in the early 1900s in a gesture of selfless generosity for the people of the world, in keeping with Pitney's instructions for his vast estate. Included in the endowment were operating expenses the *Committee* could draw on every year, but not to exceed an annual rate of $50 thousand for fifty years, and then to increase each year by five percent.

Pitney held that individual sovereignty was a false premise, and that included the American states. He said the world should adopt one government to oversee the affairs of everyone, to govern, tax, and administer a global front of police and military forces. "This," said Pitney "would once and for all end the burdensome economic hardship to maintain armies for all nations. It would spread the cost to finally end the risk of war forever, and protect all people from terrorism." He was well ahead of others to recognize the rising influence of religious fanaticism that might occur from the Islamic sphere of manipulation, and from fantasy-motivated mystics that contaminated the entire world even in Pitney's time.

Pitney's master plan called for the enactment of a consortium of nations in his one-world government concept, to have for their use a common headquarters in America, where he preferred New York City. Years before the actual birth, Pitney coined a name for the new alliance: The Unified Nations Commonwealth, to become the United Nations.

In his recommendations to the *Committee*, he suggested they start to infiltrate governments with a covert practice of secretly supervising some of the affairs of state of small nations as a training exercise. The ultimate goal was to begin running the governments of these minor countries, but to remain invisible and undetected. They would graduate to larger countries year-by-year, ending in Europe, with France. Along the way, they would inculcate the British people for an even bigger change, to gradually groom them for an end to the monarchy, and then further their success more strongly in America. News outlets would contribute glowing reports to convince voters to elect a Progressive president and Congress for the full takeover. All of these events would bring about the full takeover across the globe, and the final fall of capitalism.

Casimir Zgonina, the President of Russia and head of the entire Russian Commonwealth, had visited the United States many times. His last stopover was in May for a summit meeting at Camp David, where he met with President Crawford to discuss their joint appearance before the U.N. in February of the following year. He was a new leader with new ideas, new attitudes, new philosophies, and his message was clear. The time for continuous confrontations in the world was over as far as he was concerned, specifically for Russia. This was after the era of Putin, Medvedev and the Russian invasion of Georgia. The new alliance was to assist Russia with its ongoing terrorist and criminal elements. It would also lend a hand to General Tso in forging a new world path for greater security in China, and the payment to them of owed debt. However, Zgonina would preserve his higher status in the new alliance. He was many things, but he was certainly no fool.

The Russian President announced that it was crucial for all nations to learn they could not endure a continuous quest for crushing power. This was even truer in a time of such enormous technological advances in weapons of mass destruction. It was also accurate when considering the on-going development of the European-based American defense system and the highly mobile weapons of Zgonina's predecessors. In private, however, he insisted that his own weaponry be secretly increased and refined even more substantially.

He made frequent declarations that governments should act for the collective interest of everyone. They should work together in common partnership to establish common ground and common goals for all people. America had proved the value of peaceful coexistence between certain aspects of socialism put in place with inventive features of capitalism. It worked very well for the masses of Americans, especially since the election of Barack Obama, but they could not use the word socialism, as it was plagued with negative overtones in America. Progressive and democracy would replace it. To be successful, the words would instruct people worldwide, for they believed them to have the same meaning, and in America's history, the two words infected the language with the full acceptance of political and media leaders, and the general populace.

Zgonina was exhilarated when he received the call from Cantrell. Though he had great reservations about the D/CIA, he was acutely aware of the close, out of the ordinary bond Cantrell had with Crawford. For Zgonina, it was also a double-edged sword, but still he looked forward to the secret meeting. He was eager to get on with their business and put the final steps of the super-plan into operation, unless of course a better one could work its way in for Russia, which he did not talk about, but drove toward all the same. It would bring the world under their full control and supervision with the newly created power. He would just have to monitor the treacherous Cantrell closely.

In recent years, Zgonina had become an outspoken supporter of the Committee on Foreign Affairs, even in his speeches inside Russia. He said the *Committee* was wise in working with the brilliant David Rockhold and President Crawford to bring the world's population and diverse cultures ever closer together.

The meeting began on the second floor of the mansion in a room reserved for functions of the highest security and secrecy. It would be the final chapter for the full elevation of the *New World Order*. The planners seated themselves around a massive oak table, with David Rockhold in the traditional center position as leader.

Though he suffered from Dyslexia, Rockhold managed to overcome the affliction with super-human effort, along with his extremely small physical size and his refusal to use contractions when he spoke. This made his use of words appear stilted to most people. Precisely because of his lack of contraction verbiage, however, it was easier for Zgonina to follow Rockhold when he spoke.

He swept through college at the head of his class, and then began a dynamic approach in the family-owned business, oil. From there he moved into publishing, where he scored his greatest coup. This was where he would one day be extremely successful in causing enormous changes in textbooks children would read in public schools to favor progressivism. It was made easier with Teddy Roosevelt on Mt. Rushmore. Rockhold's power would resonate across the globe, as his success was about to gain general acceptance from national leaders in academia.

As the Rockhold wealth and influence increased in America and around the globe, the family was successful in placing their own people in high government posts to enable them to continue building their bonds to an even greater depth. He could not have achieved his exploits without the multi-year efforts of his ancestors that began in 1900, working to elect TR as president, but he expanded and improved them in ways his family tree could never have imagined. Now they were on their way to become a controlling unit of secret corporate rulers of many policies of the American government. One of Rockhold's protégés, Dr. Hartan Kaiser, a little-known professor, quickly emerged as a dominant force at the highest levels of government. His influence would even surpass that of his super-wealthy friend and mentor. Kaiser would go on to become a driving force for American's to accept collectivism, and, by extension, the word democracy. It would take place at all levels of government. Even educated Americans would jump on board the democracy train. It became a convoy for an entitlement mentality of goods and services for everyone—a non-threatening and benign word that even the Founding Fathers used to spread the wealth of all citizens, as Americans would not understand the mechanics that the riches they were intent on spreading was their own.

The men at the table clung to the words of David Rockhold. To his left was the D/CIA, Clifford Cantrell, and across the table the man whose arrival in America was a closely guarded secret, Casimir Zgonina, helping to make the non-government summit rightly appear to be extremely sparse at the substantial table.

Zgonina was a squat, burly man with a round face dominated by a square, flat nose and bushy eyebrows with no separation of skin between them. He was a chain smoker who greatly enjoyed American cigarettes, and, who had the habit of holding one in the corner of his lips, even when he spoke. His hairline and eyebrows had long since discolored from the continuous flotation of smoke around his face, and he held the permanent odor of tobacco in his clothing and skin.

Press releases inside Russia told his countrymen that Zgonina would be absent from the nation on a working holiday to help him prepare for an address he would give at the United Nations the next year jointly with the President of the United States.

With the smoke swirling around his rotund face from the ever-present cigarette, Zgonina pondered the question that was uppermost in his mind, and then aloud. He spoke English phonetically, crisp and distinct, and with no apparent accent.

"Gentlemen," he said pointedly. "What assurances do you offer that the leader of the Supreme Command of China, General Tso, and the President of Western Europe, Salvatore Ripoli, will follow our lead and *acquiesce* to the international alliance? If we are to be one, as we all certainly believe we must be, we should all agree. That has been a large concern of mine for several months. Let me also add that my unease is genuine, and I am looking for *definitive* answers."

Rockhold said, "Mr. President, as you know, the World Council Group has been in communication with the three leaders for many, many months, along with President Crawford. They all consider the president to be the proper choice as the *first* leader of the alliance, as do you, I might add. They have all become very close over the last several months. They are also like-minded with each other. For all intent and purpose, the *Group* has been the unofficial government of several countries for *many* years. It even applies to the United States, though in a much smaller way, and we *do* have all of the mechanisms in place *to* succeed. We have it written and we have tied the International Constitution *to* the treaty. You have all *signed* it, including General Tso and President Crawford. Tell me just what more could you ask for in this life, Mr. President? It is already done!"

"I am aware of that, my good friend. The part I am the most concerned about—what I am most *fearful* of, is that the implementation of the treaty is not *before* the presidential election. Suppose for a moment that

President Crawford does not *win*! What then? Can you personally guarantee she *will* win, and do you have any contingency plans if she does not? It is my understanding that you have not had a great deal of success—that you have made little progress and have not been *effective with* Senator Principle! Is that correct, and if it is, what will you do if she upsets the president?"

"If Principle *does* win, Mr. President, she *will* come around. They always *do*, Republican *or* Democrat, just as they have for more than one hundred years. But she will *not* win, and because we *know* that, we have no contingency plans. Director Cantrell has assured me the president *will* win, and he has been most consistent in the past. Regardless of how popular the senator becomes, she will *never* be president, and that *is* a guarantee! Or do you know something I do *not*?"

"*What* I know, *how* and *when* I knew it, my good friend, I will keep to myself at this time. It is not necessary to reveal what I *know*."

"Mr. President," said Cantrell, his lips forming his usual scowl. "What you are unaware of in regard to the polls is this. My organization *outside* of the CIA has been working behind the scenes with other groups to make it *appear* that Principle is ahead, when in fact she is not. In that way, it will be possible to induce greater grassroots participation for President Crawford. It's all in place, and the president will easily win. Take my word you have *nothing* to worry about."

He paused, wondering if he sounded confident enough to keep the Russian from seeing the deception, then he continued.

"I won't deny that we were surprised by Principle's popularity. We clearly *were*! However, as I said before, the truth is exactly the opposite of the published reports. And while I cannot be specific, there *will* be a revelation in just a couple of hours that will stop Principle cold, and that is my guarantee."

After the meeting, Cantrell immediately left for Washington and his rendezvous with Dominick Caputo. This would be Caputo's spot to kill the presidential candidate, and he would disguise his true purpose from the gay minister, Father Paul.

St. John's Church, known as the *Church of the Presidents*, stands opposite the White House on the north side of Lafayette Park on 16th Street. On the night before the CFL rally scheduled in the park, Caputo made his way to the uppermost loft of the church, accompanied by the overweight minister Father Carlo, a backer of the WSC organization. Carlo was a bitter opponent of both Sara Principle and Thomas Farley, having read nearly every piece of literature ever published on the two leaders, as well as all of the books written by Farley.

Carlo was an active member of the gay community, and worked with their lobby to enact gay-rights legislation to make federal grants available for treating the disease, HIV/AIDS. It would pay for the entire treatment of drug therapy for the life of the patient, over and above the Affordable Care law. He was certain that Principle and Farley were anti-gay, and devoted a significant amount of time working with WSC and Father Paul to disrupt the CFL rally from the beginning, to help prepare the way for Caputo.

The CIA operatives Shawn and Phillips approached Carlo a few weeks earlier to enlist his help in making the rally as disastrous as they could. It would embarrass Principle and help the president, and for this, Carlo was eager to assist. To accomplish the goal, they needed access to the church loft to enable Caputo to take long distance photographs of known criminal elements who worked with the CFL. Then, in full view of TV cameras, district police would arrest all of the leaders of the anti-Crawford organization.

Carlo's lover, Father Paul, himself a vehement foe of both Principle and Farley, was the minister of St. John's Church. Through him, they arranged to have the church closed for two days under the guise of having a weak section of the tower roof inspected. Phillips instructed Carlo to take Caputo to the loft then go to the park and actively participate in the counter-demonstration with Paul. At midnight, Paul would fire a gun with blanks, and then meet with Phillips to retrieve Caputo's gear. Paul did not know the gun would have live ammunition, though Phillips was certain it wouldn't matter to him if he did know.

By midday, the recently arrived thunderstorm had ended in D.C. The sun broke through the clouds with its fading warmth, and in the White House, President Crawford met with the Russian Foreign Minister. Across the planet people waited for governments to come together for the benefit of the entire world. Demonstrations signaled that the time for action was overdue. In America, the long-awaited announcement by the president could eliminate the possibility of a nuclear and biological holocaust if the talks were successful. It was what the people wanted. It was also the biggest promise Crawford had made in her first campaign. Chet Forbes would issue the message.

Principle sat in front of the television in her alternate office with Armando and Thomas Farley. They were finished writing Farley's speech for the rally but could not overlook anything coming from the White House on this day, the day of the first debate. Everything was now ready for them, and nothing could stop the oncoming Principle avalanche, not even Presidential grandstanding.

The air in the White House briefing room was electric as reporters gathered for the important announcement. Word had quickly spread in newsrooms that a major breakthrough in the negotiations had occurred suddenly. Even some members of Congress were present in a room overflowing, with practically no place to turn for space.

Chet Forbes appeared apprehensive as he approached the dais. "Good afternoon, everyone," he said, reading from his notes. "Today a bright light has risen and will shine its radiance on the whole earth for all time. This is the message you have all waited for.

"The president has worked diligently on the problem of nuclear and biological weapons of war over this past year. At this very moment the president continues, much to the harm of her re-election campaign, which is why she is not here now. She *wanted* to be here because it is such a great personal triumph for this woman whose principal focus is world peace in *our* time, not in the future.

"Today I am pleased to tell all of you that President Crawford has concluded informal talks with the Russian Foreign Minister as the *direct* representative of President Zgonina, to begin the final preparations to dismantle *all* nuclear and biological weapons worldwide. Further meetings will be necessary with General Tso and President Ripoli, approximately one week after the election. Those meetings will result in a gathering of representatives of the United States, Russia, Western Europe, and China, in Geneva, Switzerland. On that occasion, one document will be finalized and signed. This will enable the four leaders to begin the actual process of dismantling *all* of these weapons of mass destruction, even in the Middle East including Iran, and in North Korea. Moreover, there has been *another* breakthrough. It is so huge I cannot even quantify it accurately. Islamic countries will now recognize the right of Israel to exist.

"I am not free to answer your questions now. I'm sorry. I know you have many. What I *can* say is that this is perhaps the most significant achievement about weapons of war and peace in world *history*! The president hopes to announce the progress toward the *full* agreement in February, and to give a specific timetable as to when those weapons will no longer exist. We will obviously keep you up to date as to the final disposition, and of course, that will take place sometime next year. Hundreds of news outlets will cover it, and with those *signings*, we will have peace in our time. This will not be the *end* of these terrible weapons, but to paraphrase Winston Churchill, it will be the *beginning* of the end. The process of destruction, however, will take many years to complete. It will not happen overnight because it is far too big a job to risk dangerous mistakes."

It was an incredible statement. No leaks of any kind had slipped out. With the exception of the D/CIA, no one had the slightest indication the statement would be of such magnitude. The president had completely sealed off all access to any information in a record execution of total secrecy. Known for his congeniality and easy access, Forbes uncharacteristically turned from the podium and left without further comment.

Members of the media descended on the White House as news of the announcement began to spread. Washington was jubilant. Everywhere people left their jobs, joined in the frenzy by their superiors to congregate in the streets, loudly praising the president. Few Americans ever believed they would ever hear such a stunning announcement. America was delirious. In several snap polls, Crawford's popularity rocketed to remarkable heights, with nearly all professional pundits in agreement that the election now belonged to the president. It had taken a woman to end war on earth.

Following the initial shock of the statement, Principle's staff began to print notices to disperse in Lafayette Park to announce the suspension of the CFL rally until further notice. The update to the gathering would happen as soon as they could arrange a new location.

Thomas Farley sat on the corner of the desk in stunned silence. The impact of the Crawford statement was only partly responsible for his immobility, for there in Principle's private and secret office was Mo Dobrosky, the National Security Advisor. He had arrived unnoticed amid the pandemonium around the building, and the senator embraced him as though they were old and dear friends.

Farley was horrified. Was it possible that Principle was not what Thomas thought her to be? She had just welcomed the enemy like a long lost brother. The surprised consternation registered on Farley's face was not lost on the senator. Principle gestured Dobrosky to a seat and then turned toward the troubled Thomas Farley.

"Tom," she said. "I'm sorry! I know what you must be thinking, but Mo is not *against* us. In fact, he's *one* of us, and he has been for a very long time!"

Farley nearly fell from the edge of the desk. He was unable to speak. Armando stood by his side, quietly urging the professor to stay calm and listen to what was coming.

Dobrosky extended his hand to the stunned professor and said, "He's *right*, Dr. Farley. I'm *not* your enemy, and I want you to know that. I've been a member of the Principle Coaching Staff for a long time."

He turned to Sara, his expression changing to a look of intense fury, uncertain as to possible repercussions to follow because of the Crawford statement. Privately, he felt the campaign might be in for hard times, possibly to a point where it could not recover. He did not state it, but he had to let his feelings on the announcement ring out, and in the open.

"They sprung it on us, Sara," he said. "I had no idea they would make this kind of proclamation today or any other day, before the election or *after*! *No one* did. It took all of us by complete surprise. Even Chet wasn't told 'til the last minute, and then it was too late to do anything. Not that I *could* have, but if I *had* known I could have at least *warned* you that it was coming.

"The lid was kept tight on this. I think only the president knew, and if you stop and think about it, it was a masterful stroke of political engineering. She must have been feeling the heat so much that she had to come up with a blockbuster, and let's face facts. This is the thump she needed! It may even turn things around for her that we can't repair. I also think she had it planned for some time!"

"It's okay, Mo," said Principle. "But first we have to fill Tom in on things. He's in a state of panic seeing you here."

Sara walked to the bar. Pouring a shot of bourbon, she gave it to Farley and said, "Tom, get hold of yourself and come over here and sit down!

There's a lot to tell you. We'll get to some of it while we're here, but other information will have to wait 'til later. There's just not enough time for everything right now! So be sure you just sip that drink Tom!'"

Thomas reluctantly sat down, still regarding Dobrosky with suspicion. It had been a long uphill struggle for Thomas. The price he paid for his position with Principle was ostracizing by much of the black community. He decided early on that he was willing to pay the tab because of the importance of this election. The result was that many blacks now regarded him as a traitor to his race. They followed the lead of several high-profile pastors who, after their experiences with Barack Obama, would no longer allow another well-known black person to freely skate on their positions. This was in direct conflict with their love for Obama, but they had subconsciously learned from him to charge an opponent of doing bad things for America, even as they mirrored their own actions. Obama became a master of deceit in labeling his opponents support of anything as unacceptable, even as he supported the same issue. Doubletalk came naturally to the former president because he quickly learned in the weeks and months of his first term that the mainstream media had swooned because he had won the White House, and they would not hold him accountable for anything.

"Tom," said Principle. "The Solution is bigger than you know. A *lot* bigger. It may even be bigger than *I* know. We started with seventy-eight people, and now there are *millions* of us. We span the entire nation with citizens who will come out to vote, and Tom, we *will* win this election, and trust me when I use the word *we*.

"Mo has been a part of the organization almost from the first day. He's also been something else in recent years, and that's one of our personal insiders that we couldn't have gotten this far without. And there are others, like *Matt Weeks*, Johnson's right-hand man at EAD. The list also includes *Chet Forbes* and *Cecil Price*! The other major one is Wilson Keyes. We have people on the inside working with and for President Crawford. They've infiltrated some inner positions of the White House in several key ranks. Some of them are even on the board of the *World Council Group* and in the Crawford *Cabinet*! They're virtually everywhere. They've been responsible for the constant flow of information we've always had. It's helped us in all our planning to direct several things we've done to gain in popularity with the people all over the country. It's not *over* by a long shot, Tom. We're not just going to *win* this election; we're gonna win it *big*! Bigger than anyone can imagine."

She turned to Dobrosky. "Did you bring all the papers, Mo?" she said. "And do you know what's going on with Chet? I wasn't able to speak to him before the briefing."

"No, I didn't bring *all* the papers, Sara, and I only talked to Chet for five seconds when we passed each other in the West Wing."

"Were you able to get any of the documents on the U.N. military force, *and* what about *Cantrell*? He worries me more than just about anyone or anything right now. I am certain he is working on something big. But I don't have a clue what it is."

At the mention of the United Nations military, Farley snapped his face toward Principle. "What do you mean? What's the U.N. military got to do with *anything* having to do with the election?"

"That's something else you don't know, Tom," said Principle. "Not because we don't *trust* you, but because *I* decided that the fewer people who knew some of these things the better it would be for all of us, *and* it would also be a lot *safer* for everyone concerned!

"This little package Chet announced today is a prelude to the actual implementation of the world government. Without the military, they wouldn't be able to make it stick. And how about *this*; it even includes our *own* forces, who won't know what's really going on, but we have *Wilson*. That's to *our* advantage. I think he has a lot more control over the troops. Even more than Crawford does, and we won't have to worry about *our* people as long as Wilson's there.

"Like Castro did in Cuba, they plan to disarm any country that has anything remotely resembling a WMD, and turn it over to U.N. control. In that, way they'll rule the world without firing a shot. They'll install a progressive government. That means moving *beyond* the Constitution even more, and enforced in the strongest terms. Think TR, Woodrow, FDR, and Obama rolled into one. You remember Obama's war on *guns*, don't you?

"The biggest problem we have is the American people. If we try to expose them without the documentation, it'll make us look like a bunch of raving lunatics. We also have to keep our own organization alive and secure at the same time, and never, ever forget that the people just do not understand what has happened to their own government. It wouldn't have gotten this bad if they *did*! We *must* have the documentation. That's what Chet and Mo have been working on, among other things. They didn't know Crawford would spring any of this before the election. We grossly underestimated her, and it's probably going to help her tonight in the debate. I don't know what Chet has, but I do know I'll hear from him soon. Mo, let's see what you've got."

"I can't go over this now, Sara. I have to get back to my office. I *can* tell you this much, though. Cantrell's *already* started to transfer power to the U.N., but just how far he plans to go *before* the election is unknown. He's also involved with something else almost as big, but I don't know what it is. We're working on it, and I should have an answer soon. You've cancelled the rally?"

"Yes. We're gonna have it later. I've sent word to the volunteers to expect another location, but that I don't know when it'll be. Maybe it might even be the *big* one late at night."

"All right. I have a meeting with Matt tonight. In the meanwhile, I think you should have someone find out about that New York hooker, because I haven't been able to locate *any* information on that house. My gut says the house and Cantrell are connected, and he's one dangerous son of a bitch. I'll talk to you in a couple of days."

Chet Forbes had been President Crawford's press secretary since the time Crawford was a candidate for governor. He was a trusted lieutenant in the cadre of personnel and was privy to a wide assortment of classified information. Just before the briefing with reporters, Crawford handed him the documents that contained the signed treaty of the Quadripartite Federation. It was then up to Forbes to write the appropriate announcement for the press and clear it with the president. When he was finished, he would immediately go in front of reporters.

As he worked on the statement, he knew he must be prepared to take the greatest risk of his life—a gamble not just for himself, but for The Solution as well. If he failed, the information would remain secret and never be used against the president. Somehow, he must find a way to duplicate the document.

Surprisingly the opportunity came almost immediately when Clifford Cantrell arrived in his usual huff. Understanding that Forbes had not been given sufficient time to prepare, Crawford sent him to the study adjacent to the Oval Office. Crawford's nonchalant trust of Forbes did not even take into consideration the small office was equipped with a copy machine.

TWELVE

On the morning after the NO MORE MISSLES announcement, leaders of the Committee on Foreign Affairs met in closed session to discuss the ramifications of the White House report. Now things were different. The statement was a brilliant sign of the President's leadership qualities, and the *Committee* must do everything in its power to retain the strong wave of approval. They would continue cultivating the support of their media partners. Those who came before when a large number succumbed to the administration of Barack Obama and abandoned all remaining journalist parameters made this easier—a feat that would bring them even more of what they had sought for more than one-hundred years that now included the ongoing and strict control of the Internet.

Headlines blazed across newspapers and online blogs. A flood of telephone surveys indicated the president had managed the impossible. Once again, she was leading in the polls, and now by a substantial margin. The *Committee* must do what it did best and create a glut of attention and misinformation with their media lackeys. It would be their steady role to make voters believe the opposite of the truth, to enable and assist the *Group* in their climb toward world domination. They were close to final victory in using a process they were intimately familiar with, and one they had used repeatedly to achieve their aims.

"Good morning, gentlemen, and thank you all for coming on such short notice. Even with the announcement of the impending new treaty, we have a most serious and pressing problem that we must address *immediately*! With the election literally just around the corner, we cannot rely on the statement alone to continue to assist us in the fight against Senator Principle without more input and effort on our part. All of our *Internals* say this is not only true, but *urgent* too. We are not yet *finished*, gentlemen, but we will be very soon, and when we are, the legacy handed to us by our ancestors will finally be realized. Just think that after more than one-hundred years the end is in sight to capture the biggest prize on the planet...America.

"We have made several attempts through intermediaries to persuade the senator to accept our *stated* public goals, with no success. She is not a woman we will be able to manipulate, and for us, this is new. In the past, a candidate's political affiliation has not mattered as far as we are concerned. Both parties have served us well, but Principle is unlike any we have tried to work with in our entire history. There is definitely more to this woman than meets the eye. What it is specifically I cannot say, but for our purposes it is very dangerous indeed. She may even know our *true* agenda. I cannot confirm that with any degree of accuracy, but I *do* want to make this next point perfectly clear...*abundantly* clear! There will be no place for us in a Principle administration regardless of the successes we have had with other president's in the past!

"Do not become beguiled by the sudden surge for the president. She is no Barack Obama! Also, there seem to be events taking place all across the nation that have confounded the usual political trickery. One of them is a surprising increase in travel by our fellow citizens that is much more extensive than normal. The other is what appear to be *skewed* polling results that we cannot account for in the usual way.

"Another major problem because of Principle is that we will not be able to successfully stage-manage public opinion as we have in the past. Yes, even if Principle wins we will still control the Senate, but not her. This is a new and very *different* election. Either directly or indirectly, we have controlled the previous seventeen administrations *without* their knowledge, with emphasis on Republicans. We were very successful in using Ahmad Chalabi to help create the Iraq invasion, clearly an unconstitutional act on the part of George W. Bush and Congress. We got away with it because we literally *own* many politicians. Now we are in the final phase of what our ancestors created. Principle has hurt us with her work in the Senate, even though a great conspiracy is far easier to sell than a lesser one. The bigger the lie the easier it is to hawk it to the American people. Now we must act *strongly*! This was supposed to happen in the middle of Crawford's *first* term. We are now two years behind our own schedule.

"Under the quadripartite agreement, President Crawford will be the *initial* president of the federation, and I stress, *initial*! The four leaders know this, but rest assured she will not be in that position long. *She* does not know that, but now *you* do.

"Wherever WMDs are stored, U.N. forces will take them over, even in *America* and *Russia*, but obviously with the assistance of their own leaders. The federation will oversee all activity and take fitting action against any offending country. American, British, Chinese, and Russian officers will assist us, as we have purchased abundant individual *loyalty* with extremely large sums of cash. The *bulk* of their own forces on the ground will not know the details. We will simply be giving the people of the world what they say they want; an end to the arms race, a world without risk, and full collectivism for everyone. Worldwide the people have spoken. It has been especially true since Obama, who helped us not just in America, but also because he became so popular worldwide—a citizen of the world, as he described himself. *We* will now have elections with known outcomes all over the world, as we continue to solidify and leverage opinion and effect the manipulation of *all* the governments."

The speaker was Dr. Hartan Kaiser, the presiding Director of the World Council Group, a position he held in secret for three years after rising through the ranks of government. He became a driving force to solidify a progressive mentality, but sold himself as conservative both in government and in law, and with the vast consent of the majority of Americans.

Kaiser served in two positions, the first of which was as a special presidential advisor. With Hadley R. Crawford's election, she quickly moved to place Kaiser into the newly created position as the General Ambassador of Goodwill. His role was to work with various governments around the world to promote the end of nuclear and biological weapons with a form of diplomacy that involved constant travel. Kaiser was just as fine with that as he was with being a bachelor.

Crawford instructed the obliging Kaiser to maintain a high public profile, which he accomplished with the assistance of a highly connected, but well hidden public relations firm. Behind the scenes and fully concealed, Kaiser quietly worked for the establishment of a worldwide federation of nations. President Crawford never learned of Kaiser's lofty position in the *Group*, or of his ultimate intent.

A naturalized citizen, Kaiser was a student, and then a professor of world history at Yale University, and a member of the secretive Skull and Bones. With the support of David Rockhold, he authored eight books detailing the cause and effect of world crisis. All of the books concluded with the same supposition. The only way to eliminate crisis was with a collective philosophy of governments working together with a modified byproduct of capitalism and socialism. It would not, however, be sold in that way to the American people. Instead, they would use a word that society embraced and declared to be a good word, democracy. They would continue to push for democracy because they discovered that most people misunderstood the definition and intent of the word. Voters were comfortable with the *idea* of democracy, and even saw it as a necessary ideal—that it is synonymous with freedom. They lacked the ability to see that majority rule, democracy, in its true sense, is collectivist, statist, anti-freedom, and not called for by the Founding Fathers. They insisted the nation must be a *federal democratic republic*, not a democracy, as the *Group* acted to make Americans see that a republic, with three branches of government, was identical to a democracy. With their creation, the *Group* instinctively understood that the word democracy was an easier *sell* to human brainwaves.

"The final climax," he wrote, "will eventually be a single government to supervise the masses of people simply because they require supervision, and majority rule takes citizen responsibility out of the equation and gives it to the collective majority." This would give the people what they wanted and what they continued to vote for worldwide; control by a remote, unknown entity, the majority, and not themselves, to rescue them from difficult decisions. It would also maintain their personal individual and collective need to be controlled.

The academic community greeted the single government theory with open arms, as they had done for more than one-hundred years, simply because one of the most respected academicians of all time touted it. Its only drawback was the need to thoroughly indoctrinate citizens to its call of compassion and goodwill for all people; to fully instruct them to the goal of democracy, the supreme word that meant equality for everyone.

To the casual observer, which certainly included most Americans, Kaiser meant for the world to have a democratic democracy. The people never understood that their own Constitution contained some undemocratic features, the most important of which were the Electoral College and senators chosen by their state, not elected. To Kaiser's brethren, it was a signal from the Wizard of New Haven that the time had finally arrived for the *New World Order*—a phrase purposely chosen by a Republican president years earlier to become subconscious verbiage among politicians and the public, made imminently believable by merely repeating the slogan with great frequency.

Americans had clearly shown themselves to be politically illiterate time after time. They continued to lack the necessary knowledge to see the slow deterioration of their government, and were now an electorate happy with the slogans created by public relations executives and political hacks whose positions were whatever they could sell in their own self-interest, in line with the benefits to their off-stage masters. Kaiser's books became bibles for the usage of the power-seeking political class who would spread the all-encompassing word of the new oligarchy to every nation, and the word was democracy.

Following his term at Yale, Kaiser swept into Washington in the manner of a visiting monarch—the new media darling, in demand and pursued by reporters for interviews and appearances on television. Armed with an array of impressive credentials, he quickly gained strong support for his presidential advisor role, where he served for two years before launching his new career as America's emissary of goodwill. His place in the forefront of national politics swelled even more dramatically with all of the media support he received, in addition to the legislative branches of government, President Crawford, and Kaiser's wealthy mentor, the New York banker, David Rockhold. Their armored knight had arrived.

Kaiser finished his speech to the *group*. He then announced the Rockhold family would match the $20 million put up by the *group* for the final thrust—the cash to be funneled into the Crawford war chest through 527s for the remaining weeks of the campaign, exclusively earmarked toward a flood of television commercials. They would blitz the airwaves with an abundance of vignettes showing a concerned Crawford contributing the weight of her office to help children, linked to her quest for a permanent end to weapons of mass destruction.

Bill London, the erudite publisher of the Albuquerque Sun, was one of the panelists chosen for the second debate in five days. Unknown to anyone outside the committee charged to select panelists, was a surreptitious plan. London's selection was for only one reason, and that was his fiercely written opposition to Sara Principle that began when Principle campaigned for Mayor of Las Cruces.

London editorialized that it was far too early to measure the most recent polls, as they could not be adequately quantified to determine if the latest upsurge for the president would last. However, he was now certain the people would completely make up their minds after the second debate, and the third one scheduled would be overkill. Honesty, he said, played a significant part in the electoral process, and the candidate who came out on top in that one area would more than likely be the next president…or so it seemed at that moment in time.

Sara Principle was subdued in the first debate. For the most part, she simply repeated her campaign themes, refusing to comment on the treaty or its merits. She appeared to have resigned herself that a skillful President Crawford had simply upstaged her.

Allen appeared on the Barbara Langdon program for the second time two days later. Langdon worked in TV news for twenty-five years, and unlike other journalists, believed the presidential announcement would not hurt Principle in the long run. Allen refused to respond to questions on his private life with the senator by previous agreement, except to reiterate the length of their marriage and that they were happy with their lives. Personal questions were out of bounds.

Near the end of the show, Langdon leaned forward and said, "Why do you believe Senator Principle will win in light of the startling announcement from the White House? We all know every politician says they *will* win even when they are certain they will *not*!"

Allen breathed deeply. He was on a frenzied schedule across the nation speaking to large and small groups from every political persuasion. Everywhere he went his superstar status followed, even though he had not made a theatrical film for five years. Commentators, however, continued to report, using their built-in, progressive bias that the large turnouts were due more to Allen's fame, plus the astonishing popularity of his latest film, a powerful political drama made as a mini-series for television. People wanted to see him, but Allen was intent on building up support for his senator-wife in her own right. In a supreme effort of self-discipline, he endured a barrage of insults in Boston, vowing to increase his appearances on television, and across the nation.

"Yes!" he said forcefully, his dark eyes full, wide, and passionate. "I believe she *will* win! I also believe she *should* win because she is definitely the better candidate.

"I believe she'll win because she's for the *legal* and *rational* freedom of *all* people, and that is a rare quality for a politician in this country. Oh, they all *say* they're for liberty, but they really aren't. They are for control, and they support force. I also think she will win not for what she would have government do for the people, but for what the people can do for *themselves*. Asking people to do for their country is a ridiculous statement anyway. Kennedy used it because it *sounded* good. What it really means is to do for the politicians in power. People can best do for America by being free to live their lives with only self- regulation. That's also the best way to be *productive*. As to war and wars weapons, the *people* have not caused these great threats. No, that has been the role of *politicians*.

"I think there's much more to what the president has said about the arms reduction program and the treaty. She hasn't said *everything*. She thinks the government should be the end that justifies the means. The means she speaks of are dollars *unconstitutionally* taken from individual Americans to spend for what the *President's* ends are, and that means she does not believe the *people* know what is best. She thinks the *collective* knows what is right...a collective *brain*. If they give her another four years, she will use that power wantonly against the Constitution. If it happens, her control will grow much stronger and a lot more extensive than anyone can now dare to imagine, just like Obama in 2013.

"America is supposed to be the United States of America, not the United *Socialist* States of America, or, the United *Progressive* States of America, but since eight years of Barack Obama we just might as well change the initials to the USSA or the UPSA and quit living in a *dreamland*! We have a *Constitution*. We also have Bill of Rights that is there to limit the *government*, not the individual *citizen*, and to protect the *rights* of individual citizens. It is sad and infuriating that the Constitution has been so extensively violated that it no longer matters to so many Americans, *or* their political leaders. Sara wants to change that, and she will when she is president and has a good working relationship with the new Congress. That will happen next January 20."

THIRTEEN

Following his appearance on the Barbara Langdon show, Allen returned to Las Cruces for one day of relaxation. This was the time to catch up with old friends and relax—a time to renew old bonds, tell tales of family and careers and daring achievements, and spend many important moments with anyone who might be faltering from the White House statement. This was their day of many yet to come, in an effort to restore their government into the one intended by the Founding Fathers. The long awaited day had arrived, with the appearance at the largest Harrington warehouse of many associate members of The Solution for their final reunion before Election Day.

Jim Miller's advanced age and recent health problems made special arrangements necessary to move him cross-country, but nothing would hold the former Plymouth dealer back, not age, health, or an arduous trip from Indiana where he still lived.

Sara, Allen, and Russell, sat together with Miller in the office before the members began to arrive. They talked about the beginning of their long, upstart adventure that had no possibility of success in their natural life, or the lifetimes of any of their offspring.

"You know, Jim," said Principle. "I *remember* all those talks we used to have when I was a kid; every *one* of them. Maybe it was because I *was* a kid. Did you ever think that forty-years would pass and we'd still be *at* this? I know *I* didn't when we went over ideas for the hundredth time when I was still in *high school*!"

"No way, absolutely no damn way!" said Miller, his eyes twinkling with the mischief of the secret backroom broker he had always been. "If someone had predicted it then, I think I would have told them they were *nuts*! We *were* nuts, you and I, so I guess it also means that we were both *wrong*, because we *did* make it Sara, and this country will never be the same again. Obama's fundamental transformation was child's play compared with what we will be doing. It's gonna be great, but only if you win the election and have full congressional support! That's the key!

"I sold cars and you went to school and conducted yourself like an adult when you were a *teenager*! Maybe that's the most surprising thing about all of this, even more than being female. I always said you have an old soul Sara, yet here we are, forty-years later, and no one *knows* we're here but *us*, and you *know* damn well they're looking! And even though they are looking, they won't find us 'til it's too late! Damn it's great!"

"Remember when we used to talk politics in your showroom on Broad Street? We did that a lot. And you used to shut me up when people came around 'cause I got really excited! It was *hard* for me to be quiet. It was even harder when the new models came in and you were busier! Remember? We had to watch it even more then! Remember *that*, Jim? Those were very special days."

"They *were* special, but not long after that the town began to die because Chrysler sold their parts plant to Mercedes, then *they* closed it and for all practical purpose the town was killed in the process!"

"But how in the world did you ever come up with this screwball idea in the first place?" asked Harrington. "You wanna talk about a wild idea— it was *brilliant*, but it was *wacky* too, and the word crazy doesn't even *begin* to describe it. I know I've thought about it at *least* once a day from the start, and that's a long time!"

"I'm not sure how *brilliant* it was, Russ," said Principle. "But we're all older now and we have to see that we haven't gotten there yet. We also don't know how the voters will react if we *do* win! Anyway, I started thinking that if enough people got elected who believe like we do things could change. It really *was* that simple, and I *still* believe it. Somehow, though, we could only do it as members of the two parties. There was no other way. The Libertarian Party that came along had it right, then, but they could never get enough power because not enough people *voted* for them. And that was the biggest part of the whole thing. It was the *key*, getting enough people elected to office, and so, I thought it had to be with the candidates running as though they were members of the two parties without them knowing they were something else, and that's exactly what we've *done*! We've also returned a *huge* block of voters to the polls; those who just dropped out and didn't vote, and millions are coming back to vote for us…and I *do* mean *us*! There will be a greater percentage of voting age people going to the polls, even more than the historic election of 2008, and that's something the two parties really don't want, though none of them would ever *admit* it. With our huge base, we shattered online contributions that even surpassed what Obama did. He started mainly with *new* voters in the old block of Republican, Democrat, and Independent. *We* started with our own *members*, and now there are *millions* of them.

"I guess the real turning point in *my* mind came when I met *you*, Russ. You provided the seed money, along with what Jim was able to add. Less than you because he wasn't as *rich* as you are.

"I also remember how shocked you were when I started telling you about the Constitution. You never imagined that anyone could *think* such a thing, especially a college girl! I guess no one did. Another thing I remember is how taken aback you were when I told you that Washington was the first president to *violate* the Constitution, and how you suddenly just jerked your head backward really *hard*! Then, when you agreed to study with Jim, it just all came together after that, and here we *are*! You and Jim were the *key* to all of this, not me. You guys were the *fountainhead*! I just had the *idea*, but you guys had the money, *and* the will."

Allen said, "I was always amazed at how much Sara knew about politics. As unlikely as it sounds, we used to talk about it for hours on end. She even had a following in college, but a lot of students thought she was just plain weird…*good looking*, but weird."

Sara laughed and said, "That's *true*, but it was really *Allen* who came up with the secret party-within-a-party idea. *He* deserves the credit for that. It was probably the artist in him, along with his take-no-bullshit personality. If we win though, we're gonna need to be ready for an intense reaction we'll get. This won't be like all those so-called fiscal cliffhangers they used to play games about. This time it'll really happen, and the public and the politicians have *no* idea what's in store. I think we'll even see some riots, and Allen agrees with me. He's seen the *speech*, and I tell you now it isn't *finished*! We have to be ready for anything that comes along, because it will."

Around the main warehouse location, the desert grounds looked more like a meeting site for world leaders coming together in the arid climate of the Middle East. It did not resemble a homecoming of everyday Americans devoted to a program that most people had never heard of—a plan of action that would completely alter their government, their Constitution, and the Bill of Rights.

Then the members began to arrive. Gone were the cars of teenage boys and girls. They left that part of their lives behind to pursue families and careers. Replacing the worn out beaters and jalopies were significant examples of achievement. Some traveled in limousines from the airport. Here and there, scattered among shiny sedans was an occasional exotic sports car, along with one classic Mercedes 500-K roadster, the mark and distinction of the wealthiest member, Russell Harrington, El Paso-raised oilman-turned United States Senator. The Solution had arrived.

"Sara," said Miller. "All those letters you used to write were a great source of inspiration for me, but I also felt bad for you 'cause I didn't think you, *we*, would *succeed*. I even remember thinking that it was just the pure joy and dreams of an idealistic collegian who couldn't possibly understand the extent of what she was trying to put together. But you *fooled* me, and so far, I guess no one knows about us. Is that even *possible*, and if it *is* possible, how has it been accomplished? Or is it just something the youngster knew that the oldster *didn't* know? I think it was. No, I *know* it was!"

"Nobody *does* know about us, Jim, and it's partly due to protecting our cyber footprint that none of us had any idea would even come into existence when were still in the 20th Century. And when I went to work in that office in Las Cruces, I didn't think we'd make it *either*, but we sure *have* made it! We really have! I'm sure we're going all the way now, but it *was* a pipe dream then, even for me! I told Russ he was probably wasting his *money*! He told me that he had a lot of it so what the hell; and he wasn't even a *billionaire* then, but he did make a bundle on his book. If we pull this off it will really be something! *Nothing* like this has *ever* happened before. At least as far as *I* know, that is. It's the greatest coup in history…if we make it!

"When you think about it, though, it's amazing and sad at the same time that we even had to *start* this project. Just look where we are! We have a government that keeps on spending and regulating with unconstitutional laws simply to buy votes, and it *works*! The people didn't wake up from all the illegal stuff the Obama administration did. The average person has no idea they do these things just to stay in power. There've been a few books that tried to wake them up but they got nowhere, and the people just keep voting for the same clowns over and over. The *irony* is that we've had to make them believe *our* people are just like the ones they've been voting for all this time. It's absolutely *nuts*! We have to keep the conservatives convinced we're just as conservative as *they* are, and the same thing with the *liberals*. If we *do* win, I hope they'll be able to handle the change, 'cause it'll be more dramatic than anyone can imagine. I really do think there'll be some violence that we'll have to control. Obviously, I don't know how *strong*, but I'm convinced it'll happen! The change is just going to be too dramatic for a lot of people to handle, at least right away, because they are still in an attitude of how much they can get from government, and they can't conceive of another way…the *right* way!

"We also have to be very careful *today*. We need to make sure that none of the reporters who're outside sneak in and hear *anything*. We've been successful at keeping everything on the web and all the e-mails locked up with J.J's. software and other stuff I don't have a clue on— bouncing and disappearing email and web sites. Also, journalists all over the place are doing everything they can to get information, including the Help-a-Reporter website, but so far, we've *stopped* them. I don't want anyone letting their guard down or agree to talk to them or give interviews, and here's something else. Isn't it *also* ironic that we have to continue to deny the Secret Society charge, while Skull and Bones doesn't have to do the same thing because everyone already *knows* they're secret? It's strange to me that the public seems to be okay with that. Our fellow Americans never fail to amaze me on a daily basis. J.J. has his people always working to check and hide all of our networks throughout the whole organization. It has taken up more of his time than just about anything."

Fred Spans was tense with the arrival of the members. His team of fifty security men continued to listen to his admonitions to leave nothing to chance. Some members might have become disenchanted, especially those who were struggling with their lives. It was highly unlikely now, but still possible, and this caused him some concern, but he had uncovered no one who might slip.

When each new vehicle drove in to the warehouse compound parking areas, staff repeated verbal explanations drivers received with their written instructions and bar codes that each had received electronically. The procedures were necessary due to the size of the gathering and the nature and number of threats against the candidate, as this grouping numbered just over one thousand people. Chauffeurs experienced a background check, and were then directed to an area reserved for them exclusively. They were instructed to stay in that building. Members walked to an adjacent building for food and drink.

As with any family, there was success and failure in personal lives and respective careers. With the original merger of talent each member agreed not to seek any government aid, but to call on their extended family of The Solution for help they might need. It happened many times. On more than one occasion, requests went out across the country and even around the world for financial assistance and help with some problem or crisis, but the members were only human. They were not living in a cocoon of self-indulgence and glorification, but a real one in common with each other to reach their final goal. Some dropped out along the way and unsuccessfully tried to gain attention by writing books and talking to journalists. No one was successful, and with the members un-divided, the theme of unity and code of silence remained for all. Some people who did not stay with the organization also received help from actual members, even after they had dropped out and gone their separate ways. All agreed to this ongoing guiding principle.

One of the major surprises in light of their vast size of millions, was their learned ability to control the outcome of divorces, as they related to the organization. The biggest part were funds to help individuals and entire families with jobs, yet through all of that personal upheaval, most of them renewed their pledge of secrecy and commitment to the driving purpose of the organization. All new recruits agreed with these procedures in advance.

The main body of affiliates remained a growing, close-knit, though very large clan that operated for themselves individually, and for their personal extended group. They took care of their own in a myriad of ways with both financial and individual emergencies, and in the long road the wealthiest member frequently came to the rescue of individuals and businesses of all colors and stripes.

Russell Harrington was a constant and prominent backer of many members. Along with others who had accumulated great wealth, Harrington frequently offered financial assistance, and because all were in accord, the former oilman, and the others, profited. Whenever someone received monetary help, that person would repay the investor at a profit. It enabled Harrington to increase his sizable holdings in an even greater way. The price for his aid was either a specific interest, or a percentage of the individual's business. One of the members, Joseph Jacobson, J.J. to everyone, was a computer prodigy who nearly lost everything but for Russell Harrington, who put $2 million in the business in return for a forty percent ownership of the company. J.J. also became the head of computer operations for The Solution. He established web sites for individual members and businesses, with coded, disappearing and bouncing email systems. He was also instrumental in setting up the headquarters in one of Harrington's warehouses in Las Cruces where his company became profitable and flourished worldwide, to emerge as an international operation. The system of self-help and voluntary assistance worked with complete predictability.

As the replacement for Robert Wilcox, New York Governor, Jack Kayne obviously wanted to be victorious in his home state. The latest polls gave the lead to the president in New York, but in a diverse way for this election, the state had evolved to become a battleground state like Florida or Ohio. In addition, the polls did not reflect the special way millions of people would be casting ballots in the entire country. Throughout the network of The Solution, the call went out to deliver New York, but to bring it into the Principle camp in the way that was necessary to confound the polls by using the absentee ballot. It had largely taken place, and it would rock the system like nothing before. It had happened earlier, but never to the extent of this year's election.

Principle was conceding most of New England, but not New York. This year the voting patterns had changed dramatically, in a process that began with the FEMA mismanagement after Super Storm Sandy ravaged the east coast in 2012. New York was now in play and as vital to the campaign as Ohio and Pennsylvania. Paid staff and volunteers from more than twenty million online donors came together to modify the state like an invading army. With the assistance of the Republican National Committee, phone banks measured and coordinated needed transportation for some voters. The process was being set in place in the same way the two parties always conducted business for their standard-bearer. More than four-hundred thousand members of The Solution took leave of absence from their jobs to spend the remaining weeks getting out the vote in a similar way with those provided by the RNC. Laura Hammond set up a command center in the alternate D.C. office to coordinate the Western strategy for members. Twelve Western states, along with Nebraska, Oklahoma, and the entire South would carry strong for Principle, which left the Midwestern industrial states as the key to victory. They were certain they would win Florida to make victory for Crawford even more difficult. If they won all of their targeted states, they would squeak by with a single vote win in the Electoral College. With New York, the total would jump to more than three hundred, leaving no opportunity to steal the count, as had been tried in the last election in the attempt for a new Amendment to finally eliminate and remove the Electoral College from the Constitution. Progressives had finally lost one area to reality.

They sat in the office with notes and charts to outline the possible tally, and were startled when the telephone rang. No calls to this number were supposed to be forthcoming from the campaign or anyone. When she answered, Sara quickly pressed a newly installed button on the side of the desk to alert Fred. The graininess of the smoker's voice and odd syntax made her body rigid... *Cantrell*! She *was* right the first time! Why did she not make the same recognition when she spoke to the president? In the same instant, she knew she was at least one-step ahead. The D/CIA would be comfortable now, believing he was not recognized. Because of that, he might make a mistake.

"Senator," said Cantrell. "Do not bother to respond. I know your Miss Hammond has been with you for many years. We got that much out of her already, and I know you will act to protect her. This is what it has come to. You have not been practical. Well, then, we have her, and we are *deadly* serious! This is not like the last time. That was just a demonstration. This isn't! I will give you ten minutes to check it. Be assured, Senator, we can do what I say. Withdraw from the race or we will kill you, *after* we kill your Miss Hammond. You're going to lose anyway, and we really do not *want* to kill you. That kind of executive action makes things a lot riskier for everyone."

The line went dead. He must be right! Who would know more about this kind of thing than Cantrell? A violent eruption of compressed anger erupted in her brain. She glowered at the receiver, numbed by the knowledge they had somehow penetrated Fred's security. *No*! *No, goddamn it*! *This just can't be true. It's impossible*! Hadn't Fred told him that? *What now...what more insane madness can possibly take place now*? *I have to think of something*!

But Sara Principle was fixed in place. She stood as a statue, immobile and icy, as Allen dashed to her side. In the same moment, Fred charged into the room.

"We didn't have enough time to trace it, Sara," he said.

Principle looked at her security chief with a blank, unseeing stare, as though Fred wasn't even in the room. All she could think of was Laura. *Do they have her*? *How*? *By now, they must know.* They could not believe she would comply with their demands regardless of who was at risk. Without speaking, she dialed the number. Fred quickly slammed his hand downward to cut off the connection. Principle glared. Her nostrils flared open and closed as her penetrating eyes burned through Fred's like a laser beam.

"Are you *crazy*!" she yelled. "What in the hell is going on? What the fuck do you think you're *doing*?"

In all the years, he had known Sara Principle it was the first time Fred had witnessed his boss's loss of composure. He sometimes thought Principle might just be a person with no emotion behind her actions. She always seemed to take any setback as a positive signal for needed focus to reach a specific goal...and she seldom used profanity.

"Sara," said Spans, quietly, firmly. "Just calm down and *listen* to me for a second, because I've made different plans, very unusual plans, and I've arranged to keep *all* of you out of danger. I have fulfilled my responsibility. Some were just recently set up and I haven't had an opportunity to tell you and go over them."

"What does that mean now? You didn't hear the *threat*! Laura is in danger...*great* danger."

"No, she isn't. He said the words matter-of-factly. "One arrangement involves the Russell building office and Laura in particular. We have to sweep *both* offices each day, and even then, we could overlook the creative placement of a bug. These people are *pros*, and it's probably going to get *worse*! Do you remember *Watergate*?

"I know this is going to sound like something right out of a spy movie, but I've given Laura a code. That's right, Sara, and I know it's corny, but her code is Starr. When you call, you have to ask for Starr, even though any member of your staff would easily recognize your distinctive voice. There are no exceptions, even for you. Laura will not accept a call that uses her name for the duration of the campaign. Quickly now, call her. Tell her that you're here and she should call you back in sixty seconds. I assure you Sara, she is all right."

Principle's face softened. She dialed the number. There was great urgency in Fred's voice, but he must have everything under control. Fred asked her if the person would call back, and if it was Cantrell. Principle nodded.

"Listen, Sara," said Spans when the short conversation was over. "When Laura calls back, tell her that you just wanted her to know that everything is going well here. Tell her you will speak to her later in the day, and then I will give you the explanation I don't have time for right now. This is very important, so do as I ask."

Before the return call from Cantrell, the head of security cautioned her to say only that she would need more time. Afterward, Fred was the first to speak. His voice was steady, his manner of supreme confidence. He knew what he was doing and Principle would have to trust him.

"Sara, after that first call I put a plan of action together and this is it. I gave the code to Laura because I thought she could be in jeopardy. Turns out I was right. We're even tighter than this for the Big Night. When a call is received and the caller asks for Laura by name, they are put through to one of my agents who looks and sounds like Laura, even to someone who has briefly met her. When I spoke to her after you a few minutes ago, she said the agent has been out of the office for more than two hours, which probably means they *do* have her. We told her to see anyone who tried to set up a meeting with Laura. We wired her with very sophisticated equipment to transmit her location in case something like this might happen.

"I've been in touch with Mo, and he knows how we're running the operation. He's agreed to make his resources available anytime. We have it under control. When the right time comes, we will move in to find and rescue the agent, but Laura is all right. As for you, we have to be extremely careful now. This is a move on their part to get to you. They are deadly serious, Sara, and for the rest of this campaign you must wear a bulletproof vest. The same goes for Allen. But like I said, we have it under control."

FOURTEEN

Russell Harrington was the last visitor to leave. It was urgent that he return to Washington to collect a wealth of valuable information that would be vital to the outcome of the second debate, and printed in time for full distribution. The hour of full exposure was closing in fast and the amount of work was daunting for the urgent task now at hand. Everything must proceed like clockwork, as this could be the most dangerous part of the entire forty-year process. All pieces of the current puzzle needed to be present and at attention for full consideration. This would shake up the works big time.

When Harrington had left the Principle residence, Allen realized they were alone as they had not been for a very long time. No crisis would now intervene. For a few hours at least, there would be no need to catch a plane, give a speech, or answer reporter's questions. It was a first after months of running, always trying to stay ahead of the pack to elicit one more convert and claim one more vote for a cause they could not fully reveal. If only they could. Allen often fantasized over the prospect. One day a nation so deeply set in tradition, so naively controlled by conformity would hear the truth. He hoped they would somehow come to understand the changes ahead, because the tight, risk-free world of sameness they now seemed to crave was about to be turned topsy-turvy and wiped from the face of their personal map. For a time they would not recognize their own government or that tradition simply for tradition's sake would no longer be the order of the day…at least for the near future. The country they themselves had personally designed and developed along with their ancestors, people who worked to create space not for political leaders, but for politicians over citizens would never look the same. It would also never be the same, because they were about to be handed a government that was never seen in all of human history.

However, the people were not the real fight. If The Solution actually won the election, the battle now fought for votes would be a far different conflict than the one to follow. It would not be just against the government when the curtain closed down the current show, but also the self-delusion of the people themselves, whose votes and lack of interest had created the mess in the first place.

"Everything's going to be fine, my darling," said Sara softly. "I know it's silly for me to ask you not to worry, but things will be okay. We'll make it just like we always have."

"You know," he said. "I often wonder if we should have even started this in the first place. Don't you?"

"Yes, I do, once in a while, but even when I *do* think that, I keep coming back to what's happened to our country and I know we had to act. Something *had* to happen in some kind of way. Even if we lose, at least we will have *tried*, and we *will* have made *some* kind of impact. We *had* to do it, Allen. I'm absolutely convinced that that's as true as anything, especially after the immoral acts of Bush *and* Obama."

"Sara, what do you think will happen with us when it's all over?" He looked puzzled, at odds with his own feelings, with his own emotions. "I think about that a *lot*!" he said. "We've spent a *lifetime* together working for just this one solitary goal. Oh, I know I've had my career too, but we've spent *so* much time on *this*! I'm not complaining, but I *am* tired. You must be *completely* exhausted!"

She watched him walk outside to the terrace without speaking. She knew that he needed some time alone for reflection—personal time, and she decided to hold back, content with just having him there. She loved him so much. Then she shuddered, looking at him, feeling not just her own reactions and emotions to everything, but his as well.

He watched the fading sunlight. How many times had they stood here to witness this changing sequence of nature where the sky met the earth? It was good to be alone. Suddenly the appearance of a security agent startled him as he came around the corner of the house, bending his head downward in apology for the intrusion.

They were not alone! They would not be alone for another four years—years akin to another lifetime, foreign, unending and constant; a span of time that would rob them of their personal moments together even in the residence of the White House. They would not be able to escape the natural restriction for occupying that structure.

In the deep, emotional part of his brain, he wanted her to win, believing with every ounce of his being that she would. Still, a small voice echoed the long, and many nights of believing they had lost too much in the fight. It was possible. He was frequently filled with the knowledge of his own mixed emotions—impressions that countermanded logic and the reason they had gotten into the contest in the first place. *No! She has to win! She must win.* But the silent doubts lingered in his mind just as surely as the setting sun sat suspended, nearly touching the horizon. They could be together for the rest of their lives to do only what they wanted to do and be just for each other where time had thus far not allowed...but only if she lost the election.

He wondered what had kept it going for them. What had sustained them when other people might have ended the relationship long ago because of too many outside pressures? It had to be more than just love. What was it, really? He could have rationalized and self-examined forever, but the fact remained that the years had passed and there was no turning back even if he wanted to...and he knew he did not want that now, or in the future.

A hodgepodge of emotions clanged back and forth in his head like an out of control pinball that bounced and ricocheted along the walls and through the many gates of a machine with up and down, side-to-side movements. He even thought about a pinball machine as he thought about his own long career. He had made enormous contributions to the performing arts, the latest of which was the momentous completion of his most recent project, and that was the filming of WASHINGTON: A CAPITOL OFFENSE. It was, arguably, the finest performance he had ever given—an augmentation to the art of filmmaking, to the teaching of politics that continued to this very day, and to the secret plan of his wife to change America forever. He thought the film would help to achieve the ultimate goal, and because it was truly noble in every way, that was the reason for its creation. Still, it would be a huge undertaking.

He insisted the film be shot in sequence as a better way to enable the actors to live their roles as they would on the stage—the *boards* he had developed such an intimate relationship with in his youth, and now, in the twilight of his career. When the final scene of CAPITOL was over, and he heard the director call to print, the entire cast and crew leaped to their feet, wildly cheering his ultimate performance. The most surprising part was that it came in a studio with several heavyweights from the movie capital Hollywood; a tangible sign they had made inroads with filmdom's elite citizenry, an intentional part of the entire process because they also clearly understood that citizen perception equaled citizen reality.

The film left the story unresolved, giving the audience the time to form their own ideas based on the presentation of a vast amount of information. It showed the massive corruption and pork-barrel projects of both political parties that was the legislative process in Washington.

CAPITOL, made as a mini-series and seen by nearly fifty million people in prime time over three successive nights, was even more than they imagined it would be. The film was a valuable public relations effort for The Solution, developed five years prior to its production. It would become an unconscious reference point to consider and remember with pointed clarity when a person who had seen it was alone in the voting booth. The making of the series was a cumulative effort in Allen's personal quest to elect not just his wife as president, but also several other members of The Solution running for the House and the Senate on the national level, and for statewide offices. This was his own special attempt separate and apart from the campaign to change the face of government and the Constitution, for he was the writer and producer, as well as the lead character for that one solitary goal.

Everyone's favorite scene was the final one, *catching* the emotions of the audience and the storyline, as the picture and sound faded into nothing. In the film, he played a junior senator, after winning election with a stunning percentage of the vote. His character was sitting in on his first Appropriations meeting for resolution with the House of Representatives. The scene called for him to listen by innuendo, strongly suggested by the most senior professionals, to learn exactly how bills are resolved in D.C.

As the meeting progressed, he heard the lineup of senators and representatives barking out figures willy-nilly from the previous budget. They had all been in Washington for many years, and they were ready to help their handsome new rookie learn.

Allen watched and listened. The implication they were dealing with vast amounts of money did not register on his character's face until the meeting was nearly over, and then as a sudden revelation after he heard similar comments from all of the members. He remembered his lines as though he had said them only moments ago.

"Gentlemen," he said in the film. "I will stay silent no *longer*! I actually find it very difficult to believe what I am seeing and hearing, and even though I'm the new kid on the block here, I *will* have my say. Please don't even *try* to interrupt me! It is extremely difficult to believe what I have heard in this room.

"Senator Reeves. *You* just said that the appropriation for the last item was 1.4 last year so we should increase it to 2.6 this year. You even had the audacity to call it an *item*, and not its *budget* name. Apparently, you did not even base your increase proclamation on *facts*. You simply *decided* that an increase for the *item* was essential. You are talking about *millions* and *billions* of dollars! These are *taxpayer* dollars, and you even have most of the work in this effort performed by your *aides* while you primarily pose and posture for the *cameras*!

"I have been watching you so-called *honorable* men spend the wealth of this nation as though it was nothing more significant than counting beans in a jar at a *carnival* show, and you all have participated in this thievery in the same scurrilous fashion! You are a *disgrace* to this institution and to this country. I also know that most of you are people who *fill* these bills with Earmarks to use for one single purpose, and that is to *buy* votes back home!

"Tomorrow, gentlemen, I will hold a press conference to announce this outrage to the voters, and I will suggest that they conduct a series of recall campaigns against you regardless of party, if that is possible in your states. I will name *names* and recommend they begin to *require* the members of both Houses be present for a *full* reading of every bill before you can vote, instead of the constant *wave-reading* phrase I always hear, in a *Read the Bills* resolution I will soon introduce. That would be a giant step to stop some of the shenanigans I have seen in this room, and it would almost surely reduce the size of each bill.

"I will suggest that voters require *written* disclosure from the entire Congress as to how you appropriate these taxpayer funds, and that you make available to the *providers* of these moneys a *written, mailed,* and *online* audit. I will recommend they *demand* an explanation as to why you spend their money with such wanton disregard, and I will instruct my staff to issue reports to expose the fraud perpetrated in this room. The people hired you to *safeguard* their interests, not *squander* the resources they give you! I wonder if any of you deal with your private funds in such a capricious way, and if I were like *you* I would be *embarrassed* to call myself a senator!"

The scene lasted a full ten minutes without cut, with Allen holding court as he slowly walked around the room. The camera showed the startled expressions of the committee members in extreme close-up. From there it faded to the front of the Capitol where Allen held an impromptu press conference to announce some of what he had just witnessed, with as many details as possible presented to the American people in a few days. The picture ended as a fade-out, with Allen walking back up the steps to re-enter the building.

The film recalled scenes of *Mr. Smith Goes to Washington* in its idealism, stirring audiences across the country to mount a massive letter and email campaign, to insist on full disclosure from the Congress.

CAPITOL was a smash. Members of both Houses were inundated with mail, and the CBS network deluged with requests for an immediate re-run. Senator Russell Harrington, a consultant on the film, held a press conference to confirm the authenticity of the production and to hail the actor, producer, and writer, Allen Davis, for having the courage to turn out such a blistering indictment of the Congress, never seen before this film, even by C-Span viewers.

Allen was riveted to the past and to the spot in the sky where he watched the setting sun reach down to touch the horizon, remembering even further back to a point in their lives that took place nearly ten years before this day. Throughout their marriage, it was the only time away from the everyday affairs of two careers and the building of The Solution. Sara was then the Mayor of Las Cruces, while he continued to pursue a variety of film and stage roles. At the same time, they both devoted many hours in the ongoing effort to increase the size of their secret organization, with both associate and non-associate members. The one thing they did not know was if the numbers would ever be strong enough, great enough to work. It was something they were never certain of, and was always a constant concern.

In the beginning, it was clear that a run for the White House by one of their members might necessitate an early course of action or none at all. But ten years before this day, both Allen and Sara needed a break to be alone and beyond the reach of careers, the goals of The Solution, or anything except a substantial amount of time together. Their long-standing friends, Joseph and Amy Jacobson, would be in Europe for an extended trip. It was the perfect opportunity to use their California ranch for the extended Principle outing.

Allen Davis and Sara Principle arrived at the ranch high above the Santa Barbara coastline incommunicado, and far away from the glare of Allen's fame. They were alone for the first time since college. No urgent messages awaited, and he would make the most of a glorious situation. He had insisted they receive no communication from anyone. They must be completely cloistered and alone, and this requirement would include any member of The Solution, even a cantankerous Texas senator.

Each morning they ate breakfast on the patio. They swam nude and made love in the brilliant sunshine and warm water of the pool. They made love often, luxuriating in the newly found wealth of time created expressly for them—a time without specific purpose or interruption—a time just for themselves because they were there and loved each other. For one entire month, the minutes did not disappear in the blink-of-an-eye, eluding their passions and their need to be together. The days remained etched in his memory, indelible and valid, as if they had just happened. He wanted those moments again, and he often thought about that one sensational part of their lives as perhaps a prelude to a time when she would no longer be seeking public office.

When their month was over, Allen rushed back to his hectic schedule. Several projects were on hold and he had to move. It was then that the idea for the TV project began to germinate, but would require several months just to get the script on paper, while Sara flew back to New Mexico and her role as mayor.

"You were thinking about Santa Barbara, weren't you?" she asked softly, touching his shoulder.

Quickly her words brought him back to the present. He slipped his hand into hers without answering and led her into the house. After so many years, it still surprised him. She always seemed to have the unique ability to know what he was thinking. It was amazing. If he were troubled or just quietly happy she knew, she always knew…but now he did not want to talk. The reminiscences of their month-long hiatus worked to excite his senses. Now he wanted only to feel his body next to hers stripped of all material covering, with nothing between them but their own skin. He wanted to feel her response to his touch; to know, at least for this brief period that this was their time, and it would belong to them exclusively…and for a short time America would be excluded from their lives.

They often made love in the swirling warmth of the whirlpool just as they did now. He had taught her the lesson of the natural demulcent qualities of warm water laced with light oil years before. It was their prelude to moving to the brass bed, still exciting, even after so many years together, and even with advanced age.

The water aroused her, and then the freedom of the brass bed where nothing could restrain the touching lips and fingers, across and into the most sensitive parts of their bodies, to make the mind forget what was about to happen in America. *We must forget*! *We must not forget*! Even what she would do in Baltimore—what Russell was preparing that would be so strong.

The next morning brought an urgent call from Fred. "Sara," he said. "We got lucky and found out where Laura's double is being held. It looks quiet there. We probably won't move for a while, and she can get some information on them. We'll just keep an eye on the situation for now. I'll get back to you as soon as I can. In the meanwhile, give 'em *hell* in Baltimore! We'll all be watching."

Principle thought about the call and dialed Harrington. "Hi, Russ," she said. "Is everything ready?"

"Sure is! Everything's all finished and ready for distribution. The material will go out to the various locations by express service, which is one of *our* people. It'll go out late tonight and all day tomorrow. The networks will jump on it right away and try to turn it against you, except maybe CBS and Fox. We'll make sure they all get copies. Then we'll do the e-mails. Incidentally, I've gotten word that they're all goddamn *cocky* at the White House. They think they've put you on ice and all that's left is to wipe up the drippings! But you just *wait*! *Oh boy*, after what you *say*! They thought *their* October Surprise would *finish* you, but they didn't know about *ours*! I wish it was gonna take place right now or in the next five minutes. *Boy*! And hell, I *cain't* be there! You sure I cain't? Someone could do what I— no, I guess they couldn't."

"Thanks, Russ. I'll be in touch then, unless the troops and Samuels need to come to my rescue. What I say tonight is going to cause an explosion heard 'round the world. It will be interesting to say the least! Let's hope it doesn't blow up in our faces, though. I think we need to have Howard appraised of the situation and be sure he's there. Call him, Russ. Has Mo been in touch with Wilson?"

Harrington thought for a moment and said, "Yep! Wilson's *with* him and it's gonna be *great*!"

Two hours later Principle left for Baltimore. Allen warned her that the consequences of her statement could backfire into charges of sedition. She must remember that it had been a very long time since Nixon's defeat. The people responsible for Nixon's fiasco other than Nixon himself had spent a considerable amount of time getting rid of him. Much more time than Principle had getting to a point where she could make such a risk-filled declaration. She must be very careful. To do less would further complicate the long struggle they had waged just to get to this point in time. She must also remember that even though progressives didn't fully kill capitalism when Obama ruled, they came close and would never quit. They would keep trying to convince the voters that progressivism and capitalism could coexist.

Principle understood it would never be possible, with progressivism being an immoral idea, while laissez faire capitalism was the only moral social system for any nation.

FIFTEEN

Speculation flourished extensively on the morning of the second debate. Russell Harrington threw down a verbal challenge in a prearranged press conference, daring voters to listen carefully, as they would hear a bit of news heretofore not mentioned by anyone in the media, or the two campaigns. He was not at liberty to divulge the nature of the information, but it would be a bombshell.

Reporters tried unsuccessfully to get a statement from the Principle campaign. Failing that, all electronic news organizations interrupted programming throughout the day by holding interviews with people associated with the candidates. No one could add to the speculation. Whatever Principle had to say would have to wait for the actual debate. According to a number of national polls, the sudden mystery increased viewer potential by thirty percent. It was also facilitated by the intense commentary on talk-radio that still existed, long after progressives had lost numerous efforts to restore the so-called Fairness Doctrine.

Barbara Langdon sat behind a small desk in preparation for the opening of the debate. Both candidates were in complete accord that Langdon, a non-partisan, was a fair choice to oversee the affair as its moderator. She watched as the digital clock reached the precise hour for the Countdown, while listening for the signal through her earpiece, and then she began with her opening introductions.

"Ladies and gentlemen," she said. "We again welcome back the Commission on Presidential Debates as our sponsors for this election season. They and the television networks are pleased to bring you this presidential forum, the second in our series. We would also like to offer our thanks to the people of Baltimore for providing this Town Hall, and to the candidates for appearing here tonight. We know they have had grueling schedules, but we believe this is an integral part of a uniquely American process, especially in light of a recent decision by both of them that I can now share with those of you here in Baltimore and the millions of people around the world watching on television and listening on radio. This is a *very* important debate for America.

"As you know, three debates were scheduled for this year. However, President Crawford has informed the Commission that because of the delicate nature of the non-proliferation talks, she will be unable to attend any further deliberations. She has also put the panel on notice that she will try to answer questions about the initiatives as fully as possible in her opening remarks. She has told us the talks are highly classified and sensitive, but she will cover as much as possible.

"Senator Principle has notified the Commission that her remarks will be of a delicate nature, and that any further comment beyond that which she will say tonight would be superfluous. With that in mind, she has called our attention to her previous statements that she believes the debates are unfair by rejecting other candidates with arbitrary percentages of the actual vote in the last election, and potential numbers in this one, and that she too will not participate in any debate after tonight.

"The long standing policy of the Commission is to include only the two major parties for what the members of the Commission believe to be just and honorable reasons. We regret additional forums will not be available, but that is beyond our control. However, we offer our sincere apology to those who are watching and waiting around the world.

"We have invited the CBS news anchor, Terry O'Neil; commentator Stanley Schwartz; and the publisher of the Albuquerque Sun, Bill London, to present the questions in this historic presidential debate between two women tonight. Due to the unprecedented refusal of the candidates to appear for the rest of the schedule, we are extending the program tonight to four hours after receiving agreement from both candidates. We will begin with individual statements, followed by the first question from Mr. Schwartz. Since Senator Principle was first with her opening statement at the previous debate, we have given that position to President Crawford tonight. And so, may we hear your opening remarks, Madam President?"

Crawford's face gleamed with confidence. This would be a fitting climax to a lifelong effort of working for others to conclude her final election as the President. With her numbers now soaring in the polls, she felt more positive than she had since the convention. Now she was certain her stunning announcement had ended the Principle ascent for good. From this moment forward, the election would be a cakewalk. In less than three months, she would achieve the zenith of a lifetime—her own personal sacrifice for her country. In a world filled with political mediocrity, she would tower over all others who had come before her by bringing peace to the world. Many had tried. All had failed. But Hadley R. Crawford would not fail. Poised and confident she looked directly into the television camera to begin her statement. This would be no debate. More than likely the people would not even hear what Principle had to say. This night belonged to Hadley R. Crawford, the incumbent President of the United States of America and the oncoming landslide that would soon occur in her favor.

"My fellow citizens," she began. "First, I would like to extend my thanks to the Commission for their thoughtfulness in sponsoring this debate. I also want to send a huge *thank you* to the American women. We are so proud of the wives and daughters of this great land for their insistence to end the threat of weapons of mass destruction. They, more than anyone, deserve the credit with their never-ending perseverance for a safer world. Unlike my opponent, I applaud the Commission for creating a *necessary* limit in the debates. I understand why you have done so, and I support and agree with your decision.

"Because of the success of our bold initiatives, the signing of the international treaty will end the gathering threat of terrible weapons of war. This will take place in February. The arms race will then become just a terrible memory of the past.

"While keeping our differences clear and the needs of the people at the forefront, we have formed an alliance to dismantle all nuclear and chemical weapons, which will begin to take place sometime after the signing of the new treaty. We have nearly reached the *ultimate solution* in our talks. We are going to achieve the dream that all humanity has longed for, for more than seventy years. We will have a world at peace, and we will end the *nightmare*, the *tragedy*, and the *senseless* killing in wars. I also trust that this will be my legacy when my second term as your president is completed, and I pray we *do* succeed.

"I believe my record stands on its own as a testimony for all of the people! In *my* heart I know that when the voters look to *their* hearts, they will come to understand that I am not *perfect*, but I am for all of our American families, *especially* our *innocent* children."

Crawford's eyes did not stray from the camera as she spoke. Deeply engrossed in her television posture, she did not notice Armando approach the platform holding a large manila envelope, which he quietly handed to Principle who examined the contents and returned all but four pages to Armando, who then turned and left the auditorium.

Barbara Langdon broke a sharp round of applause, and when the camera focused on Sara Principle, she appeared relaxed, and moved easily to her conversational style of speaking.

"Ladies and gentlemen," she said, firmly, yet softly. "I also offer my thanks to the Commission. I just wish it had been extended to other candidates who might have had something valuable to say just as what took place many, many years ago when Ross Perot was included in the debates of that year. Isn't that the way it *should* work, together and *inclusive*, not *exclusive*? But that has not happened since that time when the Commission took over and eliminated candidates with *arbitrary* rules that favor both Democrats and Republicans. As the Republican candidate, I know it benefits me, but somehow, as a nation, we have chosen to ignore all points of view except those of the two major parties. Since the president claims to support the rights of minorities, you would think she would have given the green light to include at least *one* of them, and if she had, I would not have opposed it. As far as the women of our country are concerned, I look forward to their strong support. They have fought nobly for their freedom, and one of the most important things they have gone to battle *for* is to be seen as *serious* people and not talked *down* to.

"This election is the clearest difference between candidates in the past *one hundred ten* years! It is a true alternative for the people against the special interests of *both* parties who have effectively ruled our country for a very long time. However, most Americans do not yet know who they are. They have had no publicity. We will certainly *tell* you who they are just as soon as we can, but they are *not* your elected officials. I understand how that might confuse you, but I promise it will be obvious very soon."

With a clear view of the audience, Principle was able to see the bewilderment on their faces. "The announcement from the White House about the end of WMDs" she continued, "tells only one side of the story, which is usually the case with government officials. It was not my desire to reveal this information now. I believed that if I did it would come across as so unbelievable it would make me look like a scare-merchant. I have changed my mind. The president, in a desperate and obvious last-minute attempt to resurrect her failing campaign has herself chosen to make this information an issue. Because of that, I will too.

"As to her assertion that she has at hand the *nearly* signed treaty for the end of weapons of mass destruction, she has not given you the full story, and listen closely—she has not told the *truth*. She has *lied*! The treaty, ladies and gentlemen, in an action to bypass the constitutionally required Advice and Consent of the Senate is *already* signed!"

She turned, defiantly glaring at Crawford. A loud murmur began to build throughout the audience. Principle raised both of her hands to ask for quiet, and slowly the Town Hall audience moved to a still, tense hush, with a feeling that something very dangerous was about to take place in front of their own eyes.

"When President Crawford stepped in to nationalize certain businesses two years ago and thus follow the far left-wing actions of Barack Obama in *violating* the Constitution, she initiated Executive Order 51490. More than likely most of you do not know what that edict is because you have never heard of it, and elected and un-elected officials have done an exemplary job of keeping it quiet. Aside from being *unconstitutional*, the Order confirms that the president can, when she alone deems it necessary or *preferable*, take away your property and prevent you from leaving the country merely by making the *declaration*! No judge is required, just as no judge is *initially* required to *spy* on American citizens before taking a request to the secret FISA Court that is several stories beneath the Capitol Museum, but that is not a part of the Order. These are but two of a wide range of actions the Order permits, like preventing you from leaving the country and confiscating your property. In that context there are documents that show her *Peace at Hand* report to be a fraud, and unadulterated political opportunism as the final part of that equation, to *selectively* take your liberty away from you by the order of *one* individual. That establishes a *dictatorship*!

"The full story on the treaty is this: The documents show that President Crawford; President Zgonina; General Tso; and President Ripoli have formed an alliance not for peace, but for the purpose of ruling the *world* with President Crawford as the ultimate *leader* of that ruling body! All four Heads of State have signed the document. The only thing they wait for now is the outcome of this election. It further states that no nation will hold its own sovereignty; the only military power will be in the hands of the United Nations; and that a new *World* Constitution through the U.N. will rule the day. When that happens, President Crawford will have achieved the dream of all of history's despots. She will rule the world without ever firing a shot!"

Crawford's face twisted to an ugly grimace of hate, as she shrieked out to interrupt Principle's remarks. The audience looked on in stunned horror, watching the first female president become a violent mirror image of her longstanding example of non-violence and quiet deportment. Amid the intense picture taking, Crawford completely lost control of all of her emotions. She shouted out at the panel of reporters and television people, calling Principle a liar and a traitor, as Barbara Langdon helplessly tried without success to call the debate back to order.

Suddenly Crawford raised her hand in an obscene, violent gesture, then wagging her index finger at Principle. Her body shook with rage as she screeched out instructions to Secret Service personnel to place Principle under arrest and confiscate the material she held aloft in her hand…the papers delivered by Armando Munoz.

Pandemonium raced throughout the hall engulfing the entire audience. Leaping to the stage in Principle's defense was the noted criminal litigator from New Castle, Indiana, Howard Samuels. Before a shocked and frightened audience, federal agents placed handcuffs on Sara Principle's wrists and in the scuffle, knocked Samuels backward off the stage and onto the edge of the table with the panel members. People in the audience screamed out in terror, pushing and shoving in a desperate attempt to flee the hall. In seconds, military police swarmed throughout the Town Hall, ripping television cameras from their bases and from the shoulders of the mini-cam crew. MPs began to confiscate discs and tapes according to orders screamed out from the president, and across the nation and the world, all television screens went blank. The table with the three panelists was overturned. One of the legs caught Terry O'Neil on the temple, splitting the skin. Then, almost as quickly as it had begun, the uproar was over. MPs escorted the remaining audience from the auditorium, as Secret Service agents placed a quiet, nearly serene Sara Principle into custody. They said the Justice Department would try her for treason, holding the papers delivered by Armando as evidence of stealing classified government documents.

Fifteen minutes later, a boisterous and smiling Russell Harrington held a press conference in front of the White House, and another *Harrington Court*. In his hand were several pieces of paper. When asked of their content, Harrington declined to make a comment until all television crews were in place and fully operational. When he finally began to speak his voice was gravelly, sly sounding and gruff, and the shape of his lips curved with a roguish, defiant expression of disgust, as he boldly pointed the papers toward the assembled reporters. He motioned for them to observe the White House, and then he said...

"Friends, you all know who I'm for in this election. I haven't made that a secret to anyone. The pages I hold in my hand here are copies of the ones that Senator Principle raised in the air at that farce that just ended in Baltimore. You know what I mean—the sheets the President's storm troopers *arrested* her for, but the actual papers were from her staff to help her in the debate that never took place. They were *not* government documents the senator held on the Town Hall stage, but it wasn't somethin' that would have been illegal if she had actually done it with government papers, *either*!

"The president, true to her *real* colors, had the senator arrested thinkin' the papers were top-secret documents. They were no such thing." He quickly switched to the papers in his other hand and said, "*These are*! What Senator Principle had were reports about the progress of her campaign in certain states, along with a variety of notes to help her answer unasked questions. As for the papers, well, as far as I'm concerned, they were *stolen* from the senator!

"The documents the senator *described* are a type of pact between our president and those three foreigners she's been in cahoots with. Its purpose is to guarantee those four people the complete and absolute control of the entire *world*, and that is what I hold here in my hand, a *copy* of that agreement. This is *proof* of that contract. This is the evidence of *evil* masqueradin' as a carin' President of the United States, but is the exact *opposite* of that. She is just like former President Obama was in thinkin' he could move *beyond* the Constitution willy-nilly, and even more than what existed when she *got* here, and now she wants four *more* years to *hurt* us!

"Now, before the president's goons rush to arrest me too, let me add this little tidbit of information. These papers—these *White House Papers* were handed to me on the streets of Washington just as they are now bein' passed out on other streets all over the country and *mailed* to newspapers that are still in business and television stations to *expose* this sinister plot. This is *whistle blowin'* time! This document, this covert lust for power that has been residin' in the hidden personality of President Crawford and bears her seal of office and personal *signature*, is absolute proof she's broken her Oath of Office! This evidence *commands* that she be impeached and *removed* from that office, although it's probably too *late* for that...but we can *hope*!

"She promised to *protect* the Constitution. Unfortunately, our highest law doesn't require her to *obey* it. Our Founding Fathers just thought other presidents that followed them *would* obey. Well they sure were wrong.

This president has worked with a group of people in and out of government for the sole purpose of placin' herself on the throne of a new, one-world government. That's what she means by her phrase the *New World Order* that you've heard her say time after time, but *Hitler* invented it! It's all here in these papers—these *Hadley R. Crawford* Papers! It's here for everyone to see and *think* about when they go to the *polls*! The choice you have in this election is now up to you voters, for this conspiracy will affect *all* of you, as well as your *children* and *grandchildren*, and I speak the *truth!*"

With the public disclosure of the papers and the arrest of her opponent, Crawford's actions were now in the open but still unclear to most people. Attorneys for both sides met, which resulted in Principle's quick release from custody.

In the Oval Office, Crawford met with the Chairman of the Joint Chiefs, General Wilson Keyes, Cecil Price, and the Secretaries of State and Defense. For more than two hours, they discussed the idea that the president resign. As they talked, Crawford wondered if she had enough support to institute a coup by using the military, but she did not discuss it with the abrasive Wilson Keyes.

The meeting concluded with the assumption that not enough time remained for the House to institute impeachment hearings. Explanations would be given; fences could be mended; denial would be stated and commercials would be aired. Victory might still be possible.

SIXTEEN

Central Park is an expansive sprawl of 843-acres set aside in the mid-1800s as a recreational spot for all of the people of New York City. It was there on the site of the 13-acre Great Lawn that the CFL began to prepare for speeches by Thomas Farley and New York Governor, Jack Kayne, the Republican candidate for vice president. Held with speeches by Principle and Allen Davis at the Hollywood Bowl in California at the same time, the two events would begin concurrently. The joint venture was to be a cooperative tribute to the American spirit as THE LAND OF THE FREE. The affair would be a gala night with endorsements from noted personalities in the entertainment industry, a surprising outcome of progress for a Republican candidate that for some recalled the Reagan era. This would be Allen and Sara's first joint appearance of the entire campaign. They would give speeches after acts by a variety of comics and singers, with the climax for the evening to be an exit performance by the Los Angeles Philharmonic and their personal salute to America. The New York and Hollywood extravaganzas would be coordinated and shown on cable television and the Internet, alternately, and on split screen, with some speeches synchronized to enable viewers outside the live venues to see and hear all of them very late at night because of satellite coordinating needs.

"Tonight's the night, Dominick," said Cantrell. "You make sure Principle is no longer around, and make goddamn sure you get her this time. I don't want another fuckup. That was the first one for you in all these years, and after you get Principle, it'll be Kayne's turn. See to it!"

With each passing day, the president was growing increasingly tense as pressure mounted in the media to address some of the charges of corruption in her administration. Even with her strong media support, the force of notoriety still kept the White House staff occupied in dealing not just with the Republicans, but also the President's own party. The notoriety of a White House scandal was very similar to that which happened in 2013 to President Obama, who was successful in disavowing all of them.

As Crawford concluded her public day, Sara and Allen tried to rest in their hotel suite after they had been fitted with bulletproof vests. This would be their next-to-last public appearance, and Fred assured them all bases were covered. The same was true for Thomas Farley and Jack

Kayne. The opposition had shown they would continue taking extraordinary steps to achieve their objective, especially now that the truth about the president was out in the open.

Dominick Caputo walked casually around the Hollywood Bowl with other tourists and curiosity seekers—star-struck groupies who eagerly anticipated the evening arrival of their celluloid heroes. He did nothing that would set him apart from the bulk of celebrity lovers. Even though he quickly thought he saw where he would station the gay minister, he would follow his assassin's visceral instincts that would help him discover if security people were already present, as he suspected they were, and then to evaluate the location for Paul.

Having no previous experience with the Bowl, he was nonetheless pleased with the location. Not only was it out in the open, which was what he preferred, but also because millions of people would see the kill, something that had not happened since Houston many years earlier. He enjoyed it even more knowing he would evade capture simply because of the presence of the gay minister, and he very much enjoyed getting a homosexual into trouble. He called them queers, and loathed them almost as much as he hated women.

Ignoring the posted signs at the band shell, he followed the lead of others and hopped over the iron railing. He walked up the steps to the center of the stage. The Bowl was open in the morning hours to allow visitors access, but not in the afternoons when entertainment was scheduled for the evening.

He looked out from the stage at the benches that fanned out right and left on the slope of the small hillside. The location of the stage in the section at the bottom created a bowl-like setting and was perfect for Caputo's needs. Then he remembered his other major hit many years before this day. It was more difficult than here because the target was moving. Tonight would be a snap by comparison.

On the furthest section of the seating area, he moved along the walkway behind the last row of seats. He would go up in the Hollywood Hills behind the bowl and make the kill from there, with one possible difficulty. If any people also went there to watch the show, he would have to kill them as well. Then he would simply have an easy exit and a panicked audience in a stampede from the seating area. That would then leave Paul alone and arrested, primarily due to the weapon in his possession. Because of that singular fact known to professional detectives with insider knowledge, was that another patsy would pay for a crime he did not commit.

It was a perfect scenario, and much better than in Chicago where he had found it necessary to expose his face to possible identification. That was a problem he did not have here, with an easily arranged scapegoat. This hit would be the most effortless of his career, but he still had to check the spot where he would place Paul, and be absolutely certain of that decision. His participation in the assignment was fundamental for Caputo to remain undiscovered and unknown.

He continued around the seating area to look at the site more closely, stopping at a small, green building. He decided it was where the electrical equipment for the stage was located. The building was unobtrusive in the setting and would be a superior location for Father Paul. He would first make his way around the surrounding terrain in the developing darkness to reach the low, flat roof of the building while carrying his own weapon. Then he would be in place for his part in the assassination and become Caputo's newest pawn. The gay minister was completely unaware of the weapon technology that would seal his fate. When signaled, he would fire his handgun that was technically identical to Caputo's rifle in every way, even in its bore markings. It would make him the easiest flunky ever.

Luther Johnson telephoned Mo Dobrosky. "I followed Director Cantrell!" he said, running the words together as fast as he could speak them. "He went to Kennedy and caught a flight to L.A. I'm on my way in from the airport now."

"Okay. Go back to your place and wait. I'll call if we need you."

When the phone rang in the hotel suite, Principle stopped pacing. This was what she was waiting for to tell them what to do and how soon to do it. Now, she must place all of her trust and confidence with Fred Spans without any question.

Allen's recent mood swing troubled her greatly. As long as she had known him, he never expressed fear outwardly. Something more than just the parameters of the election was bothering him, but she did not know the source, and he was not speaking of it. She would have to find out when they made the time to talk with each other.

She pulled the plans over in her mind, backward, forward, side-to-side, up and down, trying to see if anything had gone unnoticed. The voting method had to work. It was such an important feature they had devised to defeat the entrenched forces of political insiders. It might be their only chance, considering the typical patronage by political hacks acting not for the good of the nation, but in their own self-interest. Even Obama couldn't shut it down in Pennsylvania in 2008, with the constant demand for *Street-Cred*, translated to mean cash.

The patterns for the voting plan had begun years before in California, and it was there that she first envisioned the idea for this year. When put into operation, the way millions of people would be casting their ballots would confound all the experts. Never again, would anyone place any substantial amount of trust in local or national opinion polls—not after the multi-pronged attack, for the sampling would be decidedly wrong this year. It was a sophisticated undertaking requiring constant monitoring and supervision in the command center in Las Cruces. It also involved millions of voters who were unaware they were being used to further a cause they were not privileged to know or even understand. The definitive success of the program depended on the mails and early voting, and the participation of the Republican National Committee.

She instantly recognized Fred's voice. "Sara, I have everything ready," said Spans. "I want you and Allen to stay put 'til tonight. When you finish with the festivities, return to the suite. We'll get your flight ready. I'll phone you later because you and Allen will need to leave the hotel on time. As of now, I'm not certain when we will make our move on that warehouse where they're holding my agent, but it will be soon, and don't forget! Cantrell has someone *stalking* you, and it's probably the dark-haired guy—the one in the pictures."

Principle thought again of Allen as she replaced the receiver. They had tried many times to explain their relationship to other people with little or no success. Perhaps it would be just as difficult for her tonight. She needed to explain all that had gone wrong with America's politics in a co-gent and easy way to understand.

As far as she and Allen were concerned, their mutual love was simply a system of shared values that certainly included emotion, but also with reasoned principles. They never supported the romantic idea of uncondi-tional love, for it had no rational value to them. True love automatically required stated, self-interest conditions. She did know that Allen, above all others, had exercised a considerable amount of both physical and mental effort. More than anyone, including Russell, he had helped to make it hap-pen, but now she could tell that something heavy was on his mind that he was not sharing with her. From his melancholy expression from time to time, she even thought he might be regretting what they had tried to ac-complish. *No*! *That's crazy*!

Exhausted and mentally drained, she needed a nap to help replenish her strength and collect her thoughts more fully to sort out what she would say to the people, and the two, long, non-stop flights to come. What more could she say? It would just have to be more of the standard Stump Speech words. What else was there? Somehow, she must try to make the words sound fresh and alive. She had never written her speeches down, preferring instead to deliver spontaneous ideas with a much deeper conviction than just reading words from a sheet of paper or a teleprompter, but that did not include the Big Speech. Her attitude was also to hell with any gaff she might make. People expected gaffs, but written lines for her were never as real as natural speaking. It was different for Allen. He was an actor. It was easy for him to deliver written lines, even if someone else wrote them, as was usually the case.

David Breyer began to make needed arrangements to cover the rally in Central Park. It would be, they said, one hell of a show. He had already voiced his support for Principle and wanted to cover her in California, but that was impossible because of scheduling problems. He would have to settle for the Great Lawn and the Thomas Farley/Jack Kayne speeches. And in spite of being on the inside, he had no power to change the schedule or intercede in any way. He even wrote a number of columns about the difficulty factor.

Breyer had covered political races for nearly fifty years; thirty of those as an active member of The Solution, but he had never seen a contest like this one. Perhaps he never would again. Even 2008 when the first black person won the presidency paled in comparison to this year, though voters had no obvious clues about that contrast.

He thought about the crusty Texas senator who spoke out for change with reporters in front of the White House, and, being an insider, Breyer knew the talk of change would be far different than anyone else could ever foresee in their wildest imaginings, including reporters.

Thoughts of Harrington's last press conference with the *White House Papers* filtered through his mind, then back even further to another time of presidential scandal. That one was against a Republican president. It was not the campaign he thought of, but the television images of a disgraced Richard Nixon, defiant to the last, as he moved his arm brazenly before boarding the chopper, no longer the president, and because he was no longer the Commander-in-Chief he was not on board Marine One. Now another president was under the same kind of intense bombardment. Even liberal commentators were calling for actions against Hadley R. Crawford with the same self-righteous vengeance they had for Nixon's head. Yet Breyer could not help but wonder. An inner voice kept repeating that this would not be the last thing for the president. Hadley R. Crawford was an astute, political animal. She had survived for a very long time. Perhaps it was possible she could still pull a rabbit out of what was now a very tall hat, and one strong fact about her remained...solid popularity.

In spite of her sudden and dramatic fall from grace, Crawford seemed to be coming back. Regardless of how it appeared on the surface, Principle should not pack her bags for the White House just yet. The final tally would be close, and for the senator to think otherwise would be to grossly underestimate Crawford and the massive power of an incumbent president to make many things happen. This was especially true now with her explanation that she had only made a preliminary agreement on the treaty before submitting it to the Senate, and already something major was taking place. Crawford's popularity was surging again. It seemed to Breyer that his television repetitively blasted him with new commercials purchased by a 527 group, making it obvious that Crawford was not going to go away meekly, nor would the vast army of supporters. Many political fortunes always rested on the coattails of an incumbent President of the United States.

The day of reckoning would come in less than three days, with the most recent polls giving Principle a razor-thin lead of 48% to 46%. The vast climb upward since the Baltimore fiasco was a tribute to Crawford's natural popularity, and Breyer could not help but think that the impossible of just a few days ago with the president, might turn into the achievable. This election was turning out to be the most unpredictable he had ever seen, and he had inside information pollsters did not have. He had also witnessed a multitude of elections with which to compare.

Crawford met with David Rockhold to discuss the latest poll numbers, and the likelihood of beating the odds in three days.

"Hadley," said Rockhold. "Without our $40 million you would still be at rock bottom. We put that money with hundreds of local chapters of the Concerned Citizens Action Committee, and you are back and nearly on top. The *Group* and the CCAC have asked me to convey this message. Leave the rest to us and we will get you there. We have done it several times before."

Crawford watched the tiny man leave. Even in her youth, she did not like him. Rockhold would do anything to further his own ambition, but now things were different. The people were rallying behind their president. Crawford would allow the *Group* to spend the money. Then, on January 20 she would put them and the nasty little man where they belonged...out in the cold with the rest of the world's greedy people.

They all thought they owned the president—believing she was their monkey, successfully obedience trained. David Rockhold did not know the president had discovered the *Group's* real plans over many years. Crawford was angry with herself that she had been so naïve for so long. They had simply used her from the time she was a very young girl. Now, she would use all of her powers against them for the good of the nation, not for herself, and when it was over, she would still call all of the shots. She could not wait for January to arrive. When voters gave her another four years, she would summon the little man to the Oval Office to meet the attorney general. Then she would end the cozy relationship with the United Nations and the quadripartite attempt. When that was finished, she would look into the charges Principle made after first re-reading the Constitution several times, but as far as the election was concerned, nothing and no one could stop her now, and that included a pompous senator from a backward state like New Mexico, or a vicious, greedy little banker from New York.

SEVENTEEN

Dominick Caputo used the tickets Cantrell had supplied him and entered the Hollywood Bowl with Father Paul. Together they mingled with other spectators gawking at the array of personalities seated near the stage, ready for the coming program that was now just minutes away. Earlier Caputo went up in the Hollywood Hills, where he concealed his deadly weapon in perfect alignment to center stage.

He spotted the security men. They always had their own peculiar mannerisms, making identification easy for the trained eye of the knowing, professional assassin.

Caputo had earlier sent Paul to a well-known shop not far from the Bowl to obtain a variety of wigs and beards. Caputo's face had not been on display for a lifetime, but he would still take no needless risk of discovery. If nothing else the Chicago experience taught him to be even more meticulous, and he always operated with the same careful methods that helped him stay alive. More than twenty-five years before this day, the Houston hit was his most spectacular job, and was clearly dramatic testimony to his thoroughness and dependability. Then, the CIA had forced him to make the best of his circumstances with no other option, but now, the taking of a human life that had once been the ultimate high was reduced to the status of just another job. It would have remained so except for missing his main target in Chicago. He knew he had been ham-fisted with that one.

Before Houston, Caputo worked with a firearms ballistician to design the ultimate weapon for assassination—a weapon all experts said was impossible to manufacture, and for which the CIA paid the interior ballistics man a total of $3 million to produce. The discovery was a manufacturing technique that made it possible to create one or two high-powered rifles and handguns with identical markings to the bores before the temporary computer software failed. The Company provided him with the current mainframe methods of the era, and for months, he worked with ballistics, coefficiency and curve, with tables and waves, struggling with density to find the right path. The solution to the problem came almost by accident as many discoveries do, simply from an off-handed remark from Caputo. From that moment, the CIA took charge of all of the information, cautioning the expert to forget about the project regardless of any major news event. Two weeks later the man lost his life in a mysterious automobile crash never thoroughly scrutinized. Everyone in charge agreed that federal agents had interfered in the investigation, repudiating stronger evidence and intimidating the local authorities to close the case down.

Central Intelligence applied the newly discovered ballistic codes by developing a full arsenal of top-secret rifles and handguns, creating a vast munitions storehouse for use around the world many times, in a long series of unsolved murders. When Caputo made his hit in Houston, he used a local political organizer to take the fall for the outcome. He was a known activist and the first in a precise pattern to affix the blame for the murders. Caputo would go on to use the method frequently, with no discovery of his own existence.

He stationed himself outside a civic auditorium, sheltered from any observation by a half-dome sewer cover that was in a direct line to the on-coming motorcade. He placed his flunky in a vulnerable location where the convoy would pass. In his irregularly shaped shoulder case, Caputo carried a .38 caliber Smith & Wesson handgun, along with a powerful rifle that duplicated the ballistics of the one he gave to his partner. The activist was only to fire a distracting shot. Acting with precise synchronization, Caputo fired the fatal bullet and easily escaped through the large sewer line in the ensuing pandemonium. The patsy pleaded for his innocence, but matching ballistics showed his guilt, even after witnesses lined up, unsuccessfully, to testify, but were turned away. They all claimed they had heard another shot from much closer to the official, and from a different direction.

Sara Principle awoke from her nap somewhat refreshed and slightly more at ease with all that rattled around in her brain, but the concern over Allen's behavior persisted. Following their speeches, they would fly to Las Cruces and it would be all over except for Election Day. She would discuss it with him then, after getting some sleep on the plane. After tonight, they would not be seen in a TV interview at their home as previously reported, but correct that they would appear in downtown Las Cruces when they cast their votes and Allen gave a short speech. Allen also thought they would appear on television, but those plans were changed, and he would not know of it for three days. It would fall on Election Day, and the changed plans were all under his wife's directions.

When they left the hotel, Allen felt not only his own anxiety from the weight of the bulletproof vest, but also from his wife's sudden immersion into herself. It was completely out of character for her and he wanted to know the reason. But he would not ask until they were alone in New Mexico. She had enough on her mind for now. He knew she was preoccupied with something, but what it was he could not make sense of. She had not confided in him for some time. He wondered how she could have changed so rapidly.

She remained silent, seemingly transfixed with something mysterious. It was almost as if she had mentally seen their failure.

One block from the southeast corner of Centre and Grand Streets in New York City, General Wilson Keyes quietly assembled one dozen crack shooters to work with six of Dobrosky's agents. On the experienced feet of men used to conducting silent operations, they quietly began to reconnoiter the area, finding the black limousine parked outside the entrance to the huge warehouse building with the mansard roof. The driver was reading a newspaper. It was 1 a.m. One block north of the warehouse, Keyes and Dobrosky sat in a plain black van with the latest equipment to monitor everything that took place around the building.

"I'll tell you one thing, Wilson," said Dobrosky. "This thing is sure getting to be right out of the imagination of some *spy* novelist! If we made the facts known to the American people, I think they'd say it was completely unbelievable. I'm not sure *I* believe it, and without a doubt, no one is *ever* sure of you! Of course, this dog and pony show at this time of day is absurd. It's all because of booking the satellite for TV."

Keyes simply scowled as Dobrosky continued. "We've taken the necessary steps for Principle's protection, and we have three men watching that guy we think killed Robert Wilcox. If he makes a move, we'll get him. Hell, we'll get the motherfucker even if the goddamn son of a bitch *doesn't* try anything. He's *finished*!"

"*Congratulations*, Mo!" said Keyes. "Do you also know that he's been used in other operations and usually has someone working *with* him? I just found that out *myself* right before we met tonight."

"*What*? Shit!" Instantly Dobrosky was in a state of panic. He said, "Then I've got to get in touch with the boys out there! They have no idea the son of a bitch is part of a *team*! They think he' a *solo* hitter. Goddamn it Wilson, we don't need this shit! I have to get in touch with Fred first, and right *now*! Then I have to reach Joe Gaines out there in California. It's a hell of a lot to do, so let's hope I get to them so something *really* bad doesn't happen!"

At the Hollywood Bowl, Caputo watched the three agents. One was near the entrance and one was standing behind the last row of seats. The third agent was trying to look like a member of the audience. *He doesn't know*! *He's trying too hard*! *It gives him away*! One should never be too obvious, but no matter. He would be no problem at all. In fact, the agents were making the contest even more exciting—a splendid competition where Caputo would finally be the clear winner this time, just as he was used to being in the past. He had never made a hit in the presence of anyone who knew of his presence, but they did, and now they even had him in sight in spite of his disguise. They seemed to be waiting for him to make the first move. This would be the best he could ever have hoped for, and maybe, just maybe, he would pack it in when he was finished. But now he would have to lure the agent to a spot of Caputo's own choosing to make things ready for the kill to come, a choice made even earlier in the day when he did his walk around the entire Bowl.

He confirmed his earlier decision. Walking out through the main entrance toward the public restrooms on the outside of the actual Bowl, he determined the area would be perfect for what he had in mind. It was now dark with very dim lighting, and filled with enough people milling about who had not yet taken their seats on the inside. A small group of men congregated near the men's side of the restroom building, apparently waiting for one of their party. Caputo would do it there.

The agent followed at what he believed to be a discrete distance. Caputo suddenly veered off in the direction of the building, stopping abruptly by a group of shrubs and briefly out of sight. With lightning speed, he reversed the bright red jacket to the opposite side of black and tossed the beard and wig into a nearby clump of trees. He watched, then headed toward the building as the man inside rejoined his friends.

Just as quickly, the trailing agent lost sight of the red jacket. His target had simply vanished. He walked slowly, hesitatingly, toward the building, eyes darting from side-to-side. Once he stopped and spoke rapidly into his communicator. Fearful he had lost track of the man he was calling for help, but he first had to check the building.

Slowly he crept through the entrance, his body tense, cautious. No sound of voices or running water penetrated the night air to help the agent know for sure if Caputo was there. He decided that his quarry must have passed the building but he had to be certain. All at once, the soft movement of a foot behind the dividing wall of exit and entrance diverted his eyes. It was too late. He had rounded the end of the partition. His eyes never saw the glistening stiletto blade that was thrust sharply upward into his sternum and aorta, and then through his throat. He was dead before his body hit the floor.

Without hesitation or even a glance at his victim, Caputo wadded up the protective plastic that shielded him from the spurting blood and joined in with a group of people on the outside as if he were one of them. He engaged two of the men in conversation, and watched for a few seconds as another agent ran past, calling out to his partner through his communicator. He heard no response. Satisfied with what he saw, Caputo left the group and headed through the automobile entrance at Highland Avenue to move to his place in the Hollywood Hills. He smiled as he walked; energized from the fresh kill and from the one to come…the one he had missed in Chicago.

By now, Paul had already made his move and was comfortable on the roof of the small green building, ready for his part in the crime. Caputo had given him the handgun with the duplicate ballistics and reinstructed him to listen in his earpiece for coordination as to when to fire the distracting shot. The sounds of weapons fired from two distinct areas, Caputo told him, would allow the gay minister to get away in the excitement. Unknown to Caputo, however, was an important fact. Paul was getting into his role and wanted to make the hit himself. He just wished he could make it on Thomas Farley, the man he really loathed. If only he had the opportunity to take Farley out. Paul did not know the roof was not the safe place he thought it was, but Caputo knew. He had his own solitary exit from the city planned to the last detail. He overlooked nothing. As he made his way upward to his spot, Caputo laughed aloud at the stupidity of the gay minister, wishing he had Carlo with Paul. Then he would know that two homosexuals would go to prison for crimes neither had committed.

The affair in New York began as the capacity crowd listened to a rousing rendition of Stars and Stripes, the opening, identical number playing at the Hollywood Bowl. Colors of the flag abounded. All of the box seats were overflowing with personalities as familiar to Americans as their own families, and just as untouchable as the real stars in the sky. The atmosphere was electric. Now the show would begin.

Caputo was ready and Paul was in place, lying flat, completely out of sight. How he hated Sara Principle. Such a person did not deserve to live, and certainly not become the President of the United States. Even more, he hated the black professor—despised him with a heated repulsion of all that Farley stood for. If only he could have convinced Carlo to come here, then Paul would have tried to find a way to get Farley in New York. But no, his fat lover would not hear of actually shooting someone. *The black devil— the black heretic*! The black fiend would live to see another day, and Paul would have to deal with Carlo when he got back to New York.

Joe Gaines, the agent in charge of the Bowl detail, was speaking frantically on his communicator, screeching out for help. He found his partner with his throat slashed and his chest split open, lying in a pool of blood. Switching to a cell phone, Joe reached Dobrosky in nearly the same moment as when Mo had finished talking to Fred Spans and was preparing to phone Gaines with the new information.

"It's all *right*, Joe," said Dobrosky, trying to calm the distraught Gaines. "Don't worry! Find him. That's all you can do for now. I'm sorry."

"*Goddamn* it, Mo!" shouted Gaines. "Scott is *dead*, and we've got to call this whole fucking thing *off*! Don't you see what I'm *saying*? For Christ's sake, *Mo*, I don't even know where the son of a bitch is! He's vanished like a *goddamn puff of smoke*!"

"I know, Joe, but it isn't necessary. I've just talked to Fred and he has…" "*Goddamn it, Mo*! What the fuck is *wrong* with you? Don't you *understand?* We've *lost* the motherfucker! He's killed one of our men and we've lost him! He came here to kill Principle and by God, Mo, he's going to succeed! We have to call this *off*! You've got to have Fred get to Principle and make her *understand*!"

"Damn it, Joe," shouted Dobrosky. "Just shut up and *listen*! I'm sorry about Scott but there's nothing I can do for now, and there's nothing *you* can do. Fred's made plans outside of what we're doing and it's okay. Just try to find the guy and keep him under observation, but Principle won't *let* it be cancelled. I already *tried* that with Fred. Just find the son of a bitch if you can and keep him under surveillance, but don't *take* him 'til you hear from me or Fred! Repeat, don't *take* him!"

Dominick Caputo was at his secure hilltop sanctuary listening, as the orchestra finished its opening number. Everything was in place and ready for the final moment of the kill. He leaned against a small tree; eager for his move to come and secure in the knowledge his position was inviolate. The deathblow was ahead of schedule with the helpless situation of his opponents. He would amuse himself knowing the agents were in a state of panic. With only two men left to protect Sara Principle, he wondered how many frantic transmissions to home base were going on. When they captured Paul, they would know he was not the one, but they would convict him because of their need to protect an illusion of being moral, and life would go on as it always did for men such as these. It was always there, the need to protect the bogus appearance of being even-handed, forthright, and balanced.

Three thousand miles away on the Great Lawn, the point in time was set. As the strains of the same musical introduction that was being played simultaneously in the Bowl faded out, the New York audience gasped at the sight of Barbara Langdon, who walked out to the center of the platform, her arms lifted high.

"I know that my being here will surprise many of you who do not *know* me!" she shouted. "But I have been a personal friend and quiet supporter of Senator Principle for more than *twenty years*! I know what you're thinking! Not quite the nonpartisan you thought I was, right? Well, we *had* to keep it secret."

The roar was thunderous. The area was filled to overflowing, pushing the boundaries of the Great Lawn to capacity. It was not at all like a typical rally for a politician, with the exception being for Barack Obama in 2008 in Chicago. Once again, perception was reality to TV viewers and in person live. The stage was enormous, with giant screens and superior sound amplification. Hundreds of lights radiated, making the early morning hour more like a time for lunch.

"We have a gigantic *surprise* for you tonight!" she shouted over the blaring crowd. "It is a great coup for a great *city*! You came here expecting to hear some familiar names tell you why you should vote for Senator Principle. Well, that is true enough. You may have even thought *I* am a *liberal*. I'm not, and I am also not a *conservative*, but I do love this city, in spite of its communist ruling class. I also love what Senator Principle stands for, and that *does* include some *liberal* positions. Well, onward New York, because you also thought you would hear from the professor from the Golden State, Dr. Thomas Farley, and your own Governor, Jack Kayne. Well ladies and gentlemen, one part of that duo is here but not the other. Professor Farley is gearing up at this very moment to deliver his speech in his home state of California at the Hollywood Bowl! To repeat for those of you who might not have heard, Dr. Farley will be speaking in California!"

The audience reacted with a mixture of mild boos. "*No! No!*" she shouted. "We will not disappoint you! We really *won't*! We've made a slight change—a necessary, last minute change in light of recent events that have created great danger here for Dr. Farley, as surprising as that sounds. We have some fabulous entertainment for you, so settle back and enjoy the night, because this is *New York*! So now, give it up for your favorite Governor, *Jack Kayne*, who *will* be the next Vice President of the United States!"

"Ladies and gentlemen," said the speaker at the Hollywood Bowl. "We have a big surprise for you tonight. I know that many of you who *do* recognize me think I have been *against* the candidacy of Senator Principle from some of the articles I have written in my newspaper, The Albuquerque Sun, *and* from some ideas that have been *attributed* to me at the outset of her career. Well, I honestly have to tell you that those words had a *specific* and *definite* purpose, but I will not elaborate on that here in California. However, I assure you that I *do* support her wholeheartedly and my paper has endorsed her today. I also have to tell you that a change has become necessary. For her own safety and for our protection as well, Senator Principle will not be here tonight. It is simply too dangerous for *her*, and for all of *us*!"

Bill London waited for the roar of disapproval to subside, refusing to fight the audience for attention, and from his hilltop position, Dominick Caputo heard the statement and quickly bolted upright, watching the stage closely through binoculars.

"Instead," London continued, "we have one of your own with us. He is in fact an institution here in the Golden State. You all know him to be a professor on leave from the university. This change is essential for the welfare of both Senator Principle and one of your featured speakers, Dr. Thomas *Farley*. Please welcome him."

At the mention of Farley's name, Paul snapped his head higher in the darkness. His eyes pierced through the air full of hate and rage. So much the better…they had done him a favor. Slowly he raised his weapon, gripping it so tightly his hands began to shake, completely forgetting his role in the assassination attempt, and not even hearing Caputo's voice through his earpiece to abort the mission.

Jack Kayne spoke and others entertained on the Great Lawn. The New York Governor repeated several of his renowned diatribes against the president and her giveaway administration. Expectations were high as Barbara Langdon returned once more to center stage.

"Ladies and gentlemen," she shouted. "It is now time for a *very* special speaker who has also been on my television show. He is one of the finest actors in the *world*, and my *friend*! Please give *a city that never sleeps* welcome to *Allen Davis*!"

The confident, purposeful stride was unmistakable, as Allen walked to the center of the stage. Seen on countless movie screens and live stage productions for more than twenty-five years, he was nearly without equal. Few performers commanded the same level of respect and admiration. He had said no to any compromise throughout his life, and always refused to alter his appearance, except for the stage or in movies. He said to take him for what he was with all of his *warts*. He wanted no confusion between the real Allen Davis and the roles they saw him play.

He stood proudly before the mass of people, his hands held loosely by his side, standing in the presence of his largest live audience. The applause enveloped his senses in ways he had never before experienced or considered, filling him with awe. *This is not the same*! *It is unbelievable*!

"Ladies and gentlemen," he said repeatedly, in a futile attempt to quiet the crowd. His cries for silence fell on the deaf ears of people who demanded they be heard for as long as they chose to roar and applaud. Before the cheers slowly subsided, he stood at center stage for a full five minutes, hearing the ovation, and then he began to speak.

"I have not come here tonight to be in the spotlight for myself or my craft. My role on this very early morning is *supportive*. It is as a man who cares deeply about the rights of *all* people to live in peace and freedom, *and* to live in the country our ancestors bequeathed us. I am also here to tell you that we do not have that kind of country, and we haven't had it for a very long time. But we *can* have it again. We really can, and I am married to the woman who will help us get it *back*!

"I am here to tell you that Sara Principle is a woman committed to the ethical and high-minded principles established in this land more than two hundred forty-years ago. Our Founding Fathers introduced ideas that this nation, this wonderful land of mixtures and natural resources originally enshrined as a place for freedom and *individual* rights, will continue to live on after we have departed, and that we the people will prevail and *return* to those ways. They *did* make mistakes. No one goes through life perfect, but their missteps were extremely small when compared to the *intentional* ones of yesterday, today, and at this very hour!

"If you believe in liberty, stand *with* us. If you believe your life and property are yours, and not the governments, stand *with* us. Stand with us if you believe in the real McCoy idea! If you believe that you may walk this earth as your own master, stand *with* us, because you have only one choice to support that point-of-view. It is therefore my honor to introduce your *featured* speaker. She is the one force who will stand with *you*! She is the *only* candidate who will not sell your rights down the river of political opportunism. Ladies and gentlemen, I present to you my wife, the next President of the United States of America, *Senator Sara Principle*!"

He waited while she crossed the platform, embracing her, as he had never done before in public. She was so much more than just his wife. He kissed her softly and then took his place on the front row of seats, still feeling the weight of the bulletproof vest on his body, and her striking aloofness on his mind.

The standing ovation continued unabated for many minutes. Several times the orchestra tried to interrupt the audience approval with short bursts of rapid-fire Stars and Stripes music used in their opening number, but nothing would stop the crowd. They were jubilant; needing to burst their lungs for the one person, they believed would bring them what they wanted. Others had come before with the promise of change, but the wrong change. This time it would be a different and bigger tale. Now the politicians would lose and the people would win. Not yes, I can, but yes, I will!

Hordes of individuals from the swelling army of The Solution members and non-members had taken valuable time from their jobs and families to attend the function. Their goal was to put on a show of unity and to send their message across the country. Americans should get used to the inevitability of her election. The will of the people would prevail this time around. The most recent polls indicated the election was too close to call, but the volunteers believed they knew more than any pollster did. They knew the big voting method that was only now starting to earn a glimpse of notoriety on the back pages of newspapers and television news programs. It was not a trend, they said, but perhaps reporters should monitor it more carefully.

Following the show of support, Principle spoke for ten minutes, repeating her familiar theme of the evils of big government and calling for an all-out effort throughout the nation. They must send the message to the towns and cities and farms, and then they must bring it to Washington to declare that the time for taking the people and their just rights for granted was finished. The people would win this time, and the old style of progressive conservatives and progressive liberal positions would lose, and that even included a rehabilitated New York state.

In her closing she said, "I want to talk with you now about two things that I have said repeatedly. Not just in this election, but in all of the rest of them I have ever been in—the Constitution, and the fact that our country was created as a federal democratic *republic*, not a democracy, not a *progressive* democracy or a *representative* democracy. The difference is *huge*, and you need an understanding of that distinction! There is no more important concept in the United States of America today. Believing we are a democracy gave us our previous and present political opportunists.

"For many years your leaders, your trusted news people, and those who teach your children have succeeded in *obliterating* the Constitution while they *sold* you and your kids on the words, democracy, conservatism, liberalism and progressivism, because they discovered those words are somehow more meaningful to you than a *federal democratic republic*. They also decided that you are not smart enough to know the difference, and even think they are the *same*. They are not. When you recite the Pledge of Allegiance you do not say, and to the *democracy* for which it stands, do you? The word you use is republic. That is because a democracy is *not* a rule of law system of governance no matter how much you want it to be, because it is *majority* rule, which many of you think is a good thing. It isn't, and the Constitution provides several *undemocratic* features for a *reason*, starting with the Electoral College and senators appointed by their state. It *prevents* majority rule, along with other parts we will correct.

"In a rule by the majority, so-called public money is transferred from some individuals to other individuals to appease fifty-*one percent* of the population, but not the *entire* population; just the fifty-one percent of people who *vote*! That gives them power, and that power leads to never ending spending to buy your vote with your own money. In return, the perception is that majority rule is a good thing. It is not, and democracy, in its truest definition, is *unlimited collectivism*, or *statist* power!

"Now for some history…Thomas Jefferson began to realize the direction of the new government as regards the spending of money in 1778, and he did not like it. In a letter to the Virginia Senator John Taylor, he wrote these lines."

'I wish it were possible to obtain a single Amendment to our Constitution. I would be willing to depend on that alone for the reduction of our government to the genuine principles of its Constitution; I mean an additional Article, taking borrowing ability away from the federal government.'

"Don't you think Jefferson knew more than today's politicians? That was a simple solution answer to what our government does day in and day out. It incurs debt because it exercises the raw power to *force* us to give it money for bad and *illegal* policy. I remember listening to President Nixon give his first inaugural address when I was a girl. This is what he said in part.

'We have shared our wealth more broadly than ever. We have learned at last to manage a modern economy to assure its continued growth.

'In this past third of a century, government has passed more laws, spent more money, and initiated more programs, than in all our previous history.

'We shall plan for the day when our wealth can be transferred from the destruction of war abroad to the urgent needs of our people at home.'

"This was a Progressive *Republican* president *admitting* to a progressive approach to government with transfer payments that progress *beyond* the Constitution, just like *Barack Obama* and Hadley R. Crawford. It was incredible that Nixon chose to fess up to what was mostly unknown. Usually they try *not* to admit it just like Obama did. On the other hand, Obama slipped up in 2013 by admitting that if you had $3 million in retirement that was enough money for you. So think about it, because it isn't difficult to figure out if you just give it some *logical* thought. Listen closely. Free people do not need to have their money *managed* by anything more technical than a free market and their *own* decision. Going *beyond* the Constitution is what created the great recession of 2008 *and* the Great Depression in 1929. Free markets do not employ the use of force in any way. Free markets are *voluntary*. *All* of the transfer of wealth not authorized by the

Constitution is, and always will be, illegal, regardless of how much you might like a particular program. What creates that program—what makes the transfer possible, is *force*, and government *is* force.

"Former Senator, Phillip Hart, who was from the state of Michigan, said this long ago. 'It is not politically hard for me to vote against say, a new aircraft carrier. But if the shipyard were in my state and five thousand people were waiting for work, I would be examining very closely, and perhaps less critically, all those reasons why the carrier might be essential to national security.'

"What he really meant was this: the taxpayer money that was used to create those jobs probably meant five thousand votes for *Phillip Hart*, because that's what it's all about with professional politicians...*votes*!

"Many presidents are very inventive with words. President Bill Clinton started to say invest, not spend, because the two words have different *connotations*. This took deception to a new and more creative level not seen before Clinton's time, even by FDR. Obama expanded Clinton's dishonesty with the words, *saved* or *created*, and more *revenue* instead of higher *taxes*. Is this lying? *You* make that decision.

"The major point I'm trying to make is this: The only people who deserve your vote are those who will not spend *your* money to further *their* ambitions!"

As Allen rushed to her side, he was unaware of the news from California. Barbara Langdon was distraught, trying to get Principle to hear what she was screaming about over the noise of the crowd, and then she heard. Thomas Farley was in the hospital after having been shot in California, but Principle could not go there. She would board a plane in New York for an extremely long flight that would require two days, and had to be completed before Election Day. The flight would take her to her second face-to-face meeting with one of the men who could start World War III.

EIGHTEEN

Mo Dobrosky's office transmitted an urgent message to the van in New York. President Crawford was looking for Wilson Keyes, and it was serious. The Pentagon had received numerous directives from the White House, and there could be no acceptable reason for delay. Keyes was to report to the president at once. Unknown to either Dobrosky or Keyes was the knowledge that Crawford knew of their location and mission. The order was simply one part of Crawford's strategy to gain control of Keyes with a presidential summons. It would shake up the world of everyone who worked with and for the gruff general.

They quickly agreed to stop the operation. Keyes must respond, but he also wanted to be in on the rescue of the agent and arrest of Cantrell, if it was possible to arrange. At this point they would do everything they could to placate the president. All was in readiness to keep Cantrell sequestered until after the inauguration, and then, the D/CIA would go on trial for treason, along with other officials.

Crawford met with William Patterson, the Director of the FBI, as they awaited the arrival of General Keyes. Patterson's agents were conducting an intensive interrogation of Chet Forbes in the study adjacent to the Oval Office, the study made famous by Bill Clinton. The facts were clear. The press secretary was the only person to have direct access to the treaty. No possibility existed to circumvent the incriminating evidence against him, and he might as well make his complete confession now.

The president was eager to confront the defiant general. The harsh sound of the buzzer alerted Crawford to Keyes' arrival, while Director Patterson moved to the study where he would further interrogate Chet Forbes and wait for the President's signal to re-enter the Oval Office, and deal with the powerful general.

Keyes wanted to get down to business with Crawford and return to the warehouse. He did not like the president, but he would tolerate her, as one would indulge any set of circumstances in which nothing of value could be firmly achieved, except the necessary time to pass on to other business. And it was the other business that was uppermost in the General's mind. If only he could get along with the woman as he had managed to do for a few months at the start of the administration, but the need of both people for power had helped to degrade their rapport that even included the Secretary of Defense. Now Keyes especially despised Crawford, and the feeling was mutual for the president. In this meeting, Keyes believed he would make short order of Crawford and get back to New York, for there was still much left for them to do in a quickly vanishing timeframe.

Wilson Keyes was a four-star general who had served his nation for thirty-five years. Due to his own successful maneuvering at the time, he became the most logical consideration for the Joint Chiefs Chairman for political reasons. Now, however Keyes, the defense secretary and the president all knew their time together would see a natural end as customary after the second term began. Keyes had achieved his post with great aplomb in the quest of The Solution to infiltrate the inner workings of the administration, and became a driving force in the accumulation of essential intelligence for their own political agenda.

An exceedingly large man, Wilson Keyes stood nearly six feet nine. He openly scorned all public notoriety, preferring to command the notice of other public figures with an unrivaled physical presence. Speculation abounded that Keyes was even more powerful with the military than either the president or the secretary, maintaining his own special cadre of influence in all branches of the service. On this day, the general did not know that the meeting he was called for would not be one of the typical occasions where the president would continue to remain intimidated. Today, Crawford would finally complete her specific purpose—a tour de force she had long coveted where Keyes was concerned. No longer would the fiery general find a reticent Hadley R. Crawford unwilling to exercise her considerable authority and power as had been the case in the past. This was to be the President's day, with a bold move against a powerful adversary.

As their personal animosity grew exponentially, they decided to see less and less of each other, and now the huge general was there, glaring down at the president as he always did after arriving at the presidential desk on his giant two-for-one strides. It was what Keyes intentionally did when he was infuriated, knowing that his size would quickly define his authority, as he so obviously wanted to do at this moment. Now things were different, and he would not be particular in how he dealt with Crawford, whose presidential days were numbered as far as Wilson Keyes was concerned. He would enjoy making the president feel embarrassment, and he would do it quickly, with no consideration for the office of president or for Crawford personally.

Keyes spoke first and said, "Madam President, I came here because you so ordered, but also for another purpose of my own, and I want to get to that now. I'm here to inform you that if you actually *win* this election, I will not be available to continue in my present capacity. I have not yet discussed the matter with the secretary or anyone else at the Pentagon, but I will in due course. You may even find that he is not happy too, so I ask that you be brief, as I'm on a tight schedule. It's very early in the morning, so let's not beat around the bush with polite pretense. We both know where we stand with each other."

He remained standing, pointedly refusing the silent hand gesture by the president to sit down. He glared at Crawford to force a response. When none was forthcoming, Keyes continued. He said, "I think you will *lose* this election, and quite frankly I hope that you *do*. So let's get on with it. I need to get back to what I was doing before you summoned me, and I do not have time for unimportant things."

Crawford smiled and continued to look upward. She knew Keyes would persist with his belligerent insult, but she wanted him to see that this was a different Hadley R. Crawford—a confident president the aggressive military man had never seen, and she also wanted to savor the moment of power she had never before displayed with the huge military man.

Finally, Crawford spoke. "General," she said, "I am aware of many things that go on in my administration, and you would be wise to remember that fact. Having said that let me just add that things are not going to go well for you today...not well at all. Rest assured, General, I am acutely aware of your dislike for me, and yes, the feeling *is* mutual. There will be no pretense."

She paused, using the silence to her fullest advantage. Now she had the upper hand, and the general was where the Chief had wanted him to be for a long time. She would amuse herself for a short while and play with Keyes' exorbitant use of power. Wilson Keyes was about to experience the wrath of a presidential hammer crashing down on his head, but he did not know it, nor did he think it was even possible from this president. In Keyes' mind, this would be just another day where he would continue to have his way, but he was wrong. This was to be Crawford's day. This was a time of retribution and payback. For the very first moment in the nearly four years of her presidency, she did not feel inferior to the powerful Wilson Keyes, and as she thought about it she suddenly wondered why she had been so afraid of her own underling in the first place. She quietly made a vow to give it some serious thought later on.

"I am also well-versed about something else, General," she said, speaking very slowly and deliberately. "I am *wise* to the conspiracy in my own administration from you and others, and I am also aware of your *present* objective." She leaned backward, her hands clasped behind her neck, her body now free of all tension. This was wonderful. Her day of justice and tit-for-tat had arrived, and it was the most delicious of any moment she had known for a very long time.

The astonishment on the face of Wilson Keyes was genuine. As Crawford had suspected he would be, the general was dumfounded and stunned by Crawford's words. He quickly made a decision. He decided to go on the attack like the military man he was, and regain the upper hand by ignoring what she said, even as he knew it would not happen just from the expression on her face.

"Madam President," he said, haltingly, cautiously trying to mask the uncertainty he felt from his voice. "Before we go on I want to tell you something you will not enjoy hearing, but I will certainly take great pleasure in telling you.

"Regardless of what you *think* you know your position is at best tenuous. We both know it, so let's not try to *kid* each other. You are going to *lose*, and I hope you *do*; but if you're thinking about using the military in any way, forget it, because it will not work. I *guarantee* it."

Crawford smiled even more broadly and said, "I'm pleased that you've decided to be so candid General. I understand your position, and now you will understand mine. It's going to be a delight on my part, to watch you over the next few minutes.

"Soon, I will re-introduce you to a man you are already acquainted with, and I think you dislike almost as much as you hate me, and I *do* know that you hate me. However, my positive numbers have returned and I think you're wrong...but that doesn't matter.

"The message of the quadripartite is not what you think it is. Its purpose is not to give me power. Yes, that will happen, just as it does when one reaches *this* office, but that is not its principal objective.

"Since the development of recent space technology, along with all of the sophisticated *new* weaponry, high-level meetings have taken place—*secret* meetings to prevent a nuclear blowup and maintain some control of North Korea. You have not been part of them, but those discussions are continuing. They are also about the ongoing proliferation of terrorism, the legacy handed down by one of your pals in the Republican Party, George W. Bush, along with other matters that put us in great danger. However, I will not discuss them with *you*. Whether you like it or not, the agreement for the new alliance is essential regardless of *who* is in this office, and it *will* go to the Senate. Oh, I know it won't be an *easy* sell, but we still control the Senate, and the movement *is* necessary for our nation's long-term survival, and it is up to me to *make* it happen. The change has to take place, and it must be *soon*."

Keyes was furious. For years, he had listened to the rumors, but never before had he witnessed this kind of arrogance at the presidential level. It was inexcusable, and certainly intolerable. Even Crawford could not believe what she was saying.

"Madam President," said Keyes, scowling ferociously, his hands extended above his head. "That is the highest pile of horseshit I *ever* heard! You *can't* be serious. If you're talking about a possible invasion of the Middle East or Europe, you can't sell that crap to me under *any* set of circumstances! We've been *over* this! You know the Russians and Chinese are not capable of such a thing! You *know* it! That's just a figment of your imagination and an intelligence ploy by Zgonina and Tso to use you, and you've taken the bait! You are walking down a road that has never happened in America. It's *incredible*!"

"It may be incredible, but it is also true. It's been true for some time now General."

"And what would they expect from America? They know we wouldn't allow it. They also know that Europe is primarily a People's State, and China is more collectivist than *we* are, if that's even possible. Europe doesn't *have* a credible military! Have you lost your *mind*? This would be completely unbelievable from *anyone*, but it's even more so coming from the President of the United States!"

Suddenly Keyes' expression changed from a look of anger to one that seemed to show he had just discovered something new that he had not considered. Yes, that had to be it. His voice became a whisper as he said, "You're going to use this trumped-up charge for your own political *lust*, aren't you? That's *it*, isn't it? It's all part of a complex *ruse*! Just what the fuck are you trying to pull?"

Crawford was astonished. She stood and then began to pace back and forth. She turned her back to Keyes because she wanted to be certain to hide her face that might have a telltale expression. Keyes was turning out to be more astute than Crawford thought he could be. Still overall, it was a perfect day with a cool temperature. Believing she had fully composed herself and retained the ability to continue the subterfuge she turned, glaring at Keyes.

"*General*" she said, a confident and steadfast sneer on her lips. "I know you think you're privileged to know just about everything of a military nature that happens in this government, but you are *wrong*. One of the problems the world has had is that military geniuses like you have kept humanity in a constant stage of armed conflict. That is now *over*! Never again will people like you have access to power. There are events that are unfolding behind closed doors, General. Things you know nothing about. Diplomatic discussions, decisions, and yes, I *will* win this election and there is not a damn thing you or your conservative buddies can do about it.

"I'm telling you this because I want you to know that I am aware of the secret plot against me, and because I wanted to see your stupid face when you hear me tell you. I also know that a secret group does not do what they do because it is in the best interest of America, but because it is in their *own* best interest. This is a mad world, General. It's made even madder by men like you! It's up to people like me to find a way out of the military insanity, and that's exactly what I *am* doing and what I will *keep* doing! If I'm not successful, the world will not survive. Make no mistake, General. The only way out of this mess to prevent a major catastrophe is for the enactment of the treaty. The threat of war is *very* real no matter *what* you think.

"Both President Zgonina and General Tso have no *personal* ambition to invade. They are men of peace, but they are hamstrung by a bunch of old men in positions of power and by military idiots like *you*! Zgonina has tried to change official opinion in the independent states but he has *failed,* and he knows it. In fact, I must tell you that I'm expecting a call from him soon, which is why I am up this early. Now you know that I see your position clearly, but also know that I am no longer intimidated. Now, you will see *my* position clearly."

In one smooth motion, Crawford walked to the study door. She opened it and said, "General, I believe you know Mr. William Patterson and some of his colleagues." Keyes watched, as the head of the FBI walked into the Oval Office followed by his agents, pushing Chet Forbes ahead and in front of them.

As they encircled the astonished general the president said, "You see General, I also have people who are loyal to *me*! You and Mr. Forbes would not be in your present position if you had exercised the same good judgment. I do not like you General. I saw to your appointment out of political considerations, which was *my* mistake, but I do not like you, and it will please me greatly to get *rid* of you. You are a very greedy man who is concerned only with yourself and military power and to hell with anyone who gets in your way.

"And you had better hope that I *do* win. If I don't, all of my people tell me that Principle will not accept the treaty. If that happens, there may be no world left for *any* of us. For now, though, you, Mr. Dobrosky, and Mr. Forbes go off to Camp David, confined like the common criminals you are. If I'm still the president when the election is over, you will all be tried for treason. If I'm not, well then, it might not even matter, but *your* days of holding command are *finished* General. Never again will you have *any* power!"

Wilson Keyes was aghast. He looked as if an army tank had just run over him, leaving tracks across his body.

Crawford said, "Don't look so surprised General. I *am* the president, and as such am fully capable of keeping track of people. Did you think your movements were not monitored? Right now, while we are talking, the Director's men have taken control of that warehouse in New York. The only person who successfully misled me was Mr. Forbes. So now General, I bid you good day. Kindly go with Mr. Patterson. As I said, I'm expecting a call from President Zgonina, and you may not hear any part of that conversation. However, you might want to think about *this* while you are in captivity! When the votes are in, I will be winning re-election! Think about *that* General, while you are at Camp David waiting for your *trial*."

Crawford sat at her desk and waited. She was pleased when the voice of Casimir Zgonina came through the secure line. Even with all of the modern technology and security at her disposal, the president always marveled at the clarity of hearing someone from so far away.

"My dear President Crawford," said Zgonina. "It is good to hear your voice. From all of the reports I have received about your election, I see that your standing is better—that it has dramatically improved, for which I congratulate you. However, I must bring your attention to the gravity of the moment that is now here, and one in which very serious consequences *can* occur. It is not what either of us desire, even though it is the reality of our time, and must be dealt with now. It is severe. It must be handled quickly!" Zgonina nodded to his guest seated across the desk from him.

"I believe," he said, "that my previous communications with you and the others has not left a lasting imprint—that you are not convinced of the terrible things that will occur if you are *not* re-elected and the treaty *fully* implemented. There is unanimous and *stupid* agreement in the Central Committee to invade and occupy, and so I fear it may happen. If it does, we *will* partner with General Tso who will conquer Arabia, even if that means they will have to confront *your* troops in the area, and of course we know they will."

Crawford listened, her mind unable to visualize such an act. Even though she was convinced the threat of war was just a threat, all of the different phases of intelligence revealed it might be more than that. In every fantasy the president had ever felt, she could not have predicted the state of secret tension that now held court in the world. She was also unable to see the sly, nearly sinister smile moving to the corners of Zgonina's lips, where he inserted, and lit another cigarette. He stared at his visitor and waited for Crawford's response to his explicit warning.

When the president remained silent, Zgonina continued. He said, "I must also inform you that the Central Committee issued a directive that is in line with the other heads of state, and that is they will not stand for any corresponding action from America, even as I know you will be *forced* to respond in kind. So, you see, if you lose there will most surely be a war, especially in the Middle East, where, as we know, oil is king. Speaking of kings, Tso will remove *all* the Arab kings from power. Consequently, I must make this suggestion for—please forgive me, a *final* solution. Unless you can assure me of your victory beyond any *reasonable* doubt, this is my plan. I admit to you it is not a good plan, but it is a plan nonetheless, and I strongly urge you to give it your best consideration.

"In a few hours we will make it appear that we are beginning troop movements, something that will clearly take a great deal of time. The only statements from General Tso will be in support of the operation. You will call for an emergency session of the Security Council. Historically your people do not change presidents during a time of crisis as long as one of the candidates is already in office. It therefore holds that if we create an even *greater* climate of fear, your victory will be assured and we will have our *treaty*."

Crawford's face suddenly paled to a ghostly white, completely without color except for the bright redness that erupted on the back of her neck—a crimson color of anger that made her instinctively lean forward, her elbows super-glued to the surface of her desk. A heated flare-up of a rush of mixed emotions burst through her brain from the insinuation by the Russian. Crawford was a woman of peace. She had used fear, but only for political advantage, never for personal gain. Any such action that Zgonina was threatening would violate all of her standards of ending war. She would not allow it to take place.

Her political history flashed before her in vivid waves of disaster and carnage—of untold nights of lost sleep over such a cataclysmic event taking control of everything she had ever worked to achieve. It seemed as though the world was falling apart; crashing down around her like a dangerous bet in a high-stakes game of poker, and Zgonina was calling her hand by raising the wager with a 2 a.m. phone call.

"*Casimir*!" she pleaded, suddenly blurting out the Russian's name. "If I lose, and there is *every* reason to believe that will *not* happen, you must rise *above* politics. You *cannot* allow yourself to be held hostage by a few old men in the Central Committee with no vision or brainpower to logically inform them of the consequences."

She quickly thought of how she would end the power of the *Group* after the election, but decided she must not say such things to the cunning Zgonina. "You need to think about the *Group*, Casimir," said Crawford. "Remember this—there has never been a president who did not eventually come to terms with them! It is almost a *foregone* conclusion. The American people do not know this, but you and I *do*! Senator Principle may, when faced with the awesome responsibilities of this office and the complete naturalness of the federation agree, and come to a full support of the treaty's implementation. Also, do you remember that quiet conversation we had when I told you in person how I would be able to be a lot more accommodating after the election?

"But I really do think we're jumping the gun. I haven't lost yet, and I'm *certain* I will win. So I repeat. Don't *do* it! Wait for the results! *Please*! Even if Principle wins, what is the point…mass suicide? We cannot let it come to that. If you do this thing, Casimir, you will have gone too far and I will not be able to stand with you, treaty, or no treaty." Crawford's expression tightened to a firm resolve. She said with finality, "And when push comes to shove the others will desert you too…even *Tso*."

With the pervasive cigarette smoke swirling around his face, Zgonina pressed the button to cut off the connection, pleased that his guest had heard the entire conversation over the speakerphone.

"Mr. President," said the visitor. "As you are aware, you and I are the only people other than our aides who know of our *first* meeting *and* this one. Let's keep it that way. There must be no leaks whatsoever. This knowledge must come only from me. Agreed?"

"Yes, I do agree."

"And do not underestimate me, sir. I will keep the bargain we've made. If you do not, rest assured that what I've told you *will* happen, and I will not be the one who regrets your decision. If you *do* keep the agreement you will reap benefits beyond your wildest *dreams*. And that is a promise I think you *know* is true."

Zgonina reflected, watching the smoke from his cigarette as it drifted upward and said, "I am pleased that we are able to do business. I look forward to the good results, but if Crawford *does* win, the quadripartite *will* become a reality, so you see, either way I cannot lose, but I much prefer our arrangement.

"Thank you for making this very long and possibly dangerous trip, Senator."

NINETEEN

CBS news decided to air the story on the same day Crawford and Zgonina held their telephone conversation. They made the commitment early in the day to go with the unfolding, dramatic events, using network promotion time every half-hour to tantalize viewers. The promo tease was about a major story that might become an even greater surprise to every American and turn out to be a bigger chronicle of the nation than the election or the political parties. It quickly made the rounds to other news outlets on radio and television.

Terry O'Neil read an apology from the White House at the start of the evening news about the injury he had sustained during the debacle of the second debate. He then reported that it had been beyond the President's personal control. O'Neil was satisfied and began with his usual, "Welcome to the news of the day" greeting.

"It has long been the practice of this and other networks to conduct exit polls, especially in presidential years, and this year will be no exception. It does seem likely, however, that the biggest story may not come from these exit polls this time. Another event that may overshadow not just the polls but also the election itself is the incredible size of the absentee ballot all over the nation. The number of votes coming in through the mails amazes political veterans. These are not just isolated cases, but *everywhere*, urban *and* rural. We have reports from a few key states. Before we bring them to you, here is some additional information that may give you a better understanding with what *seems* to be taking place.

"Never before have so many people chosen the mails for their vote. This is due in part to the fact that all states now allow *early* voting. Some reports have pegged it to be sixty percent to seventy percent of the total vote, which would make it historical to any previous year and well ahead of the *thirty* percent total in 2004. It also appears that an equally large upsurge in travel is underway for this time of the year, so far ahead of Thanksgiving, with hotels reporting no vacancies in many areas not known for those kinds of numbers, and not just in cities. However, we do not know if they are in any way tied to the election. Perhaps it is something else, but online reservations for all forms of travel and lodging increased rapidly six months ago.

"We *do* know this campaign is one of the most vicious on record, and poll watchers cannot accurately measure voting trends because of the incredible size of the absentee ballot. This is so serious that we may not even be able to call the winners. It may have reached what some might call epidemic proportions, depending of course on your personal point-of-view. In this year, like no other this correspondent can recall, there seems to be a changing nature in the political landscape that is far-reaching and mysterious. I can also tell you it is very exciting for all of the reporters who are covering the candidates. We have several reports, beginning with Jed Coltrane in the heart of the Chicago Loop."

"Terry," said Coltrane. "I'm standing here at the intersection where the tragic murder of Robert Wilcox took place just five weeks ago. I have talked to many people about the election, and most of them are not concerned at all. The national races have always taken a back seat to the local contests, and one gets the very strong feeling that Chicagoans mostly care about what happens here—that it doesn't really matter who is president, only who is the *mayor*. They also say it has *always* been that way here, except when President *Obama* ran."

Reports continued much in the same vein throughout the first five minutes of the program. Even the most experienced reporters were befuddled. They heard people overwhelmingly tell them they would go to the polls on Election Day, with very few using the absentee ballot route. The stories did not match up with known facts, but reporters had no answers and no explanations for the contradictions.

On the morning after the Great Lawn spectacular, Allen awoke in Las Cruces at 8 a.m. A brilliant November sun blazed across the un-curtained bedroom windows in a dazzling display of illumination and warmth. Suddenly he realized he was alone. No sound came from the rest of the house. The lack of footsteps or television did not surprise him. Sara was probably out for a walk around the grounds to think and reflect about the possible results on Election Day, and the necessary steps for an orderly transition of power if she actually won. She might even be working on tightening up the Big Speech.

He decided to take a shower. When she returned, he would seduce her. Forty-five minutes later he was still alone and starting to get anxious. She was never this long, and he could not see her from any of the windows. He abandoned his original idea and went to the kitchen to make coffee. Then he saw it. Leaning against the coffeemaker where she knew he would go first was a note. Quickly his fear of her recent mood swing gripped him. She never left notes. He snatched it up. The first line had the opposite effect of its intended purpose. "My love," the note began. "Please do not worry because I'm not here. I am fine, and after what I finally thought, I want you to know that.

"This morning it finally hit me, but I didn't want to wake you. I've been worried about you and what I was thinking were some fears of yours, and then it dawned on me that you were probably doing the same thing about *me*. I'm sorry. I guess we just missed talking about it with all of the excitement in Central Park. One of us should have known, but I guess we were too tired or too excited, or both.

"I called the hospital. Thomas is okay. The wound wasn't serious, and he'll get out in a day or two. They caught the shooter. He's an unlikely fellow, though, a member of the clergy. It sure *surprised* me, and no one knows *anything* about him. They have no idea how or why he managed or even wanted to do this. It's a complete mystery to everyone. I'll be home sometime on Election Day. Armando is with me."

Just what in the hell is going on? She had not told him of any travel plans. Why had she left without telling him? The television people were supposed to be coming later in the day for one last conversation. Allen twisted and interlocked his fingers, remembering Robert Wilcox and the emotional effect it had on his wife. He wanted it to end...now and forever! It was no longer worth it! *Sara! Where are you?*

He dialed the Washington number. Before the first ring had finished its cycle, he answered.

"Allen?"

No surprise—no astonishment in his voice—he was *waiting* for his call! He *knew* it was Allen! Something was wrong.

"Russell," he said. "I just got out of bed only to find that Sara has gone. She left a note that makes no sense whatsoever. I had some important things to talk to her about and now she's *gone*! What is going on? Do you know?"

"Yes Allen, I do. I spoke to her right before she left Las Cruces. She thought you'd call. So did I, but she just didn't want to wake you, especially since you went to L.C. on separate flights at the last minute."

"All right," he said his voice hesitant and unsure. "I can accept that for now. Where did she go? Why didn't she say?"

"She wants no trace of where she is."

"Why?"

"Why doesn't she want any trace? I can only tell you that the reason is it's too *dangerous*."

"What does *that* mean, Russell? If that's the case she *still* should've woke me up. So what does it *mean*?"

"I cain't *say*, Allen, and I think that you should remember a few things to know *why* I cain't say anything."

"I'm getting really tired of this Russell, and I want to know where my wife is. So which is it, can't or won't?"

"*Won't*, but she's absolutely safe and the less you know about it the safer it is just in case somethin' *does* go wrong. But it won't."

"All right, Russell, I think I see." He wavered, remembering the bugs that were in the house and said, "Then let me ask you this, Russell. Can you get in touch with her?"

"No Allen, I cain't. I'm not tryin' to be *evasive*, but your questions just cain't be answered *now*!"

"What's it all about, Russell? Can you at least tell me *that* much? If I've ever been pissed off in my life, this is it!"

"I cain't say, even to you, but it doesn't have anything to do with keepin' *you* in the dark. There are other matters. But if what she's doin' is successful it'll really be somethin,' man oh man!"

"Then that means you *can* get in touch with her."

"No, Allen, I cain't get in touch…I really *cain't*! I wish I could for your sake. Please take my word, I just cain't."

"Okay Russell. I'll go along for now. Do you think she'll say where she's been when she gets back?"

"I'm not sure…probably. Maybe not, though, but it's a really long trip and she'll be really tired. More than you've ever seen by a substantial stretch, so be prepared."

He replaced the receiver. Visions of more than forty-years flooded his emotions—intense, powerful images of the long and sometimes torturous path to the present moment. She was an extremely complex woman, tormented at times by her own intellect. He was still learning new things and new ideas from her. Now he was angry. She should have told him, but she must have a very good reason. At least the way she was preoccupied was not serious. The knowledge of that important piece of the puzzle made him feel less tense, but still with some anger and questions left for her to answer when she returned.

He thought about the people who would not go inside the voting booth. They were the supplemental, the deciding factor; The Solution Factor for the ultimate victory of a long effort that would fulfill the dream of an army of members across America with a legion that had grown exponentially and swelled to number millions of individuals and tens of thousands full-time groups.

The Solution had spent many years organizing in every state to expand legislation for mail-in voting based on the successful Oregon model. Afterward, they turned their attention to lobbying for Internet voting. Their own computer expert, Joseph Jacobson, whose business had been saved so long ago by Russell Harrington, worked to develop a complex system to protect everything electronic to defeat all government spying programs like PRISM, and make their data disappear while being collected. Thousands of members believed in the dream and knew exactly what they were doing to reach the goal; leveraging millions more to simply follow with the members who had brought them in to the alliance to do some of the work, as had been done openly within the two parties. They were now a full-fledged parallel to Republicans and Democrats, while remaining top-secret.

The inspiration for the final run germinated from a presidential race many years before, although that was minute by comparison. The concept of the absentee voter being a pivotal component to the level it would be this year would shake the foundations of old-style politics forever, just as the original Obama campaign of 2008 changed the way donor contributions were obtained. Now the system would never be the same again, and the absentee voter could become its own driving force in the future. Networks would make projections based on what they could determine through exit polls, but the staggering size of all of the mail-in ballots would alter the results. In this election, the majority of those votes would go to Sara Principle. Regardless of the tally, both sides might challenge the final total, and a national re-count could very likely be underway and take many weeks to fully complete. That would make the 2000 results of Bush v. Gore and the illegal interference by the Supreme Court look tame by comparison. Principle would also have to deal with the Court, as it had been fully stacked with collectivist's and post constitutionalist's by Barack Obama in his final years, and Hadley R. Crawford in her first term.

Russell Harrington waited in his office for the one interview he could no longer ignore. Perhaps it was even a positive sign at this late date. It might also reveal an interesting idea to the American people—to show them that the results of the soon-to-be-held election would not be a complete surprise to anyone.

"Senator Harrington," said Terry O'Neil. "Since her very quick rise to national prominence, Senator Principle has repeatedly been asked about the existence of a Secret Society that she might be a part of. I now have documentation that a meeting did in fact take place many years ago that *both* of you attended. It even shows that the two of you may have been the *principals* at that meeting, but it doesn't give information on the agenda, and, sir, you know yourself the rumors have been around for some time. So my question is does that have anything to do with this so-called Secret Society? What was the *purpose* of that meeting? Don't you think you and the senator have been disingenuous in not telling the American people about your involvement in a *secret order?*"

O'Neil could not contain his gloating expression, even as the Texan glared at him, his eyes severe and unwavering. Then Harrington threw the news anchor a curveball with the sudden, gleeful smirk he had shown to his colleagues in the Senate many times, in surprisingly demeaning the bill of the moment with his celebrated, sharp discourse.

He said, "I've always known that you are one fine reporter Mr. O'Neil, and you sure are *right*! There *was* a meetin' and you found out about it! But to tell you the truth, I actually *forgot* about it 'cause it happened so *long* ago. Yes, sir there *was* a meetin' but it doesn't have a damn thing to do with this *election*, and if I'm not mistaken, sir, that was *three* questions, not one."

When Harrington admitted to a meeting, the force of the confession caused O'Neil to jerk backward in his chair. He said, "All right Senator, then tell us what it was about and why you have kept it a secret all this time if there is nothing *to* the accusation!"

"Oh, please! First, I'm just amazed if that's what all you folks are talkin' about today. Surely, you all have a lot more important things to say than *that*! I forgot about the meetin' 'cause it happened so *long* ago, but it's not somethin' we've kept a *secret*! All that nonsense is just somethin' you folks in the media have pumped up for your *sponsors*. *I* know that, *or*, maybe it was for somethin' *else*! But hell, we haven't talked about the damn meetin' 'cause it ain't relevant to anything *I* know of. Hell, it happened more than *forty-years* ago when we were just *kids*. Senator Principle probably forgot about it too. Maybe you should ask *her*. Surely, you're aware that *everyone* in the country knows where *we* stand on the issues, or is that a *mystery* to you Mr. O'Neil. Hell, we've been in the leadership of the Republican side of the aisle for some time now. Come *on*! Take a breath and get *real*!"

"But Senator, that still doesn't explain the *meeting*!"

"Okay, then! Here it is, but first let me ask *you* a question. You weren't satisfied with my answer so you repeated what you asked the first time. I watch you and others get similar responses all the time, and instead of goin' back to the question when you don't get an answer, you just go on to the next one. *Why*? How come don't you repeat 'em like you just did with *me*?"

O'Neil simply shrugged and Harrington smiled.

"You see," said Harrington. "I can play gotcha *too*! But okay. When we were still young, we thought we'd like to try to get other young folks involved in the political process. They weren't much different back then than they are today. Most of 'em just didn't wanna hear a damn thing about politics, but we *wanted* 'em to hear and get *involved*. That's all. And somethin' else just occurred to me. I guess it *does* have somethin' to do with this election, 'cause we've been workin' to get 'em involved *this* year *too*! Some of the folks who were at that meetin' are Republicans today, and some of 'em are Democrats. At least I *think* that's true. But seriously, most of 'em was just regular folks who wanted to *know* more. The meetin' was just a get-together to persuade 'em to get involved in the politics of their country. That's all. And one *more* thing. One of the ideas a lot of folks have today just like they did back then is that they have hard and fast rules *not* to talk about politics when they get together. I wish they didn't think like that."

"So you are saying that there is no Secret Society and all of the rumors are just that—*rumors*?"

"*I* sure don't know of one, and I really think it's slap-happy to even *consider* such an idea for a United States Senator, don't you? As to rumors, we sure cain't control *that*! What do *you* think?"

"It doesn't matter what *I* think, Senator, but it *does* matter if the two of you created some kind of Secret Society."

"Well, maybe it *does* matter what you think. You've got a whole lot of influence bein' on television, and a lot of people watch you! I think I could easily make the charge that you have some secret agenda *we* don't know about. Maybe you're tryin' in some covert way to make political hay for the *president*! That's happened a lot and everyone *knows* it. I'm not makin' the accusation mind you. But *if* that's what you try to do on the sly, then *you're* the one who's bein' disingenuous, and that's what *I* think. You *are* a liberal, aren't you? But really, it was just *kids* for the most part. I haven't *always* been an old coot! It was no big deal at all, unless of course you count gettin' folks more involved in politics and in knowin' more about how their government works. I know *I* do, and *you* should too, but the meetin' was forty-*years* ago! Man! If I were you right now, I'd be *embarrassed*!

"Mr. O'Neil, you also need to know that I just thought of somethin' else that *might* shed some light on this. You folks over at CBS have a lot of *other* folks who do investigations on things, so let me ask *you* a question. Isn't it true that they even check up on communications we've all made to each other over the years? I know there are records on all of that stuff that you all get on *other* people, and especially since the evolution of the Internet and email. If there *was* anything, it sure seems like you would have found somethin' more than just a dusty old tidbit about a meetin' we had when we were kids. Don't you think so? Surely you could spend your time better on somethin' else!"

Sitting before the fireplace in one of the many cabins at Camp David, Mo Dobrosky, Chet Forbes, and Wilson Keyes talked quietly among themselves. Keyes and Dobrosky were playing chess and talking back and forth, and with Forbes.

Keyes looked up from the chessboard. His concentration was not on the game but the hour of the day. It was nearly 2 p.m. If his plan was to succeed, they must leave on the hour, for no one had ever breached the security of Camp David. To do less would further complicate the reality of their captivity. They must proceed with extreme caution. Not every Marine knew what was to take place on this day, and take place very soon.

Keyes stood up, seemingly uninterested in the game. "Let's go for a walk, guys," he said, heading toward a small closet. "I'm not used to being confined like this. It is all right, isn't it?" he asked the Marine at the entrance. The reply was a crisp attention stance, as the two men obediently followed the massive general.

They put on their heavy coats and waited for the inside guard to confer with the one on the outside. They were not in prison, and could walk around the grounds at will. Always present, however, would be a select cadre of Marines to exercise all necessary control, for Camp David would be their residence for an undetermined time. For now, they were free to do as they pleased as long as the military personnel were with them wherever they walked throughout the large acreage. The air was cold, not freezing, and it would be invigorating to walk and stretch their legs.

Keyes gave a noticeable sigh of relief as they passed through to the outside, receiving a smart salute from the Marine standing to the right side of the door. All three men had been to the presidential retreat many times, and as they walked, they were aware of the music. Situated every fifty yards were large speakers with elegant, classical pieces playing softly. Installed many years earlier, their purpose was to entice foreign visitors to relax in a subliminal atmosphere of tranquility. The pristine and rhythmic sound of a Bach Brandenburg Concerto played, accomplishing the goal of serenity in the camp's setting.

It was a typical autumn day in the Catoctin Mountains in Maryland just seventy miles from the White House. A light snow covered the ground. The soaring hickory and maple statues that populated the countryside were beginning to show their reaction to the coming of winter with a change in wardrobe. The military escort of three Marines stayed behind them, at a discrete distance of twenty-five yards as they walked, apparently with no purpose or intent as they neared a section of chain-link fencing that surrounded the camp. They talked quietly with each other, not wanting any part of their conversation picked up by the many microphones scattered throughout the acreage and perfectly camouflaged.

Without warning or even understanding why, Dobrosky felt a chill engulf his entire body. The hairs on the back of his neck rose to full attention, but were not put in that position by the cold air. He was suddenly, and mysteriously frightened, but of what he did not know. He turned. Behind them, the Marines had vanished as quietly as the recent snowfall had arrived, suddenly, as though they had never been there in the first place. They had made no sound in leaving.

"What the hell?" said Dobrosky, quickly silenced by the firm movement of the hand of Wilson Keyes who whispered, "Both of you just follow me and do not speak. Soon we'll be out of here."

Keyes searched and then found what he was looking for. Nearly hidden from sight was a small ribbon flapping against the nine-foot-high chain-link fence. It looked as if the wind had just blown it there, but it identified the opening in the fence, created when the wiring in the main security room was changed. From there it was just a short hike to a waiting automobile, where they hurriedly scrambled into the rear of a white Lincoln sedan, the flawless precision of the silent escape executed simply, quietly, with no mistakes.

The white sedan drove toward its destination on Wisconsin Avenue in the Historic District of Georgetown. From there the general could direct the movements of all branches of the military in a private, highly secret facility. He believed the president would not try to impose Martial Law when informed that Keyes was no longer in custody. Upon his arrival in Georgetown, the four-star general first briefed his aides on the seriousness of their position. He then transmitted a terse message to an Air Force pilot who was on the ground waiting for his non-military passengers. The communiqué said, "Do not fail with your mission." Then Keyes began to inform officers around the nation, and the world.

In Moscow, the freezing winter wind roared through the city rampant and unrestrained, as two people hurried along the deserted Russian walkway, shrouded from the icy winds with heavy fur coats to protect them in their very short jaunt. Their only desire was to reach the shelter they were seeking for relief from the frigid air. A sudden winter storm had swept across the city with blinding speed, bone-chilling and dangerous, forcing all living creatures to stay inside except for the two solitary figures whose sheer presence and consummate power was enough to open any door...at least for one of them.

"From here," said Casimir Zgonina breathlessly, the cloud of vapor from his mouth quickly disappearing as they settled into the black Mercedes, "you will be taken to a private airstrip that is for my use exclusively. Do not fear; the plane *will* be able to take off.

"I congratulate you for having the wisdom and the courage to put yourself at what could have been seen as a great risk by coming here. If leaders had met like this in the past, perhaps the world would not be in the shape it is in today, but openly, I mean, not in secret. I am not certain of that, but it *could* have been possible. Your aide is already at the airstrip, and I firmly believe your journey has not been in vain. We are in full agreement, and I wish you a safe return home, Senator."

Forty-five minutes later the G650 Gulfstream owned by Senator Russell Harrington was ready. Cleaned, refueled, and de-iced, it climbed above the winter storm. Its passengers, drained from nearly two days without sleep slumped into their seats mentally and physically exhausted from the long, historic crossing, fully completed and now waiting for the ultimate answer from American voters. The plane would reach its final destination and land at the airport in the desert metropolis of Las Cruces, New Mexico. The two passengers would then transfer to Harrington's limousine for the final trip home. They would be a mere two hours behind schedule for a rendezvous with destiny. It was time for the United States to select their next president.

Armando fell asleep instantly, but not Principle. Just over the Sea of Okhotsk, she remembered. On two separate occasions, Zgonina called her comrade. Old habits were often hard to break, even in this era where the demise of the old Soviet system had taken place many, many years earlier, and as the need for sleep began to pull the needed curtain of slumber around her, she remembered. She also had to confess that it was an astonishing, two-day summit. For a full thirty-six hours, she had conducted a non-stop collaboration with the President of Russia, a historic meeting of the minds that would astonish the world generally, and more because of her sex. She listened in on a conversation with the President of the United States. It was definitely a time of great triumph and *true* change.

Every poll reflected an even split in the vote on Election Day, with most experts now in agreement the president would pull out a win in the end. She held a slim lead in New York, Ohio, and Pennsylvania, with an even larger spread in electoral-rich California. Odds were being set in Las Vegas, with President Crawford the clear favorite of practically all political forecasters who echoed the Vegas line. In the end, the people would not oust Hadley R. Crawford, especially when she was on the verge of achieving such a stunning breakthrough on the most dangerous weapons of war. It would be their response to her explanation when she said that she had simply gotten the treaty to a point where she could submit it to the Senate. When given the alternative in the privacy of the voting booth, the people would choose to retain her as the one certain way to have a world with no nuclear weapons. Crawford was clearly a person of the people, a president who cared about the middle-class. Principle was too dumb and too strident, according to the media.

Preparations were ongoing in downtown Las Cruces to welcome their senator and her famous husband when they came to cast their votes in a newly constructed booth. The city gleamed with freshly scrubbed streets, in a boisterous show of support for its former mayor. They had decided to make the day a holiday. Shops and offices would close to celebrate the occasion when one of their own would win the presidency. This would be their answer to the elites of Massachusetts and Illinois, that their time of influence in Washington had run its course.

The mayor of Las Cruces and Allen Davis would give separate speeches on a specially erected stage. He would speak solely as a private citizen on where the nation would go if his wife became the new president. Several buildings offered clear vision to the new town square, and in one of the taller structures, Dominick Caputo gained access to a fifth floor location, his mission still incomplete.

The new Civic Center adjacent to the speaking area had closed on schedule the night before, and would not reopen until the day after the election. Caputo was in touch with Cantrell to let him know he was in Las Cruces to assure the D/CIA he would finish the contract this time. Now it was a matter of personal pride for Caputo, brought on by a dim-witted mistake of his own, and by others, along with the constantly changing events that were beyond his control. This was the worst episode of his entire career, but he would make it right.

He thought about the stupidity of the gay minister. It was typical for a crusading queer, he thought. Now, for only the second time in his career and still on the same target, he was alone with no patsy. He would have to be even more careful, but still he was pleased. His line of vision from the fifth floor was unimpaired. The only problem he could foresee would be to exit the building unobserved. Because it was in lockdown, he could easily maneuver, and even better, it was a very good angle to an adjacent structure. Anyone who made a connection would choose the other building as the more logical site for a sniper. It would require time to discover their mistake, and by then he would be in another part of the city. Overall, the caper was becoming exciting again, and this time there would be no escape for the target. Everything would go according to plan. He would succeed, and then get back to New York and hope his funds were strong enough to retire to either Cuba or Sicily.

In Washington, Russell Harrington issued a final statement before his flight home to Texas where he would cast the one vote he had dreamed of for a very long time. From there he would spend two days in Las Cruces, and then return to Washington to begin setting up necessary procedures for an orderly transfer of power. He also took the time to issue an odd statement from his candidate. It read that there would be no press conference or television appearances on Election Day or the day after, or for any single person or network. Principle would make a definitive declaration only in the form of an inaugural address.

On the plane, Harrington relaxed with a neat whiskey. His mind swirled with the multitude of tasks that lay ahead. Everything had reached this point in time for the ultimate decision of the voters, and he could not wait for their answer.

His mind leisurely traveled backward to his first meeting with the idealistic Sara Principle. He remembered the long, complex studies with Jim Miller. Before meeting those two people, Harrington possessed only a potential—a natural, auspicious talent to produce wealth, combined with an innate, yet unconscious knowledge that something was very wrong with his government, and that someone like he might be able to correct that wrong. By some strange, unexplainable and wonderful set of circumstances, the fate of Russell Harrington became the task of one who was young and one who was older, but not old. They would teach him what he needed to know to contribute his own native skills, and because of those two individuals, America was about to experience its second birth.

The primary figures of The Solution believed that millions of people did not bother to vote for a multitude of reasons, each one different from the other but valid in every mind in which it resided. Many people simply did not want to be ruled by anyone, while others believed that a vote for a minority party candidate was a wasted vote. Their answer was simply to sit out election after election, but this year they would return as voters to make a genuine difference, while millions more would come out for the first time.

At the airport in Las Cruces, the two exhausted travelers made their way to the limousine, all energies spent from the protracted journey. It was 2 a.m. Soon they would be home.

TWENTY

"My friends," said President Crawford, as she and her husband made their early morning pilgrimage to Boston to cast their ballots. "My. husband and I thank you for your gracious and steady support. I am confident about the outcome of the election today, and then we can get on with the urgent task of our mission to make the world a safer place not just for us, but for our children, our grandchildren, and *all* of the generations yet unborn. We *must* end the continuous and gathering threat of war. On this issue there can be no legitimate delay, for the ongoing buildup of horrible weapons affect all of us."

She was a beleaguered president with a reluctant smile—a woman who had seemingly lost control of her own destiny based on events in which she had no control. It was an uneasy situation for her, made even more unbearable by a long night without sleep.

Many months had passed since she had tried to spend a night with her husband. She had not even entered the Queen's bedroom that he now occupied, believing he had discretely replaced her with some unknown lover. But this night would be different. Even though she was now an elderly woman, she would at the very least try to rekindle a physical bond with him in some kind of way.

She made the decision early in the day to go to him with no prior arrangement. It would not be difficult. Their communication during the course of a day was now virtually non-existent. They had in fact very little interaction in these waning days of the administration, and she was certain he no longer cared about the estrangement that plagued their lives. She also believed that if the American people actually knew of the lack of physical intimacy between their president and her husband, they would probably grieve along with her, for in spite of all that had happened in her life, she was still very beloved throughout the entire nation, and now she was even favored to win re-election.

In the Oval Office, William Patterson said, "Madam President, we have had no success in finding Keyes, or Dobrosky and Forbes for that matter. They just seem to have dropped off the face of the earth. I *think* we'll locate them, but I'm less confident than before. We can't find *anyone* who might have information as to where they might be."

Crawford's expression was essentially blank. She seemed not to care. She said softly, with no color or expression in her voice, "Bill, just let me know. I'm not sure it even matters, and it may be very difficult. Keyes has many options and many friends. They couldn't have gotten out of Camp David if that were not true."

Following the meeting with Director Patterson, Crawford talked with Cantrell. "Cliff," she said. "Get in touch with Patterson. See if you can help him find Keyes."

Cantrell dialed the number from his limousine. "Get a flight ready for Las Cruces and have Phillips see if there's anything he can do to help Patterson at the Bureau."

The president finished her day at a private dinner with Senator Kendall in the White House residence. Except for ambition, they were very much alike in many respects. Crawford greatly admired the Pennsylvania senator, and often wished she could be more like him. Kendall never opted for a higher office than that of senator. He was a prominent figure in national politics for more than thirty years, working his way upward in his party from the position of state senator, well before moving forward as a United States Senator. He was also the principal member of Congress who had spent the most political capital in helping the president obtain positive exposure for her domestic programs. Kendall knew how to get things done...but he was slow and laborious.

"Ed," said Crawford. "You know my relationship with Alfred has been strained for some time, but tonight I'm going to go to him in spite of all that. We haven't made love for years Ed," she whispered.

"Maybe you should wait. This is something you need to take some time for, Hadley."

"No! I've waited long *enough*! I know I'm an old woman, but I want him *now*! He's my *husband*, Ed!" she said, with painful, murmured words, like those of a woman looking at the end of her own personal life and longing for any form of positive reinforcement.

Kendall was well aware of certain indiscretions by Alfred Bradford, but managed to keep the information to himself as being in the best interest of his dear friend Hadley. He decided he would not be the one to tell her the truth about Alfred, especially after she had once beaned him in the head with a glass ashtray on board Air Force One.

He said, "You have to do what you think is best, but I say, wait. It's been such a long stretch since you were on good terms. Take it slow. Give it a few more days Hadley. I know they call me *wait-a-while Ed*, and maybe that's true, but sometimes the slow approach is the *best* approach."

By the time Kendall had left the White House, the two consumed three bottles of red wine, a Kendall tactic to keep Crawford away from her husband. It did not work. No sooner did Kendall disappear through the door than a very drunk Crawford walked down the hall of the residence, after first telling her military aide with the nuclear attaché case to stay put because she wanted privacy, and that she had the codes with her.

Still with a slight amount of control, she proceeded on cautious, wobbly feet down the Center Hall, then the East Sitting Hall and the entrance to the Queen's sitting room. The door to the bedroom was slightly ajar as she entered. Reaching for the doorknob, she heard soft muffled voices. *What's this, a visitor? How can that be at this hour?* It was 11 p.m.

She tiptoed closer, thinking that the sound might be coming from the television, but no, Alfred hated TV. She could not discern who was there but it was not the television. It was just an instrument for fools he had said often enough. *How can he have company this late in the day and in his bedroom no less? He is the husband of the first woman president! Has he forgotten that!* It was not a question.

Just about ready to retrace her steps she heard the nearly imperceptible, yet familiar sound. She had heard the sound before in better days—the faint, and then loud cries of pleasure from years gone by, the sounds he made when she excited him with her mouth. She stopped short, suddenly very sober, as if she had consumed no alcohol at all. She was now as alert as she had ever been.

Can he possibly be so unthinking, so uncaring, and so insensitive as to actually bring his lover to the White House? No! Oh, God, no!

She turned, wanting to leave the ultimate humiliation—the final rejection, but she could not. The sounds were beginning to elevate. *My God, I can't take this! Why! Who?* Faster and faster came the cries, and she knew without any doubt. Some unknown woman was making love to the husband of the President of the United States in the White House in his own bedroom. She also knew that he was returning her attention with the same reckless abandon he had always shown with his wife in better days—wild, emotional, vocal and loud, with no concern of discovery by anyone, especially by Hadley R. Crawford.

She peered through the small opening of the doorway. One dim light burned some distance from the bed leaving the bulk of the room in darkness. Her eyes would have to adjust. She stood there silently, moving the door ever so softly for a better view. Then she saw a figure in shadow. It was Alfred. It was unmistakable. He sat upright, his knees bent, his hands clasped behind his head, as another head moved rhythmically up and down over his engorged penis while cupping his testicles in her palm. Then she realized. It was the head of a male. *My God! A man! A man is in the place that used to be for me—a man with long, dark hair and groping hands, feeling hands, stroking all over Alfred's body, moving his head more rapidly up and down.* She could not move. It was as if her feet were nailed in place and she could not even breathe.

Jesus! The son of a bitch is having an orgasm, calling out to his lover! Goddamn it! Who is it? Who the hell is it? Soon Alfred moved, turning his body around to position himself on his hands and knees, while the other figure moved behind him. Then suddenly it was clear to her as she saw the man mount Alfred from behind like a dog in heat, having anal sex with her husband! She watched them for a period, wanting to leave but unable to do so. They changed positions after what seemed like an eternity, as Alfred lay on his back, taking the man from above him. Then she saw clearly. *My God, it can't be true, but it is*! *Now it's obvious*! *Ronald*! *He's having sex with my male secretary*! She wanted to throw up. She always assumed it was a woman that Alfred was having an affair with, not like this, the two men jointly in an unnatural lust! It made it worse somehow. She could not bear to look or to turn away, and she could not confront them.

Weakly, she retraced her steps down the Center Hall. Halfway to her bedroom her emotions took over. Her knees buckled as she fell to the floor, helped up by her aide. Her body shook uncontrollably, wracked with an ever-increasing pain, intense, red-hot pain with throbbing temples and a hot, dripping sweat, and the anger, the hatred! *Please*! *Not like this*! *I don't deserve this*! *Not in the White House*! *I'm the President of the United States of America*! *I'm Hadley R. Crawford*! *I'm the most powerful person in the world*! *This cannot be happening*!

When the valet came to wake her the next morning, he found the president sitting in a leather chair staring blankly into space. She was still in her clothes from the day before, and through the night, she had one single, recurring thought...revenge. She would have plenty of coffee, and then Alfred's day would come, and it would come soon.

Everything was closing in around her. What a laugh people would have had—the greatest hysterics in the history of the world.

Casimir Zgonina was a patient man. It was a necessary trait for anyone in Russia, especially the head of state. Under his orders, the military command had maintained a close observance on all of America's reconnaissance satellites. Regardless of Crawford's proclamation to the contrary, America had greatly expanded its eyes-in-the-sky capability to monitor events around the world, and the on-going use of drones all around the globe. It was apparent that Crawford was covering herself, and Zgonina was pleased with his agreement with Principle. His self-fulfilling plan of action was coming to its natural conclusion, and it would shock the world. Crawford would not become the supreme leader of the new federation unless she won re-election, and all of the instincts of the wily Russian told him that Crawford would lose in all ways, including the election. The American people were many things, but they were not completely stupid. The results of a Sara Principle victory would be even more fortuitous for Russia than for any country, including the United States and China, though his own citizens were clueless to that part of the equation...and so was General Tso. Zgonina hoped the changes he knew were coming from a Principle victory would arrive quickly. He was certain the American's would choose Principle. For Russia, it was right. It was time, now, and his country would be a far richer place for everyone concerned with the death of democracy in America finally achieved.

In the early morning hours before sunrise, Fred Spans assembled his team of fifty agents in downtown Las Cruces. Some of the men looked like tourists, eager to be a part of the coming spectacle, and were equipped with communicators to a central command post. Ten of the agents posed as members of a working television crew, their eyes constantly searching the surrounding structures for any sign of activity out of the ordinary. They would interview people on general interest and whom they believed would win the election. Fifteen would mingle with the crowds to remain as inconspicuous as possible, while other agents kept looking, still searching for one elusive face.

Twenty-five agents split off in groups of five to check and re-check buildings, looking for the image in the picture they all carried. For five hours, they went through a systematic procedure, satisfied that if the man had come to the city they would find him. No one knew Clifford Cantrell would soon arrive at the Las Cruces airport.

It was nearly 9 a.m., as Sara Principle emerged from her shower still tired but more alert than when she arrived home. In the bedroom, she stopped short. The sight of Allen lying nude beneath a sheer sheet surprised and delighted her. Even though they were in their sixties, it seemed like such a long time since they were together for any lovemaking. She could not recall the last time they did make love without the need to run off in opposite directions. Whatever the amount of time, far too much of it had passed since she felt his still eager body next to hers without the everconstant obligation to be elsewhere.

She glanced at the clock. It was always there, the need to check the time. In little more than one hour, they would have to leave, and her need for him was clear to both of them. She felt wantonly aroused by the look of his still slender body—a body she knew so well and could explore forever, never tiring of his touch and scent even after many years together. And as she saw him, she wanted to forget the many long nights alone—to remember only now and this moment—to feel her emotions take over from the public face of logic she always wore, to see the crimson color of hunger that spread over his face and mouth in a ripening passion of pent-up desire.

They made love for twenty minutes and Allen did not know if he could move from the bed, or if he even wanted to. If only they did not have to leave. He bellowed, "To hell with the goddamn election—to hell with the goddamn speech, to hell with the goddamn Solution, and to hell with the whole goddamn world!" But it was a fantasy, and commitments must be kept...the steady, always present need to keep promises made.

In the Civic Center, Dominick Caputo stirred from his position on the bare floor. It had been a long night and the floor was hard. He knew he could not hold out for the beginning of the ceremonies and still be fresh when the moment came. He must shake the knots loose from his body, leave the building, find a place to eat and mentally ready himself for the job at hand.

He walked down the stairs to the rear door on the first floor, never forgetting his role as a paid killer, or that someone could unexpectedly enter the building. If it happened, he would have to make an additional hit. He removed a blonde wig and a pair of dark glasses from his backpack. His opposition would have an even larger force than they did in Hollywood. Privately he admired the unknown man who handled the security for Principle. He was obviously a professional, even though he had lost one of his men. It could happen to anyone. The man was running the operation to the best of his considerable ability, and Caputo would not make the mistake of underestimating him, or the situation in which he now found himself.

Not satisfied with the look, he removed the dark glasses and wig. With the precision of a makeup artist, he fastened a thin mustache to his upper lip and put on a pair of large-rimmed, clear spectacles. He checked the look in his mirror and approved the results. His expertise at camouflage was perhaps his second best talent. Then he went through the door to find what he was looking for.

Walking toward the front of the building as if he belonged there, the trained ear of the professional assassin heard a high-pitched conversation through a communicator near the corner of the building. Someone was checking the entrance. "Okay, Fred," he heard the voice say. "The Civic Center is secure and locked up tight." Caputo had wondered what his foe's name was. Suddenly he heard what sounded like a response, shrill, tinny, and piercing. It was good they stayed in touch with each other. It would help when he made the hit. With a bit of luck the back and forth conversations would be frantic, and help to cause mass confusion to tie up security men after they heard the crack of his weapon and saw the damage it produced. They would all be on the horn at the same time. It was perfect.

In El Paso, Russell Harrington awoke from a restive night ready to begin a full day of activities that would open with an early morning press conference. He methodically went through his grooming rituals, taking extra care to be certain he looked the part of a United States Senator. In all of his sixty-seven years, he could not remember ever feeling the emotional high of today, and that even included his first oil well. That was his time of youth when everything was possible but not permanent, all at the same time. This day was unlike any other that had ever existed. It will be a second beginning, he thought. When the rest of the world learned what kind of government America was about to have for the very first time, with new policies laid down by a new breed of political leaders, people everywhere would eventually demand a similar system for their own country...but not right away. It would frighten them at first, because the changes would be more dramatic than any person could imagine, and Principle was probably right. There would likely be some violent behavior. It would come at them from a badly informed electorate who did not understand what their select-ed leaders had done to their country. And while each American held most politicians in low regard, they still deluded themselves in believing that the majority of those same officials held the best interest of the country fore-most in their actions, especially their own representatives. It helped the rigged staging that favored the re-election of incumbents.

His driver delivered him to the polling place at 7 a.m., and he gingerly stepped from the back seat to a large assembly of reporters ready to record still another *Harrington Court*. Before going inside with his driver, he in-vited all to form a circle.

"Folks," he said; his voice even more rasping than the last time he stood in this spot. "Somethin' great's gonna happen today. It really will be a new beginnin' for our country. That's not political hype. You all know that's *not* what I'm about, but the results of *this* election are gonna be big-ger and more far reachin' than any of you can imagine. I won't do any electioneerin' today, so the remarks I *do* make will be real short, and you all know I'm a first class *windbag*! So let me just say that you all should vote and I hope you'll vote for my candidate, Sara Principle. She's the one who'll work to restore all the rights we've lost over lots of years. I *think* she'll win, but it's all up to *you* now. So, don't think with your *hearts*. Use your *brain*, and have your voices heard from here to *China*! They only lis-ten to the vote, not letters."

It was a very short speech for the crusty Texan. Refusing to make any further comment, he turned and disappeared into the building, returning with his driver straight to his limousine.

TWENTY-ONE

Allen Davis arrived in downtown Las Cruces a major film star and the husband of a presidential candidate. He was pre-eminent among his fellow actors who were politically active, and a man who constantly strove to reach the pinnacle of his own personal story. Sara Principle's Senate career was over after this day. Her life would return to that of a private citizen, or she would become the next President of the United States. For the Hoosier-turned-New-Mexican, there could be no turning back. The great oddity was in being a conservative Republican with *any* of liberal-leaning Hollywood people as supporters.

Fred Spans looked at his watch. It was 10:45 a.m. Fifteen minutes was the scheduled time for Allen and Sara to be on the stage. Too long, he thought...far too long to be exposed. It would almost be an open invitation to the man they feared. Still his operatives reported that all was normal and the downtown area buttoned up as tightly as possible. Could it really be anything else? It was just too quiet for Fred's own comfort level. There was no way the opposition had abandoned the goal of assassination. It was just too damn quiet for everyone's good. Then he thought of something and summoned Joe Gaines to bring five men to the van immediately!

Gaines walked into the van that had been set up as a control center. Spans said, "Joe, I want you to go to the airport. Take five men with you and ask questions. Show the picture. Check everywhere, including the restrooms. It's probably too late, but do it anyway."

Joe left without comment; ready to comply with orders they both knew were too late. Fred was grasping at straws. If the man they were hunting had come to Las Cruces, he would have arrived long ago, and if he had, he would have decided where and how to do his work. Then the unexpected alert arrived. An urgent call came from Georgetown just ten minutes before Allen and Sara were to go on the stage, and as he listened, Fred began to invent and consider a new plan; not one that had been analyzed and thought out, but one that lacked the quality preparation needed for the work...and Fred knew it.

"We just got information that Cantrell is on his way there," said Mo Dobrosky, "and he may even *be* there by now. It just wasn't something we could monitor with any degree of regular activity or accuracy, but from what we now know, he may have already arrived. I just don't know. I'm sorry, Fred."

Bang! The missing alarm Fred needed to hear that remained silent had just rung as loud as it was possible to ring. He had arranged to check the airport for the assassin, but not for Cantrell. At least he managed to keep his friends from the stage until the very last minute. That should help now.

He quickly ended the call to warn the men. Now he was certain the dark-haired man was here, perhaps waiting for Cantrell and final instructions. Maybe they even had a meeting place wired in. He barked out new orders to re-check all buildings and overlook nothing. Joe Gaines was at the airport when Fred signaled, ignoring the intricate security procedures, he alone had created.

"*Joe*!" he shouted. "These are new orders! Repeat *new* orders! Return to the van at once! The guy has to be here already because we just found out that Cantrell is on his way, and I don't want to stop him at the airport. Have your men link-up with the others in re-checking the buildings and you come here to the van...and *hurry*!"

Principle was listening. She expected Fred to try to talk her out of being on the platform and was surprised when Spans said, "Sara, as much as I would like you to cancel, I think you can't right now. You have to go out there and be with Allen. If that bastard is here, we have to catch him and end this madness! We can't let it keep going and going, and when Cantrell gets here, we'll grab him. But you have to go out there, Sara! I'm sorry, but it's just that simple, and I'm also sorry I've realized it so late. We can't let it keep on going like this, with a different fear each day."

Even as Fred said the words, they both recognized the inference was that Fred was willing to use the candidate as bait. Then Principle said plainly, "I made my decision before you finished with Joe. It won't take long, and don't forget Fred. We have the vests. The guy's probably not here anyway. That's what *I* think. If he *was* here, I think you would've found him by now and have him in custody. Don't you?"

Back at his position by the window, Dominick Caputo was aware of everything. He understood the moment was near. He assembled his weapon; not one of the newer, high-tech firearms preferred by many of the younger members of the Company, but a specially constructed .357 Magnum with 9-round capacity and a telescopic lens. It would find its target with deadly accuracy and take the life of Sara Principle in spite of a Kevlar vest. Now he was certain he would complete his mission this time. They could not be positive he was even in Las Cruces. They could only speculate when, or where the time would occur, or if it would happen at all. This would give Caputo a clear advantage for the most important assignment of his long career, the death of a presidential candidate.

In the White House, Senator Kendall tried to soften the blow to the president. Kendall knew of Alfred Bradford's homosexual affair with

Ronald Davenport for two years, as did most of the people around the president, yet everyone had managed to keep it hidden in a mutual covenant for their beloved boss and friend.

"Hadley," said Kendall. "I'm not sure it wasn't something that just happened by accident. I'm certainly not trying to make *light* of it, but that's probably how it occurred. I know that doesn't make it any easier, though."

"It's been going on for some time, Ed. I've resigned myself that I could have done nothing then *or* now. I'm not even sure I'd *want* to, even if I could. I had a long talk with both of them and we've reached a mutual compromise that I think will be to everyone's benefit. I don't know if it's worth a damn, but we have to do something, and I have an idea."

Once again, Kendall adopted his wait-a-while position. He said, "Hadley, please don't do anything hasty! Try to think it through a while longer. Don't do something you might regret and lash out in anger. You know yourself that only *bad* decisions come in the heat of the moment, not good ones! Anyway, it's not as if you *have* to decide now! Surely it can wait 'til after January 20!'"

"Ed, I love you, but you're always saying wait. Maybe you've just been in that long-winded Senate for too long. At least you aren't one who loves the sound of your own voice. Whether I'm angry or not, and I sure as hell *am*, it wouldn't make any difference, and no, it *can't* wait. They were both adamant. They will not give it up, and I can only go so far. They've even threatened a public scandal, and we all remember the problems Clinton had. But I asked you here to do me a favor you might not want to do because it *does* include you."

"Name it, Hadley. You know I'll do whatever I can! You only have to tell me what it is."

Crawford's jaw was rigid—unyielding in her resolve to rid herself of her perfidious husband. Her face was that of a woman who had to come to terms with the reality of her life and reveal her innermost emotions—private, intimate feelings that made it necessary to bare her personal soul to her closest and male friend...he was, perhaps her only friend.

"Now it is *you*, my good friend, who should not be so hasty," said Crawford. "But I honestly can't think of anything else."

"Like I said, we've been friends—close, close friends, far too long for *anything* to get in the way. I'll do what I can no matter what it is."

"Okay, but you still might want to turn me down after I tell you, and if you do, don't let our friendship get in the way because what I'm about to ask *could* be misconstrued once the word gets *out*. So don't be so hasty yourself Ed, not that I've ever known you to move fast on *anything*! You are the most careful person I know. "

The president rose and began to walk around the Oval Office slowly, deliberately, with decision-time in the making. She was now uncertain about the outcome of everything in her life—perhaps everything she had ever thought or done. All things being equal she was still the president, but her husband was making a fool of her. The indignation spread on her face, raw, painful, with no understanding as to how she had gotten to the position she was now in.

Standing near the corner of her desk, her eyes betrayed the sadness of a woman having arrived at her last moments with the man she had once loved more dearly than any living person or thing—even more than the tremendous climb, she had made in politics, and the world stage, to become such a powerful person. Now, however, all she wanted was plain revenge, female revenge—a clear retribution, and she would extract it with all the power of the presidency at her command. It would also happen even faster than either Alfred or Ronald could believe possible. She also knew it had to be fast, because she just might lose the election.

"Ed," she said her voice barely above a whisper. "I can't stand the sight of them. I don't know what I've done to deserve this. If I lose, there will be an immediate divorce. They both know it. They also know that it's out of the question if I win, at least right away. Anyway, I want them out of the White House *yesterday*!

"If you will agree, they can move into your Connecticut house for at least six months. The press release will say that you and your wife have given Alfred the house while he spends some time writing. Someone else will take over his First Gentleman responsibility. When it all blows over, then we can get a divorce. As liberal-minded as I've always been, they disgust me more than I can say. If anyone had told me something like this could happen in my life I would have told them they were nuts, especially with a man who is sixty-seven years old!"

Throughout his many years in politics, Edward Kendall thought he had seen and heard everything. Nothing could surprise him at this late stage, not even this. So great was their friendship, no request was too imposing. Words of consolation between them were not necessary. Crawford must do what she thought best, and the house was Alfred's for whatever amount of time they needed for the President's benefit. In that moment of mutual trust and closeness, Edward Kendall was certain that Hadley R. Crawford would not continue to reside at 1600 Pennsylvania Avenue. The next four years would belong to Sara Principle. It would help keep their liberal position, and that the Democratic Party would still control the Senate, along with Kendall's position as Majority Leader. Quite possibly Crawford could rise in four years, but for now she was finished, and more than likely would never make a political comeback.

Hector Madeja, the Mayor of Las Cruces, completed his short speech. When he was finished, he introduced Allen & Sara and watched as they stood with their arms lifted upward in a salute to the people. Minutes before they walked onto the platform, Fred's men took Cantrell into custody. They moved him to the van for questioning, but did not get the answers they wanted or needed.

Fred spotted him first. He instructed his men not to move until he signaled. He wanted to watch the D/CIA—to see where he looked, hoping for any sign of recognition. Finally, he ordered him seized. They would interrogate him while Fred remained on the outside watching the crowd and the adjacent buildings. Now he was certain. It was no longer just a possibility. Now it was a fact. The assassin was here, of that, he was now convinced...but where? Fred had carefully scanned the surrounding buildings with binoculars for more than two hours, looking at all levels, with most of his concentration on the roofs and higher floors, made easier because of the scarcity of very tall buildings. Nothing was out of the ordinary, and he was certain the man was not in the audience. It was as though he did not exist even as Fred knew that he did. The assassin was there to complete his unfulfilled task to take the life of Sara Principle, Republican in name only.

Dominick Caputo was ready. He carefully opened the window he had kept purposely closed. The white mini-blinds had fully secured his position from the ever-present eyes of the men who wanted to stop him. The time was now. With deadly precision, he leveled his weapon at the figures standing at the center of the platform, smiling, waving, and absorbing the cheers of the audience as if they thought they were in friendly territory since they were in Las Cruces, with no danger in store for them, now that the campaign was over. *They must think the worst has ended. They are foolish people who do not deserve to live because they are stupid. Now they will die!*

Hector Madeja retreated to the seating area on the stage to give his two friends their moment together. The days of secrecy were nearly over. Soon they would be able to unveil the existence of The Solution to the entire nation and complete the mission laid out more than forty- years earlier. It would now be open for all to see and learn, and wonder if they had made a good selection.

Principle looked down at her security chief standing on the street level in front of her, still fully engaged in the process of scanning the entire area. They would be all right, she thought. She had already stood there with Allen for nearly five minutes and nothing had happened. Nothing would. Her husband would soon give his speech, and then they would leave the stage to end their public exposure. Everything would be finished to await the answer from the voters.

She felt composed and relaxed. She thought about how Jim Miller had taught Russell Harrington, and what they were now going to teach the American people. They had indeed arrived. The second American Revolution was about to start on this November day. The Constitution, with all of its original and amended flaws was about to be restored as the Supreme Law of the United States of America.

As her eyes looked out on the surging crowd, they did not see the panic that suddenly crackled across the face of Fred Spans. She was not able to hear the frantic screaming into the transmitter, as Fred's eyes suddenly locked on the window just seventy-five yards away. Her ears did not hear any of the short, staccato sounds of the high-powered weapon over the noise of the cheering mass of people, as bullets found their mark. She knew only the smell and taste of blood that spewed over her face, gushing forth to flood the surface of the surrounding stage with the sickening smell of death, as she crumpled downward to the floor.

In the pandemonium of hundreds of terrorized people, each one desperately trampling the other to find refuge from the onslaught of the formidable firepower, Fred's eyes left the window only once as he raced through the erupting mob consumed only with their own safety.

Running toward the building, he shouted orders through his transmitter. He paused for a brief glance backward at the stage and the bodies lying in a pool of their own blood that glistened on the painted wooden floor of the platform. *My God*! *The goddamn son of a bitch*! But he could not stop. Others would take charge. Fred was needed elsewhere. He screamed into the transmitter. "Report! Report!"

Dominick Caputo instinctively understood that his time was over. He saw the fierce scrambling to reach the building and knew he had miscalculated. There was no place to go as the security force closed in. He would surrender without protest. Finally, it was over.

Quickly the agents reached the building, weapons at the ready. Joe Gaines led them to surround the perimeter and cover any escape route. Then he unlocked the front door, as Fred burst through after him with no regard for his own safety—consumed only with capturing the assassin and then find out if his friends were alive or dead.

"Could he have gotten out before you got here, Joe," shouted Fred. "Joe! Could he have gotten *out*?"

"No way, boss, no way!" said Gaines, his composure far greater than Fred's. They hastily conferred on procedure. Someone yelled out from the back of the building. The man was coming through the door, his hands clasped behind his head in an attempt to make it clear he had seen the security force and was giving up.

Fred raced to the rear leaving Joe to guard the front. Spans had known Sara and Allen for many years, and protected her with a small force of agents until this year. He loved her and all that she stood for. This maniacal lunatic had killed two people recently, and now, perhaps a third or fourth. He was a crazed fanatic who did not deserve to live or have protection of the law, and certainly not handed over to a corrupt court system that might let him go unpunished.

On the CBS television network a harried, unshaven Terry O'Neil sat at the news desk anxiously waiting for his cue. It was a typical charge for the intense, extremely competitive journalist who had cut his teeth as a cub reporter many, many years before this day. His fervent dislike of Sara Principle had recently gotten him into trouble with charges of losing his objectivity. Today, however, his on-air passion was tempered and subdued.

The anomalous mixture of Principle's puzzling conservatism tantalized the liberal anchorman from the beginning of the Senator's sudden, and mysterious rise in popularity, and, as the many years passed, it became a constant battle of truth and justice as defined by Terry O'Neil. Still, this day was different. He understood his personal views must stay in the background, unspoken and private. O'Neil was about to bring a stunning announcement to a scattered afternoon audience brought up watching soap operas and game shows. He must rise above all personal considerations and opinions and present only the facts as he knew them to be—facts now being reported on by every major news organization from the desert metropolis of Las Cruces, New Mexico.

He began, grim-faced and somber. "This is Terry O'Neil in the CBS election center. We interrupt all programming to bring you this report from Las Cruces, New Mexico. Very serious events have just taken place there, and recorded as they happened. We caution you that some of the images may not be suitable for children, but we believe they are an important documentation to these events, and parents should allow older children to see the scenes recorded in Las Cruces. Here then are those pictures, with my voice-over.

"From the beginning of her quixotic attempt to reach the White House and unseat a popular sitting president, the first woman in American history elected to that office, the strident political style of Sara Principle has, throughout this campaign, suffered many surprising turns and tragedies. At 12:15 p.m. eastern time, shots were fired in downtown Las Cruces where the candidate and her husband, actor Allen Davis, were appearing today for her speech to the citizens of that city.

"Video clearly shows the senator and her husband both falling to the floor of the stage, but we are not clear as to the extent of injury at this point. What we do know is this: a would-be assassin, who obviously missed his target, that being Senator Principle, shot Mr. Davis. This is what we have learned.

"According to Armando Munoz, aide to Senator Principle, a lone gunman hidden from view on one of the upper floors of the Las Cruces Civic Center, fired the shots. Senator Principle was standing with her arm interlocked with her husband. He apparently turned both of them at the precise moment of the first shot, placing himself in the direct line of fire. In a state of extreme and justifiable panic by members of the audience, Senator Principle's security chief Fred Spans and his agents, surrounded the Civic Center. The alleged assassin was taken into custody—his name is being withheld for the moment. Mr. Davis is in critical condition at Memorial Center hospital. Senator Principle was not injured.

"Once again we have a national government official being fired on by a sniper; an assassin, in the past fifty-plus years; three presidents and one United States Senator, one of them successful, in the most recent history of our country, a violent, gun-toting populace. Just a few minutes ago, William Patterson, the FBI Director, issued the following statement, and I will now quote from that statement in its entirety."

'The tragic events of the candidacy of Senator Principle have been and continue to be, under investigation by this department. I cannot divulge the extent of our inquiry except to say that we have given it top priority. We believe these events have been the work of the single individual captured today, and that he was not a part of any organized plot against Senator Principle. We believe he worked alone. A full report will be released when the new Commission completes its investigation, but from what we now know, no one else was involved.' What the director did not say was a simple fact. Dominick Caputo was in the custody of Fred Spans at an undisclosed, secret location, not the FBI.

From the first notification of the shooting, television networks made the decision to preempt all local programming. In its place, they would compensate for the habitual lack of news on Election Day with non-stop coverage from Las Cruces, and on voter turnout. The other major story centered on the massive number of absentee votes. State and local officials were concerned that the national election could negatively affect local contests.

In the hospital, Allen clung tenaciously to life. A despondent Sara Principle sat by his side. Her once piercing eyes were now drawn and heavy, as if all life had left her, as she stared at his motionless body. They had pursued the goal of the ages. Now there was nothing left.

TWENTY-TWO

In the brilliance of the sudden heat wave that swept into the nation's capital, November seemed both far away and only moments ago to Sara Principle. It was now Inauguration Day and Washington, normally dressed in its winter clothing, but caught off-guard by the surprising sixty-eight degree temperature. A new order was ready to emerge for the world to marvel, as when France presented the Statue of Liberty to America in 1886, saying that Europe should look to the shores of North America for a new moral compass in the affairs of a nation. The statue lighted the way to freedom for the entire world to see; casting aside the immorality of right by birth or right granted by the collective, to full freedom and rights of the individual for the first time in history. However, as the chronicle attests, Americans did not keep it. Freedom nearly disappeared in 2013.

The temperature was a shock to everyone. Nature had chosen to honor the new era with its fickle fashion of surprise, and it was justly fitting for the occasion of change by citizens whose record was to seek out and elect self-serving politicians—not leaders and statesmen, but standard political hacks who were definitely not builders of freedom. With their explicit invitation, the people continued to maintain their on-going ignorance about America's highest law…the United States Constitution.

Looking out at the multitude of people unaccustomed to the sudden warmth, her thoughts were not of the speech to come but of Allen, seen in all his magnificent splendor—almost as if she was observing him through the translucent film of a sheer curtain. His image saturated her emotions. The people in Washington and around the world with radio, television, the Internet, and smart phones, would hear her inaugural address.

Allen managed to hear the speech in the hospital in those horrible hours, forcing her to read it in its entirety. She had never put a speech to paper in its final form. This was the first one, and he had heard it all, weakly giving his complete approval. When she finished, she looked at him tenderly, as she desperately tried to see more of him than her tear-filled eyes would allow, and with the compelling force of his courageous will to live, he heard the speech to its conclusion. They had made it after all. In the more than forty-year odyssey, they had made it all the way to the executive seat of government in Washington D.C. and the White House.

He visualized the new age that would come while she read the speech. He was without pain now. He knew they had fully reached the pinnacle, and he was content and happy. Then, with all of the memories of how they had gotten there, of the long, secret plan from his then young wife, Allen Davis died, at peace with himself and with the world. The dream would live on in the reality of the new days to come—an era that would shake America, and then the entire world to its very core.

The lingering visions of him occupied her mind as she stood there, her hands resting on the lectern for support of emotions that were still shaky, her jaws tightly clenched to control all of the rampant feelings lying so close to the surface of her thoughts and memories, as she worked to manage and direct them. She had not yet mended from the brutal devastation of November. Perhaps she never would. They had both worked for their country's restoration behind the scenes, secretly, and with noble inspiration. But she was alone now, never to see his living face again. Looking out on the people and the city of Washington, he touched every part of her, and then she began to speak.

"My fellow Americans," she said, trying to force her brain to focus only on the speech and not on memories of her husband's final hours, horrible minutes and seconds of the life of a great artist, and a life that was ending. "Some time ago I decided not to honor the custom of giving out copies of this address to the media, or to anyone. They, like you, will hear it for the first time. As you can see, there is no teleprompter, for that would have meant the necessary publishing of the speech you are about to hear.

"It is with a deep sense of personal loss yet profound pride that I stand here as your president. Many years of effort on the part of both public and private citizens have reached this climax of our November election. Now we begin, and the beginning will be to cleanse government and restore what our Founding Fathers first created. Washington and Jefferson formed a rule of law, *federal democratic republic*; a *constitutional* republic that fully *obeys* our highest law, not a democracy, which does not, in spite of what you have heard not only from your elected officials and so-called political experts, but also from those who teach your children.

"This is not the kind of speech you have ever heard, nor have any past generations heard one like it. There are no applause lines for personal aggrandizement. There is no pat on the back for those who came before me, because this is a harsh speech—an *angry* speech, an accusatory speech, but I fervently urge you to hear and heed its *complete* message. Just as important is to *understand* it. I say this knowing there are people watching and listening who will be enraged and want to turn me off. Don't do it. *Listen*, because you and I are crucial to taking back our country.

"Some of you may have wondered why I did not take the Oath of Office with my hand on the Bible. Here is one reason. It is because of Article 6 of the Constitution, which says in part that, 'no religious Test shall ever be required as a Qualification to any Office or public Trust under the United States, and they are the *last* words of the Article. Is there a distinction? There is for me, and that is to use a religious book, *any* religious book, *implies* a religious test or affirmation, and is therefore unconstitutional. I will have more to say on this matter later in this address and in the weeks and months ahead, but religion has no place in a *moral* government. Our founders knew this, and now, so do you.

"Some of what I say will be based on fact and some will be my opinion, and as someone once said, you are entitled to your opinion but not your facts. My first opinion is that the greatest American in our history was George Washington. He was also the first president to *violate* the Constitution by *adding* the words, *so help me God* to the Oath of Office. For me, the next greatest American was a person who *chose* to become an American...a Russian Jew from Saint Petersburg. Her name was Alisa Rosenbaum, better known as Ayn Rand. She was born on February 2, 1905 and died March 6, 1982. She came to America in 1926. She was a writer/philosopher who created Objectivism and taught it to *some* of us. My first *facts* are that this speech is very long, and I am not as good a speechwriter as was Abraham Lincoln.

"Throughout this speech you will hear quotes from Ayn Rand, and the reason behind giving you these quotes will become apparent directly *from* the quotes, the first of which is this one. 'I swear by my life and my love of it that I will never live for the sake of another man, nor ask another man to live for mine.' That quote comes from her 1957 prophetic vision of the future in her magnificent book, Atlas Shrugged. If you have not read any of her books, I strongly urge you *not* to begin with Atlas. Instead, begin with The Fountainhead, and then include all of her non-fiction books.

"Elected and non-elected people have urged you, many, many times, to listen with your hearts. That means your *emotions*. Today, however, I ask that you listen *objectively* and with a passion for *reason*, and know and *understand* that reality exists. I ask you to do this because some of the things I have to say will be frightening to those of you who do not appreciate the state of affairs that exists in the world in general, and in Washington in particular. I am also very sorry to say that that means *most* of you! The reason I say this is that it is clear that entertainment and socializing are more important to you than what your leaders are doing in turning your government into one that is *secret*, *illegal*, very *dangerous*, and that charge is also against *all* who came before us who sold you on the idea of collectivism...and you *bought* it! The reasons you accepted collectivist actions are many, but the main one is that it was just *easier* than being responsible.

"Many of you have also forgotten what the *true* purpose of government is *supposed* to be in the very *first* instance, and I tell you now that it is not to transfer the wealth of some to the coffers of others. Another *political* saying is that the first responsibility of government is to keep you safe. That is not true. It is to keep you *free*! Others have never correctly realized why people actually *need* a government, yet the answer is very simple. It is for protection from physical acts of aggression here in *America*, not abroad—to protect the *Rights* of Americans. There *are* several subtexts, and I will speak to *some* of them in detail.

"Most of you *instinctively* know the American government has become a grotesque, colossal leviathan in its raw power to coerce, to spend the money all of you and your posterity work so hard to earn, and until today, no elected official has come forward to actually *reduce* the size of that monster through a process of *elimination*. Many have talked of it. No one has acted. *We* will, and we will do it quickly, because the time is long since passed when a *lack* of action will further deteriorate the necessary repairs on this behemoth we call the federal government.

"There are many reasons why this horrific growth occurred that start with a simple truth. The creation of our oversized complex in Washington is *your* fault. That's right. It is *your* fault! You were the only power that could have stopped it, but you didn't, and *that* is why it is your fault. There *were* movements like the Libertarian Party and the Tea Party, whose idea of returning to constitutional government you largely ignored in favor of a person who was very good at *reading* words from a teleprompter that others had written. This was all part of the *style* they used to make you believe their actions...that perception *is* reality. *That* is why it is your fault. You did not stand up and declare that it must *end*! You left it in the hands of the people you *voted* for, and they acted in their *own* interest, not in yours. It has been this way for a very long time, but it will be that way no longer.

"From the early 1900s we have seen the staggering growth of our government become the *opposite* of what it *should* be in a free society. Today, we will witness the necessary diminution of this same government, and *this* time it will actually happen because we now have the *power*. I will explain that statement soon.

"*Some* of the people who originally came here did so to escape what they thought of as religious persecution. Then a number of *those* individuals formed groups and established their *own* methods of bigotry, racism, intolerance, narrow-mindedness and chauvinism, to name just a few. The *starting* place for this immorality was in denying reality in the first place, and then using religion to *suppress* religion. It continues on this day by those who insist on the suppression of natural, *fundamental* rights, or who even believe those rights do not exist. I am here to announce that they *do* exist, and no amount of *force* can make them disappear. Natural Rights *are* the Constitution. There is only one purpose for government, and that is to protect these Natural Rights.

"Then more individuals came here who did *not* support the new American mind-set of prejudice because they really *did* believe in freedom. They journeyed here with a hunger for liberty. They had not yet learned that *individual* rights were above all! That is something they *instinctively* understood; that groups may not claim, and then receive rights over an individual, because groups do not *have* rights, except when immoral politicians try to make it so. Rights are strictly for individuals with *no* exceptions. There are those in our country who think they rule government, and I'm speaking here of *unions*. Perhaps they once did, but not any longer!

"Many settlers wanted nothing *more* than freedom. However, they did not generally have a clue as to what a *huge* commitment and undertaking that desire would entail. The sad commentary is that in *all* of the generations who came before us, America has not been that kind of country. We have *said* that it is, and it almost was. We have shouted it to the world, but we were only kidding ourselves. Others knew this basic truth long before *we* did, and some of you do not know it even at this moment. You did not know it yesterday and you will not know it tomorrow. It has been chiefly true since the era of Franklin Roosevelt, but it actually began well *before* his time. He was just a great salesman, but nothing more than that. As far as presidents are concerned, the greatest of the Twentieth Century *was* FDR. But that is only if you begin with the usual paradigm—that the Constitution is simply a document to be used and manipulated not for America's benefit, but to laud government officials for going *beyond* it. To *transform* it into something it was never meant to be, as a document not for *freedom*, but for *control*, and *both* political parties were at fault. Roosevelt and others spoke of something being constitutional only when they thought it would help advance their progressive cause of the moment. But they did not believe politicians should follow the *letter* of the Constitution! Roosevelt and *all* of the presidents who came before him *and* after him have *used* the Constitution, they have not *obeyed* it. There has been a consistent and continuous violation of the written text by presidents and all of the many editions of Congress and the Supreme Court throughout our *entire* history, and there is a multitude of evidence to *prove* that charge.

"With their unconstitutional standards came a concerted march to a hybrid mix of socialism and capitalism they have called a democracy, and that is clearly *not* what our founders envisioned. They did not create or *want* a democracy because they understood a democracy essentially is a corrupt, malevolent system of government that should not be desired by *anyone*. This is why they created a constitutional republic, even though some of *them* chose to use the word democracy. Misunderstanding is not exclusive to *our* time, but one thing *is* clear. Our leaders and members of the media have continuously pelted the American people with the word democracy. So much so that they surrendered many years ago, and believe the wrong things. You have fully accepted the word democracy and discarded the words constitutional republic, *or* you believe a constitutional republic *is* a democracy. I am here to say it *is* not, and *will* not ever *be* a democracy, and simply repeating the claim constantly does not make it so. That being the case, democracy ends *today*!

"A democracy is a system of governance that represents the rule and power of the *majority*, not the rule of law, and is *collectivist* in its nature. Rule of law cannot *exist* in a democracy, because whatever majority is in place can change and interpret *any* law, thus turning a law into a *guideline*. A democracy *denies* individual rights, because the individual rights of people and democracy are not compatible. The result of this constant violation is that this geographical part of the planet we call America has become a full-blown, socialist, corporatist, egalitarian, fascist state, but it will be that way no longer. We are going to begin to *obey* our highest law and return America to a nation of *limited* government. And when we are finished, states will once again be where they should be in our country...*sovereign*! Some very powerful people are going to lose jobs and will have to re-apply to private enterprise companies. Understand me, America—only individuals have rights, not groups, and today is when we begin to recapture what our Founding Fathers first created, and we are going to do it all in *four years*! When you hear people say that Social Security is a Ponzi scheme, know they are *right*, but so also is a progressive *income* tax that is also one of the planks in the Communist Manifesto!

"Most first term presidents begin their official duties by directly getting ready for re-election because they want a second term more than just about anything. When they are successful, they spend those years in the self-absorbed plan of action to create a *legacy*, in a type of *keeping up with the presidents*, and to decide where they will put their library. Do any of *you* have a library? You probably do, but for you it's a place to go to borrow a *book*, not sprain your shoulder by patting yourself on the back. It's all about *them*, America. It is *never* about you. It is never about the best interest of our country. Oh, they *say* that it is, but it's a *lie*. If it was about what is best for America, they would *obey* the Constitution, but they do not and have even *admitted* it in recent years. The presidents and their cohorts in the Congress spend their days *violating* our highest law, but things are different now. As stated, I will not seek re-election, change my mind, or modify my statement. My term will be spent restoring our Constitution. Your government has not obeyed the Constitution for many years. Some elected officials have even joked about it, saying the Constitution is old and out of date, and that most of what transpires in the Congress has nothing at all to do with being constitutional. Our founding documents are even more relevant in today's world, than when they created America.

"Your elected and non-elected leaders have taught you that government may grant you your rights, although they have not put it in those words. You have also heard this from many members of the media that curry their favor, by your unions, and by *corporate* America. They *wanted* to enslave you, and they *did*!

"You have been taught these things by your school teachers. They also taught you to conform to the image and demands of others in the name of being for the *common* good—the right thing to do, and combined it with a most insidious and misunderstood word, *equality*! They taught you that if a *majority* of people declare something is good then it is automatically good for everyone. If it weren't, they would have to find a way to live with it, the same way it is with immoral union contracts. Why do I say immoral? As with all collectivism, it transfers individual rights to the collective. That is democracy—*majority* rule. However, rights *always* belong only to the individual, not collectivist unions or even countries.

"You have been taught that your property could be taken from you and given to others both here and around the world on a continuing basis, under the cloak of being in the common interest, the *human* thing to do, the *right* thing to do. You have been taught that it is *moral* for government to spread the wealth, by *force*, if necessary, and without *individual* consent, and you were taught some of these ideas even by former *presidents*! That is the *essence* of collectivist democracy and majority rule.

"You have been taught that groups have rights and that group rights trump *individual* rights—that there is *virtue* in the rights of groups. This is what caused *collective* bargaining to become legal, in spite of its inherent immorality. When you accepted *that* idea, you forgot that you are all individuals regardless of the groups you may be a part of, and that the more of you who have your rights taken from you the greater the crime. You even had a president tell you that we must stop *considering* the individual, and that same president exhorted us to do what is best for *society*. That same president came up with the absurd proposal of something greater than your own self-interest—something greater than *you* are. That is *tribal* thinking and it is democracy…majority rule. We are *not* a tribe, and there is nothing greater than your own self-interest, which is a needed lesson Americans need to embrace. These are all part of the feel-good slogans and verbiage designed to appeal to emotions of the moment, and then they use it in *reverse* with feel-*bad* language…feel good, feel bad, the order of the day. That is a lesson that most Americans need to learn, and we hope they will. Collective bargaining will soon be *illegal* because it *should* be illegal because it is *immoral*.

"Democracy is *not* synonymous with liberty. It is an actual *lynching* of liberty. Those political leaders who believe in democracy have great *disdain* for liberty, and prove it with their actions day after day. You succumbed to the recommendation that democracy *means* freedom, instead of learning to understand it is *anti*-freedom.

"You have been taught that government may send your dollars to faraway places without your individual approval under the guise of *preserving* freedom, the right thing, and the *human* thing to do, but that is a direct contradiction. Ayn Rand tried to teach us a very important truth…a contradiction cannot exist. When you think you have found one, check your original premise. That is when you will find an error in your own thinking, and she was *right*.

"One day in the summer of 1985, musicians around the world raised more than $50 million for hunger relief, and they did it once again twenty years later in 2005. The money was not confiscated. Individuals voluntarily *gave* the money, and that even includes people like me who loathe rock music. *That* is freedom. It was a prelude of sorts to the astonishing amounts obtained on the Internet by Barack Obama in 2008, and again by Mitt Romney in 2012. I will explain something in a few short minutes. It was unknown at the time, but we were doing something under the radar that enabled us to surpass both of those campaigns, *combined*! Perhaps there is a better way I can put this, and that is by saying that the path to change *and* solutions is when they are accomplished by free *individuals* on a *voluntary* basis, not from force used against them by their own government *employees*! I really think our citizens *forget* that they are the employers. We saved the money in a few secret vaults for the person we chose to run against whatever individual the opposition party threw against us.

"Ladies and gentlemen, the ideas your leaders have taught you are preposterous and even evil beliefs that are not true today, were not true yesterday, and will not be true tomorrow. However, I am pleased to inform you of the way politics will be from now on. Our Constitution is in place and we will finally begin to honor it. America will once more be a nation where government *obeys* our highest law, and those laws it makes *you* follow…no more better deals for members of Congress, for example.

"Now I would like to tell you how this administration actually got started for it is not today, but many, many years ago in a revolutionary series of events that will change the course of America even more profoundly than when it was born. America slipped the bonds of Europe to establish *individual* rights and changed the world the right way, not the wrong one by Obama. Our Founding Fathers also firmly rejected rights established by birth! This is the second American *Revolution*, beginning today, and unbelievably, we kept it secret until this moment!

"On a summer weekend more than forty-years ago, some of us understood that our government would continue to pursue the developing mixed economy; socialist/progressive system in place then. We believed they would continue to follow it month-after-month and year-after-year. Many people revere the famous phrase by John F. Kennedy that urges you to ask what you can do for your country. However, it does not mean what you *think* it means. The people who wrote the line meant that you should ask what you can do for those who are in power.

"A truly great man, Milton Friedman, said this about that statement. 'Neither half of the statement expresses a relation between the citizen and his government that is worthy of the ideals of free men in a free society.' I agree with Professor Friedman.

"Most Americans are also not aware of another event—that your leaders have adopted in practice and in law, in part and in full, and you have *accepted*, *all* ten planks of the *Communist Manifesto* to some degree. It's *true*, and we knew it more than forty-*years* ago. At that time seventy-five people, youngsters for the most part, met with me, and two other men in a secret seminar in Lordsburg, New Mexico. If that meeting had not taken place I would not be here now, and our government would still be on the destructive path of wanton disregard for the rights of *individual* American citizens.

"The purpose of our meeting was to formulate a strategy to elect individuals who believe, unswervingly, in a government led by the *Constitution*, and represents the *people*, not the Republican and Democratic Parties, who do not. They strictly represent themselves. We went on a hunt for men and women who believe in the natural right of every person to reap the rewards of his life and to retain *all* of the fruits of his personal labor. We will soon have full, free markets. Our ultimate goal is to restore America to that envisioned by our Founding Fathers, starting with those individuals elected to a federal office who work *with* our Constitution and actually *obey* the document, unlike most of the people you have voted for in the past.

"The first responsibility of our *national* government is to provide a military to *defend* America to keep us *free*! This is why we do not have a department of *Offense*, although many administrations have acted as if we do. It is then natural to reason that we do not have a military that acts as a worldwide police force. We have had one for many, many years, even though it is unconstitutional. So also, is attacking countries that have not shown aggression against America, and so is *occupying* other nations. The second part of that equation is to have order within our *own* borders, and the third is to administer a system of justice through our courts. Those three points, in conjunction with the limited ones in Article 1 Section 8 are the only *legitimate* areas for legislation in our federal democratic *republic*.

"This cannot be challenged on *rational* grounds, and it is also not for what some might call a *perfect world*, for that will never be. One area that is certainly *not* a proper purpose of government is to attempt to spread freedom around the world, as was highly proclaimed by President George W. Bush. For as difficult as it may be to understand, there are actually people who *prefer* dictator rule, and that is *their* business, not ours. I also say to you that those who want a despot are more than likely people who have been brainwashed just as effectively as those in other parts of the world have been, including *America*—programmed from early childhood in many different ways.

"There are many so-called leaders who crave power more than just about anything, but they do not want you to know it. That includes most of the people you have ever voted for, and they then act in their *own* interest because voters have not held them accountable to *constitutional* responsibilities…but *we* will. With this past election, we have reached the time in our electoral life where we can achieve what our Constitution authorizes, and we will get there very quickly. There are very big changes ahead. You may not think so at first, but just as we had our *original* Revolution with the creation of America, a new and even stronger one is now at hand.

"Ours was a gathering of young people in joint effort who believe in *freedom*, not in sacrifice. Though we are no longer young, we knew then that when you subordinate what you value for that which you do *not* value, that *is* a sacrifice. I say this because the word is badly misunderstood, and let me make this analogy. The failure to understand the word, sacrifice, is very much like phony people who proclaim the greatness of a trite cliché—that serving a cause greater than your own self-interest is to be revered. It is not. It is strictly a misguided, feel-good emotion of the moment…it is doublespeak. Those who say it do not practice what they preach, but they want you to do it and believe *they* do. The more you act in your own self-interest, the better it is for America. Collectivism is bad for America.

"In our meeting we agreed to contact as many people as possible who believe in *complete* personal and economic freedom, and guide them to run for elective office as *either* a Republican or a Democrat, and we did not care which party they chose. In other words, they would become members of those two parties in name only. But whichever party they decided on they would act like the majority, and never reveal what they were up to while hiding in plain sight. We did this because we understood how thoroughly conditioned you are—how completely inculcated you became over the years to only vote for them in large numbers, solely because of their *party* name, not because of what they stand for *individually*. So what happened? Well, we *lied*! We joined in with the *programming* and convinced you that we were loyal members. We talked about issues you *think* you care for. We made you believe that we support defying the forces of nature at the expense of others as you do now, and as you have done for so many years. Then some of us stayed with the actual line that all politicians *should* be with, and that is with an *Objectivist* philosophy. Our Founding Fathers were *classic* liberals, completely unlike modern liberals *or* conservatives. As the years passed a few of us were elected, and you sent us here to this great city in the same way you have done for years—blindly, and for the reason I previously mentioned…you thought we were members of the two parties. That is the *only* reason we were acceptable to you.

"The name we chose for our small organization is The Solution. The only way massive reform was possible from our perspective, was to have our people secretly supported within the two major parties. The policies we embrace are *not* those of the duopoly of Democrats and Republicans, but of Washington and Franklin—not the policies of Bush, Clinton, Bush, McCain, or Obama, but of Adams and Jefferson! We support *freedom*! The two parties do not. We support the *Constitution*! The two parties do not. *Many* Republicans from the past are right-wing socialist's and Democrats are left-wing socialist's, and they all will come out against us, after having once *praised* us. They believe your money belongs to them; that it should be reassigned to other citizens in some form for the sole purpose of keeping them in power with the constant brand of feel-good/feel-bad language. This is what gives them their power because you have become what Franklin most feared—an uninformed electorate. The fountainhead for modern progressivism actually began with Teddy Roosevelt, with various stops along the way. It finally arrived at the doorstep of Barack Obama, a smooth talking, non-threatening, progressive Confidence Man of the Teddy Roosevelt/Woodrow Wilson/Saul Alinsky Community Organizer school, on a direct mission to kill capitalism and permanently install a gross, wicked, depraved, corrupt, dissolute, immoral government they sold as one that cares. They don't care. They all possessed a soaring rhetoric and actually said what they wanted to accomplish, but ill-informed voters missed it, and bought in to their *salesmanship*. Then, voters did not hold their feet to a *constitutional* fire, and with their silence, declared it was fine with them.

"As to Republicans and Democrats, those who are not part of our organization are not your friend. They simply want you to believe they are so you will continue to send them to Washington to rape you with your own consent. Will they now start to attack *us*? You bet, and you may even agree with them at first, or even later, for a number of reasons, because we are going to do what the United States government needed to do for a long time simply because of all the things they did that they should *not* have done. We will right the Ship of State in four years, and while we are in the process, you should remember that citizenship carries responsibility that many of you have shown you do not want. I think this is true simply because you are lazy, and open to the confidence-pedaling politicians who just want the power that comes with elective office.

"Toward the end of the 1970s, nine of us were elected to the Senate and twenty-seven to the House, along with eight governorships and numerous other more minor offices at state and local levels, like mayor and alderman. We talked the talk and walked the walk of the two parties seriously, but once again, we were a part of them in name only.

"The purpose of developing candidates in this way was to eventually elect one of us as president and to hold a *controlling*, filibuster-proof, two-thirds majority in *both* Houses of the Congress. We have now *achieved* that plateau because we organized in every congressional district. I will now reveal who we are, but first I want to mention another matter. Soon I will tell you of a different Secret Society. They are primarily responsible for the death of my husband, Allen Davis, and they are more powerful than words can adequately describe. They are comprised of political insiders who hold enormous power, but they will not hold it much longer. The politics these people call a *game* is over, because it is *not* a game and it has never *been* a game.

"Allen worked with me for more than forty-years to reach this moment. The torch has now been passed not simply to a *new* generation, but to a new, yet *old* breed of public servant. We are the new Founding Fathers *and* Mothers, some of whom will even be involved in recommending and crafting legislation that will be introduced to the House and Senate via *email* and the *Internet*. We will restore the *real* American Dream, and I assure you it is not a house in the suburbs with a four-car garage and a heated swimming pool. It is *freedom*! Now I want to show you the men and women of our organization, The Solution, *and*, I want you to give serious thought to the real reform we bring with us, for it is really coming, and we will not stop until we have restored full *constitutional* government.

"I have asked all the television networks to focus on the House of Representatives first, and then on the Senate. The Solution now holds a *controlling* majority in *both* Houses, and you are about to see *constitutional* majority rule in action. With this new majority, you can be certain we will prevail. This should also help to explain to the former Majority Leader of the Senate and Speaker of the House just how they came to lose their positions earlier this month, in the surprise of their legislative lives."

The new president reached the natural pause in her speech. Turning, she gestured toward the members of Congress. Slowly, one-by-one, men and women rose from their seats, as television cameras began to focus on them. As they stood, each person held a small sign to identify themselves and the states and districts they would represent. Suddenly the reality of the moment exploded on millions of television screens, reflecting the incredulous expressions of the members who stayed seated. She actually meant what she said.

The seated legislators were wild-eyed with the sudden awareness of the historical setting, mortified by the breadth of her statement. Their faces reflected enormous astonishment, as they looked first at each other, and then at their standing colleagues. Around the nation, millions of Americans came to full attention in their homes. Only a few minutes old, the speech began to produce shock waves, felt not just in the United States, but also in homes and businesses around the world. Parents moved closer to their televisions, firmly silencing children, as they quickly turned up the volume in stunned apprehension.

When the cameras shifted back to the lone figure of Sara Principle, her eyes moved slowly across the expanse of people. The ten minutes spent showing the new Congress helped her to more fully collect her thoughts, and then she looked directly into the camera.

"What you have just witnessed," she said, "is unprecedented in the history of America. It may be even *more* profound than the Constitutional Convention! Those who remained seated are some of the people you hired who have fostered the something-for-nothing demagoguery of professional politicians. Many of them have spent several *decades* here in Washington. That is *not* what the founders wanted when they created this nation. They incorrectly believed that *principled* people would serve America for a short time and then go back home and get a real job, unlike one senator who was here more than *sixty years*!

"These people are not evil. Instead, like you, they are uninformed as to the nature and function of a *moral* and reasoned government. They are uninformed on what government *should* be as *authorized* by our *Constitution*. Unfortunately, so are most of you. I think the reason so many people are so poorly educated is also very simple—it has just been this way for as long as any of you can remember, and you got *used* to it being normal. All of you will learn that it is no *longer* normal, and should never *be* normal again. There is a new status quo here in Washington. The policies of those who *lost* their power nearly led America into an alliance long revered by liberals as simply a *unit* in a one-world government with a single currency worldwide. Their term for this was the *New World Order*, a Hitler-like, an FDR-like, and an Obama-like set-up for a few to control the many. The record will also show that progressives and *some* conservatives desired this approach, going down separate paths to reach the same outcome. These people worked to give you another immoral creation, the North American Union. The operative word here is *union*…collectivism.

"This one-world spirit has tried to convince you that we all would be destroyed in a nuclear or chemical war. You cheered their actions when they announced the end of those weapons. What they did not tell you was the ending of that military hardware was not real, and the armaments would wind up with the only military left on the planet under the banner of the United Nations. The Quadripartite Federation of this New World Order would then own the world and your freedom along with it, in *addition* to holding *all* of the weapons of mass destruction.

"You have listened when they told you of your civic *duty* of helping others, all the while hiding the fact that the real meaning behind their pro-nouncements is the transfer of wealth from some people to other people to successfully buy votes! You are thus to blame for the havoc they have wrought because you gave them the only thing that matters, and that is your vote. With that vote, you gave your approval to grant you the natural rights *all* of you possess at *birth*, but not *before* birth, in exchange for vio-lating the rights of others. By giving them your vote, you have authorized them to enter into the affairs of other nations, and to finance those excur-sions with your own money, or the money of generations unborn. But your vote was not the *biggest* thing you gave them. *That* was your consent to *intentionally*, and *systematically violate* our great Constitution.

"When an official says that something needs to be corrected or solved or provided, that is only that person's opinion, and *opinion* is not author-ized by the Constitution. Said official will then want to make the correc-tion, solve the problem, or provide the means with what he calls *federal funding*. This is not a battle to help *you*, but to benefit *politicians*, because *they* understand these actions will persuade you to vote *for* them, not *against* them. It is *taxpayer* funds, not federal funds, and government may not collect any amount of your money for any reason not authorized by the Constitution, and then the same from everyone. It is so *simple*, and when you hear a member of the House or Senate speaking about doing some-thing that costs money, the simple thing is to ask a simple question. Is it *constitutional*, and isn't *that* simple?

"By itself government has no means of support except to expropriate your wealth. Government is a non-producer. It can only take wealth from its citizens by *force*, directly, and from the market. They then spend money in a wide variety of ways on feel-good programs to create a permanent dependence, because these plans are *for* you, and then paid for *by* you. The overwhelming majority of these programs are also unconstitutional. If you paid for them directly, they would cost less and be superior at the same time because of *competition*. However, if they allowed you to find this out you might discover that you don't *need* them, and they don't want you to *know* that. On the outside of government force, free-market competition brings better products and services for *anything* at lower cost. It has always worked that way and always *will* work that way. Remember—*competition* is the key to lower cost and superior products, *not* government intervention, and certainly not government programs.

"These practices will now come to an end. I can say to you without equivocation that your new government will put a stop to those actions and begin to rewrite the face of politics. Your employees will once again work for *you*. To paraphrase Harry Truman, this time the buck really *does* stop here, and it will stop *suddenly* and *dramatically*.

"The first stop will be income tax. Because it takes time to repeal a constitutional Amendment, we will take another path to restore constitutional government. Income tax rates will change to the same rate for *all* taxpayers, thus ending *progressive* income tax. Ultimately, we must repeal the Sixteenth Amendment, but the progressive rates are no more. We look to the changeover in June of *this* year to an initial rate of fifteen percent down to *zero* by years end. You are entitled to one-hundred percent of your income. This means that some of those words or phrases that have crept into the verbiage of some politicians, like *fair share* and *balanced* must be re-examined by all of you. I hope you will, and I want you to see that these words and phrases are intentionally directed at your *emotions*, not to your *reason*, and are literally *meaningless*. They can never explain their full significance as it relates to reality, the *Constitution*, or to you.

"Politicians have such a vast storehouse of euphemisms to lead you down a path of *their* choosing to make you believe the opposite of what is true. They reel you in with throwaway phrases that *sound* important and moral. From our perspective, fair share should mean the *same*, but it doesn't with these people. When you *balance* two people on a seesaw, the result is a *level* device, not a *tilted* one. This is why the same tax rate fits both phrases, but you have been lead to believe those nasty rich people do not *deserve* a balanced approach. Make no mistake—the fair share charge is only a beginning for the collectivist. They ultimately mean *one hundred* percent of what you earn as described by Obama Sr. They won't say it, but that is what they eventually want because in their minds, you are not smart enough or good enough to manage your own wealth. That is the Marxist way, as history has shown, if we care enough about our country to learn.

"Today we begin the cleansing process *away* from a socialist democracy to *privatize* our country with the only economic/social system that is moral and works for everyone, and that is the *free enterprise* system. Only this time it really *will* be free. The real solution to personal and economic progress is not *more* government but the exact opposite—more freedom, *less* government. The only *moral* economic/social system is complete and total *unregulated capitalism*. The reason this is true is that capitalism does not employ the use of force against anyone, but operates solely on a voluntary basis of exchange. Only with this unregulated capitalism, which has never existed in any major country, including America, can we soar to the highest economic achievement possible. We were very close to this ideal when we became a nation, but it did not last. And hear me now, all of you who are employed in banking. You will not receive bailout money to save you from bad business ways, and you will be like all other businesses if you break the *law*. Some of you committed the greatest financial crime in our history in 2008, and if you repeat it, you will then be imprisoned.

"The subtext of *regulated* capitalism is the use of government force—power that declares the collective knows what is best for each citizen and our nation. It doesn't. The free market is where superior knowledge resides with *individual* rights, and yes, some actually get hurt it they do not exercise due diligence or if they are defrauded, a direct act of physical force.

"Force is force, regardless of *how* it is implemented, such as our national government forcing Americans to pay other Americans in *any* way, even with natural disasters, foreign or domestic. That takes money. And while we can all empathize with those who suffer from natural adversity, that ability for compassion does not make it *moral* to confiscate money to pay for rebuilding from hurricanes, tsunamis, tornadoes or floods. That is the use of force, and it is *always* wrong! It is *immoral* to have a system of governance that forces citizens to hand over their property to others except for self-protection, which is *self-interest*. You will hear me say this several times. It is moral to *respond* to force but immoral to *initiate* force. In all of this, I am speaking here only of our *national* government. Regardless of how much you might want to believe it is right, you cannot *rationally* justify the use of force to fulfill the *belief* and *opinion* of *anyone*. As this applies to force used *against* us, we will certainly *respond* regardless of where it comes from. We will not *start* a fight. We will fight *back* against *any* entity that starts a battle with us, and we will *finish* that fight.

"If Americans want to provide rebuilding funds to *any* people in time of disasters, the moral method is one that is voluntary. This also applies to the continent of Africa, the country of Haiti or anywhere. The American people did not create their HIV/AIDS, poverty, or genocide problems. *They* did! It is also important to know *this*. Money taken from future generations of Americans does not go to the people the politicians tell you it goes to, but to foreign *politicians* who are just as corrupt as our own. If our citizens want to help citizens of foreign nations, they can do it *voluntarily*, on their own. It's an easy concept to understand. Isn't it?

"In 1913, the Sixteenth Amendment gave Congress the power to tax our income. It was immoral then, and it still is. Unscrupulous politicians and other so-called leaders of the era sold Americans this bill of goods, and put in place another feel-good proposition. The Seventeenth Amendment that same year changed the method senators were selected. Until that time, a senator was chosen by the *Legislature thereof* in their state. The founders made this provision because the role of a senator was to represent his state government, not the people, to keep the states sovereign. The House of Representatives was the branch of government to represent the people, hence, the name. That is just one of the reasons for their two-year election cycle. Of all of these events, think Presidents Theodore Roosevelt and Woodrow Wilson, the grossly immoral, racist, anti-America progressives who wanted to move the United States *beyond* the Constitution, and then eventually discard the document altogether. It did not work, as it did not work when President Barack Obama tried very much the same thing nearly one hundred years later…but it *almost* did. Next was The Federal Reserve Act of 1913, illegally creating a *fourth* branch of government. The Constitution authorizes *three*. Over the next four years, we will end the Federal Reserve and restore the gold standard.

"When I was a very young man, former President Jimmy Carter talked about the disgrace of our tax system, but I suspect that what he had in mind was another progressive idea that the so-called rich did not pay enough. That is just my *opinion*, but it *is* where they always go. Just tax those awful rich folks and then everything will be wonderful. However, what now takes place will be different with our new majority. We will do something to restore *freedom*, not collectivism. Those who followed President Carter didn't believe in freedom either. They all believed in the *power* of government *force*, not in the *right* of government, but *we* do, and we will begin to install it with our newly elected power to pass legislation, according to the precepts of our Constitution.

"Patrick Henry said 'Give me liberty or give me death.' That spirit must once again flourish. It must echo its cry across the width and breadth of this bountiful land, for it is not like a part-time job, on one day and off the next. The spirit of freedom must rise from the ashes of our great ancestors and actually *mean* something again!

"We will modernize our country into one the world has *never* seen, and we will do it by putting government back to its proper role of protecting our lives and property. Restoration by looking backward may even bring back *manufacturing*, and those with money offshore should be *ready* to bring it back *immediately*. Government that transfers wealth to create programs beyond our Constitution will end. Our nation began that way with the work of our Founding Fathers, and today we are issuing the burial certificate of Big Brother! As for the legislative powers of the Congress, they will return to those seventeen items delineated in Article 1 Section 8 of the Constitution. I do assure you the Congress can, and will stay busy that way, and they will be working six days a week just as soon as rules are changed. They will spend only two months per year in Washington. The remaining time they will be in their districts, and begin a wholesale repeal of regulations and laws as far back as 1900, and that means *all* of them.

"No more will special interest groups have a direct line to government. No more will elected officials weaken our currency spending our taxpayer dollars in ways not authorized by Article 1 Section 8. No more will individual rights be sacrificed to the desires of some, for if even *one* person receives special privilege, the ultimate ramification is that others must pay the bill. Said another way, the free lunch is over for everyone who has been eating at the public trough, and yes, that means the immediate end *today* of food stamps and all other so-called government goodies.

"Our citizens will no longer be required to pay for something others want. If a product or service is desired the person who wants it, must pay the bill directly, or through insurance, and obtain it from the *private* sector. A *free* society works that way—voluntarily, and without the use of force by government officials and their progressive and conservative sympathizers. Many, many years ago, the former head of the American Communist Party said in part, 'America is getting socialism on the installment plan.' Progressives will not like this, but that statement is no longer true. I know they will keep trying. I also know it is painful and difficult to admit that America *is* a socialist nation. Perhaps it is even *impossible* for many of you. To those who do not believe, I ask you to define the redistribution of wealth for anything other than the points covered in the Constitution as something other than socialism/communism, for it is not!

"This day will mark the rebirth of what our founders intended and then lost. The only system that enables everyone to reach his or her full potential regardless of background is here at last. This is the arrival of laissez faire; or, let it be free, government. It is also time to add the separation of *economics*. With the wholesale repeal of regulations, the law of supply and demand will operate freely in the marketplace of goods and services, *and* the birth of *ideas* the way it *must* be in a free nation. We do not have it now, but we soon will, and that also means completely junking government healthcare. When Congress created Obama-Care, they used Al Gore's mathematical model. The real, unspoken goal was to create a single-payer health insurance, with government as the controlling power by eventually taking one-hundred percent of your wealth. We will repeal this immoral law, along with the rest of them, and work with the American people to amend the Constitution to prevent it from happening again.

"Government officials have convinced you they are against monopolies, and that anti-trust laws exist for your security. The truth, however, is exactly the opposite. Instead of *preventing* monopolies, they actually *create* them, and they do this in some instances, by protecting certain companies and *guarantee* a profit for them.

"In a nation where freedom truly reigns, the greatest equalizer in business is competition, or *potential* competition. Only government can create a monopoly. People need government protection for their life and property, which does include their business. However, they cannot rightfully protect your business at the same time they are attempting to destroy it. In the environment that has existed for many years, Americans actually need protection *from* the government, because in the case of anti-trust laws, government regulators are out to get your business in favor of their friends and associates. That being the case, all anti-trust laws will be repealed by acts of Congress and I will sign the legislation...*immediately*!

"One of their most *unsuccessful* monopoly creations from the standpoint of *not* being excellent is the public school system. Schools are not a legitimate purpose of government, and as of today, government is out of the school business. If cities and towns want to establish private schools in what are currently government buildings, they can enable private individuals or companies to put a business plan together and get on with the *moral* education of our children. I recommend they not include unions, but it is *their* decision to make. Teachers unions have not served our children well. Yes, there are fine educators who belong to the teachers union, but the union is *not* fine and now, *all government* unions are out of business.

"Aside from being both immoral and beyond the justifiable realm of a government of *free* people, minimum wage laws have *never* protected any person who wanted a job. Instead, they have caused widespread *unemployment* by effectively eliminating a variety of jobs whose value is not as high as the law dictates, especially among our youth. What *does* protect an employee is the freedom to sell his skills in the marketplace. If he has no skills, it is up to him to acquire them because it is *his* future at stake. Minimum wage is simply another in a long line of edicts to make you *feel* good, and feel-good policies *never* benefit those it claims to help. It *does* help those who conjured up the idea in the first place by giving them a job. However, the *moral* part of that equation is that *no one*, including the government or your brother-in-law, has the *right* to tell an employer what he *must* pay his staff. They have had the *power* but not the *right*. Now they no longer *have* the power. Minimum wage laws will be *repealed* immediately, and so will forced union membership, which sure as hell is not fair *or* balanced! The thugs at SEIU and other unions will need to find *real* jobs.

"In a *free* environment, competition that is not controlled is self-regulating. Free markets keep the quality of goods and services higher and prices lower. It *always* works that way. Free competition also does not violate the first principle of a moral government—to *initiate* force is certainly not moral, whether from a military or a protection racket union, or government. It is simply some people creating the power to *restrain*. They do this for *themselves*, not for you. It solidifies their power, and justifies their existence. It is especially true of the *heads* of unions.

"This purging of government regulation is nowhere as important as in the healthcare industry. That is the business of each individual, not the government. By removing these people from power, you will see your healthcare costs *dramatically* reduced. The marketplace works in *every* area. Hospitals, doctors, and the medical community will have the ability to forge their position with excellent products and services. For this, individuals and businesses will reward them. It will be just the opposite for those who do not offer quality, and the word *will* get out. It always does. People will notice who deserves their business and who does not. Drugs, hospital stays, every phase of every treatment will be less expensive in a free market. The industry will not address their service to government dictates...only to the individual patients they serve. This also includes unions and insurance companies. Paid health care is *not* a right; *living* is. Lower income individuals will have *charitable* protection and service.

"Regulatory agencies are devices—tools to help the bunch of hooligans in power. They restrict entry into a variety of businesses and cause higher prices and lower quality. This is because they are very effective in their *intentional* tactic of depressing competition. These officials frequently exalt non-profit organizations because they somehow believe that profit is a dirty word. What is more accurate is that they want *you* to believe it. They immorally put regulations in place and refuse to accept a sound and provable fact against those rules. They *cause* the *opposite* of what they *say* they want, and they *know* it. People in high seats of authority actually *want* higher prices and lower quality. It provides increasing power for politicians and justifies their careers to the public. Therefore, the thousands of alphabet agencies like the EPA, IRS, FCC, HUD, and others will be legislated out of business, along with the 1887 Interstate Commerce Act!

"I know many of you will find this an extremely bitter and hard-to-believe pill to swallow. When politicians try to sell you the bill of goods that groups have rights, answer them with a firm and steady voice that only *individuals* have rights, and you can prove it.

"In the 1930s, Franklin Roosevelt said this about *controls*. 'Government has the definite duty to use all its power and resources to meet new social problems with new social controls.' I say to you in a very serious and frank way, *really*, that is a *literal* bunch of *hooey*! Roosevelt then proceeded to establish what was eventually called the Third Rail of politics. The Social Security Act became an untouchable to politicians who wanted only one thing, and that was to be re-elected. It made it necessary to stay away from Social Security because old people vote and politicians want power...that's why they are politicians! Older Americans have also lived the entitlement mentality all of their lives, and have refused to acknowledge the Social Security program is one that was forced on them along with Medicare. So what were those *resources* FDR mentioned? Tax dollars imposed on American citizens who had no choice in the matter, like health insurance in 2010, as well as a gigantic bank of dollars for politicians to raid to buy votes to help them stay in power in Washington.

"Ladies and gentlemen, Social Security is a cruel and *immoral* fraud. It doesn't need *mending*...only *ending*, and end it we *will*. *How* we end has not been completely worked out. We no hardship on individuals, but I believe we have a secret weapon that involves so-called government owned property, and here is just a hint. It is not a proper purpose *or* function of government to own property. Because that is true, vast amounts of what is referred to as government owned property will be *sold*. A portion of the proceeds from this going out of the real estate business sale will be rebated to our people at a rate and age group not yet determined. When it is, those individuals involved will be completely removed from the Social Security roles. As that happens, an equal number of younger people will be removed from participation. As we develop this program in different ways, *all* citizens will be removed from Social Security *and* Medicare. Some will receive checks and some will not. Those who do not receive checks will no longer have that Social Security percentage deducted from their paychecks, and medical expenses will be a lot less expensive.

"I do acknowledge it is a complex and time consuming process, and certainly, changes will have to be made, but Social Security will be ended for everyone. Government forced it on us. That is the *power* FDR cited, and, my fellow citizens, FDR did not really look at *need* when he concocted the scheme, for he was a just a stage-master extraordinaire who only cared about progressivism with government in charge of everything.

"He looked at actuarial tables that showed you probably would not even live long enough to collect, only to pay, so he would make you *feel* good while he stole your property at the same time. We of the new majority believe that government has no duty to *force* us to provide for our old age or *any* age, or to institute so-called social controls to meet so-called social problems. Nor do we believe it is the role of government to create in the minds of Americans a permanent dependence on anyone other than themselves. Social problems do not *exist*. Only *individual* problems exist, even when in the middle of a group. It is up to each person to take care of their *own* problems, not have them taken care of by his neighbor under the threat of force or the full *use* of force. Physical force must be banned and *individual* rights fully recognized by *all* members of our government.

"George W. Bush began his second term as president in 2005 to try to establish what he called *personal* accounts in Social Security. And while I give him credit for trying *something*, that is wrong too because it still gives officials the power to force Americans to participate in what is actually a *Ponzi* scheme. Long ago government made it illegal for *citizens* to develop a *private* Ponzi scheme, which is fraud, and an *initiated* act of aggression against the property of another. Therefore, that makes it illegal, just like Social Security. Yes, I just said that Social Security is *illegal*, because it is not constitutional, and additionally, it is evil because of force. Ayn Rand said: 'Evil, not value, is an absence and a negation, evil is impotent and has no power but that which we let it extort from us.'

"In the same time frame when President Bush wanted to have the personal accounts, Federal Reserve Chairman Alan Greenspan, once declared that, 'If we have promised more than our economy has the ability to deliver to retirees…as I fear we may have, we must recalibrate our public programs so that pending retirees have time to adjust.' He probably meant those pending retirees would receive *recalibrated* checks that would be smaller than they *thought* they would receive. I *think* he used to be more like members of The Solution and me, but that is my *opinion*, not fact.

"President Bush and the Congress passed a new prescription drug benefit in 2003, expected to cost more than $540 *billion* over a ten year period, and of course it was higher. This was simply a continuing effort to buy your vote by force, and with your own money. A progressive Republican president accomplished this assault against the Constitution.

"The national treasure was robbed from future generations by the moronic and *criminal* invasion of Iraq, *and* destabilized the Middle East. When I say this, I do not refer solely to dollars, but also to lives. American citizens allowed this incursion by refusing to demand that those responsible for that unconstitutional act face accountability in a court of law. The Congress did not act because they were complicit with Mr. Bush, and citizens could not institute Articles of Impeachment against them.

"As we enter this new phase of logical and *moral* governing, all other forms and functions of wealth transfer will be ended, with some *phased* out, while others face an immediate end. I think that once you get used to the idea you will be pleased that someone finally had the guts to act. One of our first priorities will be to begin the process for new Amendments to our Constitution to end the income tax, return to a gold standard, repeal the seventeenth Amendment and eliminate the Federal Reserve. Congress, like you, will have a full time job. They will work year 'round, six days a week, because there is a lot to repair.

"Some of these measures will take time, but we *will* get the job done. Except for military veterans, Americans who receive welfare payments of *any* kind will have to begin meeting their own needs. It is not up to your neighbors to support you, for if you receive something from government, you actually got it from other taxpayers, *forced* to participate in unconstitutional acts. As of today that will no longer be true. You are not entitled to monetary support from other taxpayers unless it is *voluntary*, and I cannot make it any clearer than that.

"Now I want to speak on foreign aid and our involvement in the affairs of other nations, which George *Washington* warned against. You are each currently paying around $0.03 for just *one* foreign aid program that seeks to promote democracy around the world. Nowhere in our Constitution will you find anything remotely resembling any kind of authority for that program, and in 2009, at least one member of the Congress even *admitted* it. As I have repeatedly said, democracy is not what our Founding Fathers created because they knew it is a bad form of government, even when called a *representative* democracy. That is still majority rule, and the rule of law does not exist where the majority and the gang in charge, *criminals*, make those decisions.

"Foreign aid was not *designed* to help foreign people. It was created to help American and foreign *politicians*. As of now, and at least for the next four years, America no longer has a program of foreign aid *or* military forces based in foreign lands. An important point to keep in mind is that we will not honor agreements to keep our troops stationed in foreign lands. You can vote us out of office in four years and restore the social-ist/communist government that we are removing, but for now, it is over. If citizens really *do* want to send money to people in other countries, they may do so directly, and of their own accord. That would certainly cut out the middleman, but the obscene flow of capital as directed by our govern-ment is *finished*! Our national policy will be benign neutrality, as it was under President George Washington.

"September 11, 2001 did not happen because terrorists hate freedom, as George W. Bush and a few radio talk show hosts stated. It principally occurred because American politicians first created an immoral foreign policy of interference in various cultures around the world that lasted for decades. The Islamist's finally responded to our presence in their country because we were there, and Bin Laden made it an issue to Muslims, be-cause *they* mean to take over the world. He continued to make it year-by-year because he had his foot in the door until our troops killed him. How-ever, if the Islamist's decide they want to proceed with terrorist tactics to inspire the Caliphate once again, they will quickly regret that decision.

"A very good example of American interference with other cultures was the unconstitutional invasion of Iraq and the slow rolling action in Syr-ia. That was covertly providing small arms. One part of the problem is that America abandoned true capitalism. You may think that statement is crazy, but here is the connection. Unregulated capitalism is the *only* political sys-tem that is *completely* opposed to war! Democracies are *pro* war, and, it is easy to document this truth with *evidence*, not with opinion. Knowing this you have to ask yourself where you now stand. Support laissez faire capi-talism to *end* war! Support the notion of democracy to *create* war.

"So we will no longer pursue any involvement in the affairs of other nations except for trade, because capitalism and free exchange is the *an-swer* to human freedom, *real* peace, and moral governing.

"We do have an obligation to maintain our national defense, and we will do that in a way that leaves no question in the mind of any potential enemy. If there is a strike against America we will act, and we will not *de-bate* or *negotiate* it with *anyone*! We believe that the typical method of conducting diplomacy by *all* nations is simply a fancy way of stating that lying and deceitful practices are just. They are not, and we will not contin-ue with that model. Your new government will be unequivocal in language it uses. It will not use *different* language for different *people*.

"All potential foes need to take stock on how they interact with this new approach, and understand that we really do believe that, as the epic poet Virgil said, 'fortune favors the bold.' This administration will definitely be bold, and our positions will be precise. In other words, we will not say one thing and mean another, and I will not be a serial liar like Barack Obama was on Benghazi in 2012, and the unconstitutional PRISM spying program on the world...but it worked!

"I am *certain* the so-called *War on Terror*, the phrase President Obama refused to use, cannot be won by *invading* other countries, but by *removing* American interference in those lands. The reason I believe this is simple. It is what the terrorists have said, *and*, it is not constitutional. However, if we find that after we remove our presence they *still* attack us, we will seek them out and destroy them, but we will leave them alone if they leave us alone. Another part of our non-interference policy has to do with using armed drones to kill people; we will not continue *that* immoral action, and we will close all American military bases not in America.

"I held two private meetings with President Zgonina of Russia *before* I became the president, and we have reached a mutual accord along these lines of clearly stating our positions. He is convinced I will act quickly to defend America, and he is *right*! He also fully understands much better than the two major political parties of America do, that the dream of Marx, Lenin, *and* the Republican and Democratic Parties will *never* work, nor will the American hybrid of some *regulated* enterprise and socialism put together as equal partners...the dream of many progressives.

"While we seek no involvement in the internal affairs of any other nation, we will take strong action against anyone who tries to use force against us. I want no misunderstanding on this point. There will be no diplomacy on the matter. We will simply act. *All* of the options we have at our disposal will *always* be on the table, and if called to the task we will answer with firm, intense resolve, with all of our power if necessary, and yes, that means what you think it does.

"Russia and China have been more open to freedom and entrepreneurship in recent years, and they will be even more so in the days and years to come. This time, however, their people will know the wonders of liberty more than they could ever have imagined, with open markets, private property rights, and substantially reduced taxes. They are now in the course of change. Russia will develop three branches of government like America, and will become a federal democratic republic, like the United States. When this process is completed, their government will have something else very much in common with America...some of their people will not like it. Can you think of a reason? With freedom comes citizen responsibility some citizens do not want, along with a loss of power for politicians. Where you find any politician, you will find someone who craves power. That is usually the reason they became politicians in the first place. We will develop expanded trade with Russia and China. We will not interfere in their internal affairs. Their politics is their business, not ours, but all three governments will create treaties that cover trade, because once again, trade is the answer, not interference or war.

"I now come to a subject that is one of the most evil to ever exist. An organization was born before the dawn of the nuclear age. They are an Anglophile network of wealthy people. Together, they have plotted a course of action designed to take over the world. The overwhelming percentage of their membership is a cabal of business people who discovered long ago that they could use politicians because politicians are corrupt. They did this in part by implanting themselves on the inside of governments worldwide, and worked to create a climate of fear and misinformation. In all of this, they managed to keep themselves *invisible*. Nuclear weapons enabled them to advance their plan more rapidly than when the organization was first formed in 1900. They created feel-good phrases and slogans for the masses of people—small, seemingly unimportant sayings to engage the public into a false sense of goodness and well-being.

"They began a concerted but subtle schedule designed to convince people the planet would be destroyed if nations continued to maintain their own individual sovereignty, *implied* in all of their publicity, not openly stated. They have existed at the highest levels of government for well over one-hundred years, and in some of the most respected corporations whose names you all know. They are devoted to the proposition of a single government and a single currency worldwide—a federation to sit at the throne of world control in their *New World Order*, and they would have had their way with more opportunities, but we have taken those prospects away…for now.

"This network was born in Paris and operates from there, and London and New York. They have affiliates of different names in every industrialized country. Their name is The World Council Group. Their American affiliate is The Committee on Foreign Affairs, with subchapters in all fifty states. For those who have not heard of them I assure you they *do* exist. They are a sinister lot with widespread power well beyond the comprehension of most people, from control of large sections of the media to your own state Houses. If you believe they are benevolent in their nature, you are *wrong*! They are the exact opposite. Progressives are also violent.

"These people are acutely aware that the key to socializing the world is to instill a global commonality with citizens, and then move to a powerful centralized government, the military power of which would have been the nuclear arsenal center of the United Nations military complex located in Brussels, Belgium.

"In the future, they will succeed in re-establishing their goals only if you *let* them. In the next elections, you would be wise not to give your vote to politicians unless they fully support liberty, limited government, and the Constitution, and make them *prove* it. This has usually meant candidates of the two major political parties, but as you can see, it might not be that way in another election. We of the new legislative majority strongly urge them to abandon their march toward worldwide socialism. We also ask Americans to do the same in all of our elections, for you are the ones with the ultimate power if you simply *exercise* that power. Some of these politicians are not to blame entirely. Like you, they have been part of the old status quo because it has been that way for such a long period of time, but as I said earlier, there's a *new* status quo in town.

"At this point I have a brief statement on the United Nations. Since its inception, the U.N. has been an organization that is anti-America. They are against freedom, free trade, and individual rights. They are *for* power for themselves and their socialist partners…the collective. So America is withdrawing from the U.N. And is there still a cause worth fighting for? The answer is *yes*; the *continuous* fight for *liberty* and *truth*, and remember—truth *can* change your mind, and so can freedom.

"Even though the Declaration of Independence says the words, we cannot cling to the absurd notion that people are equal for we are not, and we should never even *want* to be equal! We are all different, with unique skills and goals. Some of us *have* no goals and that is fine, but to be equal is to be the same, in spite of the glaring fact that many of you prefer to look, act, and think like your neighbor, and to be *in style* like *cool* people. That is something you have learned in the classroom of conformity, and the first stage of that learning comes from parents and the many religions. You may disagree and that is your right, but it is my hope that once you understand this basic, truth many of you will begin to demand your natural right to be different from your neighbor, *if* that is *your* choice made in the atmosphere of freedom. Besides, it is frequently great fun to be different, but if you haven't tried it, you wouldn't know. There certainly is a place for uniformity if it is *voluntary*, as is the case with families teaching their children, but there is also a *voluminous* place for *non-conformity*.

"As far as equality is concerned, it can never be obtained. Some people will always be seen as *more* equal, and in many cases that common perception is true. In others, it is not. The truth is that we can have freedom or a lack of it, which would come with equality. Freedom and equality are mortal enemies. If it were possible for all of us to be equal, that feat would mean the end of freedom. You cannot have both, and freedom is the most important to reach for, not one that would try to make all of us the same. It seems to me we do enough of that on our own without any encouragement from *anyone*.

"In the Declaration, Jefferson announced that all men are *created* equal. Did he mean just men? I don't think so. That was just the language of the day. On the other hand, women had very few rights in that era, but then another question comes to mind. Did Jefferson mean all when he said that *all* men are created equal? I think he did not, and here's why. The great Thomas Jefferson *may* have meant all *white* people. If it was true that he was against slavery, why did he own slaves? That is my opinion, not a fact. To be fair, he lived in a time that still had one foot in the Dark Ages. Jefferson had great difficulty with his Age of Enlightenment because of the intense hold of religion on most people, but not him.

"I think Jefferson wanted his fellow citizens to understand that people have the same *rights*, Natural Rights, which simply means they come from the *nature* of things, or as some have said, from their humanity...the characteristic of being human with inalienable Rights.

"The word *inalienable* means that those Rights are not *transferable*; they are *absolute* Rights and cannot be taken away and reassigned to someone else by force. We are either free or we are not! There can be no middle ground. Rights of life and the pursuit of happiness belong solely to each *existing* person. It is also true for money, which means Property Rights. Does it make sense for the people of South Dakota to have their dollars taken from them to provide something for people of Illinois or Utah or for those in *any* state including their own because a *politician* says it does? It is a gross obscenity for government power to *confiscate* the wealth of citizens and then *transfer* that wealth to other citizens. What is yours does not come with an *expiration* date, unless, of course, that information exists on some legal document, and it got there without the use of force.

"Guaranteed student loan programs exist through confiscated funds from taxpayers—*transfer* payments from some citizens to other citizens, and that certainly is a violation of inalienable Rights.

"The reason these plans were put in place was not to help students, but to purchase votes. Politicians only help *themselves*. The originators of these programs understood that you would feel very good that people who could not afford to pay for college would be able to go anyway because of these programs. This is just some of the feel-good politics that has existed outside the authority of the Constitution for decades. I know that some of you have become addicted to them, but they are obscene and immoral. The funds to pay for these programs do not materialize from a magic moneybox in Washington. They come from existing and unborn American citizens who had no choice in the matter. So the question becomes, why not a car, or a house, or a pair of shoes? Why not $1 million—where do you draw the line? Does a line even exist? Should money be seized from a so-called wealthy person who is about to go bankrupt and given to a struggling student? Well, if you believe the rhetoric of Barack Obama and other progressives you would quickly say, yes, but the *moral* answer is *no* because it is a violation of *Inalienable Rights*! Natural Rights! Henceforth, *all* entitlement programs are over as soon as possible, because you are *not* entitled to the property of other citizens unless they freely sell or give it to you.

"Before there was a United States, a group of people existed who dealt in criminal enterprises for their livelihood. In our own country, we have seen their numbers explode in direct proportion to the size of federal government regulations, and this has not been an *accident*. The hoods have taken a page from the politicians by *diversifying* their businesses. They acquire legitimate ones to help them hide the criminal operations. One of the ways members of Congress hide their pork-barrel politics, for example, is to include them as Earmarks in huge bills no legislator ever reads, and are very complex. They will soon *have* to read new bills because there will be new rules in *both* Houses that *require* a member be *present, online* or *live*, for a *full* reading to have the right to vote on a bill.

"Other advantages criminals have lies at the doorstep of self-righteous religious leaders making decisions that *they* know what is best for you, and who use their lofty positions to increase their control. In doing this they have caused certain goods and services to be illegal, goods and services such as drugs and prostitution. To the best of my knowledge, prostitution has existed since before humans ever created government. The reality is the mob is actually laughing all the way to the bank because we the people have permitted elected and un-elected officials to produce such immoral laws concerning human behavior, *knowing* the laws were dishonest.

"Consider the so-called War on Drugs. The government uses your tax money to mount what they call an assault on drugs, and then they imprison users and sellers. But there is an even greater issue on the line in this instance, and it produces a simple question. Is it really any of their business? The short answer is no! These are decisions that are the *exclusive* province of the individual. What *is* government's business is if you commit an act of aggression against someone while you are under the influence of one of these drugs, or commit a crime to raise funds to buy them. There are laws currently on the books that govern driving a car while drunk or stoned, but that is *after* the fact, not before when you actually take a drink or smoke a joint...and those are state or city laws. It can only be the business of the *federal* government on *federal* land, and as you previously heard, many of those properties are going on the auction block, because a proper government is not a landowner. Government can only be a renter.

"Officials know there are people who will use drugs, and that is their *right*. Benjamin Franklin used morphine for pain, yet certain politicians insist on making *national* laws against drug usage. This means that they facilitate the creation of criminal enterprises by interfering with the natural law of supply and demand, to drive the prices through the *roof*! The higher risk, along with tighter supplies, forces the thugs to sell at higher prices than would be possible if the drug laws did not exist. You can go to the drugstore for prescription painkillers, but you cannot go there for marijuana, which can be even more effective for some types of pain, with no side effects other than getting the munchies. When you are freely able to make your purchase of whatever drug you need or want, no one is going to be shot down on the street corner or rotting in prison because of immoral laws established by immoral *politicians*. Some of these men and women, because of these legislative actions, are actually guilty of murder in my opinion, but I will have too much to do to go after *them*.

"It has been clearly shown that prohibition does not work with anything, and the immoral religious forces behind the drug ban *know* that is true, but they do not care. I am telling you that we will correct this problem and take the criminal element out of drugs. It is none of *my* business if you smoke pot or snort cocaine, nor is it your business if *I* do. The prevailing attitude is disgusting. Therefore, we are issuing a new paradigm. We will release people from prison and stop the insanity. It is not your *business*, or as Glen Beck said, 'mind your business.' Get *over* it!

"We will fix it so innocent people are no longer killed or imprisoned because of the corrupt desires of some religious people and the demagogic politicians who pander to them. Listen to me, because when we have fully removed them from *political* power, law enforcement will have the resources to fight *real* crime. Government will not spend taxpayer dollars on trumped-up charges that are clearly unconstitutional. It is not up to some American citizens to tell other citizens that they may not use drugs, or to have the use of government force to back up your immoral claims. It is not up to them to tell men that they cannot use the services of a prostitute. Drug use will not ruin the country! Prostitution will not wreck the *populace*. Lack of freedom *will*, and I repeat—it is not your business, whether you are a complaining, self-righteous individual, priest, or government official!

"As we go about dismantling many parts of what government has become over the next four years, my current assistant, Armando Munoz, will be my chief of staff. He will also work with Cecil Price as a go-between with various parts of federal offices to coordinate many of our sweeping changes, along with a sensational young man, Luther Johnson. They will work closely with Vice President Kayne and Senator Russell Harrington in ongoing business with the Senate. Imagine! We now have the first *Jewish* vice president. Chet Forbes will be my press secretary. The White House press corps should be happy with that since they've had such a good relationship over the *past* four years, and Fox News will not be prohibited, and no one will spy on them.

"I now call on all Supreme Court Justices to resign, because all of you have a built-in liberal political bias. If there were any conservatives, my call would also include them. You seem to have been trying in any way you can to *violate* the Constitution, and that is the reason behind my call. When that is finished, I will appoint *seven* new justices, not nine, and it may include some of you. The new Oath of Office will include two additional words, and they are, *and obey*, to the current Oath. If you choose not to resign, the House will impeach you and the Senate convict you. If you resign, you will maintain your retirement benefits, but not if you are guilty in a Senate trial. The Constitution is our highest law, not a major *inconvenience* to any of your *opinions*, and I will give you a for-instance.

"Many years ago a Supreme Court stated that a woman has a *constitutional* right to an abortion, and anyone who reads *knows* that is complete nonsense. It is not necessary to have a college degree to know that. It is not part of the Constitution, and the Court and everyone else knew it. So also did the millions of citizens who *supported* the decision, including the immoral politicians who danced the abortion tune for votes. Abortion laws are not an issue for the federal government or the Supreme Court. Roe was just politics.

"As far as *we* are concerned, the people of the individual states have that authority, and we hope they will always be against *initiating* force, for abortion is really none of their business, in my opinion, and also objective *reality*. A living human being has rights, but an embryo does not. When a heart and brain exists, that is quite clearly a living, unborn human, but I do not know when that happens, and an abortion must not take place when it does. Here is something else. Making it completely illegal is an act of aggression against an individual, a woman, that is unrivaled by nearly every other act except murder. In that concept, I also believe that government has no role to play in marriage! It is a private matter with adults...straight or gay, and I credit Obama with single handedly ending hysteria against gays.

"Senator Harrington is giving an endowment of $20 million to create an organization to teach individual achievement and natural law on a *secular* level. I cannot give details except for who will head that corporation, and it will be Dr. Thomas Farley. Therefore, so no one will be confused, let me say this slowly. It will be a *private enterprise* institute. Taxpayers will not fund it, but it will be open to receiving contributions by thinking, *rational* people. Reason comes first.

"Our military forces serving in foreign lands will be returned to America. Many men and women suffered death or injury in Iraq and Afghanistan. The occupation of foreign lands is over, and bases will be closed. The role of the military is to *defend* America, not *occupy* other lands. If terrorists hear this message, and I know they will, understand this. We will remove our troops from your lands and we will begin as early as possible, *after* I have met with the Joint Chiefs. It will take time, but that is the new and complete mission. I cannot say how much time right now, but it will be as quickly as possible. I do not want them there even more than *you* do not want them there, and you now have this challenge from me. You have said that you attacked us because we are in your lands and cultures, only now we will be moving out for good. This will also apply to our government delegations. If you ever get beyond your immoral religious teachings and decide that you want to host an American embassy, *perhaps* we will return. However, if you attack us, you will slow our exodus, and if you do, we will respond in kind. So put your weapons away and show that you mean what you have said, because *I* do. Once again, if you do not stop your attacks against us we will respond and destroy you. We have the power. *Strong* power we have not yet used, but we *will* use that power if it is necessary. If it *is* used, hundreds of thousands of your citizens will die. Maybe more! We also now have a non-interventionist policy that will hold as long *we* are not interfered with. We will no longer be a *Crusader* nation, nor will we be a nation interfering with the cultures of nations because we are on an oil hunt. There is enough oil in America, and I assure all of you that oil companies will develop *all* of those reserves.

"One additional thing you are advised to remember are the details some of your countries have made with private oil companies. They will have *private* security forces protecting them from you to fulfill their contracts. The American military will be used only if you attack us. Remember this, or you will not survive, and know that this is a statement of fact.

"I understand this address is strong. I also recognize that it has the potential to generate massive hatred because I have spoken with reason—not superstition. It is my sincere hope that those of you who have not yet understood what I have been saying for the last hour or so will now come to know and realize what is true, and what is false, and my message is simple. However, it is only simple if you freely dispense with all of the illogical approaches you have used thus far. This is what caused all of our active and non-active members of The Solution to do what we did and spend more than *forty years* doing it, and there are now several *million* of us, individually remaining anonymous and untouched by PRISM.

"Whenever government interferes in the lives of people beyond the scope of protecting them, that intrusion opens the door to where enslavement lies beyond. It also causes a deep, permanent dependence on immoral politicians, unions, *some* religious leaders, and other groupthink, tribal-think organizations that continuously use their lofty positions to peddle immoral schemes to easy-to-fleece politicians and gullible citizens.

"I could have made this speech warm and fuzzy and gone down the typical road of deception, like those who came before me. I could have done that, but if I did, I would not be telling the truth, and honesty is sorely missing in American politics. Never before in the entire history of the world has so much potential existed for the advancement of individuals, at least in America now. Yet with all the greatness we have created so far, we have done it with one hand tied behind our backs. We were getting very close to a time in our lives when progressive liberals and progressive conservatives tied *both* hands. Now the hands are *untied*, and we stand at the crossroads of American recapitulation. Which road will we choose? The next four years will unleash a power that heretofore has been nothing but a distant glimmer of hope on the horizon. That is *freedom—laissez faire* capitalism our founders created but failed to keep—a *moral* method that does not *initiate* force against *anyone*. Only a free *capitalist* government does not use force. We will get rid of all the collectivist acts that started to occur in 2008 with the advent of the Obama administration when they thought they were going to *kill* capitalism. Now America is open for business once again, unregulated, as it must *always* be. If you think you saw an explosion of growth in the past, watch it *now*. And you will also be stunned when you see, along with *true* separation of church and state, that we fulfill the promise of our founders with full separation of *economy* and state. Capitalism will fix all of the immoral, progressive borrowing and spending that occurred for many, many years to try to create what they called Social Justice. It will not be easy, but it will *happen*, because *nothing* can stop laissez faire capitalism except government, and *you*! Complete laissez fair capitalism *is* social justice, because it eliminates all force.

"That means there will be a learning skill to develop and nurture, for nothing is more important than this. It is the crux of human freedom. Keeping this newly found liberty will not be easy! The same forces will remain against us steadfast and determined; standing by to restore their socialist/progressive/communist treachery—ready to counter freedom with the same kind of control they have maintained for a very long time. But they will not cede their power *easily*, or roll over and play dead, because in a strange sort of way they are a natural part of human evolution, and evolution *is* a fact...in all life forms. Evolution even occurred with President Obama and gay marriage. At least that is what he *said*. We think, however, that he just lied because he was a *serial* liar. At any rate, that was the *right* position. What we need to worry about now are politicians who want your freedom *and* your money. They will always be around with a thirst for power, because power is what all politicians want, and they will use all sorts of touchy-feely oratory to get it back, just as they have done in past years.

"In spite of what many Americans think, we still have a race problem in America, even after we elected Barack Obama president in 2008 and re-elected him in 2012. In 2008, Obama gave what I regard as the *definitive* speech on race except for one part. It was not a mistake, because he *knows* America is not a democracy. *I* think it was on purpose. As I have said repeatedly, our founders created a constitutional republic, not a democracy. If they had in fact built a true democracy Al Gore would have won the 2000 election simply because he got the most votes—the *majority* of votes, but he didn't win, in part, because the Supreme Court *illegally* interceded and *violated* the Constitution they swore to *uphold*. There is much to do in this country, and there is much to *undo*. Government uses force against the many to favor the few, but they sell it to you as just the opposite. That is the way most politicians operate for just one reason...to keep power.

"We should never let it fade from our memory. We must *always* remember and be vigilant toward the inclination to become apathetic and content with the way things are as it relates to those who are opposed to freedom. If we are not, they will rise again, ready to flex their power-seeking muscles. The keeper of the flame of liberty must be in all of us to ensure its lasting brilliance and *existence*. Freedom is not free, but the cost is *not* spending our nation into oblivion. It is active responsibility, staying alert, and being well informed.

"Do we choose to keep our freedom this time, or give it away as we did before? You will not maintain liberty by returning to the kind of government from which we rescued you. You must decide if you want to *keep* liberty, or if you prefer the control of immoral politicians who will illegally send your sons and daughters to fight against people who have not attacked America. You have the power to return to what you once had before we came along—to live with self-serving leaders, or move forward and fully embrace the freedom we will soon have in place the way our nation was in its infancy. So make your decision, but make it by using your *thinking* brain, not the emotional part of it that is frequently referred to as your heart, and answer these questions using only *reason*, not feelings, not emotions, and not superstitions. Demand *evidence* for your choices.

"Do we stand side-by-side with the *producers* who create the jobs and prosperity, or with those who routinely claim government can create jobs? It can't, you know. The jobs that officials claim to create are from taxpayer dollars, and most are held captive by immoral unions. They are far more costly than they would have been in a completely free and *competitive marketplace*. Certainly, if you have a government job like senator or in an office, they *are* jobs, but the money that pays your salary came from taxpayers, not investors. Government does not *invest*. Government *spends*. Government has no competition...investors do.

"Do we invite people from Mexico and other countries to come to America? Well, guess what! We *do*, we *will*, and we will make sure that America is open to those who either want to become Americans, or just *work* here. If those forces against immigration were around when our ancestors came, our ancestors would have been denied entry. As that has to do with Mexico, increasingly high fences will *always* succumb to even higher ladders and inventive human adaptability. But we *will* protect the border from any invasion by terrorists, and we will use our magnificent military to do it. That is something that came to be from a lack of protecting our border.

"Do we revert backward and elect old-style politicians who live in the murky military waters of their ancestors? Perhaps we need to put them in a re-education program so they can learn what our founders *really* established in the making of this nation. At this point in their lives, they actually believe it is *moral* to invade other lands. They do not understand that America has no right to tell others how to live simply because we have the military might to *force* them to bend to our will and to our power, just to bring military *jobs* to our *district* or *state*.

"Do we continue to send people to Washington who have convinced themselves that Americans are just too dumb to live as they were meant to live, free and unregulated, or who simply will not get the concept of personal and economic freedom in the *first* place?

"Do we choose to keep all that we personally achieve, or do we try, as some administrations did, to *reinvent* a government with the raw power to *force* us to give what we have earned to others in the name of the common good?

"Do we choose when and where we will offer some of what we have acquired, or keep all of it just for ourselves, which is our natural right? Or, do we leave that important decision in the hands of politicians and bureaucrats where it has resided for so many years? Liberals want you to feel *guilty* about your wealth, and so too do many conservatives.

"Do we choose when and where to educate only our *own* children, or with those who say that we must be *forced* to pay for other people's children in *addition* to our own?

"Do we stand with those who declare it takes a village to rear a child in addition to parents, or do we finally see the idea may just be touchy-feely *code* for full collectivism? Do we recognize that the rearing of a child *can* involve those outside the family provided it is on a voluntary basis *without* government involvement, which certainly includes the use of force? Americans have gotten used to government force, but for now, it is over. When you hear politicians praise a progressive concept, understand this: progressive does not mean progress. It is collectivist code that means to go *beyond* our Constitution. It means that progressives are *smarter* than Franklin, Jefferson, Washington, and *you*, and they will *fix* things from the awful, nasty, and greedy capitalists who endorse competition.

"Do we work with the free, unregulated market, or with the insiders who derive their unrelenting power by devaluing our dollars with unconstitutional regulations and spending programs? Do we at last come to grasp the concept that only a *completely* free market is a *moral* market because it does not employ and hide the use of force in the name of law or regulation? Forcing automobile companies to reach parameters set by politicians and unions, instead of the free market, is neither moral nor competent, and it helped some of them to go out of business in 2009.

"Do we finally begin to listen with our *minds*, which *instinctively* tell us what is right and what is wrong, or continue with what we label as our *hearts*, the emotional part of us where basic resentments lay, and frequently lead us to commit acts of aggression even against ourselves?

"Do we continue to allow immoral presidents like George W. Bush and Bill Clinton, to engage in *unconstitutional* foreign wars by attacking those who have not attacked us, instead of holding them to account with impeachment and a prison term?

"Do we allow immoral presidents like Obama, to have the power to bring about spending programs that dwarf our entire history of national debt and fully change America into a Communist nation?

"Do we finally begin to see that when you elect conservative or liberal politicians—Republican *or* Democrat, the subversion of the Constitution will continue unabated? Do we finally know it will be to achieve *their* aims, not those of the nation? Until you begin to understand this basic truth, constitutional government will *never* last.

Elected officials force you to subordinate yourself to those who are in power, your own *employees*! It makes you hand over *your* money with the many generations after you, and feel good in the giving, while at the same time, it succeeds with covert bank shots to keep you from even seeing where money came from, and that is you. These people are nothing more than smooth talking *grifters* that convince you they really care, when what they *really* care about is self-perpetuation.

"The force government has used for war mongering was at one point conscription to military service. If it ever comes again, and at least one representative has it on his mind, remember this: A nation that has to force military service is a nation that should not exist, and yes, I can prove that statement. If you disagree, can you prove your opinion? You cannot. This is why we will be ending the Selective Service Administration. Young people will no longer have it hanging over their heads, and will no longer have to register.

"Freedom is fragile. It is difficult to find in a complex world, and so very easy to lose to the power-hungry thugs who masquerade as leaders in order to take it from us. This is our second chance. Our ancestors fought and died for freedom, and I am certain they did not want their successors to take what they did lightly. Some of them *did* believe in sacrifice, which is giving up what you value for what you do *not* value. To do something greater than your own self-interest can *never* be a good thing, and that *would* make it a sacrifice. Look out for people like President's Obama, Bush, and Clinton, who want you to sacrifice, for it does not mean to them what it does to you.

"The American Dream is really only one thing, but it is wrapped in many others. It is the freedom to live your life as you alone decide, or to *end* it if that is what you rationally choose to do. If you do not own your own life, you do not own anything, and there *is* a test. The *ultimate* test of ownership is if you can do what you want with what you own and never have to get permission from someone to do it. The single caveat is as long as you do not aggress against another person, but if you have to ask for permission, you are not the owner...they are!

"The American Dream is also the right and the power to solve your *own* problems, but not those of your neighbor, unless you both *agree* to that decision. It is the right and the strength to pursue the type of business you desire without the need to ask for permission from your own employees in a variety of ways that includes licensing, and in that light, licensing does *not* protect you. They just want you to think that it does because it justifies their existence, and makes you believe they are doing their job well.

"It is the right and the ability to live as people are supposed to live, under their own direction and decision, not the directions and decisions of elected politicians and non-elected bureaucrats. And while the Constitution had several serious flaws, it still stands, along with the Declaration of Independence, as the finest founding documents in the history of the world and must never be usurped, as they nearly were. But to protect them requires an *informed* citizenry, not one that prefers to watch television, go to movies, or brag to friends about not reading books. I know entertainment *is* wonderful, but it pales in comparison to the need to be ever on the alert about what our leaders are doing, because they are doing them with your express permission, and they are doing them in your *name*. I hope you will stop saying *no politics* when it comes to conversation, as is the case in millions of American homes. Political discussions are very useful, especially when the dialogue is point/counterpoint. It helps to create and maintain an informed citizenry that is in good standing with its principles.

"Regardless of how wonderful you think any particular government program is, there is a basic fact that you certainly may disregard but cannot challenge on *rational* grounds, and that means that you can never make a *moral* justification for the taking of property without the owner's permission. Many programs put in place by the government that profess to help people may in fact do just that, but the funds for these programs are confiscated, and that means force. They do not conform to the Constitution. If this is what you want, why not just admit it and get over the notion of pretending to want a free country. You have the next four years to think about it, and I wonder if your answer will be liberty, or control by some people over other people. I do remember former Congressman, Ron Paul, opine as to why it is difficult to sell liberty. It is my hope that you will become more interested in the politics of America and listen more closely to what officials *say*, especially as it regards the Constitution—that it means what it says, not what someone *says* it means. It isn't complex. You will now have all of your freedoms back, especially those that were lost when more than one administration began to track every keystroke you made, on the phone and online. I often thought that because of those government-spying program, they must have had something on Chief Justice Roberts to make him change to declare the horrible healthcare bill constitutional. Did they confront him with information he was desperate to keep private? Only time will tell, but now, you have *all* of your freedoms restored.

"So this is where we have arrived and where I leave you to ponder. It is all in your hands. You should hold *yourselves* accountable and make *reasoned* decisions, not *emotional* ones, for if you do not, progressive collectivists will rise again. One thing *is* certain. Progressives do not quit, as was stated by Barack Obama in 2010, and he was the *ultimate* progressive. The other part of this equation is that progressive *conservative* collectivists will also rise, because both are forever busy, going down different paths to arrive at the same location.

"You can vote this new form of governing out of office in four years and restore the corrupt presidency and congress you have seemed to want for such a long time—a government with the raw power to make you do what *it* says. You can do it with the House and with some members of the Senate in *two* years. That is your right. But there is another road—the road you took this time without knowing it—the *moral* road that recognizes our nation was founded on rule of law, not on rule of the *majority*, but you can only do this if you actually *learn* and understand these things.

"I urge you to recommit to our founding documents and read books that will help you understand more about our government. I hope that in that extremely important decision, reason will always prevail over emotion *and* religion. Those who complained about Muslims would do well to look to their own religious teachings for their built-in bias and immorality. Using your intellect to sort things out will also help you see that you need a government to protect you, not force you—to preside over a nation filled with free people who can figure things out on their own, so long as they are secure, not constrained. Edward R. Murrow once told us that we are not descended from fearful men, and that is true enough, but in recent years, we *have* selected leaders who *intentionally* set out to frighten us. They made the determination that if they terrified you strongly enough, they would be certain to achieve longevity in Washington, *and* they *succeeded*! From the illegal creation of the Federal Reserve in 1910 by a few men on Jekyll Island who shilled for a few wealthy men to the present time, American's have listened to many con men. These confidence peddlers have always existed. We eagerly gravitate to them because we largely live in a type of fantasyland most of the time. President Obama declared, in a series of commencement speeches, that there is government and the individual, with nothing in between. He declared that government is our keeper. He was wrong. *We* are *government's* keeper, its *employer* and *boss*.

Many people who seek public office are loyal to themselves, not our nation. They *are* fearful people who believe in the right of the collective, not the individual. They are still nothing more than grifters; moving from program to program—from regulation to regulation, for one, and only one purpose—to perpetuate themselves. To all of you I say that these individuals—these modern liberal and conservative progressive politicians could never have founded the great United States of America, because that took men of character, not larceny."

AUTHOR NOTE

It should be obvious to any reader who has gotten this far that I am a huge fan of Ayn Rand, and I too am an Objectivist. I also believe that if she had a seat at the table when men created America, just about every American living today would be well off, and many more would be alive. Our government would not have sent our sons and daughters off to fight in unconstitutional wars, and I include the War Between the States in that declaration. Lincoln shredded the Constitution and engaged in massive amounts of doublespeak. Then, with his great ability with words, he made people think he was a great president. He wasn't.

Our money would be gold and silver, or *linked* to them, not to thin air, and the Constitution would probably insist that elected officials *obey* it in every way. I do not know that, of course, because I never had personal contact with the great woman, much to my regret. For those of you who have not read the works of Ayn Rand, both fiction and nonfiction, I strongly urge you to do so and discover one of the greatest minds that ever lived...maybe *the* greatest.

As stated in the story, our founders created America as a constitutional republic, not a democracy. The Pledge and the Constitution were the noblest founding documents ever written, even though the Constitution had some serious flaws. The biggest blemish in the text was that it did not require obedience by the three branches of government. They only have to pledge to preserve, protect, and defend. Then people quickly began the process of *disobeying*, starting with George Washington who added words to the presidential oath of office. The authors of the Constitution also failed to acknowledge that a non-white person deserved the same *status* of white people. And even though I agree with the great Frederick Douglas that the Constitution was not a racist document, the right language should have been inclusive of all people, not just white people. Rights belong to *all individuals*, not to *any* group.

Since the early days of our republic, those who were elected president, senator, and congressman, have routinely violated the Constitution in small and great ways, and nearly without exception. It became more pervasive and greater in scope as the years passed, culminating at the end of the writing of this book with a president and a congress in lock step with one another even when they were in stated *opposition*. I am convinced that the Obama administration means to *destroy* the Constitution. If he is successful, it will be because citizens are just too lazy to be informed, because they really do not care in the end.

Freedom may actually be lost in America, whose last days, I believe, are here. I also believe those final days did not just start this year or last year, but with Washington himself, and that seemingly innocuous addition to his Oath, "so help me God." It accelerated with TR, Woodrow, and FDR, then it went on a trip around the world with George W. Bush, hitting warp-drive with Barack Obama. Beyond arrogance doesn't even *begin* to describe it.

Now we have arrived at a time when Americans have collectively decided to keep believing what immoral politicians have said—that the only reason socialism did not work in the rest of the world was because it was not an *American* version.

They do not use the word socialism. They know Americans do not like that word. Instead, they use the words, progressive and democracy—that some should receive resources from the government, yet refuse to admit the money does not come from government, but from themselves. They use touchy-feely language to attempt to make people forget their plan to defeat the Constitution.

We had one president who *illegally* sent our military to Arabia on the pretext of spreading democracy. The House and Senate helped him, along with citizens and the Supreme Court. His successor sent more American troops back to Afghanistan in another criminal military incursion not authorized by the Constitution. Just what in the hell do you voters have to know to stop voting for these people? The Constitution does not give presidents the authority to declare war, and it does not authorize a *resolution* to allow a *president* to declare war. Constitutionally, it is the responsibility of the Congress.

If Obama had sent two *million* troops, or *twenty-two* million, he would not have been able to remove the infestation of the Muslim religion on the minds of Middle Eastern people. It is too late for them. They will stay in the Dark Ages forever. No amount of troops will ever change that reality, and as Rand said, reality exists. They completely surrendered to mysticism many centuries ago, but they are not our business.

In 2007 and 2008, the American financial community from Wall Street to some neighborhood banks and all large banks, committed the greatest financial crime in the history of the world, and then we elected a committed Marxist as president. With that election, we announced that we were fine with the grossly immoral *Affordable Care* package, until we awoke and slowed things down in 2010 with the re-emergence of a Republican majority in the House. But the problem with that is the members were still committed to their own re-election, not to our Constitution. Then we re-elected the Marxist president who, with his comrades in the Senate and their minority in the House, continued their war against the individual in favor of the collective. They have worked to transfer individual rights to the collective. In the case of labor, they set it with unions. As stated in the story, rights belong to individuals, not to any group, even unions or Americans.

In 2013, Barack Obama said that government is not the source of problems—that government is us! No it isn't. Government and the individual have only one thing in common, and that is both are here in the country. He also said that government is our keeper. No, it isn't, or at least it is not *my* keeper. Communist's like Obama fault capitalism with the full knowledge that capitalism is so powerful it will ultimately pull their feet out of the fire and save them, even as they attempt to *blame* it for all the problems.

I believe America should continue to live only if it returns to what the founders created with the writing of the Constitution—if it stopped electing criminals to office. If not, it should die. America, the collective, has no *natural* right to exist. The same is true of Israel or any other nation. However, *people* have that right, and the reason is simple. Rights belong exclusively to *individuals*, never to groups, including America and Israel, and that is true regardless of how many people think or say it is not true. It is reality.

www.ingramcontent.com/pod-product-compliance
Lightning Source LLC
Chambersburg PA
CBHW072220170626
46813CB00003B/1025